154

THE TESTAMENT OF THE LOST SON

The
TESTAMENT OF
THE LOST SON

by

SOMA MORGENSTERN

Translated from the German manuscript by
JACOB SLOAN
In collaboration with
MAURICE SAMUEL

Philadelphia
The Jewish Publication Society of America
5710–1950

60

PRINTED IN THE UNITED STATES OF AMERICA
PRESS OF THE JEWISH PUBLICATION SOCIETY
PHILADELPHIA, PENNA.

CONTENTS

THE TESTAMENT OF THE LOST SON

BOOK I

BOOK I

1

IVAN Kobza stood in his garden and spoke to Onufry Borodaty. They were talking about their neighbor, Shabse Punes, the horse-trader, who was standing in front of his house watching Walko Gulowaty, nicknamed "the Stallion," wash his master's small coach down with water and scrub it with a brush. It was very early in the morning. The sun, a fiery red disk, had just risen behind the roof of Kobza's barn; it resembled a full moon; near, round and cool.

"Today is no market day," said Onufry Borodaty. "Where can the cholera be riding!"

It was not a question that Onufry stated in this way. It was a declaration. Nor did Kobza answer. He made a declaration of his own.

"Yes, where may the cholera be riding today!"

Thus their conservation really did not cross back and forth over Kobza's garden. It was as though each of the farmers were sowing with suspicious words a strip of the garden that separated them, each his own strip; yet, nevertheless, it was for their common benefit.

"It's not market-day in Kozlova," said Ivan Kobza. "It's not market-day in Rembovlia. It's not market-day in the city. Where can the pestilence be riding today!"

"Tuesday is market-day in Rembovlia. Thursday is market-day in Kozlova. Wednesday is market-day in the city. Where can the cholera be riding to on Monday!" said Onufry.

They could easily have solved this problem that busied them so early in the morning. One of them had merely to raise his voice a trifle and to call over to Shabse, his neighbor. The

[3]

horse-trader would certainly have gladly taken part in the
conversation and have given the peasants a satisfactory solution
to their problem.

For, however strained and hostile the relations between the
horse-trader and the Jews of Dobropolia, Shabse Punes stood
on a good footing with the peasants of the village and the
neighborhood. The fact that his two nearest neighbors spoke
of cholera and pestilence, having him in mind, had not the
slightest to do with Shabse personally. That was simply their
way of speaking. If one of them, Kobza for example, had
gotten his wagon ready for a trip some Monday, and if Onufry
Borodaty and Shabse Punes had had occasion to speak about
this extraordinary occurrence, the words cholera and pestilence would have served the same purpose: that of giving
friendly expression to their astonishment over an extraordinary
event. But neither of the peasants cared to call the horse-trader
and question him. They could conjecture without doing so
the direction of Shabse's trip. They knew the grounds for the
trip, as well. What neither of them knew was: how much the
other might know concerning Shabse's trouble. It was this
that their early conversation was meant to ascertain. For each
of the peasants took great heed to disclose to his neighbor no
more of what he knew than the latter would confide to him.
In this way they probed one another prudently, circumstantially, and with complete distrust, before proceeding to an open
exchange of opinion concerning the horse-trader's doings.
Though it would be a hot harvest day, and the subject interested them both to the same extent, they moved towards their
goal leisurely, by way of many and heavily tangled paths and
bypaths. A simple peasant is, as a matter of fact, the most
complicated being on God's earth, whatever people may say.
And a true peasant never hurries of his own accord.

Both neighbors had their morning chores behind them.
They had foddered and spread straw for their beasts and prepared their tools for work in the field. Their wives were preparing breakfast inside their kitchens. Harvest days are hot, but

[4]

a chat between neighbors can turn up something useful. Four eyes see more of the world than two. When a neighbor loses his head — though he be a Jew — a Christian may have a chance to better his lot a bit. The less you have, the more have I.

They had both remarked that the sun had risen the height of three men above the horizon, before Ivan Kobza and Onufry Borodaty agreed on the conclusion that Shabse Punes, the sly horse-trader, had lost his head, and that was why he had decided to ride to the district capital on a Monday — apparently with the intention of finding his head there again. But it was still quite early in the morning. The night dew lay a glittering silver on the drowsy grass.

"He won't be able to do it without Mechzio," said Kobza.

"No," replied Borodaty, "he will not be able to do his horse-trading without his brother-in-law. But he soon will be done with his property."

"Couldn't Walko the Stallion do it?" said Kobza, trying to out-do his neighbor. "The powerful man that he is!"

"Oh, him!" exclaimed Onufry. "He is strong, strong as a horse. But he has the sense of a horse, too!" And to show that he had indeed appreciated Kobza's cunning, he shook his round-cropped head thoughtfully and added:

"But perhaps the cholera will do it yet."

"No. I say no; he will not do it."

And now they began the conversation anew, and it was like a musical response.

"Who tilled the vegetable garden? Mechzio!" said Onufry.

"Who tended the orchard? Mechzio!" intoned Ivan.

"Who plowed? Mechzio!" sang Onufry.

"Who sowed? Mechzio!" sang Ivan.

"Who mowed? Mechzio!" sang Onufry.

"Who thrashed? Mechzio!" sang Ivan.

"And who *was* thrashed?" asked Onufry, the slyer of the two, giving the conversation a comical turn.

"Mechzio!" assented Kobza.

[5]

He too was satisfied that a harmless joke was bringing the conversation to a close. For his massive wife now stood on the threshold of his house and loudly addressed both men:

"What is it to day, a holiday – you lazy buggers! Both of you!"

The morning meal was ready. Kobza regarded the fact that his deft wife had gotten through with breakfast earlier than Borodaty's wife as a good omen.

2

Shabse the horse-trader did not look that morning quite like a man who had lost his head. On the contrary; though it was still early, he gave the impression of being quite content, full, — in a word, fat. Coatless, his head covered with a satin cap, he stood behind Walko, who had begun the day washing the wagon, and now went on to grease the axles.

"He who greases, rides," said Shabse to Walko's bent back; and he repeated the adage at each of the four wheels, although he knew that the stooping giant was stone deaf and could not hear a word his master was saying. The horse-trader enjoyed making a display of his high spirits early in the morning, quoting adages whose proven ancient wisdom lighted the devious paths of all mankind, and not only of horse-traders.

"He who greases, rides," he said again to himself. The words were not meant for Walko's ears; at that moment he was thinking not merely of wagon grease. His thoughts were on greasing the palms of police officials and officers, to expedite the tracking down of this runaway brother-in-law. Meanwhile, however, he did not neglect in the slightest his careful supervision of the greasing of the axles. The deaf giant was not to be trusted even in so small a matter. Shabse's sure eye estimated the grease needed for each wheel and he doled out the wagon grease accordingly. Every once in a while he applied his own smoothing hand, distributing the fresh grease evenly by quickly revolving and counter-revolving a wheel, and carefully spreading, thinning and smoothing the surplus around the nub with

[6]

a stick of wood. These were petty manual services; he performed them with visible pleasure, indeed with pride. For Shabse Punes loved fat in all its forms. He loved the fat flanks of his buxom wife, the fat cheeks of his children, the fat milk of his cow, the fat dishes on his table. He loved the fat of the geese, the fat of the hens, the scum floating in the scalding soup of the Sabbath meal. Yankel Christiampoler, his mortal enemy, often gave vent to the sacrilegious opinion that the reason why Shabse Punes so proudly shouted the confessional, "Hear, O Israel," in Grandfather's Room on the Sabbath, was because those holy words were printed in the largest, fattest characters in the prayer book!

The visible self-satisfaction which his own fatness aroused in Shabse was only a sublimation of his love for everything fat. On hot summer days when he took cooling baths in the Dobropolia pond, his effeminate behavior provoked the lively, indeed mocking, interest even of Velvel Dobropolier. His very undressing was a spectacle for the children of the village, who followed the anxious doings of the bearded colossus with peals of wild laughter.

First he sought out the shadiest and coolest spot on the river bank. With careful hands, he tested the grass in the shade of the thickest tree for protuberances and hollows. Then he cleared the selected spot of every object that might press, stick, scratch or trouble in the slightest his seated or reclining bulk. The smallest dry twig was removed; his fat finger would pluck up a withered branch and throw the abomination away: who knew what horrible worm might lie in ambush there! When every peril that lurks in green sward had been plucked forth, Shabse spread a white sheet over his resting place — no man did the like in Dobropolia; over the sheet, he spread a white cloth — no girl did the like in Dobropolia; and then the second act of the performance began: Shabse removed his clothing. Every piece was meticulously hung on a separate branch of the tree and, when he was completely undressed, his last undergarment fluttering on a limb, the pure white opulence of

Shabse's naked body stood out, hung around and tented on every side.

Now began the magical transformation. The tub o' flesh, whose matted chest was shielded by the full gray-black beard, was transformed into an anxious, dainty, hopping, tittering girl. A man who was feared in all the horse-markets of the land like the Devil himself was overcome by an hysterical anxiety at the sight of every crawling and creeping thing. A villager who thought nothing of squeezing a tick from a horse's coat emitted shrill cries of terror when an innocent bee buzzed in the neighborhood of his nakedness. A conscienceless horse-trader, adept at fixing a horse's teeth to make it look younger, now did a grotesque St. Vitus dance when a gnat threatened to approach his white corpulence. And his voice suited his timidity; it was high, thin, womanly. The children clamored and danced around the screaming, hopping man. But that did not disturb Shabse; on the contrary, his histrionics were calculated to encourage the youngsters. For, while their mocking cries offended him, their antics, and particularly their swinging of branches and weeds, frightened away all buzzing and stinging insects.

The spectacle continued in the clear water. His pure white body, a mound of fat on the solid ground, was reflected as a gigantic jellyfish in the blue underworld of the water. He could not swim. This, too, was extraordinary in Dobropolia, where even the dignified Velvel Mohilevski was so good a swimmer that some Fridays, treading water in the deepest part of the pond, he would completely cut his toenails in honor of the Sabbath, a trick that left even the wild young men of Dobropolia wordless with admiration. Shabse Punes was the only non-swimmer among the Jews of the village. But he was not afraid of the water. Though he did not have the confidence to assume a horizontal position, he knew how to get the fullest delights of the bath in a vertical position. Crying with delight — ohhh! haaa! ay! vay! — he splattered and splashed with zest, clapped and spluttered, and, bending and inclining in the water, made

[8]

an almost obscene spectacle of lascivious embrace on the part of two elements, fat and water.

After he had savored the delight of the water to the full, Shabse betook himself with mincing, painfully tiny steps, treading his way through the rubble of the river bank, to his grassy couch. The children followed him with their branches and reeds to the accompaniment of soft cries, such as are used to calm down a balky stallion while it is being shod. Shabse smiled happily and stretched out, smooth and gleaming like a polished idol. After a rest-period, he dabbed himself dry with a soft cloth — then, eyes shut, sat in the cool shaded green, his padded hands on the white protuberance of his stomach, while the children danced about him in a wavering file. Once, years before, it happened that one of the children — it was the youngest of the three short-necked sons of Gruenspan, the distiller — got possession of a stripped switch during the course of the wild dance and, either caught up in the passion of play or conceivably in a childish fit, touched the sharp reed to Shabse's pure-white fatty upper arm. This took place on a Friday, when all the Jewry of Dobropolia was bathing. Then both young and old had the experience of seeing the bearded colossus break into tears at the blood-red trail left by the reed and go on to bring his wounded upper arm to the highest authority, Velvel Dobropolier, in order to make out a tearful complaint against a child. Such was Shabse Punes when naked!

Clothed, he was, despite his fleshiness, a brisk, hard business-man who never once went out of his way to avoid physical labor, as we shall soon see.

During the first stage of the washing of the coach, he was the inspector and overseer of the deaf giant; but as soon as the washing and greasing came to an end, the roles were reversed. Now Shabse sprang into action. The carriage was light and high-wheeled, but, as was usual with such vehicles in that part of the country, the short green-painted cab had no seat worthy of the name.

Shabse did not like a fixed seat, and in matters involving

personal comfort he depended on no one but himself. No stranger's hands could make the seat right for him, not even the talented hands of his brother-in-law Mechzio, to whom he otherwise entrusted everything. "A wagon seat is no bed," Shabse used to say. "A bed is good when the slightest movement of the body sets it moving, swaying, even swinging. A wagon seat must be solid, but it must also be soft and flexible. Solid and slack, soft and hard — that is what the seat must be, and it must be so as a whole, not just in parts." How does one make it so? "The way Shabse makes it," he said. — Indeed, they said so in all of Dobropolia, and in the other villages as well, where they seldom neglected the opportunity of watching Shabse build up or tear down his seat. Though there were many resident Christians, many traveling Jews, and all had seen and many had studied it, not one of them could duplicate this work of art.

Not even dull-witted Walko allowed his master out of his sight while he was helping him spread his seat. Walko brought the materials to Shabse, then stood by rolling his puma eyes; even he was eager to observe the master at work. First Shabse spread a sack full of coarse linen through the whole coach. Upon this he laid a uniform, thin layer which would bear the structure. The material was astonishing; it was such as no other man used — dry, broken flax. "That's the whole secret!" many a superficial observer precipitously exclaimed at this point; but at the master's very next move such a novice was forced to laugh at himself. Shabse's next stroke was to lay a layer twice as thick of simple rye straw over the crackling flax base. But there was a trick to this, too. It consisted in the fact that Shabse did not lay the straw across the wagon like every one else, but lengthwise. The master builder himself termed his layer, "the parallel." Next came a layer of hay. The fourth layer was of barley straw. Next came a sack of oat chaff, only half full, so that its contents might be evenly kneaded and smoothed down over the seat. "This is the diagonal," Shabse used to instruct the observers. For, just as a good cook

[10]

is glad to offer recipes, knowing that he does not divulge the essence, so Shabse loved to instruct the observers, because experience had shown him that his art could not be copied. And just as the master cook tastes the dish when it is almost done to see what it might lack of perfection, so Shabse interrupted the labor of his hands to test the seat, now almost finished, with that part of his body which was most involved, his rear. First he sat down facing the shaft and — listened. Then he threw his limbs sideways, swung his heavy body 180 degrees around, sat with his back to the shaft and again listened for a short time. Afterwards he began to press on the seat with the whole weight of his body, first in the middle and then, half rising and letting himself fall, on all the four corners of the structure. Then he covered the hard-packed seat with a coarse sackcloth, packed so well that not the slightest trace of the motley material of which the seat was comprised peeped through. Then Walko handed Shabse a horse blanket which he folded three ways and bedded down in the middle of the seat, thus caulking the sackcloth.

The next to the last layer consisted of a light straw sack — filled not with straw but with soft horsehair — which to the astonishment of the observers now perfectly fitted the contour of the apparently improvised seat. The last layer consisted of another horse blanket, one which, not being folded, covered the entire seat both fore and aft; not being tucked in on any of the sides or the corners, it resembled a loose throw. That was the topmost layer. For, the striped coach blanket with which Shabse crowned his work was but an ornament, which served more to flatter the eye of the observer than to serve the pleasure of the rider, thus esconced for his journey.

Shabse builds his seat the way one makes layer cake, was the opinion of the pious Czarne Gruenfeld, the mother of the innkeeper and grain-dealer, Shmuel Gruenfeld, whose layer cakes were unsurpassed; you mix something loose with something thick, something light with something heavy, and enclose the whole securely in a tight frame. But of what avail are comparisons, however apt? One comes much nearer to the truth, if one assumes that, in building his seat, Shabse followed the same instinct that guides a bird in building its nest. Here, too, the technique is as primitive as the material, but the greatest tapestry-maker in the world cannot imitate the nest of the lark in the grass of the steppe, or the raven's nest in the branches of a beech tree. This opinion was shared by Shabse's newest friend, the communal secretary, Vincenty Lubasj, who found himself on the farm of the horse-trader with a shabby portfolio under his arm at the very moment when Shabse was at the point of spreading his striped horse blanket over the finished seat.

"Good morning," Shabse greeted him, without interrupting his creative labors. "Good morning, my dear friend." Then he took the portofolio from the communal secretary, placed it behind the seat under the horse blanket and, with a ceremonious, mocking gesture, invited his guest to try the seat. In contrast to the good-humored, fair-spoken horse-trader, the communal secretary was bad-tempered in the morning, and climbed unwillingly into the cab.

"There's a seat for you," he said with real approval. "There's a real seat for you. Bravo, Mr. Punes!"

"He who travels with me, travels in comfort," said Shabse. "This, as you see, is a seat for two. When I travel alone the seat looks about the same, but, at bottom, is made entirely differently. Just wait a moment. When I sit down next to you, you will see what comfort means. For this seat is built for two. Not for one, not for three, but for two. What do you say now?"

The two friends were now sitting side by side.

"What else can I say? It's wonderful!" said the secretary. "Count Potocki does not sit any more comfortably in his Rolls Royce than we two are sitting here."

"Comfortable, that it is," said Shabse. "I make it comfortable for myself. Comfortable, no more, no less. For, you see, Mr. Lubasj, what does a man want out of life? He wants to eat. First of all, to eat. His second need is for women. These two

[12]

needs are not to be ignored. As a rabbi once said: 'You can break your neck and your limbs, but you will never break yourself of a habit or repress an instinct.' But man has still a third need, the need for comfort. According to the inexplicable will of the Creator, this third need, however, can be, I will not say ignored, but postponed. Why? Because this third need exists in order to serve the other two needs. Is that not so? A man must eat in complete comfort. A man must lie with his wife in complete comfort. But, because this need for comfort can be postponed, because it is its nature to be postponed, the fools believe it can be ignored with impunity. There are many Jewish fools, especially, who believe this. Have you ever seen a peasant eat in discomfort? No. But a Jew takes a piece of bread, a pinch of salt and a clove of garlic, and runs to the market, gobbling it down on the way, like a dog who has stolen a sausage. Now the peasant — so help me God, isn't it true? — the peasant throws a woman on a heap of straw and there they couple like dogs on a dungheap. That's why there is so much heart disease, and there are so many madmen among the Jews, and there are so many village idiots and cripples among the peasants — for they all commit sins against the need for comfort. As for me — I never commit that particular sin."

"Not the sin against comfort," said the communal secretary, pressing the horse-trader's elbow with his hand. They smiled at one another.

"Often a good friend profits, too," said Shabse, "or are you perhaps sitting uncomfortably? If you are not comfortable," he added with feigned alarm, "if you don't find it as comfortable as you wish, I can build up your seat and make it better still."

"I have never sat so comfortably in a wagon. On my word," said Lubasj.

"Like Count Potocki in his —"

"Rolls Royce," Lubasj interjected.

"In his Rolls Royce," said Shabse.

"The only difference being that when Count Potocki sits in his Rolls Royce in the morning, he has a good breakfast in his well-bred stomach, while I must go riding with my stomach gurgling."

"You have not yet had breakfast?" asked Shabse in a soft voice dripping with sympathy.

"Where can you have breakfast in this godforsaken place? Mr. Gruenfeld only opens at seven, the great Sergeant Shmulko!"

"You'll settle accounts with him for sure," said the horse-trader.

"As sure of that, as my name is Lubasj. In six weeks at the latest, in six weeks I shall have the inn license and —"

"— and I shall have scraped together fifty per cent of the capital for the business, as my name is Punes. But let's not talk about it here. My wife, you know —"

"Your wife, I know — she is Mechzio's sister. She is pious, industrious and holy."

"You will have breakfast with me, today, Mr. Lubasj, but not a word about the inn license. We'll decide all that on the way, and conclude the business in the city. Let my wife believe we are riding to the city only to look for her dear brother, Mechzio."

"Is breakfast ready?" the secretary inquired; he sprang out of the wagon as lightly as a young man.

"Slowly, Mr. Lubasj," Shabse, who was not so nimble, calmed him down, "everything goes like clockwork with me, but everything goes slow and easy. He who hurries too much is not my friend."

To appease his business partner, Lubasj courteously helped him out of the wagon and they both went into the house; Shabse slowly and thoughtfully, Mr. Lubasj slowly and fidgeting.

"The communal secretary will breakfast with me," Shabse called through the open door of the kitchen, and bid the guest enter.

"Good morning, Mrs. Punes," Lubasj greeted Shabse's wife, who was just packing the children's buttered bread for school; the children, one a youth of almost thirteen, the other a boy of ten, sat at their breakfast at the kitchen table.

[14]

"Good morning, Mr. Lubasj," Mrs. Punes retored without looking at the guest, and the elder of the boys greeted the secretary with an exaggeratedly respectful nod which pleased his father so much that he rewarded his first born with a tender look of mutual understanding. But the father's look of pleasure died on his face, which clouded over with a wrathful grimace; for at the sight of Lubasj, his younger son had sprung to his feet and greeted the guest in his own way. It was a greeting that sent a shudder down the horse-trader's spine. Loudly and clearly, as though reciting a poem, the boy declaimed the Hebrew saying, which pious Jews are obliged to repeat at the sight of heathen abominations: "With revulsion shalt thou turn away from it, with disgust shalt thou detest it; for it is unclean. . . ." Then he spat three times with his childish mouth — "Tfu, tfu, tfu," unskilfully but audibly — an obvious translation of the Hebrew for the benefit of Mr. Lubasj. And with fire and tears in his eyes, the child tried to dash quickly between his father and Lubasj and out of the kitchen. Shabse caught his son with an angry grasp of his left hand, at the same time raising his right for a blow. But the calm and statuesque Mrs. Punes had caught her husband's right arm as though she had foreseen everything, and now would not let it go free. His wife lived in constant anxiety at the domestic tyrant's passion and allowed everything to pass in silence except where her Shloymele was concerned; then she was ever resolutely ready to face her spouse. Shabse knew this and calmed himself in the presence of the communal secretary with a suddenness that visibly affected Mr. Lubasj even more than the boy's outburst.

"Let me alone," said Shabse to his wife with a honeyed smile; "let me be. I won't do anything to him, that rabbi of yours."

As a sign of his peaceful intentions, he let the child go by relaxing the grip of his left hand after the mother had released his right. But Shloymele did not run away. He approached still nearer to his father and waited, with rebellion in his eyes.

"He is going to be a rabbi," said Shabse to Lubasj, "he is *her* pride and joy."

"A fanatical child," asserted Lubasj, in not unfriendly a tone. "The schoolmistress, Miss Rakoczy, has probably had something to do with his point of view."

"I am not in her class," said Shloymele in a contrary tone. But he did not speak to Lubasj, to whom he had turned his back; he spoke to his father. "I am in Mr. Dudka's class. But all the children in school know it."

"What is *it?*" asked Lubasj pedantically. "What do the children in school know?"

"All the children know," replied Shloymele, quickly turning and retreating a couple of steps to the door, then lifting his finger and pointing it at Lubasj, "All the children in school know that this man here is the real murderer of Lipale." Then he ran quickly out of the kitchen, slamming the half-open door behind him with a backward kick.

"*Her* pride and joy," repeated Shabse, "*her* Bible scholar."

"And you?" Mr. Lubasj turned to the older boy, who had remained at the table and calmly continued his breakfast, "do you know it, too?"

"I know nothing," answered Kalman Punes and regarded his father. "I don't mix in things that are none of my business." At that he stood up and placed a chair before the guest.

"This is *my* son," cried Shabse triumphantly, "This is my bringing up. Pardon me, Mr. Lubasj, I must say my prayers now, but I will be back immediately afterwards for breakfast."

"Prayers? You are going to begin to pray now?" asked Lubasj. "My stomach is grumbling." He sat at the table and acted the exaggerated disappointment of the man of the world.

"Don't worry," said Mrs. Punes without warmth, speaking with her usual calm, "my husband does everything very slowly, but when it comes to praying" — the pious sister of Mechzio sighed deeply, "— my husband is very fast. You will see soon enough."

Shabse could already be heard murmuring in the living room. Mrs. Punes took the jug of milk and the buttered bread that Shloymele had not finished eating and carried them out

[16]

to him. The boy was sitting on the bench in front of the house crying softly to himself. "Don't give him any breakfast, that Haman," he sobbed. His mother gave her son the buttered bread, wordlessly stroked her darling's forehead with her hard workworn hand and set the cap straight on his head. Shloymele took the jug of milk and stopped crying. When his mother went back to the kitchen, he continued his breakfast alone outside. He ate and drank hastily in futile wrath. Then he stood up and went into the house. But he did not go back to the kitchen. After setting the empty pitcher on a board on the floor, he opened the door of the living room, where the horse-trader was presumably at prayer, only a few minutes having elapsed since he had declared himself ready to pray. But with the unerring knowledge that really pious children have of the failings of their elders, the lad stepped into the room and found it empty, as he had expected. The holy utensils lay on the table in shameful disorder. Shabse rarely re-wound the phy-lacteries when he had finished the hasty mumble that he called prayer, rarely folded up the prayer shawl again, and frequently did not take the time to shut his prayer book. He left this duty to his first-born, who was almost a *bar mitzvah* boy now and was learning the care of the holy objects. Shabse's prayer book lay open. Shloymele cast a glance into the book. As he had suspected, the book was open to the first page of the morning prayer. On the Sabbath and High Holy Days, Shabse was one of the noisiest worshippers in Grandfather's Room. His bulky body shook wildly in rhythm, he hopped and skipped, and clapped his hands like an ecstatic Hasid; but in his own house on work days he very rarely got past the first page of the prayer book. Shloymele kissed the prayer book, shut it and laid it in the table drawer. Then he folded the phylacteries awkwardly with his unaccustomed child's hands, kissed the head and arm capsules and placed them in the satin bag where they belonged. Shabse's prayer shawl was too long for his younger son's short arms, so he waited until his older brother came into the room to put father's prayer utensils away for him. Wordlessly both

[17]

children folded their father's prayer shawl, put it in a larger satin bag, which looked like an embroidered pillow case, and placed it next to the small bag in the chest. Wordlessly they left the room together; Shloymele went out into the yard and waited there until his brother emerged from the kitchen with both their school bags. Wordlessly the brothers set out on the way to school.

Of Shabse Punes's two sons — who, like most children, showed at first glance the traits of both parents — the elder was, as the saying goes, his father to the T; the younger resembled their mother. Kalman, the elder, had his father's fleshiness; the younger had his mother's broad cheekbones in his still childish face. Kalman's face was round and padded, his narrow lips always damp, like his father's, and there was a fatty sheen in the cherry-black eyes which — like his father's again — twinkled behind beautiful long eyelashes. Shloymele had his mother's strongly protruding cheekbones and the brown eyes in his flat face were slit like a Tartar's. Had not the boy's goodnatured face been framed on both sides by thick earlocks, two braids of *peyes*, almost seeming to be pasted on, Shloymele might have been mistaken for a young Tartar. "My Tartar," Shabse used to call him in Jewish company, "my little Tartar is a real Bible scholar." As a matter of fact, the horse-trader's younger son was "a good learner," as the Jews express it. He would have been outstanding in piety among all the children of the village, had not the repute of the still younger Lipale Aptowitzer surpassed his by far. But none of the children could compare with that youth! No one had been his equal either in studies in the village school or in prayer and song in Grandfather's Room. But now Lipale Aptowitzer was dead, murdered by drunken peasants who had been incited by a foreign Haman. Only eight days had passed since that bloody Sunday on the *Groblja*, and the terror, pain and anger were still fresh in Shloymele's small heart.

It was well that the path to school did not run past the *Groblja*. Shloymele knew the spot on the *Groblja* where the murdered Lipale had been trodden to death by a mob of rioting peasants, and he was seized with anguish whenever he saw it from afar. Two days before, on the Sabbath, going to prayers with his brother and father, he crossed the *Groblja*, and although he was walking between his brother and his father, the boy's anxiety was so great that he could hear the very air screaming over the broad and silent dam . . .

The boys arrived at the eastern part of the *Gazon* where the *Groblja* could not be seen at all. All that could be seen from there was the small pond, but it seemed to Shloymele as though the clear air over the water was still shuddering.

"Why are you mad at me?" Kalman asked his brother. "Can I help it that Father brought Lubasj along to breakfast with him?"

"I heard what you said to that Haman," said Shloymele. "I heard it all right."

"What can I say when he asks me? Father is smart! We have to get along with him. Otherwise it will be even worse. Father is smarter than everybody," said Kalman.

"If Mechzio were here," said the younger boy, "if Mechzio were only here, he would show him all right, that Haman."

"Mechzio was still here when the accident happened," said the elder boy.

"He came too late. Otherwise he would have broken all their necks. The brothers Mockrzycki, Mr. Lubasj — all of them!"

"But Mechzio came too late. Maybe he could have saved Lipale; maybe not. Panko is a very strong man too and they almost did him in. They say that they may have to cut his leg off. That's the way they treated a Christian. What would they have done to Mechzio!"

"Mechzio is much stronger than Panko. Mechzio is as strong as Samson. Mechzio is one of the Thirty-Six Secret Righteous Men."

"Are you sure?" said the elder boy with a smile. "How do you know that for sure?"

"You can't know that for sure; but even our Rebbe, I asked him and he said: 'It is possible. But no one can know such a thing for sure, not even Mechzio.'"

"If Mechzio was one of the Thirty-Six, why did he come too late? Mechzio was one of the first to say that Lubasj, the Haman, was responsible for everything, and still he did nothing to Lubasj. He rode away to the funeral and never came home again. Mechzio works with the peasants and he knows them better than any of us. But Mechzio knows that we're living in the Exile. We are few and we are weak. There are only seven of us in the school."

"Now we are only six," sobbed the younger boy.

"We are six, and they are two hundred and sixty. What do you want to do?"

"They are all nice to us in school. The children, Dudka, the teacher, Miss Rakoczy and —"

"You see. But what if someday you get a teacher who is a Haman like Lubasj? Then you've got to be on good terms with him, says father. There is a teacher like that in Yanovka. The Jewish children sit on special benches. That's why father says that we must get along with him."

"That's why you were friendly with Lubasj?" asked the younger boy.

"Why else?" said Kalman. "Do you think that Lipale's death doesn't hurt me as much as it does you? Now we shall all have to go to school on foot the way we did before young Mr. Mohilewski came from Vienna and became infatuated with Lipale," the elder boy continued in complete innocence. Nor could the younger boy close his ears to this argument. For virtue and vice dwell side by side in the innocence of children, which differs in this from the innocence of adults. In the midst of all his great sorrow for Lipale, Shabse's younger son also thought of the fact that now they would have to go to school on foot the way they had done before the young gentleman from Vienna had become infatuated with Lipale —

[20]

as the grown-ups put it in the village. Almost daily, young Mr. Mohilevski had had his horses harnessed to take Lipale to school and home again. On the way, Mr. Mohilevski took along as many children as the wagon could carry. As it turned out, everyone could come along, and on the way home the children sang. It was beautiful. Now it was all over. And many children of the village were unhappy because of Lipale's death.

It took three-quarters of an hour for their short legs to make the trip to school. Still the brothers came a quarter of an hour early and at once joined the other early-comers in noisy play on the common before the class began. The younger boy did not remain on the side lines very long. He very soon forgot how the air over the *Groblja* had screamed an hour before.

3

About this time Shabse's wagon rolled slowly and soundlessly past the dusty *Groblja*. Neither of the two travelers heard the air screaming over the *Groblja*. Although they passed directly by the spot where the bloody deed had taken place, neither Shabse nor Mr. Lubasj would have remembered that bloody Sunday had they not now caught sight in the distance of two pedestrians coming their way up the *Groblja*. They were Alfred Mohilevski and worrisome Pessa, who was carrying a straw basket.

"They are paying a sick visit so early in the morning," said Shabse.

"Miss Pessa is bringing a good breakfast for Panko, the well-thrashed hero," said Lubasj.

"Have they already amputated his leg?" Shabse inquired.

"Not yet," said Lubasj. "The hero is defending himself against that with might and main. He can't disgrace his master by having a cripple sit on his coach box. That's what the hero says. That leg is going to be his finish."

"Yesterday two doctors from the city were here. Young Rothschild is paying for everything. They will save Panko yet," said Shabse.

Then they both fell silent. Alfred and Pessa were by now within hearing distance. When they came nearer, both Shabse and Lubasj lifted their hats and wished them good morning. Without favoring the travelers with a look, Alfred touched his hat with his left hand and Pessa began to busy herself with her straw basket. When they came to the New Village, Lubasj said:

"The young gentleman believes that he is helping Panko with his loving care. He doesn't know that everybody in the village, calls Panko 'Jew servant.'"

"Everybody?" asked Shabse. "Do you really think so? Perhaps everybody in the Polish Village. The Ukranians in the Old Village have a different opinion. Don't underestimate young Mr. Mohilevski, Mr. Communal Secretary."

"I shall settle accounts with the young gentleman, too," said Lubasj.

Shabse gave his neighbor a sleepy side glance from under the long eyelashes of his gleaming eyes, as a cat looks at a mouse whose neck she is holding with a light paw. Silently they drove out of the village.

In Kozlova the two travelers and the horses halted for a long stop. Though he was seeking his runaway brother-in-law, Mechzio, in the county seat, Shabse prudently made a casual inquiry after Mechzio in the little town, while Lubasj left several messages for the infanticide Mokrczycki, also a runaway, with one of his political friends. From Kozlova they took the Lemberg highway. When they arrived in Yanovka — the horses that had slowly strained up the high and difficult incline from Kozlova already cast long evening shadows over the grass-green banks of the old highway — Shabse resumed the conversation. As though many hours had not passed in the interval, Shabse suddenly opened his mouth and said to Lubasj:

"Mr. Lubasj, you are taking on too much at once. 'I will settle my accounts with young Mr. Mohilevski,' you said before. *You* are going to settle your accounts with everyone. You had barely arrived in Dobropolia (you were then boarding with me) when you began with: 'I'll soon settle accounts with old Bjelak.' "

"Old Bjelak —"

"— Let me finish. Old Bjelak is the most respected and richest peasant in the village. He has been the head of our community five times and has just been elected for the sixth. You were going to settle accounts at once. Now I say to you: If old Bjelak were to drop a few lines to the Starosta, you would be dismissed in three days. Or at least demoted."

"There you are making a mistake, Mr. Punes, you are making a very bad mistake. I have more important connections with the Starosta than even old Bjelak. Besides, I am now getting along very well with old Bjelak."

"Certainly. But, so help me God, Mr. Lubasj, I helped a little in that. Do you agree?"

"Gladly. I didn't know my way in the village very well at first. I agree to that."

"Good. You agree. Then you had a quarrel with Yankel Christiampoler. About a perquisite that existed only in your imagination, between us two."

"I shall still fight for that perquisite," said Lubasj, and his blonde mustache bristled.

"Mr. Lubasj, between us, a perquisite can only be acquired under special circumstances, not won by fighting."

"My predecessor in the office had acquired this perquisite —"

"That he did not. And you know this, Mr. Lubasj. You can't speak so childishly to me. If you want to be my partner, Mr. Lubasj, you must control your language a bit. I won't quarrel with you about your perquisites. I only mention it because you are now to become my partner, and because you said: 'I shall settle accounts with Yankel Christiampoler, too.' Why? Because he would not allow you to milk the dead cow of your dead predecessor. I am no friend of Yankel Christiampoler's —"

[23]

"I have already settled accounts with Yankel Christiampoler; you can believe that," commented Lubasj with a self-satisfied smile.

"At the same time you began to become interested in the school. You became something of a pedagogue. Soon you declared: 'I shall settle accounts with Miss Tanja, too.' —"

"This priest's daughter must leave Dobropolia, I tell you —"

"So far as we know, so far as I know, the priest's daughter would prefer nothing in the world to leaving Dobropolia as soon as possible. She will leave. But if this happens soon, she will have her father's protection to thank, not your influence, Mr. Lubasj."

"Her father has not the slightest influence with the school officials," said Lubasj.

"Let us assume that you are right. But, on the other hand, the priest, Kostja Rakoczy, has so much influence in our village and all the other villages in the county that at a nod from him, Mr. Lubasj, you could not stick your fine nose out of a window without getting a stone thrown at it."

"You never told me that, Mr. Punes," cried Lubasj in righteous indignation.

"Mr. Lubasj, your affairs have interested me before, but not as much as you believe. Now that you wish to become my partner, it is another matter. As you know, Mr. Lubasj, I am not very popular in our village myself — "

"That's very true," Lubasj quickly interjected, laughing as though his friend had told a good joke.

"But, as you must know, Mr. Lubasj, until now I have had very little business with the village, if one can call horse-trading business. But if you wish to open an inn and hardware business with me in Dobropolia, you must change your conduct, Mr. Lubasj."

"How do you mean that?" asked Lubasj, assuming an aggrieved tone.

"First of all, Mr. Lubasj, you must somewhat contract the number of the enemies with whom you have to settle accounts.

[24]

That is my good advice to you — and it is also a condition, Mr. Lubasj. That's what I wanted to tell you."

Shabse inspected his friend as though the condition that he had just laid upon him were a new article of clothing and he were trying to see whether it fitted. He did not seem very sure it did, for he added in a gloomy voice: "It won't come easy to you to change your character all at once. But you must make a serious attempt at least to change your conduct, Mr. Lubasj. First of all, no more bragging, Mr. Lubasj, if I may ask that."

For a whole year this horse-trader has had nothing for me but flattery, thought Lubasj in a sudden rage which flushed his face. How the hypocrite strained to please me in every way! Now he has to dole out his money. Then he gets nasty. A true Jew. But, to show the niggardly trader that he did not lack self-control, Lubasj suppressed his rage and swallowed the curse that he always had ready on the tip of his tongue for Jews. I will settle accounts with this horse-trader too, he decided. However, since he was far from being a master at the art of self-control, Lubasj diverted the conversation toward the very point which Shabse's future partner should have had grounds to avoid.

"As to the number of individuals with whom I wished to settle accounts, it is obviously diminishing, simply because of those same individuals with whom I have already settled accounts," he said matter-of-factly, but at the same time sharply.

"For example, Mr. Lubasj?" asked Shabse.

"Yankel Christiampoler, for example, the proud bailiff," said Lubasj triumphantly. "Have you seen how he looks since coming back from the funeral? He is really done for."

Shabse transferred the reins from his right hand to his left, raised his right hand and sternly shook his index finger several times, as one does when he warns a child. Then he transferred the reins back to his right hand, and was silent.

"What do you want to say?" Lubasj insisted.

"I am not yet ready to say that, but I will say this to you: Don't depend on your having settled accounts with Yankel

Christiampoler. For, see here, Mr. Lubasj, that old Yankel has higher connections than yours. Perhaps you are not aware of the fact that his first post as a young man was with Count Rey. That was a long time ago, and the old count is dead. But his daughter, the countess — she is no longer young either — is very fond of old Yankel Christiampoler. Every New Year's Yankel pays a visit to Daczkow, like a Hasid to his miracle-working rabbi. Only in this case, we do not know who is the Hasid and who the rabbi. It is said that when they are alone they call one another 'thou'; Yankel calls her both 'countess' and 'thou.' Are you aware of that, Mr. Communal Secretary?"

"I did not know that; but the countess' protection, as you yourself have often said, Mr. Punes, is not worth a penny," said Lubasj. "The crazy countess is sufficiently known in our national circles as a friend and protectress of the Jews, and is favored with universal suspicion. Do you know that, Mr. Punes? This countess, they will say, this *meshugene*, gave the Jewish community in Lwow one of her houses in protest against the pogrom in 1919. People haven't forgotten that, although that's ten years ago. She sees to it herself that her noble deeds are not forgotten. A year ago she did something of the sort again. She gave one of her smaller estates to a Jew and —"

"The countess sold an estate of some three hundred acres to her personal physician, on very good, one may say, noble terms. But why does that excite you so fearfully, Mr. Lubasj?"

"Why that excites me? Is that what you ask me? What is our first national task here in the borderland? We must Polonize the threatened borderland. It must become Polish. And the first aim of our national mission is to get as much as possible of the land, of the earth, of the holy ground of the borderland into Polish possession. Don't you understand that? And here comes this *meshugene* and presents three hundred acres to a Jew!"

"The doctor is said to be a good Pole," said Shabse.

"He is a Jew. Or is he not? It is enough that he is permitted to be a physician in our country. I shall soon —"

"— settle accounts with the countess, Mr. Lubasj. I know,"

said Shabse brightly, favoring his partner-to-be with a loving look.

"Make no bad jokes, Mr. Punes. The Jews have the unfortunate habit of joking about all their troubles," said Lubasj. He was now very much at his ease. The conversation had taken the turn that he had wished for a long time to give it. When a Jew becomes nasty, you can always get the best of him with the Jewish question. Then the rogue becomes insecure. "Mr. Punes, you do not seem to be completely clear about the situation of your co-religionists. As a representative of the government, I can open your eyes to the facts, if I have your permission."

"You have my permission. We people seldom have the opportunity of getting an idea about our situation from a representative of the government. If you have my permission? I beg you to do so, Mr. Lubasj."

"You must certainly remember the speech that our fine Minister of the Interior delivered in the Sejm?" began Lubasj.

"After the pogrom in Bialystok?"

"Our Minister of the Interior said: Jew Pogrom? No. We won't have that. But an economic boycott of the Jews? Quite the contrary — do you remember? — *Owszem*, the Minister of the Interior said. That is to say: 'By all means!' An economic boycott of the Jews — it's welcome! That *Owszem* has become our national economic program. Do you understand that, Mr. Punes? It means: A population of thirty-three million will carry out this boycott. You can figure out what that means. You are good at figures, Mr. Punes." Lubasj rode his national hobby horse, resolute to pull Shabse Punes down.

"I am good at figures," said Shabse calmly. "I have already figured that your number of thirty-three million boycotting citizens is not exact. You yourself will certainly allow me to subtract the three and one half million Jews in the country, against whom your national *Owszem* program is aimed, from the thirty-three million. You will allow me to do that, won't you, Mr. Lubasj?"

[27]

"I knew that," Lubasj conceded good-humoredly. "I knew that you are good at figures. That's why I want you for my partner. All right, three and one half million may be subtracted. I concede that. So there are thirty million against three and one half. Do you know what that means?"

"So there remains twenty-nine and one half million against three and one half million, by your figure. But these twenty-nine and one-half million won't remain that large very long. For you, Mr. Lubasj, are a zealous, true, perhaps too zealous patriot. And you will allow me at once to subtract from the twenty-nine and one-half million the small figure of seven million Ukrainians and White Russians, who hardly subscribe to your national *Owszem* program. Right, Mr. Lubasj?"

"Believe it or not, I actually left these out of consideration completely, I don't know why at all —"

"I do know why, and if you will permit me, though I am only a trader, I will explain to you how you found it possible to leave that out of your considerations. You true patriots have your nationalistic mouths always full of thirty-three million Poles. You scream it to the outside world to prove that you are a great power. That's foreign affairs. But in this country, between us two, you patriots continually wage a partly bloody, partly political, partly economic battle against all the minorities in the country, who make up a good third of your thirty-three million. That is patriotic domestic affairs. That, Mr. Lubasj, is why you could leave a great deal out of your considerations. Without thinking, you opened your foreign-affairs mouth, and out popped the thirty-three million of the great power. We are speaking, however, that is to say, *you* are speaking of your patriotic *Owszem* program. Let's stick to that. That is domestic affairs, Minister Lubasj. Subtract seven million from twenty-nine and a half, and twenty-two and one-half million remain. Right? Am I good at figures?"

"You are good at figures. I concede that," said Lubasj. "But, on the other hand —"

"Let me do the figuring, Minister Lubasj. Let me figure

[28]

some more. You will see that I shall soon figure to your benefit. But we have not yet come that far. Of the twenty-two and a half million, you will certainly allow me to subtract one and a half million for the small national minorities who have grounds of their own not to stand behind the boycott program. There remain a round twenty-one million. Right? But let me figure on, Mr. Lubasj. If you should help me figure, I shall surely come to the correct conclusion, but it will take a little longer. For to such patriots as you, a cipher is only a phrase which one can color one way or another, according as how it fits the *Owszem* program. Unfortunately, I must request you to permit me to subtract another round figure."

"How so? Why?" Lubasj exclaimed indignantly, and his indignation was honest. "There are no more minorities in our country."

"No," said Shabse, "there are no more national minorities to subtract. You are right there for once. But there is a political minority in our country as well that doesn't stand behind the *Owszem* program. This political minority consists of the majority of our country. Who stands behind this government? Who elected it? Our workers perhaps, whose leaders have been clapped into prison and whipped? Our peasants, whose leader, Witos, is now an emigré in Czechoslovakia because he doesn't fancy being shut up in a prison in his old age? If I were such a patriotic reckoner as you, Mr. Lubasj, I could subtract twelve from the twenty-one million. But I won't do that, because I know that a large part of this political majority who are against the government in all else, would go along with the government when it comes to robbery —"

"Robbery!"

"Pardon me. I meant to say: when it comes to the *Owszem* program. If I were such a reckoner as you, that is to say: if I reckoned only to annoy you, as you did to annoy me in beginning this whole *Owszem* business —"

"But this is — this is impossible! Why should I annoy you?"

"Let it be, Mr. Lubasj. You got up very early today, but to

fool an old horse-dealer you have to get up even earlier — and not this once for a change, if you wanted to wipe away the tracks of a murder."

"If you speak to me that way any more, Mr. Punes —"

"Let it be, Lubasj. I must figure further. You shall see that I shall draw up a balance to your benefit." It was the first time that the horse-trader had called the communal secretary simply Lubasj, and a cold sensation stole over Mr. Lubasj, as though by so doing the horse-trader had begun to undress him by force in the cool of evening.

"Please continue. I am listening," he said.

"I shall, then," Shabse continued calmly, "subtract only a fourth from the figure of twenty-one million. There remain then sixteen million. Against three and one-half. That is a fine proportion, Mr. Communal Secretary. You can be quite satisfied with this, when you consider that behind this sixteen million of yours stands a government that does not, indeed, sanction pogroms, but at the very least tolerates them; on the other hand, it invites an economic pogrom by placing the means of the state at its disposal. You can rejoice, for now we shall see how I figure to your benefit. For all these millions whom at the beginning of the figuring I subtracted with your express permission will not be active on the side of the three and one-half million Jews. Under the best of circumstances they will remain neutral, that is to say, economically speaking, they will further the *Owszem* program. But they will help to thrust the three and one-half million into even narrower straits than they otherwise would be in, and to ruin our country internally even more, this country of ours that poses as a great power in foreign eyes. Have I drawn up the balance in your favor or not? I see you are pleased. I am happy to see that."

"I hope that you don't consider me an anti-Semite because of that," said Lubasj, who was as a matter of fact very pleased with the horse-trader's figuring.

"I won't tell you right now what I consider you, Mr. Lubasj. I would have told it to you earlier if you had not suddenly come out with the *Owszem* program of our fine Minister of the Interior."

"If all Jews were like you, Mr. Punes —"

"If all Jews were like me, Mr. Lubasj, I would be ashamed to be a Jew; and if all Christian Poles were like you, Mr. Lubasj, I would be ashamed to be a Pole. Luckily, there is another kind, the crazy countess, for instance, whom you, Mr. Lubasj, don't like at all, and go so far as to think a traitress. And between you and me, there are, on the other hand, such Jews us Wolf Mohilevski. Or doesn't Velvel Dobropolier please you at bottom either, Mr. Lubasj?"

"If all Jews were like Wolf Mohilevski —"

"If all the Jews were like Wolf Mohilevski, the word Jew would have died more than a thousand years ago, and the last Jew would now be on exhibition in the world's fair in Paris at a high admission fee. Luckily or unluckily — for it really is a question whether it's worthwhile always to live among such patriots as you — there are not only Velvel Mohilevskis among us Jews but Shabses as well, resolute scoundrels like me who will soon settle accounts with such rascals as you, Mr. Lubasj."

"You have a remarkable way of expressing yourself, Mr. Punes," cried Lubasj, and moved as though to jump up from his seat.

"You wish to get off?" Shabse inquired, with a friendly expression. "Please do! We are only eight kilometres from the city."

When Lubasj replied only with an angry look, Punes added with complete calm, "I express myself well enough for a horse-trader who lives in a country where a minister talks like a robber, and a robber, you, for example, tries to talk like a minister."

"So I am a robber. But you want to go into business with me. Despite the fact that I am a robber!"

"I must go into business with you, perhaps I must. But not despite the fact that you are a robber, but rather because you are a robber. Where robbers are in power, the business man must go along with them. That is clear. Count Potocki will hardly be available to me as a partner. Nor old Bjelak, either. That is clear. But why do you want to go into business with me, Mr. Lubasj?"

"I?" Lubasj considered. "I want to go into business with you because I have no capital. That is putting it crudely, Mr. Punes."

"That is a crude truth and a crude lie, Mr. Lubasj. It is quite true that you have no capital. But why do you have none? Your fine *Owszem*-Minister places the necessary means at the disposal of every half-wit who can add one and one, to make merchants for the *Owszem* program. Hundreds and thousands of persons have been helped to become merchants overnight. A considerable part of these johnny-come-lately merchants have gone bankrupt. There's a popular name for them, already."

"I know, I know," Lubasj interrupted. "The Jews are always joking. They call them '*Owszem* merchants.' The Jews are always joking. Now, I know that I am no merchant. That is why I want to go into business with you. I don't want to be an '*Owszem* merchant.' "

"That's very sensible, Mr. Lubasj. You don't want to be an '*Owszem* merchant!' But the truth is that you could not become an '*Owzsem* merchant' because they wouldn't trust you with so much as a bad penny."

"That's not true. That is something you can't possibly know. If I had asked for a state loan, I would have received one. I have better connections than you believe."

"Perhaps you once had good connections, but things have happened since then, Mr. Lubasj. Things have happened since then —." Shabse placed the reins between his knees to get his hands free. Then he drew an envelope out of the inside pocket of his coat, took a sheet of paper out of the envelope, and read.

"In 1921 you were a cashier in the T. S. L. in Zloczow. There was a sum of 3,000 zlotys that you — "

"It was an error. I had no experience in handling money."

"Good, Mr. Lubasj, I understand. You were young. You were inexperienced, and you made an error in 3,000 zlotys in Zloczow. A year later you had some sort of patriotic post in Przemysl, and there you made another little mistake. The exact figure — I am exact at figures — was 500 zlotys. In Przemysl. Then you received another patriotic post, in Tarnopol. . . .There your error was only one of 320 zlotys. The errors, I concede, always became smaller — like the patriotic posts."

"Ah, you have been collecting material to use against me, Mr. Punes! May I ask why? Have I done anything to you? Since coming to this god-forsaken Dobropolia, I have showed you every courtesy in my office. You were apparently my best friend in Dobropolia. Now it appears that all the time you —"

"I have been collecting no material to use against you, Mr. Lubasj. I was your friend. The communal secretary's past, even if he was my friend, never interested me enough to induce me to gather information against him. But a few weeks ago you came to me with this business project, and then I informed myself about you. When you plan an undertaking with a man, you see to it that you have information about him. That is not unusual in business, Mr. Lubasj. Well, now I know what you did before you were sent out here to us in Dobropolia. But all I am interested in is where your errors had to do with money. So I took a few notes."

"Nevertheless, you still want to be my partner?" asked Lubasj.

"Nevertheless and despite everything," said Shabse, conciliatory throughout. "As my partner, you will have nothing to do with money matters. You will neither buy nor sell. And you will see only your part of the receivable net profit, Mr. Lubasj."

"You have already explained that to me a few times. That is acceptable."

"What I could not say to you before, because you suddenly tried to intimidate me with the Jewish question, the *Owszem* program — "

"That is an error, Mr. Punes. I did not try to intimidate you. One should be able to express himself freely among friends," Lubasj assured him.

"— and which you did not quite succeed in doing, as you shall soon see," the horse-trader continued calmly, "is: The second condition is that the license is not to be in your name."

"In your name, perhaps?" cried Lubasj, and his mustache trembled.

"No. Not in my name. That would be against the *Owszem* program. I am not working against the *Owszem* program. I am a patriot, too, Mr. Lubasj. Not in your name and not in my name. I have thought it over carefully. A very nice name for our license occurred to me: Walko Gulowaty."

Lubasj wished to utter a prolonged What? but he couldn't say a word. His mouth was open in round astonishment.

"W — W — Walko G — G — Gulowaty . . .?" He stammered after a moment of silence, when he had somewhat regained his voice. "A criminal, an ex-convict? That is a good joke, Mr. Punes. I say again: The Jews are always joking!"

"An ex-convict is a better and more practical choice than a criminal who is about to be a convict," said Shabse, looking at the communal secretary through a narrow slit in his eyelids; he did not remove his eyes from his companion for a time.

"You call me a criminal because I committed a few youthful sins. You, a friend?" lamented Lubasj, and looked aside, because he could not bear Shabse's look.

"Oh, no!" Shabse protested, "it is not your youthful sins I am referring to. I call you a criminal because you are a murderer, Mr. Lubasj."

"Ah!" Lubasj shouted, "now you are talking like your son. And I thought the child learned it in school from the priest's daughter!"

"Don't shout, Mr. Lubasj. See here, you are frightening the horses. When, this morning, this hand of mine —" Shabse shifted the reins to his left hand and lifted his right, spread the thick fingers, considered them a moment, then balled them into

[34]

a fleshy fist and spoke on: "— this hand of mine — may it wither if it ever does so! — was about to strike my dear child in the face, it was not, Mr. Lubasj, because I wanted to please you. Whether you believe it or not, Mr. Lubasj, I did it because this morning I thought you were innocent. I knew that you had called poor Lipale a little Trotsky. Because he had so good a head, you said. I also knew that you had been plying the Mokrczycki brothers with brandy for three Sundays before the murder. I thought to myself, he is doing this to provoke a political squabble between the Ukrainians and the Poles. After all, that's what he is here for. Or, were you perhaps not sent to Dobropolia to agitate?"

"I came — I was sent to Dobropolia to find out why the Polish peasants who had been settled in Dobropolia to Polonize the frontier were now speaking very good Ukrainian, while the Ukrainians —"

"See, that's just what I thought. He has been sent to agitate. He's doing that. What more is there to say about it? You see Mr. Lubasj, I was perhaps the only silly fool in the village who held you innocent of the murder. As late as this very morning."

"And what has caused you to change your mind during the journey, Mr. Punes?" asked Lubasj.

"You, Mr. Lubasj. Today, here, in this very wagon, you made a confession out of simple arrogance. Or do you wish to deny it now?"

"I will deny nothing. I said nothing of the sort," cried Lubasj.

"You confessed by your bragging, Lubasj. You said: 'I have already settled accounts with old Yankel. Did you see how broken he was when he came back from the funeral?' That's what you said, no less. And that is enough. Or have you again made just a small error?"

"Oh, that! And if I did say something of the sort? The woods have no ears. A man should be able to speak freely among friends."

Before, when the horse-trader had been detailing the error's in Lubasj's patriotic money dealings, the latter had, so to speak, sweated blood. But now that Shabse was accusing him of having confessed to a murder, the communal secretary of Dobropolia was not in the slightest embarrassed.

Shabse saw this and began to breathe heavily. The words that passed his damp lips were slow and heavy when he spoke again to Lubasj after a period of silence, as though the whole weight of his body were pressing on his lungs and voice.

"People — make no confessions — even among friends — when they are not murderers — Lubasj. Even a friend — must tell the truth — when he is called up as a witness."

"Ah, you're worried about being called up as a witness, Mr. Punes? Calm yourself: No trial, no witnesses. And I will see to it that there is no trial. You don't believe that I am traveling to the city with you merely for a license?"

"Now you are bragging again, Mr. Lubasj. I know there will probably be no trial. But you need not travel to the city on that account. Our pastor, Rogalski, has already taken care of it. The commission has presented its findings in such a manner that there probably can be no trial. They did not find that the child's forehead had been crushed by a bottle. Through a lamentable and unfortunate accident the child happened to get into the midst of the riot on the *Groblja*, and was simply trampled down. Do you remember the first scream at the *Groblja* on Sunday? — 'They have trampled on a dove. They are trampling on Kobza's doves.' Do you still remember that? It is now the official version. A dove was trampled to death — who can be found guilty? The child's father is guilty, a notorious sot, who had sent his son for cherry brandy on a Sunday."

"How do you know all that? I didn't know that myself." Lubasj was honestly amazed.

"I know it. I always know more than you, Mr. Lubasj. For one thing, I know everything that you know. You blurt out everything when you start bragging. Then again, I also know what I know."

"So, so," Lubasj said, wonderingly. "The deposition is not

badly drawn up. You have to concede that. I see that I have underestimated Rogalski."

"Whom do you not underestimate, Mr. Lubasj? At this very moment you are again underestimating the members of the commission, who, it is true, have drawn up the deposition as I have told you, but who will certainly have to give a report that is based on facts to the political authorities. And it is the political authorities that will have to decide whether or not a trial is in order. But should a trial take place, I shall appear as witness. And as witness I shall tell the truth, Mr. Lubasj. Mark that!"

"If there should be a trial and I should be involved in it as the accused," said Lubasj, raising his voice and narrowing his eyes as he spoke, "then you, Mr. Punes, will appear not as a witness against me but as a fellow defendant. You mark that!"

"I wish that things would come that far," said Shabse. "A defendant who stands innocent before a court of justice perhaps can prove his innocence. It is worse when one is accused but stands before no court."

"Come now, 'innocent!' You are not so innocent as you say! Who was it who called my attention to the fact that Yankel Christiampoler was infatuated with the cashier's little son, Mr. Punes? Who was it who told me that the old man clings to the boy like an old maid to her parrot, Mr. Punes? Or will you deny this in the end, Mr. Punes?"

"No," said Shabse, "I will not deny that." He took off his hat, laid it on his knee and wiped his sweating forehead with his hand. "No," he repeated, "I do not deny that. I will still be thinking of the fact that it was I who told you this when I lie on my deathbed and the death sweat breaks out over me in my last hour."

"So much the better," Lubasj remarked. "So now you know how you must behave as a witness. But have no fear; you will not be called up to be a witness. No trial, no witness."

"I know what I will say when I am called up." said the horse-trader. "I will say: I admit it is true that I said, 'The old man clings to this boy like an old maid to her parrot.' But how did I mean it? This is how I meant it: This Mr. Lubasj has a quarrel with Yankel Christiampoler, who is an old enemy of mine. Mr. Lubasj has an official position. Now sometimes it happens that a school child needs an official document. Then Mr. Lubasj will place difficulties in the way of the child's obtaining it, and the proud old man will have to soften his stand in the quarrel about a stall-and-meadow perquisite and give in at the end. This Mr. Lubasj boasts of having influence in our village school. Certainly the child has a good head, but one can place difficulties even in the way of a child with a good head, and Yankel Christiampoler will have to come to terms with Mr. Lubasj, our most influential official personage. That is how I meant it. That's not pretty, I know. It was my old hatred for Yankel Christiampoler that talked me into doing that, I know. But God is my witness: I never thought of blood and killing. It is only *you* who always think of blood and killing."

"What 'you'?" shouted Lubasj, not in indignation, but only to outshout the horse-trader, who had raised his voice at the end of his speech.

"You and your kind," Shabse shouted back, "you heathens! There will be no trial?! God will strike you dead! May a bolt of lightning shrivel you! God will punish you! The blood you are shedding will stand up against you and choke you and the freedom which you are abusing to shed blood!"

Beside himself under the onslaught of his fury, he let the reins drop into his lap, clenched his hands into fleshy fists, which he alternately beat against one another and then against his forehead. Suddenly he screamed in the high, shrill, feminine voice which he emitted only when naked at his bath:

"Great God! Such a child! Such a dear child! If I were the father, I could break you in two with these fists! I would strangle you with these hands!"

"Why, you are insane!" shouted Lubasj, who had never learned to know Shabse thoroughly. "It is dangerous to sit next to you! I am getting out!"

"I'll find my brother-in-law Mechzio in the city," Shabse continued to rage and shout. "My Mechzio is stronger than all of you together. He'll twist your necks like hens. You dogs! My Shloymele is right: You are a murderer. Great God, such a dear child!"

The horses, frightened by Shabse's unaccustomed yelling, had taken the last rise of the ascent to Yanovka with hurried steps and quivering flanks. Now, having passed the crest of the highway and finally having reached a level road, stimulated by the cool evening wind, they took the liberty, which not even a tame and enslaved work horse will relinquish, of passing water. Of a sudden they stood still, crooked their sweaty backs, spread their hind legs and sent two acrid-smelling streams splashing on the hard road. Shabse was silent and gave the horses their liberty. He sat quiet, with closed eyes and trembling cheeks. His distended nostrils breathed in the strong ammonia of the pissing horses with visible pleasure. When the horses had relieved themselves and the horse-trader had somewhat come to himself, he gathered the reins, pulled the horses up short, opened his eyes and gazed at his neighbor as though awaking from a deep dream.

"What," he said calmly, "are you still here? Get out!" And to show the speechless secretary that he was in earnest, he turned, reached back, took Mr. Lubasj's portfolio out from under the blanket, and threw it out of the wagon to the road-bank.

Lubasj sprang angrily out of the wagon and picked up the portfolio.

"I will get you into plenty of trouble for this," he cried up to Shabse, and with a threatening gesture energetically put a distance between them as he strode off in the direction of the city.

"Very well," answered Shabse calmly and only half aloud, apparently not caring that Lubasj could not hear him, "very well, I'll have plenty of trouble for this. I'll have to build my seat up again. For this seat is only good for two."

Before he disappeared around the next turn of the road, Lubasj looked back for a moment and, because he apparently did not really know his friend and opponent, he could not trust his eyes. Although Shabse was only some seven kilometers from the city, he was now actually busy rebuilding his seat. He was bending, squatting, kneeling and tumbling about industriously in his wagon, all alone on the wide horizon. Forgetting himself and all his cares, the horse-trader unmade the seat and built it all over again. He padded and ironed it with the flat of his hands, pressed it and hammered it with clenched fists, forced the loose stuff down with his elbow and pressed the tight stuff down with his knee. He did all this with a fresh, even happy, zeal, as though he wished to call nature itself to witness that at least his own drive for comfort had the creative power of an instinct. The seat was ready in a quarter of an hour. A layman would only have observed superficially that it was now narrower and somewhat higher and that the horsehair mattress did not cover the new seat lengthwise but girdled it diagonally. But as Shabse tested it with his rear, one could tell from the architect's face that the new seat was as good for one person as the old had been for two. When he took the reins in his hand again, the horses, thankful for the unexpected rest, wanted to start trotting, but Shabse held them in their places for a time. He knew the road so well that he could reckon exactly how far Lubasj must be ahead of him. He guessed him now to be on the last rise behind the village of Yanovka and Shabse wanted to avoid coming up the hill behind Lubasj. He wanted to overtake the communal secretary on the level road and at a steady trot.

After some ten minutes Shabse was close to the secretary, who had halted within hearing distance of the span and waited at the bank of the road. Shabse cracked the whip over the heads of his two young horses, and drove past Lubasj at a trot, which threatened to pass into a gallop any minute.

"Hey, Mr. Punes," he heard Lubasj calling, but pretended not to hear him. "— One word, dear friend!" Lubasj cried, and ran behind the rolling wagon. "Hey, just one word, Mr. Punes!"

Shabse let Lubasj run after the wagon for a while. Then he held up the horses and waited, without looking back at Lubasj. After a while, Lubasj came running up, his portfolio in his left hand, his hat in his right, with sweating forehead and gasping breath.

"I — have — thought — it over," he said, still out of breath, but with a friendly smile, as though nothing exceptional had taken place. "I — accept — your condition!"

"What condition?" asked Shabse, who actually did not grasp what Lubasj meant.

"The license. The license can be made out in the name of Walko Gulowaty," Lubasj explained. "For all I care," he added with a great display of nonchalance. "What do I care about that?"

In dumb amazement Shabse looked down at Lubasj. Since he remained silent, Lubasj took it as a sign of agreement. He placed his portfolio in the wagon, and began to climb up, with the intention of resuming his seat next to Shabse. But when the secretary had gotten up, Shabse said:

"Not here. You can't sit here. This is now a seat for one. Sit back there!" With his outstretched whip-stock he showed Lubasj a place on the oat-sack behind him in the cab. Lubasj stared at Shabse with the dumb look of a suffering creature, one that might well be called heartrending. But there was apparently no heart in the horse-trader that could be rent, and the extended whip-stock remained inflexible. With a sob of indignation, Lubasj proceeded to take the indicated seat on the oat-sack. The wagon set forth.

4

Lubasj was as good a realist in his way as Shabse was in his. His seat on the oat-sack was not only an insulting humiliation; it was uncomfortable as well. Lubasj no longer sat in the wagon like a traveler entitled to his seat, but squatted on the oat-sack, which was only half full and lay so flat on the bottom board of the wagon that Lubasj's chin almost touched his knee. He sat there like a tramp picked up off the street, grateful for being permitted to climb in and ride along. In this painful as well as uncomfortable situation the secretary realized that a complete change had now taken place in the relationship, complex enough already, between himself and the horse-trader. He also realized that this change was due to their verbal interchange; because he believed that it was a result of the conversation and nothing more, he allowed himself to hope that he would be able to retrieve this unfortunate change for the worse through a further conversation appropriate to the new situation. But his bitterness over the humiliatingly uncomfortable seat pushed every feasible plan out of his usually fertile mind. It was only after he had succeeded in pushing the accursed oat-sack into the back of the wagon and propping his suffering spine against the side-boards of the wagon that Lubasj found himself able to think up a more substantial topic of conversation with his moody friend. After a long period of diplomatic silence, he began to speak in righteous, heartfelt tones to Shabse Punes, as follows:

"My dear friend, you're making a regrettable error when you consider me, who am your good friend, to be an enemy of the Jews. Now, I concede there have been anti-Semites in Poland, there are anti-Semites among us nowadays, and there will, I am afraid, always be anti-Semites in Poland. No man knows how many anti-Semites there are. I certainly do not, although I began to interest myself in this problem when I was a mere schoolchild; but there is one thing I know as surely as my name is Lubasj, which is, that the Israelites themselves foolishly overestimate the number of their enemies when they hold such men as me to be anti-Semites. If you, my friend, figure it the same way, all whom you will have left in this country in the end are the crazy countess and old Bjelak in Dobropolia. Are you listening?"

Shabse gave no sign. He sat high up on his rebuilt seat and drove on. The horses sniffed the end of their journey. They knew the way. They knew that a refreshing drink from the bucket and fragrant oats in the crib were waiting for them. So they ran at a prolonged trot, their heads cleverly bobbing, their ears listening for the sounds of the nearby city.

"The fact that you, who are a man with open eyes, who has been around so much and seen and heard so much, would fall into a fit of anger at the mere mention of our national economic program was something I did not expect. You call it — very wittily, I must admit — the '*Owszem* program.' Good. But why become hysterical immediately? So help me God, as you say: What is the economic situation in this country? Walk about our cities and you cannot pass through a business street without coming upon Jewish businesses. If a Christian wants a spot of brandy, where does he go? To the Jew. If he wants a pair of boots? To the Jew. If he wants a pair of pants? To the Jew. The Jews buy and sell beer and double malt beer, Hungarian wine and French wine, champagne and Rhine wine, English beer, Polish mead, Hungarian mead, cherry brandy and all sorts of liquor. The Jews sell butter, cheese, meat, eggs, meal, garlic, onions, kindling wood, powder, pomades, tobacco, cigars, oil, lubricating oil, cobbler's paste, bread, rolls, soap, candles, vinegar, amber, pepper, safron, cloves, nutmeg, dutch herring, swedish herring, raisins, almonds, figs, dates, syrup, honey cakes, bagel, lox, olives, capers, anchovies, aniseed, citrons, sugar, paper, varnish, chalk; dyes, needles, safety pins. Silk, bands, cloth — in one word, everything. The Jews control all the business in our country. Are you listening?"

Shabse stopped his horses, turned from the waist toward Lubasj, and said:

"Were you speaking? I thought you were reading."

"I was speaking to you."

"Why, you talk like a book!"

"Congratulations, Mr. Punes! You guessed it! It *is* out of

a book, out of an old book. One hundred and fifty years old, to be exact."

"You *are* educated!"

"You know that I have a diploma."

"Naturally. The whole village calls you 'the man with the diploma.' You learned all that in school? By heart?"

"Naturally I did not learn that in school. You collected information about me. You must know that I did electioneering for a time — and I was a good speaker! I have quoted what I just told you before so often in my speeches that I could say it by heart in my sleep now."

"Marvelous," Shabse said in amazement. "But what do you mean by all that?"

"That the Jews control the whole business in our country, that's what I meant to tell you."

"Control?" Shabse repeated. He turned back again to the horses, and they drove on. Shabse was not as well versed either in politics or literature as the man with the diploma; he had no idea what Lubasj meant by the word "control." Shabse had never heard it used in this connection, and for that reason it made a stronger impression on him than the whole epical listing. The fact that the Jews dominated various things in various places — business in Poland, banks in Vienna, newspapers in Budapest — was something he had heard, or might have read in some yellow sheet. But this was something new; no longer did the Jews dominate: they controlled. Although he could never have explained why, Shabse sensed that the Jews who controlled were far more terrifying than those who merely dominated. Shabse felt the dark mystery behind the word. He, too, began to think in images. While his sturdy horses trotted toward the city, Shabse saw before him Jews with pale faces, mysteriously foregathering at midnight to "control" the business in onions and garlic. Of a sudden, he broke into pealing laughter. Like his previous wrath, the laughter of the fat colossus was hysterical and excessive, his voice again high and feminine. He screamed and giggled and clapped his hands in uncontrollable ecstasy, causing the young horses to begin to gallop in terror. Just as suddenly as he had begun, Shabse stopped. He reined in the bolting horses and drove on.

"I don't see what there is to laugh about," Lubasj complained.

Shabse did not say a word in reply. His complete attention was now focused on the horses. As they galloped Shabse had heard a clattering sound; this was a sure sign that a shoe had come loose, and perhaps was in danger of slipping off. Now as they trotted the sound repeated itself in a steady rhythm, and Shabse soon spied which of the eight hooves it was. He pulled up at the bank, got out of the wagon, went to the near horse, and examined the shoes on his left foreleg. It would hold till Zagrobela. He climbed back into the wagon, ignoring Lubasj, who now began to doubt whether Shabse had even heard his long discourse about the Jews' control over business.

In Zagrobela, one of the villages near the city, Shabse turned the horses off the road on to a side path, and stopped at the small green plot before the smithy of Red Sender. While the short-limbed sturdy smith, who had a fox-red beard and a curly black head of hair, repaired the shoe, Lubasj climbed out of the wagon to stretch his cramped legs a bit — as he said with a lamentable look. Shabse did the same. Both men stiffly walked a few steps on the green sward in front of the smithy. They carefully avoided one another's path. After a while Shabse stationed himself behind Sender, the smith, who, assisted by an apprentice who was as swift as a gnome, wielded various tongs and hammers of different sizes and was soon finished. Shabse looked at the repaired shoe very carefully, passed a calming hand tenderly over the mane of the nervous, shivering horse, paid and climbed into the wagon again. As Lubasj climbed back into the wagon, he heard Shabse asking the red-bearded smith:

"How many horseshoes do you control a day, Sender?"

"What do you mean, 'control?' Am I a customs officer? What are you laughing at, you villager? 'Control,' he says!"

"Mr. Shabse is in a very good humor, today. He has been laughing the whole day," said Lubasj, who was in a good humor himself now that he knew that the horse-trader had heard everything he had said. When they reached the highway again, the wagon stopped and Shabse turned a friendly face to Lubasj.

"Sit here next to me. You can't be lying in the wagon like a porker when we ride into the city."

Lubasj hurried to accept the invitation.

It has worked, he thought. You have only to know how to talk to him.

"It won't be very comfortable," said Shabse, as he moved over to the side a bit to give Lubasj room, "for this seat is made for one. But in only about ten minutes, I'll be done with you."

After an easy turn, they arrived at the height beyond Zagrobela. The city was visible lying on the banks of the river. The sun had just gone down. A golden dust veiled the city. A purple haze lay over the river, pent in by a large dam, whose left side was as broad as a lake. Water cascaded furiously down huge, noisy mills. Seen from a distance, this city of 40,000 appeared a metropolis. Near the river rose the thick walls of a castle, followed by yellow-painted barracks from the old Austrian days, old, solid houses, church tops, cupolas and gleaming gold crosses on church spires. The Lwowska road soon turned into Lwowska street, and there was almost a metropolitan commotion on the bridge they now crossed. Shabse restrained the horses. The street was full of pedestrians, farmers' wagons, fiacres, bicycles, and occasional automobiles. Sunburnt young sportsmen, who had spent the afternoon near the river now returned home with sunset. Older folks who were no sun worshippers began hurrying to the river after sunset, on their pale, bearded faces anticipation of the delights of a cooling dip in the shade. Fishermen who looked like apostles pulled wheel barrows loaded with open water butts where all manner of fish quivered — carps, pike and tenches. Refreshments were sold

[46]

in booths: soda water with rose or raspberry syrup, lemonade, honey cake, and other sweets. A fat marketwoman selling watermelons shouted the virtues of her fruit in stentorian tones. "Buy, Jews, buy, a food and a drink all in one!" Ambulatory sellers of ices tinkled their bells to entice the hot-eyed, barefoot children who ran about the street in noisy crowds. Lubasj smiled. If he had ordered a picture to illustrate his lecture, he could not have had one more fitting. He smiled maliciously but said nothing. He was happy to be no longer shaken up on the oat-sack and did not wish to jeopardize his relationship with Shabse again. But all Mr. Lubasj's thoughts revolved around provocation, for which he sought and at once found another occasion. They had now entered the city. To their right stood a row of houses, to their left the old Greek Catholic Church with all its soft, round, large and small onion-shaped towers painted in Byzantine blue. Lubasj looked up to the highest tower of the church and said:

"This is an old Polish city, founded by our great Hetman Tarnowski, as its name shows. But from whatever direction you enter the city, the first thing that meets your eye is the Ukrainian church."

"That isn't true, because it is only half true; and because it is only half true, it is a lie. Why must you always lie?" Shabse said calmly. He continued, interrupting himself every once in a while to greet passersby:

"If you enter the city through Lwowska street, or through Smykowiecka street, it's true. There the first thing you see is the Ukrainian church. But if you enter by way of Biala or Zarudzie, the first thing you see is the Polish church. The main street has two Polish churches, one at its head, one at its foot. In the old Dominican plaza, the main plaza, there's another Polish church. Why do you lie, Mr. Lubasj? You say that the city is named after a Polish Hetman? Very fine. But Lwow is a much larger city and it is named after Prince Lew, who was no Polish prince. Why are you always agitating? If you keep on agitating, we will experience a fourth partition of Poland, God forbid."

[47]

"God forbid, God forbid," repeated Lubasj in a kind of solemn rage, for, like every Pole, Lubasj loved Poland above all.

5

The evening of the following day they rode home. Rather than lose another day of work, Shabse decided to travel during the night, so that they might be able to arrive in Dobropolia early the next morning. Neither of the men returning home was satisfied with the outcome of his journey. Shabse had hoped to apprehend his runaway brother-in-law in the city, even if he had to turn to the police and the secretary for help. Mechzio, he had thought, should not be difficult to find in the city: one needed only to search the houses of prayer, for it was a certainty that Mechzio would be found in one of the innumerable small synagogues every morning and evening. As soon as they arrived, Shabse went to a synagogue in Lwowska street. Here he was forced to the conclusion that it was senseless to search any further. For during the course of the past week there had been many inquiries in many of the city's synagogues for a young man named Mechzio from the village of Dobropolia—they had been instigated by Wolf Mohilevski — but not a trace of him had been uncovered. Shabse soon realized that neither he nor Mr. Lubasj would succeed where Velvel Dobropolier had failed, and gave up the idea of finding his brother-in-law in this city. So he proceeded to his business and succeeded in closing a transaction of which we shall hear more later.

Mr. Lubasj also was in an unhappy frame of mind. His friends in official quarters had not been able to assure him that he would secure the tavern license which lay so near to his heart. The political prospects his friends held up to him depressed the secretary even more than his personal failure. To his great disappointment Lubasj was given to understand that there was no desire in influential circles to expedite the national frontier policy; on the contrary, the inner political circles were concerned with building closer relationships with the Ukrainians. True, his party friends afterwards consoled him with the assurance that the appeasement period would not last very long; but Lubasj was not encouraged by this consolation.

There was one satisfaction that Mr. Lubasj did derive from his visit to the city — a small satisfaction to counterbalance his failure to secure a tavern license. He managed to place an account of the bloody Sunday in Dobropolia in a journal called *The Podolian Messenger*, a rural paper, such as are common in small cities. He had composed an account of the events in Dobropolia and brought it along with him in his portfolio; now, since the editor made only a few insignificant changes in his presence, the secretary believed that he had improved his relations with the press, of which he used to brag in Dobropolia. We shall unfortunately meet Mr. Lubasj's literary work again. For the secretary's article in *The Podolian Messenger* was to have dire consequences for several persons whose fate lies close to our heart — above all, for Yankel Christiampoler and, as we shall see, for Mr. Lubasj himself. The travelers had again to traverse Lwowska street at a snail's pace for, as it had been the day before, it was good bathing weather, and lively crowds of young people moved noisily about on the street. The evening smelled of smoke and cooking, of horsedung, fruit and roses. Shabse stopped in front of a relatively uncrowded booth and ordered two glasses of soda-water-with-rose-syrup to be brought out to the wagon for himself and Mr. Lubasj. After he had cooled his throat with the fizzing cold drink and had paid for the drinks, he turned a bright face to his friend and said:

"Yesterday you forgot to mention that the Jews control the whole soda-water-with-rose-syrup business on Lwowska street."

Lubasj averted his face and with a piteous gesture of his arm said:

"He's beginning again!"

"Another glass?" asked the black-eyed girl who had brought the drinks, mistaking Lubasj's gesture. Shabse laughed, whipped the horses, and they proceeded over the bridge at a slow trot, past the noisy mill and out of the city. At the rise before Za-grobela, Shabse said:

"I am not beginning again, Mr. Lubasj. I only wanted to make you look at me. Look at me! Do you notice any change?"

"Why, you have cut half your beard off! And your earlocks are gone! What have you done?!"

"Am I changed much?" Shabse asked gloomily.

"No," said Lubasj. "I didn't notice it at all at first. You look a little older, strangely enough; perhaps because your few grey hairs are more visible. You look quite good. You should have done it long ago. You had a beard that was long enough for three Jews. I only wonder why you did it now."

"You were the one who gave me the idea, Mr. Lubasj," said Shabse, cheerful again.

"I?" said Lubasj. "Never! It never occurred to me that you would do this."

"You gave me the idea of changing my business, or rather of expanding it. I had long been planning to do so; but I couldn't decide."

"You want to change your business? The tavern license will be granted before long."

"Your tavern license is done for, Mr. Lubasj. Let's not pre-tend," said Shabse.

"It is just a misunderstanding," said Lubasj. "It will just take a little time. You'll see!"

"You need not trouble yourself any longer, Mr. Lubasj. You will never get the tavern license. But I am honor bound to thank you. You gave me a good idea."

"Idea? When?"

"Yesterday," said Shabse. "When you recited the list of Jew-ish businesses, it occurred to me that it was up to me to add an-other. You can introduce a new item to your list: Pork. Polish pork."

"What?" said Lubasj. "You want to deal in pork! No mem-ber of your faith has ever done so in this country."

"I know," said Shabse. "That is why I have decided, as you see, to enter the business of exporting pork to Vienna."

"Now you are joking again!" Lubasj said.

"A few weeks ago I received a letter from an acqaintance who is a Ukrainian pork butcher. He wrote me about a newly founded company, proposing that I join it as its chief salesman, with a certain capital investment on my part, of course. I have considered this proposition for a long time. For, as you yourself say, no member of my faith has ever done business in pork in this country. It was no easy decision. But after yesterday's conversation with you I decided."

"All because of the list I recited?" wondered Lubasj.

"No," said Shabse, "naturally, that was only a joke. But when you explained the '*Owszem* program' of our fine Minister of the Interior to me, I said to myself: 'I shall join the company' — and no sooner thought than done. In such things I move very fast."

"So you are joining a Ukrainian company," said Lubasj reproachfully. "You are getting yourself connected with the Ukrainians."

"I would join up with the devil himself against the '*Owszem* program' of our fine Minister of the Interior. I would even go into partnership with you. But where is your license?"

"The fact that you have decided to go into the pork business is your affair. But how are you going to be an exporter at this time? The frontier is closed."

"Mr. Lubasj, you imagine that you know more than I. But that is not the case. Our government has concluded a new trade pact with Austria. One can now export pork to Vienna again. Contingent on certain circumstances, obviously."

"Aha," said Lubasj jubilantly.

"What do you mean by 'aha?' " Shabse shouted at him.

"Then you need an export license," said Lubasj, fondling the word "license." Lubasj loved that word.

"Certainly one needs an export license. It has already been

obtained. The Ukrainian pork butchers have an export license. I have nothing to do with that. I am the chief salesman. I shall travel to Vienna and do my business there. That's why I cut off my beard and earlocks. When you're a pork merchant you can't look like a rabbi. The pork merchants in Vienna would wonder."

"I am afraid that it is your wife who will wonder most of all, Mr. Punes!" Lubasj gave Shabse a long look, and it was hard for him not to burst into laughter. The horse-trader looked like a shorn poodle, not at all like a pork merchant. But Mr. Lubasj did not dare to laugh, fearing a fresh outburst of anger on the part of the colossus, whose face had suddenly grown gloomy at the words "your wife." Shabse was silent. Those two words had sealed his lips. He remembered how even the Christian barber who had clipped his hair had burst into laughter at sight of the consternation with which Shabse regarded the finished product in the looking glass. But it was not the scene that he pictured as taking place in his house because he had cut off his beard and sidelocks that troubled him. Even in Dobropolia there were Jews with clipped beards — Leib Kahane, for example, who was known as Mr. "Lemberg-there's-a-city-for-you," wore a round clipped beard on his civilized person; Shmiel Gruenfeld, the demobilized sergeant and tavern keeper, was smooth-shaven, and the three short-necked sons of the distiller Gruenspan also had smooth-shaven faces and, with their mustaches and round, close-clipped heads, were only distinguishable from the young Kobzas and Zoryjs by their clothing — and that distinction was not to their advantage. Shabse's lifelong orthodox dress was a concession to his wife, the pious sister of the pious Mechzio. Now Mechzio was away. Even if he had not decided to join the pork company, Shabse would have taken pleasure in cutting off his beard and earlocks, simply to punish his wife for her brother's flight. She would have to bear it, would Mechzio's patient sister, who had come to judge her husband's piety correctly in the course of the years. She would sigh for a while and there

[52]

the matter would end. But a pork business was another matter
— Shabse knew that well. He had had a few weeks to decide
whether to accept his friend's, the Ukrainian pork butcher's,
offer. He had counted and discounted in advance his wife's
antagonism and wrath. But when Lubasj reminded him of his
home, Shabse did not see his unhappy wife. Instead he saw
his son, his younger son, the Bible scholar. How will Shloymele
take to this? What will my Shloymele say? The crafty horse-
trader had completely left this factor out of his calculations.
Now, because of that error, a sweat broke over his body in the
cool of the evening. Shloymele would not take to it. His
younger son resembled his mother in other ways. But he was
not such a patient soul. He was really *his* son, too, the little
Bible scholar. Thank God for that. These were bad times for
patient people. His children would not be Mechzios. He did
not have to worry about Kalman, the older child. He would
be on his father's side. But what would *her* darling say? Your
son and my son, that had been the game in Shabse's house for
years. He had played along. But he knew very well that it
was only a game. His wife would never know which of the
sons was his darling. Shabse himself knew better. He had
played along because it pleased him to employ the horse-trader's
craft even at home, and with a hoax to deceive himself and
those nearest to him.

The horses were already wavering shadows racing on the
gray highway when Shabse woke in terror from his thoughts.
The lights of the houses in Yanovka told him that night had
meanwhile fallen.

"I've only made a seat for one for the trip home," he said
to Lubasj.

"He's beginning again!" Lubasj shouted into the night.
"I thought," Shabse added softly, "that there was no sense
in both of us not sleeping all night. We'll change off."

"Very good," Lubasj hurried to agree. "Give me the reins
now, and you lie down a little. You seem to be very tired."

"No, Mr. Lubasj," said Shabse, "I never let the reins out of my hands at night. They are good horses, but at night you never know — a hare may scamper over the road, a horse become shy, the driver be nodding — and you end up in a ditch. No, Mr. Lubasj, we'll do it this way: first we'll have a snack; or have you already eaten this evening?"

"Not a bite," said Lubasj, "I ran around so in the city, I never even ate at noon. Have you brought a bite along?"

"I think we'll eat now. Then you can lie down, and I'll wake you up with daylight. Then I'll sleep a little. Look — back there, in that basket behind the seat, I've got a snack."

Shabse stopped the horses, took the basket that Lubasj handed him and divided the provisions he had brought along with him. He had a roasted chicken, sour pickles, and a loaf of white bread. Shabse tore the roasted chicken very skilfully into two unequal parts, handed Lubasj the smaller portion, and they ate silently in the silence of the night.

"In Yanovka," said Shabse, when they had finished the supper, "we'll have a glass of beer and then you can lie down back there."

There was still a light in the tavern in Yanovka. Shabse stopped before the door and ordered two pitchers of beer by loudly calling into the inn through the window. Refreshed and grateful, Lubasj settled down on the oat-sack, which he used as a pillow this time, and stretched out in the wagon as well as he could. They left Yanovka at a quick trot. Shabse felt more comfortable when he noted that his traveling companion had soon fallen asleep. Now he could be alone with his worries. And the worries did not keep him waiting long. They sprang at Shabse like bloodhounds at a wild boar — and Shabse defended himself like a boar.

It was a cloudy starless night. The crickets sawed their metallic music in the fields. But Shabse did not hear them. He drove past dark forests. Nightingales sang in the forest. But Shabse did not hear them. He drove past rivers and swamps. Frogs croaked in the swamps. But Shabse did not hear them. At midnight he stopped in front of a trough in a village asleep in the night. He fed the horses, but himself restlessly circled the wagon and span. It was only when the horses lowered their necks and began to nibble at the grass that Shabse became aware that the horses had had their fill. He quickly climbed up to his seat. His worries sat next to him again. One village and then another came and went; the cocks were already crowing their golden proclamation of sunrise, but he did not hear them. The horses ran eagerly at a steady pace. He did not need to drive them. All clever horses run eagerly home. When Shabse set his eyes on his horses again, they were on a sunny streeet.

Lubasj awoke, rubbed his eyes, and yawned a good-morning:

"Why, we are already in Dobropolia! 'Why didn't you wake me?"

"I don't know," said Shabse in a hoarse voice. "It was a short night," he added in amazement. "A very short night."

Shabse marveled. For, like most people who have never spent a night in anxious worry, he believed such nights to be long. Now he knew otherwise. And he was right. For, whatever complaint you may have about anxiety and worry, they are not tedious. Those people who tell tales of long, sleepless nights full of worry and anxiety have certainly never lain awake through such nights. Otherwise they would know that such nights are short, astoundingly short.

"Do you know anything about pork?" asked Shabse after a while. They were already on the main street of Dobropolia.

"I? Why?"

"I'll need two buyers for Dobropolia and the environs. You can earn some money — that is, if you know something about pork."

"I? Buy pork for you?" Lubasj shouted at him. "You forget, it seems to me, that I am a man with an education, that I have a diploma."

"For my part," said Shabse, amicably and tired. "So my neighbor Onufry Borodaty will earn the money. And my second neighbor Ivan Kobza will prove more responsible than you."

"Let me out!" shouted Lubasj in wrath. He sprang out of the wagon with his portfolio under his arm. "Drive on alone through the village. You, on your seat made for one! I am going to His Reverence, Canon Rogalski. He has already converted one Jew in the city. When I tell him that you have cut off your beard and earlocks and become a pork merchant, he will agree that you have taken the first step to conversion. — Good morning, Mr. Punes!"

6

Shabse had proposed to the communal secretary that he become a buyer for him thinking thus to induce him to be silent. For Shabse first wanted to see how his family, especially his younger son, would receive the change in his appearance. But, tired and excited, he had ruined his relations with Lubasj completely and now he realized that the whole village would learn about his prospective pork business during the course of the morning. He decided not to wait. He had barely arrived in front of his house, and was still turning the horses down the road to his farm, when he called in an overloud voice to his two neighbors, Ivan Kobza and Onufry Borodaty, urging them to come over at once, for he had something to tell them. His neighbors hurried to obey him. Shabse wishes to sell a piece of his vegetable garden, thought Kobza. Shabse wishes to rent out a part of his meadow, thought Borodaty. But they were not disappointed when Shabse told them about the pork business as he unspanned the horses, and asked them both to come along with him in the role of experts and buyers for Dobropolia and the environs. They were not disappointed; but they hesitated; they thought it over; they asked questions and both agre_d on one thing — that this was a matter one could not hurry; they would first have to talk it over with their wives. This was just as Shabse had expected. There was plenty of time, certainly a couple of weeks, perhaps as much as two months before buying would begin. His only concern was to take his family by surprise. In that respect he succeeded as well — or as poorly — as he had expected.

His two neighbors had not yet stepped into their homes to share the news with their wives, when Mrs. Punes rushed out of the house with her two children; the children were not completely dressed, for there was no school that day, the long vacation having begun. Wordlessly at first, shame and dismay on their faces, they considered the physiognomy of the homecomer.

"What has he done?" softly said Shabse's younger son and took his mother's hand.

"*You* are going to deal in pork? *You?*" said his mother.

"Yes!" shouted Shabse, "Isn't that good enough for you! Can you tell me where your brother is?! Your pious brother, the tramp?!"

"You are going to deal in pigs? You?!" repeated his wife, and detained her older son, who was about to cross over to his father.

"All my evil dreams of this night, all my evil dreams of last night, all the evil dreams of all my evil nights — may they all fall on your head." His wife spoke these words as though they were the formula of an incantation, snatched her two sons and pulled them after her into the kitchen.

Shabse stood a moment stock-still. Then he went into the stall and looked after the horses. Afterwards he returned to his wagon and took out the presents that he had remembered to bring back from the city, as was his wont. Tired and visibly disturbed, he walked into the house with the three packages. He had some material for a blouse for his wife, a tie for his older son who was almost thirteen, and a book for the younger son. He placed the present for his wife, which was wrapped in paper, on the kitchen table, handed the narrow box with the tie to his son Kalman, who began to unpack it at once, and was about to offer the third present to his younger son, when the latter, backing up towards the door, held his father off with unafraid eyes, and clearly repeated the same formula he had addressed the day before to Lubasj.

"Thou shalt treat it with revulsion. Thou shalt hate it. For it is unclean!"

"It is a book!" said his father tearfully.

"It is unclean," said his younger son.

"It is a Hebrew grammar, Shloymele!"

"In your hand it is unclean!" shouted his younger son and burst into tears. He had always wanted the grammar.

Shabse tried to catch his son but missed as Shloymele ran out through the open door. Shloymele stood a moment before the house, then continued to run, as though he had decided on a goal. At first he ran up the street; then he turned around and began to run in the direction of the *Groblja*. He was only half dressed, wearing short pants and a cap. Crying softly to himself, he ran barefooted over the dew-cool dust of the *Groblja*. When he approached the spot where Lipale had been done away with, he was so frightened that he stopped crying. He shut his eyes and reconsidered a moment whether he ought not to turn back. But he controlled himself and went on, carefully setting one foot before another, till he was past the danger spot. Then he heard Lipale screaming. Without knowing it, he screamed himself and ran past the *Groblja* with all his strength. When he knew that the *Gazon* was behind him, and he could see the small dam, he suddenly felt as light-hearted as though he had been borne over the *Groblja* on wings. Soon he saw Reb Wolf's house. He was saved.

The horse-trader's younger son was the only person in Dobropolia who never called Velvel Dobropolier by his full name or Master or Mr. Mohilevsky. With the fine sense for spiritual values that pious children frequently have, Shabse's younger son never called Velvel Dobropolier anything but Reb Wolf. And with a child's sure instinct, he had long ago discovered that Velvel Dobropolier was pleased at the name. To Shloymele, Velvel was the pious Talmud scholar, the guardian of Jewishness, the defender of all the Jews in Dobropolia. So, when his heart was troubled, he ran to his Reb Wolf.

There was not a sound to be heard in the house. All the

windows were still shuttered. The flagstones of the paved drive-way were already warmed by the morning sun and were pleasant to Shloymele's feet. He stood on the warm stones for a while. Then he saw that the kitchen door was already unlocked, and slowly walked over to it. The kitchen was empty. He let himself down on the threshold and waited. After a while Pessa came back from the flower garden. She had a bunch of flowers with her which she had cut for her best friend, Bjelak's daughter.

"Woe is me, what are you doing here so early?"

The child rose and ran quickly over to Pessa, who stretched out her arms. Sobbing, the boy fell into Pessa's open arms.

"My — father — has become — a pork merchant," he got out, between sobs.

"Who told you that, you silly child?"

"He just came home. He cut his beard and earlocks off, and now he is a pork merchant.

"Come with me," said Pessa, "come. But you must not cry. Everybody is still asleep."

The lad immediately stopped crying and followed Pessa into the kitchen.

"Have you already had breakfast, my child?"

"No," said Shloymele. "We had just gotten up. Mother was just about to make the fire. Then he came back from the city, and shouted to Ivan and to Onufry, and now all three of them will buy pork."

"Sit down," said Pessa, "sit down. I will make you breakfast right away."

"Where is the young master?" Shloymele asked.

"He is still sleeping. You know Panko is so sick, and Alfred goes to visit him every night, and comes home early in the morning."

"I know," said Shloymele, and sighed deeply. "And Reb Wolf?"

"Reb Wolf will soon get up."

"I want to talk to Reb Wolf," said the boy.

"What do you want to talk to him about?" asked Pessa.

"There's a Talmud school in Kozlova. I want Reb Wolf to send me to the Talmud school in Kozlova. That's what I want to talk to him about."

"Do you like chocolate?" Pessa set a cup of hot chocolate on the table, and pushed a chair over to Shloymele.

"Is this chocolate? Can you drink chocolate?"

"Yes," said Pessa, "just like coffee. Do you like it?"

The boy took a sip. He held his breath and looked at Pessa delightedly.

"Do I like it! It tastes like —"

"Like what?" Pessa asked, happy that the boy had apparently forgotten his troubles.

"It tastes like *Gan Eden*. It tastes like manna."

And, in rhythm, in the sing-song of Bible study, the would-be Talmud scholar explained to worrisome Pessa what hot chocolate tasted like. "Manna is said to have tasted like *tzapichit bidvash*. *Dvash* is honey. *Tzapichit bidvash* means: like *tzapichit* in honey. Nobody knows what *tzapichit* is. I asked my rebbe, and my rebbe said, 'No one knows.' Now I know: *tzapichit* means 'hot chocolate.' "

After Shloymele had smacked his lips over the last drop and licked the spoon, Pessa said:

"So, my child, now I am going to take this basket to poor Panko. You see this is Panko's breakfast. You must come along with me."

"I want to wait for Reb Wolf," said Shloymele.

"You are a clever child," said Pessa. "You know Alfred and Reb Wolf are sad now; we all have so many worries. It isn't easy for Reb Wolf to take and send you away. I shall speak to Alfred. Alfred will speak to Reb Wolf. Reb Wolf will speak to your father and your mother. Wait a few days. Wait, and don't say a word at home. Just as though nothing had happened."

They set forth and Shloymele promised not to tell a word at home about his early visit to Pessa.

"And if you get up early again, my child," said Pessa in farewell, "you can always come to me in the kitchen, and I shall make you hot chocolate."

The boy went home in a good mood. His mother was sitting on the bench in front of the house. But she did not sit as usual. She was quiet enough, but her eyes wandered as if she were waiting for someone to come and take her far away at any moment. Shabse was murmuring the Morning Prayer inside the house. Contrary to his wont, this morning he prayed almost as long as Reb Wolf.

BOOK II

BOOK II

1

ALFRED had made his first acquaintance with death. Though he had grown up fatherless, he seldom thought of his father's death. His father had fallen in the War, and his mother had told him a great deal as a child about his father who had gone to war and never come home again. But that was a childhood memory that had remained in the realm of the legendary, like everything else that he could remember from the period of his childhood. Now death had stepped into the reality of his life. It was his first acquaintance with death. We all make our acquaintance with death the first time we lose one who is dear to us. This acquaintance can be deep and real or it can be superficial and transitory, depending essentially on the age at which we make it. If it takes place when we are mature and consequently already thinking of our own death, this acquaintance can be transitory. For, the person who thinks of death in his maturity is often like the rich man who fears poverty. The rich man rejects the poor man who puts out his hand for alms because he already considers himself poor. But coming face to face with death when we are already old enough to think about death in general, but still young enough not to think about our own in particular, we may be able to enter into a deeper relationship with death, which will not cease to be terrifyingly intimate as long as we live.

Alfred was still young, his heart still rich enough, to experience the death of his small friend without fearing for his own. Thus his first acquaintance with death was very intimate. Although he discovered the whole horrible truth about the murder of little Lipale from the schoolmistress Rakoczy in Rembovlia — for even the children in the village knew what had happened and told it freely in school — he received this truth with his heart, not with his nerves. That meant that he tormented himself with pain over the absence of the dearly beloved boy, not with agony over what had happened. His heart was inaccessible to consolation, and it wished to remain so. In the painful recognition that this was the only means of preserving the memory of his young friend without falseness, if not completely without self deceit, Alfred wished to retain his pain in all its first sharpness and heaviness the rest of his life. This heartfelt desire gave him the strength and bearing at the funeral to accept the condolences of his fellow-mourners — and this astonished his uncle Velvel, who wished to send Alfred with all speed to Vienna immediately after the burial.

Alfred spent the first few days tending Panko. There was an open wound in Panko's leg that began to fester. Dr. Chramtjuk was of the opinion that the limb would have to be amputated. But Panko fought an amputation with an unconquerable obstinacy. After a few days Panko's situation was so serious that the Ukrainian doctor gave up all hope; but Alfred sent for two other doctors, and a week later it appeared that Panko would escape with both his life and his limb. It was chiefly Pessa who shared the care of Panko with Alfred. She cooked the invalid's light diet and Alfred and Pessa took turns in the night watch beside the sickbed, for Panko's mother proved quite helpless in her stunned condition. She had two sons, of whom the younger was in military service, and now the elder seemed to be on the verge of death.

Besides, Alfred had Yankel to be concerned about. The old man was completely broken up. His hands trembled, his face had turned the color of wax, and his beard had grown thin. His eyes continually blinked and, when addressed, he placed a hand to his ear and asked, "Eh?" Old Yankel had become a helpless old man. During the seven days that Avram Aptowitzer and his older son sat on footstools and ate eggs dipped in ashes,

[66]

Alfred saw to it that a prayer quorum was assembled in the house of mourning, and inquired of his uncle whether it was permissible for him to say the prayer for the dead after Lipale. Velvel answered in the negative, for Lipale did have a father and a brother who said the prayer for the dead for him three times daily.

After the first seven days, Alfred formed a permanent prayer quorum for the whole year of mourning in Grandfather's Room. It was not easy to bring the ten men together on weekdays, but Alfred spared no pains, and, singularly, it was old Yankel who encouraged him, although, because it was generally not possible to observe mourning regulations on weekdays, it was not the custom to do so. With the inclusion of the distiller and his shortnecked sons, there were nine men on the estate, for Davidel Aptowitzer, being just thirteen years of age, counted in the House of Prayer as an adult. There was need of only one more man to complete the quorum. Luckily Salman the teacher was there. On the other hand, the distiller's family could not always be counted on, for the distiller's sons were industrious peasants, sparing of their time; Alfred often had to span the gray horse of an evening and ride to the village for a tenth man; mostly it was the small Levite who filled the complement.

Mechzio had disappeared. At Alfred's request, Velvel Dobropolier had made inquiry after Mechzio in all the villages and even in the city, but nowhere had a man been seen wearing a peaked cloth cap on a diseased head. Alfred also inquired daily of the horse-trader. He would be able to inform Mechzio that his drudgery for his brother-in-law had come to an end, for immediately after the burial in Rembovlia, Yankel had suddenly exclaimed: "I will take Mechzio to me . . . I can no longer be so alone."

Like all mourners, Alfred now lived in the past. Like all who live in the past, Alfred lost every interest in reality, which — insofar as it had no connection with Lipale — had become empty, insubstantial and colorless. He became scrupulously observant. During the year which he had spent at his uncle's home he had accepted the custom of praying three times daily, but till now it had been only a habit, a practice, a courteous concession to his host's way of life. Now, after the death of his young guide in piety, whose prayerful "Amen" still lived in the dead silence of Grandfather's Room — revived twice daily by its painful absence from the murmurous prayers of the mourners — now for the first time Alfred was able to tune his voice to that of little Lipale. At least he felt it so, and his melancholy piety increased from prayer to prayer, causing unrest to his uncle. Death is the greatest missionary — as is known to all priests, both true and false, to all theologians, true and false, and to all religions, true and false. But Velvel Dobropolier was not pleased with Alfred's piety.

Evenings, after the last prayer of the day, Alfred would remain with Avram Aptowitzer in Grandfather's Room, and while the unhappy father bent and shook over the holy volumes which it was incumbent for the mourner to study and read, Alfred sat silently in a corner gazing for hours on end at the light for the dead burning in an oil-filled glass in the prayer room. In a mystic fervor Alfred would see the soul of the martyred child in the flame.

One evening — it was at the beginning of the third week of mourning — Avram Aptowitzer said to Alfred, "Tomorrow, I must go to my wife in Kozlova." Alfred looked at the pale face of the mourning father in the weak glow of the light for the dead. Not sorrow alone lay on the cashier's face, but anxiety and painful disappointment.

"Has it — reached that point?" asked Alfred, his heart stopping for a complete second, and his own face reflecting the cashier's expression.

"Yes," said Aptowitzer.

"Is it a — girl?"

"A — girl —" said Aptowitzer.

They looked at one another in silence. At that moment Alfred hated the cashier, hated Lipale's father, haunted by the thought of the dead child's mother returning home to an empty house with questions and lamentations and accusations. "What have you done to Lipale? Is this how you watched over my darling? Broken, shattered is the crown of my life!"

Pessa had already heard Lipale's mother lamenting and weeping after this fashion and Alfred, too, feared her return home. Now seeing that same fear in the father, he suddenly realized that both the father and himself were guilty. They were both guilty — the father for having sent Lipusj to the tavern for brandy that Sunday, and Alfred, because he had had no time to stroll with Lipusj in the forest. He shared the mourning father's disappointment as well, for Alfred, too, secretly had hoped that the mother would come home with a new-born son — a substitute for Lipusj. So now Alfred hated the father who had hoped to find consolation in a substitute for Lipusj, a substitute for him for whom there could be no substitute, because Alfred himself had suffered with and been ashamed of similar secret and hasty thoughts of consolation.

2

On the Sunday of the third week of mourning, the bailiff of Daczkow, Mr. Krasnianski, paid Yankel a visit. Alfred, who had heard so much about this old friend of Yankel's, was introduced to him. The bailiff of Daczkow was much younger than Alfred had pictured him. He was barely older than Velvel Dobropolier and looked even younger. He was a man of large and powerful build with blue eyes and a bushy, reddish-blond mustache that clung to his heavy-lipped mouth like a horseshoe. Despite his size, he moved about Yankel's spacious room with almost dainty grace. It occurred to Alfred that the bailiff of Daczkow treated Yankel as a close disciple does a respected master. Alfred did not remain in the room very long, for he had the impression that the two men had something of importance to discuss. He was also embarrassed in front of the stranger because of his poor command of Polish and gathered that at that moment old Yankel wished to conceal this lack of his. Alfred excused himself after the exchange of a few courtesies.

[69]

Yankel's old friend proved singularly successful in pulling
Yankel together. After his guest had left, Yankel took a turn
around the farm dressed in gleaming Sunday boots, discussed
the next week's work with Domanski, left orders for the man
in charge of the threshing, and then, walking slowly through
Pessa's garden, still swaying somewhat but not so lamentably
as before, said without any introduction to Velvel:

"Velvel, you'll have to see to it that you get the youngster
away from here for a while. And very soon."

"I've been trying to do so all along. He keeps putting it off
till tomorrow. Or else he says he'll leave next week. And he
stays on. The thirtieth is his mother's birthday. Today is
already the twenty-eighth. You speak to him."

"His mother's birthday — is that important?"

"Dr. Frankel thinks it is."

"Alfred must leave for a few weeks. While he's away, I'll
settle accounts with that scoundrel —"

"With whom will you settle accounts?" asked Velvel, frightened.

"With that scoundrel, that murderer, that Mr. Lubasj,
that —"

"Ah, Yankel, you still don't understand what times we're
living in. You still believe —"

"I believe nothing. Here! Read this!"

And with shivering hands Yankel drew forth an envelope,
took out a small newspaper clipping and handed it to Velvel.

"Read this, please, then talk!"

Velvel put on his glasses and read:

Our Dobropolia correspondent reports: Our fine peasants in Dobropolia have shown us how to make short
shrift of Jews. We have a landowner here, a Caftan Jew,
a real Croesus. One day he rides off to Vienna, comes
back with his nephew whom he has adopted and made
heir to his enormous fortune. Soon after the German
money-grubber arrives, he learns the Ukrainian tongue
with his clever little Jewish head — Ukrainian, mind you,

not Polish, although Dobropolia is an ancient Polish community — and begins to spread monarchical propaganda among the Ukrainian peasants for the House of Hapsburg. The Ukrainian peasants immediately name him *Cisarski*, "the imperial one." This bold Jew-boy, barely seventeen years old, spreads communist propaganda among the Polish population, and the Polish peasants call him "little Trotsky." On the pretense of "helping" our splendid peasants who are fulfilling a sacred national mission on the frontier "fraternize" with the Ukrainian traitors, he convokes political meetings, makes partly monarchistic, partly communistic speeches, and agitates against our government, which unfortunately still believes it is necessary to treat the Jews as citizens having equal rights. The patience of our Christian population is great, but it has its limits. Our bold compatriots from Dobropolia prove that. Two weeks ago, on a Sunday, another such fraternization was supposed to take place. But this time the Jew-boy got his due. This time the provocateur felt the wrath of the people. A volley of stones greeted the provocateur when he appeared on the common. He fell where he stood, with broken limbs and smashed guts. Israel's "Ay! Vay!" can be imagined. (V. L.)

"Well, what do you say to that?"

Velvel rubbed his dry forehead with trembling fingers, the newspaper clipping shaking in his other hand. For a long time he was silent then he said:

"Do you think . . .?"

"I know it."

"You know that V. L. is our communal secretary?!

"Yes. It's the man with the diploma. I'm sure of it."

"Where did you get the clipping?"

"Krasnianski brought it along."

"But there is no proof that V. L. is unquestionably Vincenty Lubasj."

"Krasnianski knows it. He can prove it."

"You should have let the scoundrel have the two cows," said Velvel, but not reproachfully.

"But he had *none*, Velvel. He had none of his own at all!

He wanted to place Shabse's cows in our stall. I can't allow myself to be blackmailed. But if I had known that this would harm the poor child . . . I shall make it hot for him here. But first Alfred must leave."

"Yankel, you forget —"

"I forget nothing. Krasnianski has spoken to the countess. He told her everything that has happened here. She was beside herself. She will see to it that the scoundrel is removed."

"That is good, Yankel. That is very good. But you mustn't get involved in this."

"If I don't get involved, the removal will take years in coming officially. It has to be made impossible for him to stay here."

"What will you do?"

"That is my affair. Give me back the newspaper clipping!"

"Listen, Yankel," said Velvel, and looked searchingly at the bailiff. "I don't doubt at all that you can make it warm for the scoundrel in the Old Village. But the New Village will — be on his side. I am warning you."

"We will see about that," said Yankel. "Just let me do what I want. You see to it that Alfred leaves for a time right away. He must not be around."

"I should send a special delivery letter to Dr. Frankel," said Velvel.

"And I shall speak to Alfred at once."

"You are not yet telling him what your intentions are, Yankel?"

"God forbid! Alfred must know nothing about it!" said Yankel, replaced the newspaper clipping in its envelope, and went to the door. But before opening it, he turned to Velvel again, looked at him for a long time with astonishment in his eyes, and said: "What do you say to that, Velvel? A seventeen-year-old monarchist —"

"— And a Bolshevik at the same time —"

" —A little Trotsky —"

"— Who is here propagandizing for the House of Hapsburg —"

[72]

"— What is the meaning of that, Velvel? . . ."

"That is the new German school, Yankel. Do you remember how, when I had just arrived in Vienna, I bought a newspaper on the street to see whether there was anything in it about our congress?"

"Yes," said Yankel. "You brought me right back to the hotel and left in excitement. I remember."

"Yes," said Velvel. "The report in that paper about our congress was in the style of this item. Astoundingly similar. The delegates of Agudas Israel were Bolsheviks and finance-Jews at one and the same time. Exactly as here. Every Jew a magnate and a Bolshevik at the same time. That is the new German school."

"Where are we living, Velvel?"

"In the Exile, Yankel."

"But is was different before, Velvel."

"It was a breathing space, Yankel."

Yankel opened the door and quickly went out. First he went to old Bjelak, the head of the community. The old peasant was certain, for his part, that the communal secretary was the author of the report.

"I sent a report to the authorities myself," said old Bjelak, "because I knew that Mr. Lubasj had reason to distort and falsify everything. I also asked that the man be pulled off my neck. Just have patience. We'll soon be rid of him. What are *you* thinking of doing?"

"I will go from farm to farm with this rag so that everybody may see what Mr. Lubasj is writing in the newspapers. With your permission, of course."

"With my permission, of course. Do that."

And Yankel set out on his way. He went from farm to farm, like a mailman, and read the article aloud. Where there was someone in the house who could read, he allowed him to read it aloud. First he went through the streets of the New Village, and when he was through there, already weary, he turned to the Old Village. He remembered how uncontrollably Alfred

[73]

had laughed in the field when Yankel told him that he would almost have become a mailman if he had served in the Emperor's army for the whole nine years, as his friend, the sergeant Belenoc, thought proper. No, he was not a good mailman, old Yankel. He was already tired when he slowly walked through the dust of the *Groblja* to the Old Village. Nevertheless, he continued on. It was almost night when he returned home from the Old Village. He was exhausted and hoarse from so much reading, but patently sure of what he was doing. He had really made it hotter for the communal secretary in the Old Village, where the Ukrainians lived, than in the New Village, where the Poles were — as Velvel had correctly foreseen.

That same night, Velvel did not let Alfred remain alone with Avram Aptowitzer after the prayer for the dead. He sat with a book in Grandfather's Room with the intention of pressing Alfred to leave soon, with the aid of the cashier, whom he had told during the afternoon about the communal secretary's newspaper account. For nothing had come of the conversation between Yankel and Alfred which took place in Velvel's presence before the prayers in Grandfather's Room. True, Alfred did promise old Yankel to return to Vienna soon, but it could be seen that he was not yet capable of leaving the scene of his bereavement.

Velvel leafed through a book, Avram Aptowitzer read in a book for mourners, soundlessly moving his lips. The windows were open; cool summer night breezes floated in; deaf and mute moths fluttered over the lamp, and Alfred stared into the oil wick, which was lit to commemorate dead Lipusj.

Suddenly Alfred said to his uncle — it sounded exactly as though he were giving Velvel a blow in the chest:

"Listen, uncle! I don't believe in God!"

He had sprung up as he spoke and looked around quickly, as though he were afraid of having broken something in Grandfather's Room. But when he noticed that both his uncle and Avram Aptowitzer had remained sitting in silence, Alfred

[74]

quickly sat down again and joined their silence with eyes terrified and wide open.

"How do you know that?" asked Avram Aptowitzer, after a period of oppressive silence, looking as he spoke at Velvel, not at Alfred.

"Yes, how do you know that all at once?" repeated Velvel with no expression in his voice.

"I can't pray," said Alfred.

"Could you pray before?" asked Aptowitzer.

"I believed that I was already able to pray," said Alfred.

"And why do you not believe it any longer?" asked Aptowitzer.

"Because I want to pray and I can't," said Alfred firmly.

"He who declares that he can pray knows little about true prayer. Praying means lying on the stone of the altar — lying on the stone of the altar, offering oneself up completely. He who can boast of that was never even in the first ante-room," said Aptowitzer.

"I have never wanted to boast," said Alfred, "I only said I want to pray and I can't."

"But why do you want to?" asked Aptowitzer.

"Because . . . because I want to believe."

"That is enough," said Velvel instantly.

"That is enough," repeated Aptowitzer, just as quickly.

"It is enough to say, 'I want to believe,' Sussia," said Velvel.

"It is enough. 'I want to believe.' None of us can say anything more than just 'I want to believe,' " declared Aptowitzer. He shut his book and went to the door. Already about to leave for the night, he turned back and stationed himself in front of Alfred. "May I tell a short story?"

"Please do," said Alfred, almost defiantly.

"A famous rabbi, sitting in his room, once heard one of his Hasidim, who was loudly reciting the articles of faith in the House of Prayer, continually interrupt himself to whisper, 'I don't understand that. I don't understand that.' The rabbi stepped out of his room into the house of prayer and asked,

'What is it you do not understand?' 'Rabbi,' answered the frightened Hasid, 'I am reciting that I have perfect faith — and yet I sin. How can that be? If I really have perfect faith, how can it be that nevertheless I sin? But if I do not have perfect faith, why am I telling a lie?' The rabbi answered, 'The verse, "I have perfect faith," is a prayer. It means the same as "I should like to believe, I want to believe." ' 'That is good,' the Hasid cried out. 'I should like to believe! Creator of the world, I should like to believe.' — Good night."

"Permit me to accompany you," said Alfred, who had quickly arisen and followed Aptowitzer out of Grandfather's Room. Silently they walked through Pessa's garden, which was not yet wet with dew. When they passed the smithy, Alfred touched Aptowitzer's sleeve with a trembling hand, and, pointing to a block of wood said, "Let us sit down for a while. I should like to ask you something." Aptowitzer seated himself silently on the block of wood. With sunken head he awaited Alfred's question; Alfred for his part had forgotten that he wanted to sit down too, and stood silently before Aptowitzer. After a time, Aptowitzer said without raising his head:

"I know what you want to ask me. You want an answer to the question: How can it happen that a child who cannot possibly be guilty is punished in so horrible a manner?"

"Yes," said Alfred. "Yes, that is what I want to know. How did you know that?"

"Because all these horrible days and nights I have been asking myself exactly the same question."

"And," said Alfred, "have you found an answer?"

"Have you ever heard the word, *gilgul?*"

"No," said Alfred. "This is the first time I have heard the word."

"*Gilgul,*" said Aptowitzer, "is our word for what others call the transmigration of souls."

"Do you believe in that?" asked Alfred, disconcerted and in astonishment.

[76]

"The Hasidim believe in it," said Aptowitzer.

"You are a Hasid," said Alfred, "I know. But tell me: do you believe in it? Do *you* believe in the transmigration of souls?"

"I would have to believe in it even if I were no Hasid. I have special reasons to do so. Family reasons, so to speak. As far as I can gather, it has been taking place in my family for three generations. Perhaps it's been taking place for longer than three generations, but I am not aware of it. I do not come of a family as distinguished as yours, so I only am aware of the history of three generations. But in those three generations, it has been repeated time and again."

"What has been repeated?" asked Alfred.

"In my family, not my wife's, it has been occurring for three generations. Children are born, boys and girls, average boys and average girls, not too pretty, not too ugly, not too stupid, not too clever, not too talented, not too untalented — average, good children, like my Davidl, may he be guarded from all evil! But once in every generation a child is born who is just as Lipale was — may he rest in peace! Just like him, I say: well-proportioned physically and blessed with all the spiritual gifts. Such was my father's younger brother. I did not know him, but I can show you a picture of him sometime when you come to me. You would swear it was my Lipale. The same eyes, the same forehead, even the same color of hair. The child was called Samuel and died at the age of seven of a disease of the throat. My own brother was named Samuel after that brother of my father's who had died before my brother was born. I have a picture of him, too. I will show it to you. He had the physical and spiritual gifts of his dead uncle, was the image of him, one might say. This child was trampled to death by a horse at the age of seven. When my sons were born, I was loath to give any of them the name of Samuel because I hoped to be able to break the chain. But such a chain is not to be broken. However, I assure you that I was unable to be happy for a single hour once I saw that my child was growing both physically and spiritually to be a link in that unbroken chain. — Have you already been told that I am a drunkard?"

Avram Aptowitzer now lifted his head and tried to hold Alfred's glance in the light of the moon which had meanwhile risen. "Yes, you know it. You have seen me drunk, I know. My wife told it to me. Lipusj also knew that you saw me in a drunken state. He was greatly perturbed, the poor child. Yes, I am a drunkard. Shabse, the horse-trader, informed your uncle about it, when I was about to be appointed here. For once Shabse was not lying. I am a sot. 'A quart sot,' as they say. Just like the wheelwright, Nazarewicz, Donja's father. I don't know how the wheelwright became a quart sot. He was a dragoon. Perhaps he learnt it then. But I was never a dragoon. I never understood all those years why the drive to drink attacked me like a mortal enemy every few weeks. But now I know why, and I think that you know, too. I am not saying this to excuse myself. I know that I am guilty. And you know it too . . . or don't you?"

"What?" asked Alfred. But he immediately regretted the quickness of his question.

"Don't you know that it was I who sent the child to the wolves that Sunday? My wife was out of the house, and I wanted to drink undisturbed for once. I didn't want to drink only a quota that my wife had carefully measured for me. I wanted a full measure. Now I have it , the full measure. It has been granted me according to an unfathomable decree.   I sought an escape, and I needed one. I did not trust myself to look into my son's bright face. Every time I looked at my son, I saw the black wings of the Angel of Death behind him. It went on year after year. Can you imagine that? If my wife had not prevented it, I would have been no quart sot, but a worse one. Every day I lusted for the bottle. For I could rejoice in my child when I was drunk, only when I was drunk. You knew my child only a year, but you had more joy in him than I. For there was always a bitterness mingled with my joy, and now, in escaping into drunkenness, I have run directly into the ancestral chain. You

[78]

asked me and I have answered you. And now I ask you, why did I have to be guilty, too? Can you give me an answer to that?"

"Why do you blame yourself?" asked Alfred. "We are all guilty. I am guilty, too. Lipusj wanted to go walking with me that day and I had no time for him. Old Yankel feels that he is guilty, because he had a dispute with the communal secretary. My uncle feels he is guilty because he did not settle that dispute in favor of the secretary. You are no more guilty than any of us."

Alfred, who only a few hours before had himself blamed Avram Aptowitzer, now felt a great sympathy for the unhappy father who had so many profound answers to fundamental problems, yet sat before him completely broken and dejected. They were both silent for a long period. Alfred debated with himself whether he ought not to take his leave, for it had grown late and he still wanted to see Panko, but he did not have the strength to leave Avram Aptowitzer alone with his dejection, and he sat down opposite the unhappy man on a plow-rack.

"I have not completely answered your question," Avram Aptowitzer suddenly said. "*Gilgul,* or the transmigration of souls, as others would call it, also conceives of the chain as breaking. In the course of time, a purification takes place and the chain is broken. Let us hope, let us pray, that a fourth link is not added to the three that have already been. I must return to my wife tomorrow. She still knows nothing about this, and I do not know whether she has yet the strength to bear the truth. I shall see. I shall ask. I shall ask the doctor. The doctors do not know a great deal. None of us knows very much. We know nothing. We know nothing about ourselves. I wish I were where my little son is. But I shall hardly be worthy to be where he is."

"Where?" The question slipped unconsciously from Alfred and he immediately regretted having spoken.

"The holy volumes of the *Kabbalah* tell us that children who do not learn the Torah through to the end in this realm are instructed further in the other, higher realm. One can well believe that if ever a child was found worthy of that, it was our Lipusj."

"Who instructs the children?" asked Alfred in a sort of joyous terror at this communication.

"Metatron, the 'Angel of the Presence.' The *Sar-Hapanim* instructs the children."

"Who is that?" Alfred inquired.

"It is not known. That is to say, I do not know it."

"But you believe it?" asked Alfred.

"I believe it. That is to say, you remember what I told you in Grandfather's Room, I want to believe it. I want to believe it — Good night." And Avram Aptowitzer rose and walking quickly went home.

4

After a time Alfred rose and walked through the poplar alley in the direction of the *Groblja*. His conversation with Avram Aptowitzer had made an impression on him; but now, thinking calmly about all that he had heard from Aptowitzer, he felt that he was not satisfied with Aptowitzer's revelations. It was certainly pleasant to imagine that little Lipusj, who had been so good a student on earth, was being instructed further in the Torah in another world. It was a pretty thought, and Alfred envied the unhappy father his belief in it. What a wonderful consolation lay in that thought! But Alfred did not wish to ask whether or not it was a true consolation. Are there any true consolations? It is enough that a consolation can heal sick hearts. The idea of *Gilgul* struck Alfred as strange and, in a certain sense less rational than esthetic, crude and objectionable. Although he would not have been able to tell the source of this knowledge, he was certain that his Uncle Velvel did not believe in *Gilgul*. He decided to ask Velvel at the very next opportunity. He had arrived at the spot on the *Groblja* where the child had been murdered, and for the first time walked past without a feeling of horror, although deep night now lay upon the *Groblja*, perhaps

[80]

because he was still occupied with Aptowitzer's amazing revelation of *Gilgul*. He knew that he had come to Avram Aptowitzer with a question that had perplexed the minds of all the thinkers, theologians and founders of religion more than any other problem. Why does the virtuous man suffer? Life holds no perplexity harder to untangle than the puzzle: Why had a child who could not possibly be guilty been made to suffer? All thinkers, at least all those whose answers were familiar to Alfred, had placed themselves (he now saw this clearly) on the side of Providence and openly took the part of God against man. If a man suffers, though he seems not guilty, he must be guilty. Alfred wished now to have his friend Gabriel Friedmann there, as he had wished often before when facing a difficult problem. Certainly, Avram Aptowitzer was, in a manner of speaking, a Scriptural scholar, but Alfred could not at that moment rely on a scholarship that, with its sudden assumption of belief in *Gilgul*, took on the coloration of folklore. The man who had raised the same question some two and a half thousand years before: Why does the righteous man suffer? — the man who had written the Book of Job — did not believe in *Gilgul*. That was certain. And just as Alfred had earlier assumed that his Uncle Velvel could not possibly believe in *Gilgul*, so now he said inwardly, with a decisiveness that surprised him, that the author of Job would have rejected *Gilgul* out of hand.

Alfred walked past the tavern of Shmiel Gruenfeld, where there was still light at this late hour. In the silence of the night the drinkers caroused noisily. By the light that shone through the window Alfred saw the wheelwright Nazarewicz with flushed face and a fist before his forehead sitting in the company of some peasants. It occurred to Alfred that there was something he had to say to Nazarewicz, and he decided to take him out of the inn on his way back. He turned in at Broad Street. The only light on the street shone in the house of sick Panko.

Alfred cautiously rapped on the door and walked into the house. As he had suspected, the sick man's mother was already asleep on the oven, a peasant construction of lime which is to be found in the peasant's huts throughout the east. It is a sleeping couch, which, with all the primitiveness of its construction, fulfills its purpose admirably by managing to be as warm in winter as it is cool in summer. The old woman moved in her sleep, half rose for a moment, recognized Alfred and went back to sleep. Panko lay in his bed with his eyes open. His sick leg was out of the splints. After the infection in the open wound was healed, the broken leg could be set in plaster. It now lay on the bedcover like a long, thick pipe, distinct, as it were, from the person of the sick man. The sick man was still as completely free of fever as he had been all day and greeted Alfred with a friendly smile. He is over the hill, thought Alfred, greatly encouraged. He went to the window and opened the one pane that could be opened, the peephole. All the other windows were closed tight. The peasants were afraid of fresh air. When someone became sick, the first thing they did was to guard him from every possible breath of fresh air. Fresh air was the most dangerous thing for a sick person; the village Jews shared this peasant superstition. Alfred had known this for a long time, yet he was still amazed that people who spent their lives in the fresh air did not trust it. Alfred had succeeded in opening the one peephole in the sick room only after several days with the help of the Ukrainian Dr. Chramtjuk, despite Panko's mother's opposition.

Alfred sat down at the bed and said, "It's a good night, isn't it, Panko?"

"Yes, sir. Praised be Jesus Christ," said Panko. "I shall keep my leg and not have to sit on the coach box like a cripple. No, the brothers Mokrzycki won't live to see that. No, sir. In a month I'll be on my feet again, sir. And in October my brother Petro will come back from service. We'll show those brothers Mokrzycki."

Now he is well, thought Alfred, and took his hand.

"That's foolishness, Panko. They'll soon settle accounts with the brothers Mokrzycki. That's what courts are for, and the Law."

"Yes," said Panko, and shut his eyes, "the Law. The committee of inquiry was in the village but they never questioned me. If anyone is a witness, I am. They didn't question me at all."

"Because you were sick, Panko. You had a high fever and the doctors would not have allowed anyone to question you."

Panko opened his eyes and looked at Alfred for a long time. "Did they ask the doctors?"

"I don't know," said Alfred, "it really isn't important. What is important is that you are well again. And what is most important is that you have kept your leg."

"Thank you, sir," said Panko, "you saved my leg for me."

"I?" said Alfred in genuine astonishment. "Just ask Dr. Chramtjuk. He will tell you who saved your leg for you. He was very angry at you, Dr. Chramtjuk. Do you remember what you said to him?"

"What did I say?"

"You said, 'I can cure with a hatchet too. I don't need any doctor for that.' "

"I said that?" wondered Panko. "You are joking, sir. You called other doctors. So many doctors!" said Panko with great pride. "When old Bjelak was sick, there weren't as many doctors to see him as there were to see me. You did that, sir."

"Not I, Panko. My uncle called the doctors. I told my uncle what you said to Dr. Chramtjuk, and my uncle said to me, 'Panko is right. Let us call Dr. Lustig and Dr. Brettler, who don't use a hatchet, to cure people.' So, you see, it was you."

"Yes, your uncle," said Panko. "And he has visited me three times already. Perhaps he'll come again. I hoped that he would come Friday. What day is today?"

"Sunday," said Alfred.

"Yes, that's right," said Panko. "My mother was in church today. Friday I thought the master was coming."

"Why Friday?" asked Alfred. "That's remarkable. Friday my uncle asked me whether you were already free of fever."

"Did he ask that?" said Panko. "You see, next Friday he will come."

"Why Friday?" Alfred inquired again.

[83]

"Don't you know why, Mr. Mohilevski?" wondered Panko.

"No," said Alfred, "how should I know?"

"Every Friday," said Panko, "the master and I have an important transaction."

"So," said Alfred, "I didn't know that. But if it's so, he will certainly come on Friday. Perhaps even sooner."

"Perhaps he will come sooner," said Panko. "He has already visited me three times, my mother tells me. But he will certainly come on Friday. For on Friday the master sells me the whole estate, lock, stock and barrel."

Alfred took Panko's hand, to see whether he wasn't feverish again. But he seemed quite normal.

"My uncle sells you the estate?" he marvelled.

"Surely," said Panko. "Don't you know that? Years ago your uncle used to sell the estate to my father. Every Friday. And your grandfather, too, used to sell the estate to my father. Since my father died, the master has been selling it to me every Friday. Saturday night, I sell it back to him."

"So," said Alfred, "I didn't know that at all. So you are the landlord for a day once every week," he joked.

"Twenty-four hours," said Panko. "Yes, even longer. Thirty hours, perhaps. Thirty hours a week I am the landlord," he said, picking up the joke.

"I didn't know that at all," repeated Alfred.

"I thought you knew it," said Panko. "It is this way: The master is a pious man, and in his religion it is not only forbidden to work on the Sabbath, it is also forbidden to have other people work on the Sabbath for you. So the master sells me his whole estate on Friday. I pay him for it, a deposit of ten zlotys. In the early days, when we were Austrian, my father used to give a deposit of five kronen. Saturday, when the Sabbath is over, I go to the master and sell him the estate back again, and get back double the deposit, twenty zlotys. I get twenty zlotys back. My father used to pay five kronen, and so he got ten kronen back. I pay ten zlotys and get twenty back. Every Friday. Didn't you know that?"

"No," said Alfred, sunk in thought. He believed Panko, but this mock sale and purchase struck him as a kind of farce. "No, I didn't know that."

"It is no secret," said Panko. "Everybody knows it. The overseer knows it. The cashier knows it. And everybody in the village knows it, too. They envy me the easy money, and begrudge me it, and that's why they call me 'Jew servant.' They've always called me that, particularly the brothers Mokrzycki. Naturally, only behind my back. I should like to know," Panko continued, rubbing his forehead with his huge hand, as though straining to think, "I should like to know whom the master sold the estate to when I had fever. How many Fridays have I been sick, Mr. Mohilevski?"

"Two," said Alfred, "two . . . or is it three? No, two." ·

"Two must be right, my mother says it is two, also. I suppose to Mr. Domanski. But don't ask him, Mr. Mohilevski. Next Friday the master will come to see me again. When you tell him that I am well, he will surely come."

"I will tell him that," said Alfred.

Panko breathed deep, as though Alfred had removed a burden from his mind. He shut his eyes and took long breaths. His face was grey and yellow and there were black shadows under his eyes. But it seemed to Alfred that Panko's face was not as wasted as it had been when he had had a high fever.

"Have you eaten anything tonight?" asked Alfred.

"Yes," said Panko. "I have eaten. Miss Pessa brought me something to eat. She brings me something twice a day. Yes, Miss Pessa, your uncle and Miss Pessa, if everybody was like them, that would be something. But there are also the brothers Mokrzycki. And because there are many like them, there is no place in this world for such a child as Lipusj."

"We have spoken enough today, Panko. I shall go now and you will sleep."

"I slept the whole day, Mr. Mohilevski. I slept well. I don't remember when I slept so well before. Stay a while, if you have nothing to do."

[85]

"Good," said Alfred. "If it isn't too much of a strain for you, we can talk a little."

"I want to ask you something. You were at the burial. Were there many people at the burial?"

"Yes," said Alfred, "many people. The whole town."

"That was proper," said Panko. "I should have liked to have been there. That was a child for you, Mr. Mohilevski."

"If it isn't a strain for you to speak, Panko, I should like to ask you something."

"It's no strain, Mr. Mohilevski. Yesterday it would still have been a strain for me. But not today. I am well now."

"That Sunday," said Alfred, "how did it happen you were there with a scythe when the child screamed for help?"

"It was this way, Mr. Mohilevski: I spend every Sunday afternoon in the *Gazon*. That is, if I don't have to drive the master anywhere. But when I am free, I am always in the *Gazon* in the afternoon. For, you see, Mr. Mohilevski, I would rather have been a gardener than a coachman. Don't tell that to the master, it might annoy him. I should have been very happy to have become a gardener. I always hoped that the house in the *Gazon* would be renovated and the park tended again. But the way it is now, there is no need for a gardener. On most Saturdays and Sundays I have nothing to do. Saturdays when I am free I polish the harness, both the old and the new, and the harness for the four-horse-span, though we don't use it at all. At most every fifth year, when the bishop comes. Sundays I work a bit in the *Gazon*. That is, you can't rightly call that work — the master wouldn't allow it, either. But I pull out some of the weeds, chop down a rotten branch, mow a wild plot of grass — that isn't real work. But it's a lot of fun for me. And little Lipusj, too. Every Sunday, between four and six, Lipusj used to come to me in the *Gazon*, and we would have a good time together. I would show him how to cut a rose stalk, how to dig up a flower bed, or bind a bough. And Lipusj taught me where cities lay and countries and rivers . . . What's that called?"

[86]

"Geography," Alfred suggested faintly, in a voice that almost failed him. He was overcome by Panko's information which — he was breathlessly sure at once — was of great significance for Lipusj's unhappy father — and for himself as well.

"Yes," said Panko, "geography. That's right. I did not learn much, Mr. Mohilevski. I have a poor head when it comes to study. Gardening, yes, I can learn gardening easily. But real study — that isn't for me. But Lipusj, he had a good head for study. Every Sunday he would come along with something new."

"Every Sunday, you say, Panko?"

"Every Sunday, Mr. Mohilevski, if it wasn't storming. Every Sunday. He never failed to come."

"Yes," said Alfred. "But that Sunday his father had sent him to the tavern. Do you know that?"

"Certainly," said Panko.

"So he was absent that Sunday," said Alfred, "for his father had sent him somewhere."

"Oh, no, Mr. Mohilevski. His father sent him out at about two o'clock. I saw him going. He would have returned home, and then at about four o'clock he would have come to see me, as always. The same thing would have happened to him, even if he had had no bottle with him. Or perhaps not — who can say? But he would certainly have come to me. You see, Mr. Mohilevski, for the last three or four Sundays he had been trying to explain something to me that he simply couldn't get into my head. He was still only a child. An exceptional child, but still only a child. Often he made up things, fairy tales, and called them geography. . . . For example," Panko propped himself on his arm and turned completely around to Alfred, as though he now wished to share something important. ". . . For example, he told me that the sun doesn't simply rise in the east, climb higher up the sky, go down and set in the west. But — now you can see what a child can think up — for four Sundays in a row he tried to show me that it's the earth that turns and makes the sun rise and set. At first he told it to me. Then he explained it to me. Then he showed it to me. Believe

[87]

it or not, Mr. Mohilevski, the child took a pumpkin and an apple. He held the pumpkin in one hand and the apple in the other. First of all, he scratched a mark in the apple with his nail and said, 'Here is Dobropolia.' Then he turned the apple around and showed me that when Dobropolia has turned so far that the pumpkin, that is, the sun, lies opposite it, it is morning here, the sun has risen — and he kept turning the apple — thus we have morning again and noon, until Dobropolia is on the other side, then it is night. So, he said, you can understand that it's not day or night all over the world at the same time, but rather it is day in one half, when it's night on the other. — Did you too hear or read such fairy-tales as a child, Mr. Mohilevski?"

Alfred had listened to Panko's story breathlessly. During the last few weeks before Lipusj's death, Alfred had demonstrated the movement of the earth on its axis around the sun to Lipusj with the aid of a pumpkin and an apple. So little Lipusj had had a secret even from Alfred! Alfred knew nothing of the boy's visits to the *Gazon*. Nor had he known that Lipusj had sought to share his newly acquired wisdom with Panko. He considered a moment what he should answer Panko. Should it remain a fairy-tale? Or should he, as Lipusj had done, instruct Panko? Alfred looked around the room. There were apples but no pumpkins. He looked at Panko, who received Alfred's look inquiringly.

"What Lipusj told you, Panko, was no fairy-tale. He did not imagine this — he learned it. All the children learn it in school. But they only learn that when they are ten years old. It was not too hard for Lipusj to learn it at seven. He would probably have understood it at five. He was, as you said, an exceptional child."

"You don't mean to say, Mr. Mohilevski . . ." began Panko and halted.

"What?" asked Alfred.

"You don't mean to say that it is true that the earth turns around the sun?"

[88]

"It is true, Panko," said Alfred, "and Lipusj explained it to you well. Just the way I explained it to him, with a pumpkin and an apple."

"I did not understand it," said Panko, beside himself. "I did not understand it. I thought the child was telling a fairy-tale."

"If I had a pumpkin," said Alfred, "I would explain it to you again."

Looking at Alfred shyly, Panko pointed with a swift gesture to the table.

"Could it be explained with a loaf of bread?"

"Oh, yes," said Alfred, "it can be done that way too."

"He explained it to me time and again for four Sundays, and I had to bring along a small pumpkin each time. He brought the apple. For the life of me I couldn't understand it. Explain it to me again."

Alfred stood up and approached the invalid's bed carrying an apple and a loaf of bread. Now he demonstrated to Panko, hungry for knowledge, the simultaneous revolutions of the earth and the sun on their axes, as he had learned it in school and relearned it with the aid of little Lipusj. And, either because he was a better demonstrator than little Lipusj, or because Alfred's assurance that this was no fairy-tale but a proven natural phenomenon cleared away the mist in his heavy head, Panko understood it this time. This comprehension was so obviously mirrored in his face, that Alfred, transported by his student's indescribable expression, had the feeling that he himself had now for the first time grasped the mystery in all its implications. For a long time they looked at one another as in a trance, then the invalid slowly fell back on his bed and, to Alfred's consternation, burst into sobs. Alfred waited for a long while until Panko had calmed himself. "He is still very sick," he thought. "I should not have stayed so long."

"You see, Panko, we have talked too much, we two. I should have let you be a long time ago. Good night, Panko."

"It's not that, sir," said Panko in a deeper but clearer voice

[89]

that seemed to have been cleansed by his tears. "I am not crying because I am sick, I am crying because it is so beautiful. What that child was capable of imagining! — Good night, sir."

5

The wheelwright and the peasant who composed extemporaneously in rhyme were still in the tavern, as well as sleepy Chana Gruenfeld, the wife of the sergeant and tavern keeper, Shmiel Gruenfeld. After a short conversation followed by a round of cherry brandy to which Alfred treated the two late guests, he succeeded in inducing Donja's father to accompany him home. At first they walked quietly side by side. The night was warm, and nightingales sang passionately in the *Gazon.*

"I didn't succeed in getting drunk," said Nazarewicz, "I only went to the tavern to make up with Shmielko. For, what's right is right — although I was a dragoon and he only an infantryman, Shmielko was nevertheless a sergeant, in fact, a top sergeant and I only a corporal. There must be discipline."

From the word "discipline" Alfred gathered that the wheelwright wasn't quite as sober as he imagined, but he was happy to have found him not as drunk as he had expected. For the wheelwright never spoke about discipline when he was sober. Alfred was curious to discover whether Nazarewicz would continue to contend that he had not succeeded in getting drunk or, as drunks do, would decide to act drunk. So Alfred said nothing at first.

"Everything has gone wrong with me lately. A week ago Sunday, I wanted to go to the master and give notice."

"Give notice?" said Alfred. "Why give notice?"

"I've had enough of these murderers here. Why should I live in a village where there are murderers? Murderers of children. I don't have to live in villages. I can live in the city, too. They don't need wheelwrights in the city, that's true. But I'm quite a good turner and varnisher. Do you know that?"

"Certainly, master," said Alfred, "I have a bookcase in my

[90]

room with beautiful turned legs that you made, and it has a very good varnish."

"You see, Mr. Mohilevski, I can choose to do as I wish. I can live in the village and I can live in the city. But my wife won't let me give notice and this time Donja is against me, my own daughter. She used to be always on my side. This time she is against me. And so I've not been able to give notice."

"Frankly," said Alfred, "I'm happy that you are not giving notice. We won't find another wheelwright as good as you."

"I'm happy to hear you say that, Mr. Mohilevski. Very happy. But I'm disturbed because Donja is not on my side. True, she is very well off now in the master's house. Everybody's so good to her, the master and Miss Pessa. My Donja has also learned a great deal during the year: to cook, to cook well and to bake. She can already bake pastries and sew and crochet — and her hands, have you seen them? Her hands are now as fine and white as a city lady's. And while we are speaking about Donja, Mr. Mohilevski — why are you always speaking about Donja?" The wheelwright suddenly ended his monologue on a question and began to pretend to be drunk.

"I?" said Alfred, "I don't believe it was I who mentioned Donja. Not I."

"So?" wondered the wheelwright, "It was me. But the last time — it was months ago, during the winter — it was you who began to speak about Donja. You admit that?"

"I can't remember," said Alfred, "but it is quite possible. Why not?"

"True," said the wheelwright, "Why not, indeed?"

They had now reached the smithy and Alfred saw a light in Yankel's home and another light in a window in Avram Aptowitzer's. Alfred, who had only intended to accompany the wheelwright as far as the smithy and to go home by way of the garden path, reconsidered now whether he might not be able to speak with Avram Aptowitzer during the night and tell him about his son's secret Sunday visits to the *Gazon*. So he forgot to answer the wheelwright, and said:

[91]

"I'll go along a bit further. There's still a light in the cashier's house. Perhaps he is not yet asleep."

The wheelwright said nothing and they went silently a bit together. They had almost reached the distillery and saw the night watchman, Jarema, coming towards them with his two dogs. Suddenly the wheelwright stood still, grasped Alfred by the arm and said — and now he was no longer pretending to be drunk —

"Excuse me, Mr. Mohilevski. I know very well that it was I who began to speak about Donja, not you. But I wish to ask you something."

"Please do," said Alfred.

"You remember, Mr. Mohilevski, what I said to you when we spoke about Donja last winter. It was I who began the conversation then, too. I know that very well. There was something I wanted to say to you then, and I said it. Today I want to ask you simply whether you still remember what I said about Donja."

Alfred's heart beat furiously and he knew that he remembered.

"Yes," said Alfred in a firm voice. "I remember very well."

"I said . . ." the wheelwright continued, and now he no longer looked at Alfred. He lowered his head as though he were looking for something in the grassy plot in front of Yankel's home in the moonlight. ". . . I said to you . . ."

"You said to me, Mr. Nazarewicz: 'My daughter's limbs are still too young for her to follow her heart.' Is that what you mean?"

"Yes," said the wheelwright. He ran his hand along Alfred's arm up to his shoulder, where it seemed to Alfred it rested lightly and with surprising tenderness a long, long time. "Yes," he repeated, and now he looked Alfred straight in the face, "you haven't forgotten."

"No," said Alfred, "as you see, I have not."

"I am surprised," said the wheelwright. "Can you tell me why?"

"Because you expressed yourself very well, master. I will never forget your phrase. You can depend on that."

"Thank you," said the wheelwright. "You see, Mr. Mohilevski, I knew then already that Donja would not be on my side if I should decide to give notice. And that is the way it is. But since you still remember so well what I said to you then, I don't have to give notice. I shall remain in Dobropolia, on your side, so to speak. — Good night, Mr. Mohilevski."

Alfred went to the lit window. A shutter was open. When he pushed the curtains aside lightly, he saw Avram Aptowitzer sitting at the table with his eyes shut. On the table lay a great many sheets of paper, apparently Lipale's maps. Alfred let the curtain fall, and lightly rapped on the window frame. The cashier quickly came to the window and showed his frightened face. It now occurred to Alfred that Avram Aptowitzer had been wearing this congealed expression of sad fear during the entire period of mourning. Even the knocking at so late an hour failed to intensify the mask of fear.

"Good morning, Mr. Aptowitzer," said Alfred. "I believe it is already morning. But I wish to see you, because I have something to tell you."

"Please come in," said Aptowitzer, and left the window to open the door for Alfred. Alfred followed the cashier on tiptoe through the dark room where Davidl slept. Avram Aptowitzer made a gesture as though to clear away the sketches spread out on the table. He reconsidered, however, pushed a chair forward for Alfred, and both men sat down. In the wavering glow of the lamp it seemed to Alfred as though Aptowitzer had staggered, as though he were drunk. He probed Aptowitzer with a long look and smiled in embarrassment. Aptowitzer dropped his glance and said:

"No, Mr. Mohilevski, I haven't touched a drop. I will never again drink in my life. That is certain."

"It is so late," began Alfred and stopped.

"You stayed late with Panko again," said Aptowitzer. "How is the poor man?"

"Better," said Alfred. "He is doing well. He is over the hill, I think. Today was the first time that he was completely without fever and slept for a long time, and I could speak to him. He told me something that seems to me to be important. Important for the two of us, Mr. Aptowitzer, for you and for me."

"He told you how it happened?" whispered Avram Aptowitzer, and Alfred now saw that he had erred: The expression of fear on the face of the father could become stronger.

"Lipusj," Alfred continued, and, without his being conscious of it, his voice sank to a whisper, "our Lipusj had a secret that none of us knew . . ."

"— With Panko?" said Aptowitzer. "Yes, he loved Panko deeply. Before you came to us, Panko was his dearest friend."

"Yes," said Alfred. "Panko told me that Lipusj was with him on the *Gazon* every Sunday afternoon. Panko instructed Lipusj in gardening, and Lipusj — think of it — Lipusj instructed Panko in geography."

"So, in geography. And he went there every Sunday, to the *Gazon*? That is possible. That is very possible," said Aptowitzer.

"That is positive," said Alfred. "I asked Panko expressly. Panko was positive . . ."

"What did you ask him?"

"I asked Panko whether he was positive that Lipusj would have come to see him on the *Gazon* that Sunday too."

"So he would have gone to the *Groblja* anyway . . ." said Aptowitzer. He shut his eyes. "I understand," said he. "I understand. That is just what I thought," he continued, and without opening his eyes pointed with an outstretched hand to the maps on the table. "I thought exactly that: If you have such a child with such a head as his, you must take his hand, and hold it and not let him go, and keep him by you always. But that is not possible. You see, he had a secret, our Lipusj. He never told it to you. All children love to have some secret or other. Something they can hide, a sort of toy which they show nobody. We know nothing. We know nothing about our children. We give them food; we give them books; we give them teachers; and we believe that is all they have. But it is not so. Did you have such a secret as a child?"

"Yes," said Alfred. "You are right. I believe all children have some secret or other. I, too, imagined that Lipusj told me everything. I was just as surprised as you, Mr. Aptowitzer, when Panko told me about it. I wanted to jump up at once and run to you, but I thought you were already asleep. Then I got the wheelwright out of the tavern and walked along with him till I saw the light in your window."

"Thank you," said Aptowitzer. His face had grown milder, milder and sadder, and the expression of fear had apparently been wiped away. "As for Lipusj, it's all the same. But as for me, when I travel to Kozlova today, I will not be so ashamed when I face Lipale's mother. — I was a drunk and a sinner. A sinner I shall remain. God save us. But I have not yet been reduced into a messenger of evil. 'The Lord hath given, the Lord hath taken away. Praised be the true Judge.' "

Alfred bade goodbye to Aptowitzer with a handshake. Without rising, Avram Aptowitzer held Alfred's hand tightly in his two hands for a long time.

"Panko is better, you said. That is good. That is good news. They tell me he was in danger of death."

"Yes," said Alfred, "he was badly injured. But now he is over it. And he will keep his leg. He wouldn't let Dr. Chramtjuk take it from him, and he will keep it."

"He risked his life for Lipusj. A *Zaddik*. You see, Mr. Mohilevski, a man can be called Panko Cossack and be a *Zaddik*. — Rest, Mr. Mohilevski. — Good morning."

Alfred again went on tiptoe through the room where Davidl was sleeping. As he passed he thought he saw in the morning twilight Davidl quickly shutting his attentive eyes and pretending to be asleep. Outside the air was blue with the extreme blue of morning, in which the night watchman Jarema walked slowly with his two dogs, staggering as though he were walking in blue water. The air was motionless and warm, as warm as it had been at night. Not a drop of dew had fallen. Early sparrows took their morning baths in the dust of the threshing floor and twittered angrily over the lack of dew so early in the morning.

6

While Alfred was having his nocturnal conversations with Aptowitzer, the wheelwright and Panko, Wolf Dobropolier sat till late at night at his writing table, composing a long letter to Dr. Frankl. He began first with the kind of report which he always used to send, on Alfred's progress and his way of life; then he made his excuses and explained to Dr. Frankl why Alfred had not kept his promise to visit his mother in Vienna on her birthday. He referred briefly to the mis-fortune that had occurred in Dobropolia and about which he had at once informed Dr. Frankl two weeks before, when it had taken place. After Velvel had described all the circum-stances which made it desirable that Alfred leave in the near future, he openly suggested that Dr. Frankl's personal attention was needed to induce Alfred to go. He took this occasion to remind Dr. Frankl of his promise to pay a visit to Dobropolia, which he urged him to keep, if possible, at once. That morning he would send the letter special delivery, and anticipate it with a telegram.

After he had finished his correspondence. Velvel remained sitting before his desk for a long time, deep in thought. He considered whether it was advisable to inform Alfred that he had invited his Viennese uncle to Dobropolia; but he could not come to a decision, and he finally decided to wait till noon in order to hear Yankel's opinion. Then he rose and, because it was almost time, went to Grandfather's Room for the morn-ing prayer. In the hall he met Pessa and saw at once that she must have been standing there for a time preparing to bring him bad news. As always in such cases he wanted to avoid her; as always, his attempt failed.

"Old Yankel has gone crazy, woe is me!" she said.

"What has happened?" Velvel inquired.

"Last night stones were thrown at the communal secretary in the Old Village."

"What had Yankel to do with that?" asked Velvel angrily.

"Nothing," said Pessa. "But this morning, when Lubasj appeared at Chana Gruenfeld's at the usual time, a couple of fellows were waiting for him. They picked a quarrel with Lubasj and the upshot was that the fellows drubbed the communal secretary and threw him out of the tavern."

"Yes, but what has all this do do with Yankel?"

"You will see at once, Velvel. Mr. Lubasj went straight to Bjelak, related what had happened, said to Bjelak, 'Yankel Christiampoler is behind this,' and demanded an official investigation."

"How do you know all that?" asked Velvel.

"Bjelak's daughter was just here to see me. But she doesn't want it known, woe is me! Her father, old Bjelak, shrugs his shoulders and thinks that first there must be an investigation and proof. He refused to make out a report. Lubasj left him with a threat, went to the gendarmes, and they made out a warrant."

"Against whom?" asked Velvel.

"Against Yankel, woe is me!" said Pessa. "I told you that at once."

"What can Yankel do?" asked Velvel.

"Bjelak's daughter said . . ."

"I have had enough, Pessa. Send Donja to call Yankel. I don't have to hear all the village gossip. Yankel must come here at twelve."

Pessa sighed deeply and looked after Velvel disconsolately until he had disappeared behind the door of Grandfather's Room. Then she lingered in the hall a while and listened at Alfred's door. She thought he was no longer asleep and, stepping very lightly, went to the kitchen, prepared a hearty breakfast and brought it to Alfred in bed, although she knew well that Alfred didn't at all like, would not even tolerate, being waited

[97]

upon. But Pessa was afire to communicate the latest news to Alfred.

When Velvel appeared at breakfast an hour and a half later, Alfred was already there, and Velvel immediately noticed that, as he had expected, Pessa had already loaded Alfred with the disquieting news, not omitting her commentary.

Alfred allowed his uncle to begin his breakfast in peace. He told him how well Panko had been the day before, considered whether he ought not immediately to inform his uncle about Lipusj's secret, but postponed it because he had to reckon with Yankel's early appearance. He did not want to excite the old man again. When Velvel had almost finished breakfast, Alfred said:

"I should like to ask you something, Uncle. I have been wanting to for a few days now, but I always forget. It is really irrelevant, but I should like to know whether you are responsible."

"For what?" asked Velvel.

"Whether you are responsible for Walko's guarding me on my nightly visits to Panko."

"Guard? Walko? I?" Velvel was taken aback.

"Excuse me, Uncle," said Alfred, "I thought you knew about it. I even suspected that you had arranged it."

"I know nothing about it," said Velvel, still taken aback. "He accompanies you?"

"Not that," said Alfred. "He is always where I am, every night. He follows me or he walks ahead of me, at a distance, naturally. But he is always where I am. Since he has gone everywhere I have gone for two weeks, can it be a coincidence?"

"Every night?" asked Velvel. "Or was it just last night?"

"Last night?" said Alfred. "It so happened I didn't notice him last night. Perhaps because I was deep in thought. I had a lengthy conversation with Avram Aptowitzer, and I went to see Panko later than usual. Last night I didn't notice him, but I am positive about every other night."

"You should have told me that at once. How do you know that he was guarding you?"

"I am sure, Uncle. Walko doesn't do it very expertly. On the contrary. All that remains is for him to wink to me in the dark to show me he is still there."

Pessa appeared with a tray and set another breakfast on the table.

"Hasn't Yankel breakfasted yet?" Velvel wondered.

"No," said Pessa, "it's been some time that he hasn't been able to sleep a night through."

"It was still light in his room at three o'clock this morning."

Accompanied by Donja, Yankel now passed by the window and called "Good morning" through the open window.

"How miserable he looks, woe is me," said Pessa softly, and quickly left the room before Yankel entered.

Yankel sat down at the table and ate his customary first breakfast. It consisted at this season of a platefull of radishes and cucumbers, fresh from the garden and sliced thin, which he dipped in sour cream; then followed a plate of boiled potatoes garnished with sliced, hardboiled eggs; a bowl of wild berries with sour cream, and coffee with sugar and cream. Yankel combined every possible dish with sour cream. "The Bulgarians live to an old age," he used to say, "because they take a lot of *yagurt*. I take cream." When Pessa retaliated (when there was no other cause for a quarrel) that *yagurt* was more like sour milk than sour cream, he would answer: "Am I a Bulgar?" Although he looked this morning as though he had spent a restless night and his face bore an expression of mildness, which worried Alfred by its contrast with the Yankel of old, Yankel ate his breakfast with a hearty appetite. When he reached his coffee, Velvel said:

"Have you given orders for deaf Walko to watch Alfred?"

"Yes," said Yankel, "how did you find that out?"

"It was not hard to find out," said Alfred. "Walko is no diplomat."

[99]

"You did right, Yankel," said Velvel appeasingly. "I only wondered why it had to be Walko."

"Because all the ruffians in the Old and the New Village are afraid of him. The Mokrzyckis would think twice before getting in his way."

"Has the murderer returned?" asked Velvel.

"No," said Yankel. "But his younger brother didn't even think it necessary to run away at all. The past few nights Alfred has been in the village more than at home. Mr. Lubasj is still here. I admit I have become somewhat anxious of late."

"I wish it were true," said Velvel. "I wish you had really become anxious."

"Naturally, I am not worried about myself," said Yankel. "Today I am more worried about the physical safety of the communal secretary."

"Ah, you know already," said Velvel.

"Surely," said Yankel. "I did not think it would happen so soon. So much the better. Today it became too hot for Lubasj in the Old Village."

"And tomorrow someone will be arrested," Velvel quickly interjected, "and taken to the prison in the city. And his name will not be Vincenty Lubasj but . . ." Velvel sprang from his seat in excitement, "Yankel Christiampoler!"

Alfred sprang up too and now stood between the two of them like a statue. Yankel remained calmly sitting in his place. The lamb-like calm that had so disturbed Alfred had been wiped from his face. He lowered his head and cast the look of a lion-tamer at Velvel.

"That can happen, too," said Yankel, after a moment of silence. "Where criminals rule, respectable people belong in prison."

Velvel clapped his hands over his ears and looked at Alfred with wailing eyes.

"I have been in the village for seventy years. I want to see —"

"— not seventy," shouted Velvel, "sixty-five at the most. And —"

"— I was eight when I was brought here, and now —"

"— and now," said Velvel, already somewhat calmer, "don't tell me that you are almost seventy-eight, for you aren't —"

To Alfred's astonishment Yankel's face colored a deep red. For a moment he was silent in visible embarrassment. Then he said to Alfred with a forced smile:

"Very well, for all I care. So I have been in Dobropolia sixty-five years, not seventy. I want to see who is more powerful in this village, a newly-arrived rascal, a thief, an extortioner, or I."

"Do you know that there's an official complaint lodged against you?"

"A complaint?" asked Alfred.

"A complaint for inciting to public disturbance, or for instigating a riot against an official. I don't know exactly. Perhaps our great diplomat here knows better."

"He knows," said Yankel, "that it's for instigating a riot against an official."

"Not bad," Velvel cried, "two years imprisonment — child's play for a seventy-two-year old."

"Seventy-two, yes. Old — no." And now he turned to Alfred with a wailing look. "When I was young, I looked much younger than I was. When I came back from the service, I was twenty-six. But I looked twenty. My first position was with the Countess Rey. I wanted to have more authority among the peasants, and made myself out to be a few years older. Now he's throwing that in my face, that clerical uncle of yours. He has picked the best time to torment me with it."

"What I want you to do now is to stop . . ."

"— to stop 'instigating,' " said Yankel, sarcastically.

"To stop putting yourself into the wrong. I don't doubt that in the village here, both the Old and the New, you could win your case against this rogue. But the court is in the city.

And the jail is in the city, too. There you will not be the bailiff Yankel Christiampoler but an old —"

"— an old fool, who still is under the illusion that he is living in a just state where law is law and injustice injustice. It's been that way here for sixty-five years."

"Yes, that's just it," said Velvel, no longer with anger, "but things have altered somewhat. We live in other times, and if you don't want to be a righteous fool, you have to suit yourself to the times, or —"

"— or recognize that freed slaves rule and blackmailers disguise themselves as officials."

Velvel raised his arms, appealing to Alfred, then clapped both hands over his ears and quickly left the room.

As Alfred considered whether or not he ought to follow his uncle, Yankel sat silently looking out of the window. At that moment Donja came out of the garden and smiled at Alfred. But Alfred did not see her, and, disappointed, she went towards the kitchen.

"Sit down, please," said Yankel. "A hasty mind and hasty decisions lead nowhere."

"Ought I not to ask Uncle to come back again? There's no point in quarreling just now."

"We're not quarreling, Alfred. Your uncle is right."

"So much the better. So I can ask him to come back."

"You haven't let me finish," said Yankel impatiently. "Your uncle is right, and I am right. So there is no point in talking back and forth."

"Uncle Velvel is only worried about you."

"He is not worried about me," said Yankel. "He is worried about you."

"About me?" said Alfred.

"Yes. About you. Your uncle will not be especially happy when he proves to be right and they arrest me, but he's mostly worried about you. And that is the reason why I want to speak to you. Sit down, please."

Alfred obeyed, and Yankel turned to him with a face on

which Alfred again noticed the mild expression which had disturbed him before.

"Three weeks ago we agreed that you were going to return to Vienna for a visit. Unfortunately, it has turned out otherwise. Naturally, you couldn't go away, and that was proper. You were the only one who kept his head, or Panko wouldn't have escaped the amputation, and perhaps worse. But now, plainly speaking, it's time for you to leave. Your uncle will feel better, and, frankly, I will too."

"Am I in the way here? What's really happening?" Alfred wondered.

"You just heard. I will not give in. I did not instigate a riot against an official. On the contrary. I acted with the consent of the head of the community, and he is the official here. Whether Lubasj the cur represents officialdom here is, to say the least, controversial. Otherwise I personally would long ago have sent him packing out of the village with a box on the ears. For I am still not an old man. You were here," Yankel added with a smile that enchanted Alfred, "you heard your uncle make me a good five years younger just before. I shall finish what I began. One way or another. But the best of men can't fight with a child in his arms. So, for God's sake, see to it that you leave."

"I am the child in arms?" laughed Alfred.

"Yes," said Yankel. "You are the child in arms now. I watched the other child badly. I was a bad watchman. So, that's settled, is it?"

"I must still speak to Uncle Velvel," said Alfred. "I am tired of being a child in arms. Since I came here a year ago, I have been taught everything. Taught how to eat, how to pray, how to mow, how to speak. I've had enough teaching. I am almost twenty years old now and I've decided to stand on my own feet."

"Are you going to get up on your hind legs?" asked Yankel goodhumoredly, and smiled at Alfred affectionately. "Come, keep me company for a ways. I've had a restless night. I won't sleep. But I want to stretch a bit, and we can talk some more. The atmosphere is quarrelsome here today. You ought to speak to your uncle later, when he has calmed down. Come!"

To be able to walk side by side, they went through the avenue of poplars, not by the short garden path.

"I want to ask you something, Yankel. It has nothing to do with our conversation. But since I shall soon be leaving (I can see that now) I want to ask you before I forget."

"What is it?" asked Yankel.

"Last night I was at Panko's. And he told me something remarkable."

"About Lipusj," asked Yankel. "Avram Aptowitzer told me about it this morning. What do you think of that? He had a secret from us, too."

"I assumed that Aptowitzer would tell it to you, otherwise I would have told it to you before breakfast. — Has Aptowitzer left?"

"Yes," said Yankel, "and, as well as you can tell about a thing like that, he seemed to be somewhat relieved."

"Thank God," said Alfred. "Panko told me something else. He said that you know about it, too. Panko said that every Friday Uncle Velvel sells him the whole estate. Do you think that's possible?"

"Surely," said Yankel, "every Friday. Didn't you know that?" Yankel was surprised. He stopped and looked at Alfred with a lively expression, almost sarcastically. "Still not learnt enough?"

"No," said Alfred, "I knew nothing about it. If that is true, it's the first thing I don't like about Uncle Velvel."

"Why?" wondered Yankel.

"To think that Uncle Velvel relies on such a farce."

Yankel took his arm and they continued.

"When I was as young as you — I was even younger, your grandfather was still alive, and he was no old man then — I thought the same as you. A farce. Just like you. I knew — and I needed no whole year to discover it, the way a scholar does — that your grandfather sold his coachman Matwej his whole business, lock, stock and barrel, every Friday. Your grandfather used to sit in Grandfather's Room Saturday afternoons and study, and we all knew that we dared not disturb him then. If you could have known your grandfather, it would be quite clear to you that it never occurred to anyone to approach him on the Sabbath with any subject that might disturb his Sabbath rest in the least. Your grandfather was no gentleman farmer, like your uncle. And the times were different, too. One Sabbath — it was during the threshing season — the whole harvest was reaped, the whole business capital, in a manner of speaking, amassed at one spot, when a fire broke out in a barn. You can imagine how fast it burns here, how fast it can burn in a place where everything is covered with straw, not only during the threshing season. There was no fire insurance at that time, and though I was young, I correctly estimated the magnitude of the catastrophe. I was at the threshing floor, and I lost my head. I began to run. I ran to your grandfather. I ran around the house and rapped on a window in Grandfather's Room. I must have rapped a couple of times before your grandfather opened a shutter. 'Fire, Reb Judah! The whole harvest is in flames,' I shouted through the window. Your grandfather looked at me thoughtfully, and calmly said, 'Tell it to Matwej. It's his harvest that's burning,' and he shut the window. For decades I never thought about it. Now, since you remind me with your stupidity about my own, it occurs to me for the first time that, although I lost my head, there was another thought in the back of my head, which perhaps sent me running. 'Aha!' I must have thought. 'Now we'll see this farce of the sale burst like a bubble.' I am sure that I ran to your grandfather with that thought in the back of my head, for, you see, man is always inclined to think evil of what he does not understand in his neighbor. It is almost a pleasure for me to see that you are quite as stupid as I was. Do you understand now? Or do you still think this mock sale a farce?"

"I don't know," said Alfred. "What is the point of it? Because one may not work on the Sabbath? What need is there for a mock sale?"

"You ask the rabbis that, the Scripture scholars. Your grandfather had the express permission of a rabbi to conclude such a sale. Your uncle has a similar permission."

"Would it not be better," said Alfred, "better and more dignified simply to do no business on the Sabbath?"

"Certainly," said Yankel, "certainly. But as you know, we must stop the business on Sunday, and no business can stand two days of rest. It's good that you have asked me. Your uncle will certainly have more to say to you on the subject. As for me, I have never spoken to your uncle about it. The lesson your grandfather gave me on that memorable Sabbath when the harvest burned was enough for me. What more is there to explain? 'Tell it to Matwej!! It's his harvest.' "

"Do you think, Yankel," Alfred inquired, "do you think Uncle Velvel would act as Grandfather did?"

"Exactly," Yankel supposed. "He would act exactly the same. Yet it would not be quite the same. Simply because now we are insured against fire. Yet neither of us has reason to respect your uncle's behavior the less. Don't speak to your uncle about it before you leave. When you're away for a time and stand on your own feet a bit, you'll probably come to the conclusion that you still have something to learn here."

They had arrived before Yankel's house, and they entered. Yankel went directly to a large grandfather's clock, opened it with a small key that he took out of his pocket, rummaged a bit in a small drawer of the box, returned to Alfred with a thick envelope, asked him to sit and said:

"Have a look at this. You can open it. It's not sealed tight." He went to his sofa and stretched out on it. Alfred opened the envelope and read a document written in the clear calligraphic hand of Austrian government officials. It was a short listing of old Yankel's entire estate. Paragraph one was an exact description and location of the real estate which old Yankel

[106]

might call his own in Dobropolia: there were sixty-five acres, neither more nor less. The rest in cash, bills and other valuables, was listed and described precisely. Alfred read it all through quickly and looked back at the first paragraph, which obviously interested him most. Yankel must have noticed that, for he said:

"Sixty-five acres. What do you say to that?"

"Very fine," said Alfred, "you are really a man with holdings, a real *kulak*!"

"Certainly," said Yankel proudly, "a big farmer. Sixty-five acres is a big farm. I am a real *kulak*. I showed it to you only because I wanted to tell you that I am ready to liquidate myself. In fact, I am prepared to spend everything I own to settle accounts with Mr. Lubasj, the man with the diploma. Naturally, I hope despite everything that it won't cost that much. But I wanted to show you how seriously I take this matter. Actually, I wanted to tell it to your uncle, but unfortunately he ran away. He must have sensed it. Your uncle is a very clever man. But now I hope that you will tell it to him. I also hope that you now see how serious a matter this is and make sure to leave by the end of the week at the latest. When the air here is clear again, you'll be called back. You can leave that to me."

Yankel became silent and pulled up the light blanket that had been covering his knees. Alfred saw that Yankel was in great need of rest.

"I cannot promise," he said. "I will consider it. I must still speak to Uncle Velvel. — Good bye, Yankel. I hope you will be able to sleep a little now."

7

Tuesday morning Pessa had nothing new to report; perhaps it was because she could not manage to relay her news early, for Velvel avoided her that morning with great adeptness. But on Wednesday Pessa was more skillful. She caught Velvel in the hall, as she always did when she had a mission of this sort, and said: "Bjelak's daughter was here again, woe is me!"

"And — " said Velvel, his forehead darkening.

"The Haman was drubbed in the New Village, too."

"Good, good. What else?" said Velvel wrathfully. "Have you any other good news to tell?"

"Bjelak's daughter said that old Yankel didn't do anything. He only read something in the village, a newspaper of some sort."

"So? A newspaper?" said Velvel.

"And she also said. . . "

"Who?"

"Bjelak's daughter. Why are you so angry? I am only telling it to you because I believe it is important. She said that old Bjelak had given him permission to do so."

"And — "

"So Yankel is not guilty, woe is me!"

"I knew it. There's a mailman gone to waste in Yankel. I knew it," said Velvel, and moved away with angry steps, as he always did after such morning conversations with Pessa.

Thursday morning Velvel said to Alfred:

"I have an appointment today. I had almost forgotten about it. A man wrote to me a few weeks ago. He is from Warsaw. I don't know him at all. He wished to see me on important business, he wrote. His name is — it's a remarkable name —" Velvel went to his desk and drew out an extremely stylish envelope from which he extracted a letter which he examined cursorily and handed to Alfred. "Boleslaw de Rada-Zarudski."

"Counselor to the Minister of Commerce and Industry of the Republic of Poland," Alfred read. "A ministerial counselor, like Uncle Stefan. A big-wig."

"Yes," said Velvel, and looked searchingly at Alfred. "I wrote him that I would be happy to receive him. Of course. Naturally I asked about him beforehand. I have spent some time in politics —"

"I know," said Alfred. "You were a deputy to the Sejm."

"How do you know that?" Velvel wondered.

"It was on the program," said Alfred.

"On which program?"

"On the program for the opening session of your Congress in Vienna."

"Oh," said Velvel, "on that program."

"I still have it," said Alfred. "Uncle Stefan gave it to me. Do you want to have it?"

"I am no collector," said Velvel, smiling. "But I shall save this letter. I have never seen anything like it."

"Yes," said Alfred, and gave the letter back to his uncle with a large gesture. "Uncle Stefan once showed me a handwritten letter of Mussolini's to the Austrian Chancellor — to look at only, naturally, not to read — Mussolini's stationery was more modest than this."

"The appointment is for eleven o'clock. He's coming in his car. Stay nearby. I should like you to be here. He must certainly be a very interesting man."

A half hour later the visitor arrived in a Ford which he drove himself. He had on a snow-white dustjacket, and his face was covered by dark goggles of a size for which there was hardly any need even on the dusty roads of Poland. Velvel and Alfred went to meet their guest as he stepped out of his car, and accompanied him into the house. When he removed his goggles, a face that was almost childishly innocent appeared, with blue eyes that laughed candidly. The ministerial counselor was still a young man, barely forty, tall, with broad shoulders and the light movements of a dancer. His forehead was as round and smooth as that of a young man under twenty. Only his dark-blonde hair, which was thin and sparse in the middle, gave away the visitor's age — he might otherwise have been mistaken for a twenty-year-old fancy dancer in an eastern cabaret. He greeted Wolf Mohilevski with the respect due a colleague. When Alfred was presented to him, he pressed his hand quite powerfully and not too briefly and said:

"*Enchanté, Monsieur.*"

They sat down in the living room and the conversation began. Alfred didn't understand enough Polish to follow the conversation closely, but he more or less guessed its contents.

"First, my heartiest congratulations," Mr. de Rada-Zarudski declared, to open the conference.

"On what occasion?" Velvel wondered.

"You have again been nominated as a candidate for the next election. We have good sources of information, Mr. Mohilevski."

"That is correct," said Velvel, "but there is no occasion to wish me luck. I have not accepted the nomination. As you may know, I have withdrawn from political life."

"Candidly, that is news to me," said the guest, and smiled encouragingly at Velvel. "Such decisions are usually not irrevocable, and if I may give you a piece of advice . . ."

"Thank you," Velvel quickly interjected, "there is no point in speaking any further about it. If that is the purpose of your visit, I am sorry that you have taken the trouble to drive fifty kilometers on a not very good road."

"That was not the purpose of my visit. The trouble is not worth mentioning. I would have gladly sacrificed two hours in such fine weather even on my vacation to have the pleasure of making your acquaintance. But, frankly, I have come to make you a very important proposal in reference to the Jewish question, Mr. Mohilevski — though not officially."

"Privately?" asked Velvel. "A private proposal?"

"Not entirely," said the visitor, who made a small pause and repeated with a meaningful look, "not entirely private."

"Please continue," said Velvel, "I am very much interested."

The guest opened his 100 per cent leather portfolio, extracted a Morocco notebook, opened it, read it for a moment with a very important expression, then replaced it in his portfolio and began:

"Mr. Mohilevski, we are political realists. I can speak openly with you. It is this way: Poland has always been an anti-Semitic country; Poland is (unfortunately, but it is) an anti-Semitic country, and Poland will, unfortunately again, according to human calculations, remain an anti-Semitic country. In this country we have —"

"Excuse me, Counselor," said Velvel, and moved his chair a bit away from the guest, "the fact that Poland is an anti-Semitic country is known to man and finds no favor in the eyes of God. That it always was an anti-Semitic country is not true, Mr. Zarudski, Mr. de Zarudski, and your assumption that Poland will always —"

"According to human calculations, I said, Mr. Mohilevski."

"That it will — according to inhuman calculations — remain an anti-Semitic country, is, I hope, I hope for the sake of our Fatherland, your private, not official prognosis."

"That is a matter of opinion, Mr. Mohilevski, I admit," the visitor conceded in a spirit of gracious conciliation. "And we personally hope from the depths of our heart that you are right."

"Who is we?" asked Velvel.

"Let us say 'I,' then," said the visitor. "But what was it I wanted to say?"

"Pardon me for interrupting you. I had the impression that you were about to come to realistic politics."

"Yes, certainly," said the guest. "*Eh bien*, what I wanted to say was: In this country we have three and a half million Jews. We estimate that as being two millions too many —" Velvel made a gesture as though he wished to interrupt his visitor again, reconsidered however, and withdrew his outstretched hand. "The exact figure doesn't matter," Mr. de Zarudski continued. "And this is our plan. Mr. Mohilevski, you have good connections abroad, with American Jewish circles, as well, we assume. Our plan calls for capital, large sums. Poland, which has climbed to the rank of a great power (this is confidential, please), wishes now, as soon as the international situation seems favorable, to stake a claim in the colonial field. That, as I have said, is confidential. Now we have arrived at this plan: We shall direct a Jewish mass emigration to some point (we believe we know exactly where). What we need is the interest of the influential Jewish circles abroad. You understand. We have — that is what is new in the plan, as you will certainly perceive at once — we have a national interest, not only in a mass emigration of the Jews, which would be nothing new: we have a national interest much more important than that. What we plan is not an emigration that will simply disperse the Jewish masses to all the four corners of the world — please think about this, Mr. Mohilevski — we shall gather the emigrants, the more the better, into a certain colony, and there, as Poles, build a Polish colony. With close ties to the Fatherland, of course. As a great power, we have a right to colonies. That is just. And the emigrants, as good Polish citizens, have the right, the incontrovertible right, to preserve the closest ties with the Fatherland, though far from their homeland. That is our plan, crudely put and in short. That is the news."

"You want, putting it even shorter and more crudely, the Jews, two million of them — is that correct? — to eject themselves, to pay for the costs of ejecting themselves, and to keep the incontrovertible right, though far from their homeland, to permit half-educated charlatans disguised as colonels to continue to rule them as anti-Semitically as possible. Have I understood you correctly, Mr. de Zarudski?"

"Why 'disguised as colonels?' " Mr. de Zarudski inquired; an almost tearful look of childlike hurt lay on his face. "How did you arrive at that misconception?"

"I have my sources of information, too," said Velvel, "I know on whose commission you come to me. Not officially, naturally."

"I think that there is an error here, Mr. Mohilevski. A regrettable and not undangerous error. *Eh bien?* But it's all the same. That is not so important. Whichever way I approach it, the question remains: What is your reaction to our proposition, Mr. Mohilevski?"

Velvel rose and looked across the room to Alfred, as though to ask him: What do you say to that? Alfred understood and quickly rose from his seat. Mr. de Rada-Zarudski turned in his seat and looked from the one to the other with the expression of a rebuked child.

[112]

"*Eh bien*, I understand," he said slowly to himself, and quickly rose from his seat. Velvel walked to the door deliberately and opened it. The visitor followed him. At the door, he turned around and looked at Velvel with dismay. "*Eh bien*, we shall meet again."

"Not in this world, I hope," said Velvel in Yiddish, to the lively astonishment of Alfred, "and in the world to come, according to human calculations, I shall hardly see you again."

In the terror that now momentarily disfigured the childlike face of Mr. de Rada-Zarudski, both Velvel and Alfred read their visitor's knowledge of Yiddish, Velvel with satisfaction, Alfred in astonishment. After Velvel had slowly shut the door behind their startled visitor, Alfred said, "Uncle Velvel, I could have sworn that all that gentleman could say in French was *enchanté* and *Eh bien*. How could you have guessed that he knows Yiddish?"

"Do you think that he understood it?" asked Velvel, although he knew that he had read the expression on the face of their fugitive guest correctly. He wanted to be sure that Alfred had read it correctly, as well.

"Certainly he understood it, Uncle Velvel. That is why he left so perturbed."

"So," said Velvel. "I suspected he would understand Yiddish. But I would have tried it in any event, even if I suspected the opposite. You see, Sussia, when I receive a letter of this kind from Warsaw, from a gentleman unknown to me who wishes to visit me at home on an important mission, I make an appointment to see him. At the same time I inform myself somewhat about the gentleman. Not especially because I distrust him. On the contrary, for politeness' sake, I might say. I wish to know how to speak to the gentleman, without disappointing him. So, I informed myself about Mr. de Zarudski. I received a significant piece of information: Mr. de Rada-Zarudski is, or was, a Jew."

"Frankly, that seems to me unbelievable," said Alfred. "Are you certain?"

"Yes. He was born in Lwow. His father was a high school teacher, a respectable person. Mr. de Rada-Zarudski's grandfather was a clarinet player in a Jewish orchestra. One of those orchestras that play at Jewish weddings."

"He could not have been called 'de Zarudski,' that clarinet player?"

"Piceles was his name. Hershel Piceles. Nothing else."

"Then where did Zarudski come from?"

"He took it because it rhymes with Pilsudski, I assume."

"I never would have believed that there are such Jews in Poland. There is a Jew in Germany called Naumann. I can easily believe that Mr. de Rada-Zarudski and Naumann would understand each other without any difficulty. But I would never have imagined that there are Naumann-Jews in Poland, too."

"We have them. Not so many as in Germany, but we have a couple of Zarudskis, too. — But that is not the problem that concerns me especially. I only wonder why I feel such disgust, even when he's no longer sitting here before me. I have never felt such disgust at Mr. Lubasj. Can you explain that to me?"

"I feel that he is much worse than Mr. Lubasj."

"Certainly. To us. Because he is a Jew. But that is not what I mean. I think I would have the same feeling if I were not a Jew. I wonder whether the colonel who sent him to me — not officially, that is understood — whether that superior does not have the same feeling when he sits down with Mr. de Zarudski. I do not exclude that possibility, although his superior is not the least corrupt of gentlemen. — Do you like Heine?"

"You mean Heinrich Heine, Uncle Velvel?"

"Yes," said Velvel, "Heinrich Heine."

"Frankly, I do, Uncle. Very much."

"Frankly, I do not. But Heine, you see, when he wasn't writing 'Thou hast diamonds and pearls,' was a very clever man. He foresaw everything. He must have known some de Rada-Zarudskis, too. Somewhere Heine says: 'When a

[114]

Jew is noble, he is nobler; when he is ignoble, more ignoble than a Christian.' "

"The original is stated in somewhat more concise form, I believe," said Alfred. "But the idea is accurate. Do you share that opinion, Uncle Velvel?"

"At this moment, frankly, yes. — Please be so kind as to go and tell Pessa that we shall have no guest at lunch."

Alfred went and came quickly back to inform his uncle that Pessa was very much disappointed. But he found his uncle standing at the window deep in thought, looking at the *Groblja*. He sat down in a corner of the sofa and waited. After a while Velvel Dobropolier turned around and, with a hand on his forehead, said softly to himself:

"It is an old game."

Then he saw Alfred and continued:

"I mean the game that our Mr. Lubasj has been playing here. It is an ancient game. It has always been played this way. They make the Jew a devil in the cities and a scare-crow in the country. The rest is easy. Do you know the legend of Ahasuerus, the Eternal Jew? I assume that you are aware that it is not a Jewish legend."

"I never knew that," said Alfred.

"Ahasuerus, who is the Eternal Jew, is doomed to wander through history in punishment for the sin that he committed against their Savior. Devils, that is what we are. Our Lipale was a devil, a scare-crow, an incendiary. That is the old game. The grounds given for the presence of inciting Lubasjs vary from place to place. You can call them what you will: political, economic, social — you can choose whichever you want. In this instance, this calamity of ours, Lubasj, only wanted to milk one of our cows. So, you might call it economic. It's all the same. The fact remains that the Lubasjs are always successful at the old game. And not so dark a game either, though it's of dark origin. The peasants here, you see, are human beings like us. The brothers Mokrzycki are not real murderers. They are rowdies and drunkards. But you plant a scare-crow fear in the peasant, and he reaches for his scythe in the old way. For you must not believe that such calamities occur only here."

"I don't believe that, Uncle Velvel. On the contrary: I wonder that it isn't worse in this loaded atmosphere where Ukrainians and Poles live side by side. But you are right; it can happen everywhere. Here we stand between two nations, elsewhere between two classes."

"Quite right," said Velvel Dobropolier, "that is how it is. And we cannot change it. It calms me a bit that you see it too. I feared that you would see it only when you were at a distance. So much the better. Nevertheless, it would ease my mind if, so to speak, you went on leave soon. It is remarkable: A year ago you were already here but I would hardly have been able to imagine that I would urge you to leave for a time. On the contrary. I have always been afraid to see you go away. Now I can urge you to go on leave, because I am certain that you will gladly come back."

"When do you think I ought to leave? It is already too late for my mother's birthday."

"You will decide the day of the departure yourself," said Velvel, obviously eased. "Remain here over the Sabbath."

"I should like to remain until Mrs. Aptowitzer comes home," said Alfred.

"Avram Aptowitzer counts on staying with her in Kozlova for at least two weeks, perhaps even longer. That will depend on Mrs. Aptowitzer's health."

"I shall see," said Alfred. "Perhaps I shall go to Kozlova for a half-day."

"Good," said Velvel, "you should do that."

Pessa appeared at the window and said:

"Why did you let the young man ride away? He will be hungry, woe is me!"

"He was in a great hurry, Pessa. We couldn't hold him back. Isn't that true, Sussia?"

"Never before has a guest been here on a visit around noon and not remained to eat. What kind of new-fangled manners are these, woe is me?"

"Sussia, you tell Pessa how it was."

"The gentleman was in a great hurry, Pessa," said Alfred, with a look at Velvel. "He had a new car and he had bet a friend that he could be back in the city by one o'clock. He couldn't stay."

The next day Pessa met Velvel Dobropolier in the hall at the usual early hour and said:

"Two men came this morning, on motorcycles, wearing leather gaiters and leather jackets, woe is me!"

"Apparently the commission of inquiry," said Velvel. "They were here once before. Apparently, they wish to question other witnesses."

"But they seem to be more interested in old Yankel than in the brothers Mokrzycki."

"How can you know that?"

"Bjelak's daughter," said Pessa, "was here again. What do you say to that, woe is me?!"

That morning Velvel Dobropolier had already received word from Doctor Frankl in the form of a telegram announcing his visit to Dobropolia and his arrival in Rembovlia on Sunday.

"Tomorrow evening, after the close of the Sabbath, I shall drive to Rembovlia, Pessa. We shall be having a visitor on Sunday. An important visitor. But tell Alfred nothing about it. This is a surprise."

"His mother, woe is me?"

"No. His guardian. A very fine man. Prepare the best room for him and don't let Bjelak's daughter turn your head, however good her intentions. We have enough worries without that."

In the afternoon Velvel said to Alfred, "I am going to the baths today. Do you wish to come along?"

"Gladly," said Alfred. "Do you think Yankel will give us horses?"

"I have already told Domanski. Now let's pay a quick visit to Panko. Come!"

When they arrived in front of Panko's house, Velvel said; "You remain outside for a while. I have some business with Panko. I'll call you when it's time."

Alfred waited. He had forgotten to inform his uncle about Panko's anxious expectation of his Friday visits, and he was glad that Velvel was now with Panko. When he stepped into the sick-room later, he saw that his uncle's visit had done Panko a great deal of good. Alfred had noted before that there are invalids who, though incapable of controlling their legs, still are able to sit in a wheel chair poised and proud, yes, to throne it there. But he had never thought it possible that an invalid could lie in bed proudly.

"It won't take much longer now," Panko said to Velvel. "I have no more pain. Not much. I have no fever at all. Now it's going to go fast."

"Certainly," said Velvel, "wounds heal quickly in a man as young as you, Panko. Don't worry about it at all."

Velvel and Alfred stayed a little longer. Velvel had arranged for the carriage to pick them up at Panko's house. When they heard the wagon rolling up, Panko recognized that it was Velvel's, and said, not without some melancholy:

"You are going to the steam baths, master."

"Yes," said Velvel, "who knows, perhaps next Friday you'll be sitting on the coach box again."

Velvel rose and said goodbye to the invalid. Behind Velvel's back Panko gave Alfred a sign.

"Yes?" said Alfred.

"I wanted to ask you something, Mr. Mohilevski," he whispered quickly. "When they take a leg off, do they do it with a hatchet?"

"No," said Alfred, "they use a saw. A fine, small saw. And they give you something to fall asleep. You don't feel anything at all. And when you awake —" Alfred halted. The invalid's face had changed completely. It had turned ash-gray, and the

[118]

lobes of his nose shone as waxen as they had during his bad days. "What is it, Panko? Your leg is well."

"Jesus Maria," whispered Panko. "Good that I did not know it! Good that I did not know it! I thought they did it with an axe. They chop one way; if they don't hit the right place, they chop again — good that I didn't know. Who knows what would have happened? If I had known that they put you to sleep and that they do it with a saw, so that you don't feel anything — perhaps I would have let Dr. Chramtjuk talk me into it. Good that I didn't ask at once, Mr. Mohilevski!"

"Don't think anymore about such things, Panko. Your leg is well. The wound is healing. I'll come to see you tomorrow. I can't let Uncle wait now."

"Give my excuses to the master. What a narrow escape!"

8

Before they entered the steam baths in Kozlova, Velvel said to Alfred, "I think you ought to take this opportunity to have your hair cut."

Alfred promptly followed this suggestion, although it occurred to him at once that Uncle Velvel had never troubled himself about such a trivial matter as appearance in the whole year Alfred had known him. On the return trip home Velvel mentioned in passing his forthcoming journey to Rembovlia and Alfred asked him to inquire when there whether the tombstone for Lipusj was already completed.

After having paid a short visit to Panko on Saturday night, Velvel rode off to Rembovlia. Sunday, sitting next to Dr. Frankl in the yellow carriage, Velvel gave Alfred's Viennese guardian a complete report of Alfred's first year in Dobropolia. At the same time, at home, old Yankel prepared Alfred for the great surprise. At first Alfred refused to believe that his Uncle Stefan would actually appear in Dobropolia in the flesh. Then he hurried to put on his best suit; while doing so he regarded himself in a large mirror — not his wont at all — as though to

[119]

assess those alterations in his personality which Uncle Stefan would certainly perceive. He was seized with an impatient excitement and thought of taking the *bitka* at least as far as Polyanka to meet both his uncles.

At last Dr. Frankl actually arrived in Dobropolia. Looking short and very tired Uncle Stefan climbed out of the yellow carriage with the remark, "If the mountain won't come to the Prophet —" and then wanted nothing but rest for a while. It was six o'clock in the evening. Even Pessa appeared before the house to greet the new arrival.

"Such a frail gentleman, woe is me!"

"And this is Pessa," Alfred introduced her to his uncle, "the good soul of our house."

"Yossele's friend," Pessa whispered with pale lips. "You are very welcome." And large tears rolled down her faded cheeks.

"We shall soon be ready for supper, Pessa," said Velvel, and Pessa ran off to the kitchen.

"Is she a widow?" Dr. Frankl inquired as they entered the house.

"She is an old maid. A relation. A poor old maid," said Alfred. "You can call her simply 'Pessa.'"

While Alfred helped him at his toilette, Dr. Frankl said, "You look as though you had been born and had spent all twenty years of your life here. And that Tartar mustache! A real country-gentleman!"

"All the men wear mustaches in the village," Alfred said apologetically. "How is Mama? Is she very angry at me?"

"She is all right. Whenever she isn't in a particularly good mood, she plays the neglected mother a bit. But she's all right."

"You haven't changed at all, Uncle Stefan. I can hardly believe that you are here in Dobropolia. What a wonderful surprise! At that, my birthday is still two months away."

"I've brought you something for your birthday," said Dr. Frankl, looking meaningfully at Alfred.

"You could have taken your time about that, Uncle Stefan.

[120]

We'll be in Vienna together around the time of my birthday. Or do you intend to stay here two months?"

"I'll tell you that tomorrow," said Dr. Frankl. "I'll stay here a week for certain."

They ate an early supper and went directly to bed. On Monday Dr. Frankl saw the house and the estate and the old neglected park; then he sat in Grandfather's Room for a long time with Velvel Dobropolier. Dr. Frankl appeared at supper refreshed, in sober dress and with a fat portfolio under his arm. After supper he took a sealed packet from the portfolio and handed it to Alfred.

"Here is your birthday present. It's not from me. I'm only the intermediary. Actually, I accepted the invitation to visit Dobropolia only to transmit this present to you. For it is only proper that this event take place here, in this house."

Alfred took the packet and held it for a moment, not knowing what to do.

"Why so solemn, Uncle Stefan? You usually don't care at all for birthdays. Anyway, today isn't even my birthday at all."

"It is your father's testament," said Dr. Frankl. "I received this sealed packet from a notary from Zloczow in 1916. It is meant for you. In an accompanying letter your father asked me to pass this manuscript on to you on your twentieth birthday. I don't know what your father has written to you, but it seemed very important to me that it should come into your hands in this house. Your father gave me permission to open the packet and decide whether you ought to receive it at all and, if so, when that should take place. But his letter to me was obviously written in haste and confusion; I did not feel myself obliged to take his permission for a command and to open the packet myself."

"You have never looked into it?" wondered Alfred.

"You can see that it is sealed. As I've told you, I'm not even sure that you ought to read it. But your father left the decision to me, and I have thought about it long enough. Now you have the packet. Decide for yourself."

"Oughtn't we to read it together?" asked Alfred, casting a glance at Uncle Velvel, who was suppressing his excitement with great difficulty, although apparently Dr. Frankl had already told him about the manuscript in Grandfather's Room.

"I think that would be a good idea," said Dr. Frankl.

Alfred carefully opened the packet and showed the contents first to Velvel, then to Dr. Frankl, then to Yankel, who was no less excited than Velvel.

"Let's go into Grandfather's Room," said Velvel and quickly went ahead, opened the door and ushered Dr. Frankl in before him. Alfred followed him. Yankel was about to enter when he turned around, placed a hand on Velvel's shoulder and said half aloud:

"Velvel, every time we have a difference of opinion about something, I am right for a day, but then it almost always turns out that you knew better. Let me be right for a day this time, too. You have no idea of what the packet contains. Let's read the manuscript in your room."

"For me it can hold nothing that is not good. I knew my brother better than all of you."

Pessa appeared in the hall. "I have set coffee in your room, Velvel."

"You will be right again for a day, Yankel. Let's go into my room."

"Please begin, Uncle Velvel," said Alfred when all four men had taken their places in Velvel's room. "You must be most familiar with the writing."

It was a large manuscript. They read all evening and half the night and would have read on till morning had it not been for a midnight interruption. First Velvel read, then Dr. Frankl, then Alfred.

It was Joseph Mohilevski's testament to his son, written during the last few days before his death. It took the form of a letter, in which one paragraph was crossed out and could be read only by Pessa. For the rest, the letter ran as follows:

My dear Son,

You are now almost six years old and everybody loves you. Your mother, your father, your grandfather, your grandmother — everyone. It's a shame you only have one grandfather and one grandmother. At your age, most children still have two grandmothers and two grandfathers. But you have only two grandparents. This letter, these pages will explain to you how it has come to pass that you only have two. Perhaps you, dear child, will say. "What is there to explain? One grandfather and one grandmother have died, so I have only two grandparents." But I shall tell you where and how the other two grandparents lived and died, and when you will have read to the end about how they lived and how they died, you will then comprehend that you really always had only two grandparents, your mother's parents. For your father's parents never knew anything about you, and, if they were still alive today, would want to know nothing about you, although, of course, you have never done them any harm. I alone am completely at fault for what has come to pass. I know that now, today, as I write to you. Unfortunately, I know it only now, and that is why I am writing it down for you, for you alone. I wish you to understand me, to try to understand me. You are still a little boy now and naturally you can't; but when you become my grown-up son I wish you to learn to understand me. I beg you to try. It is my last wish.

This is war-time. Yesterday we had our first skirmish with a patrol of cossacks, and I looked death in the eyes for the first time. Now it is constantly in my mind. Tomorrow, who knows, perhaps death will be in my heart as well. I shall, I hope, receive it calmly. I already owe death a debt of thanks. It has shown me my confused life clearly; it has made me aware of my guilt. I don't mean to say that I am thinking of rushing forward to meet death; not that. This will perhaps vex you, my son. I can imagine a well-bred son feeling that his father's early death was an act of treason against him. I hope very much that you become such a son. You see, I shall write nothing here for you but the truth. The peasants in Dobropolia used to say that death won't be cheated, and I feel no desire to do so. What I am writing now is not meant for you, my son, not for the child you are today. But when you actually have these pages before you, you will read them and know that they were written for my son when he should be able to read and understand them, for my grown-up son. For I am leaving a request that you be given these pages to read when you enter your twentieth year. My friend, Stefan Frankl, will guard these pages till then. He has chosen a profession which has a happy relationship to the war. During the happy time of peace, he is busy with war; but during war time, he is busy with peace. Uncle Stefan, as you call him, is in the diplomatic service, and so he has a good chance of surviving the war. God bless the day when he chose this profession! I could not think so calmly of death if I did not know that my only friend was out of danger. He will be your guardian. He will be your father. Perhaps even a better father than I would have been. I was a bad son; how should I be good enough to be a good father? Uncle Stefan also loves you very much, my little one, and this love of his will, with the help of God, be of great value to you. I do not urge you now to continue to love him. If such admonition has become necessary, it comes much too late.

ii

There shall be no tears on the pages I write — that was my decision when I bought this notebook in the bookshop of Samuel Zuckerkandl. Here in Galicia you buy writing paper in a bookshop. There shall be no tears on these pages, I hope; but this hope may not be fulfilled. Not because it is impossible to think about one's own death without sorrow. There is no death, there is only dying. And so long as I can write in this notebook, I am not a dying man. But sorrow does not come from dying. It comes from remembered life. While one lives his life, there is no place in it for sorrow. But when one *thinks* it, there is so much sorrow that the sorrow contends with life for supremacy. The soldier during war time, it is supposed — and supposed stupidly — the soldier in battle is a man engaged in the highest activity, that is to say, in the true reality. It is not true. The soldier shoots and stabs and kills. He acts as in a dream. It is not his reality. It is only for the onlooker that the soldier's shooting, stabbing, killing is reality. To the soldier himself the only reality lies in his thoughts about life. That is his truth. All else is sound and fury, self-deception and a lie.

Yesterday I was in my first battle. We were attacked by a cossack patrol. There was shooting and stabbing. We repelled the attack. I can't say how that happened, nor do I want to describe the fight. What I wish to describe is certainly more remarkable than a small skirmish on the Russian frontier. I had to defend myself against a cossack who attacked me with a lance and actually wounded me in the left arm: it is a minor wound. I defended myself with a sabre. The cossack had lost his cap during the battle and I swung the sabre at his bared skull. That was at the very end of the skirmish. My Uhlans captured the wounded Russian. There were no acts of heroism performed, least of all on my part. But I was in a skirmish for the first time; it was my baptism of fire, as they — in my opinion sacrilegiously — call it. I shall never forget my *first* impression so long as I live. How extraordinary! What do you suppose I thought of at the moment when I swung my sabre at the cossack's blond head? Of death? Of my death? Of the Fatherland? No. It was not that way. It was not that way at all. Strangely enough, it happened that I — all my physical strength concentrated in my arm, in the saber-holding hand, in the eye, at the sight of the blond-headed cossack — that I was suddenly forced to think of an event from my childhood years. At that moment I thought of my brother, my brother Velvel.

I must break off now. I am on duty.

My brother Wolf — we called him Velvel — was a year and a half younger than I. We were very close as children. We lived in the tumult of freedom, the way only village children live when school and the intoxicating studies of East-European Jewish children are over. As the elder, I was the leader in all games, also the one who seduced him into all sorts of forbidden paths. My younger brother was a quiet, soft child. It would never have occurred to him that one could ride at a gallop as many as ten horses from the horse-pond in one evening, up the hillock to their stall. But he went along with me, and because he was so soft and docile there was rarely any argument between us. This was not my fault, for I had enough arguments and exchanged enough blows with the other youngsters in the village. Only once — so far as I remember, only this once — was there a dispute during which my brother Velvel and I actually came to blows. It was my fault, certainly it could not have been otherwise. Since yesterday and my encounter with the cossack, I have remembered this experience very clearly, although I never recalled it before. The dispute with my brother was over a calf.

My dear child, naturally you can't understand how one can quarrel with his brother over a calf. What is a calf to you, you city child? But what a shame that you never were in the village where my brother is still living today! What a terrible shame that you will never be in that village! There is no finer, better place in all the world for a real youngster to live in than such a village. The only real villages are in the East. I didn't know that before. A war had to break out for me to return and see that. . . .

The calf which we quarrelled about, and came to blows over, was really not a calf, but a cow, a three-years-old cow. But it was still a calf to us, though it was a grown cow. We called it, "The Calf." For she was our calf, not one of the many cows in the stall, but it belonged to my brother and me. We had

[126]

raised it with our own hands, or, to be more precise, with our own fingers. For the calf had no mother. There had been a difficult birth in the stall, a cow had died, a rare case that touched us closely. When we children were shown the calf that had been saved, we were very much moved. The newborn calf was snow-white with black ears and a black forehead; it had a delightful black nozzle, and it lay quite weak in a corner of the box where a couple of livelier sucklings tumbled about on their calf legs.

"The poor orphan," sighed my brother. He was eight years old then and had a great love for all cattle, especially foals and calfs. My father, who was present, usually an unsentimental countryman, gave us the newborn calf as a gift.

"If you can pull this calf through, it's yours. Andrei will show you how to take care of it. But if I should hear that you are thinking about the calf during your studies, the orphan will be slaughtered," he added quickly, a threat which pierced us to the heart.

The strict admonition accompanying the gift surprised us children less than the gift itself, for as long as we were children our father kept us strictly away from everything that had to do with the stall and the barn, the field and the field labor. We had to study. Now I understand the motive behind the gift: it was an act of pious pedagogy. Caring for the poor, particularly caring for the widowed and orphaned, is a large chapter in the book of Jewish piety. In my brother's sigh of sympathy at the sight of the orphaned calf my father saw an expression of piety and he, who was far from having an exaggerated love of animals, gave the calf to us children as a practical exercise in caring for the orphaned. I understand that only now. It is also characteristic of me that it occurs to me only now, as I write, that my father actually gave the calf to my brother Velvel in the first place. I had done nothing to deserve the gift. Nevertheless, I considered that I had an equal right to it. I can only say in extenuation that I was but ten years old at the time, and that until yesterday I have had no clear recollection of the calf.

Must I first describe to you in detail, my little son, how tenderly we minded and cared for the orphan? Had not the stall-keeper, Andrei, supervised our ministrations, the little calf would certainly have passed away after a few days under our over-anxious care. Since the calf had no mother and knew no udder, it didn't know how to drink. In addition, during the first few days of its life it was weak and drowsy from the difficult birth. Following Andrei's instructions, we fooled the calf into drinking: We placed a pan of milk before it, stuck our fingers into its mouth, my brother and I jealously taking turns, pressed its mouth into the milk and thus taught it to drink. What jubilation when after a few days the orphan capered on the straw no worse than the other calves! When it grew bigger and began to eat, we stole everything for our calf that it could swallow, everything that our eyes could spy in the estate, house and garden. The calf thrived in that particularly fortunate fashion in which human orphans also thrive when they have the exceptional good luck of being adopted and taken care of by a worthy person — an object of envy to rich people with unfortunate progeny. Weaned from its mother's teat, that is to say, our fingers, the calf grew into a heifer. We had so spoiled the orphan that when all the other cows drank, it only dipped its mouth into the water, but would not drink if we did not give it our finger. It was always a source of huge amusement to the stall hands when one of us children had to be called to the trough because the orphan, now almost as large as a cow, had gone on a thirst-strike.

By giving us children this present our father had, so to speak, killed two birds with one stone. To avoid any suspicion that our caring for the orphan was interfering with our study, we both studied for a long time like — like real East-European Jews! I am not exaggerating; if I can still recite a large number of Hebrew psalms by heart, it is the calf's fault. Our love for the calf drove us to extraordinary feats, particularly during the first few months of its existence, just as his love for a woman supposedly spurs a man on to great deeds. Cows are generally dull animals. But our orphan — perhaps because it was fed so well — was no dull animal. She rewarded our tender care as calf and heifer with a fine appearance and, as a cow, with quantities of fat milk. The orphan was the best milker in the stall. She repaid us with love. Even as a calf she knew us the way a dog knows its master, and she went to us and followed us about like a faithful dog. When she was a grown cow she would run home from the meadow at the head of the herd. She knew our study room, which was not in our house but in the office, and she never went to the trough on her way home in the evening without paying us a visit. She stole away from the herd — no herdsman, however adept, could have hindered her — and came trotting in front of the office, stuck her black head with the powerful horns through the window and terrified our old teacher, Rabbi Motje, half to death with a tender tremulous moo.

Certainly, memory transfigures everything. What man who ever loved a cow would admit to having loved a stupid one? Perhaps my memory does transfigure quite a bit. Our calf was an exceptional cow, I can't allow that to be denied. What cow in Dobropolia ever swam without being driven unless it had to — while ours swam the whole pond to the opposite shore, to the *Gazon*? Or what other cow ever swam the whole powerful current of the river Strypa? Not one. But our orphan, "the Calf," did!

When two people must share a love, though it be only the love of a cow — naturally, jealousy arises. One fine day an idea occurred to me — to me, mind you, not to mild Velvel — at the Devil's instigation, and I proposed to my brother: "Let's see this once whom the calf loves more, you or me."

"How can we find it out?" asked Velvel and averted his eyes from mine.

"When the cows come home from the meadow in the evening, let's stand on opposite sides of the road. We'll see whom the calf goes to first, me or you."

"Good," said Velvel. "But you must promise me that you won't beat the calf."

"I?! Beat the calf? Have I ever beat it?!" But I saw at once what he meant, and Velvel's confidence in victory enraged me.

" 'God withers the hand that is raised against an orphan,' Reb Motje says. You know. So you must swear that you won't beat the calf."

I swore. To avoid observers and accidents, we decided to have the trial take place elsewhere than on the schoolroom path. We took advantage of the orphan's love for swimming. We waited for the calf on the bank of the pond exactly opposite the cows' watering place. Holding our hands behind our backs according to our agreement so that the calf might not be confused by a gesture that promised a delicacy, we stood, a distance of five paces apart, on the shore of the pond and waited for the calf. There was a difficulty at the very beginning. On that particular day the orphan had no desire to swim the pond. The pond was fairly broad and perhaps she didn't see us at first. We helped our cause by encouraging shouts.

"Sirota!" I shouted first. *Sirota* is the Ukrainian word for orphan. We spoke Ukrainian to the animals, the way the peasants did.

"Sirotka!" Velvel shouted even louder than I, and more tenderly. He thought my shouting an underhand stroke, for we had not agreed that shouting was permissible. So we shouted in rivalry, each of us being very careful that the other did not shout more often than himself. It was a fine evening after a very hot summer's day. Before the many-colored herd of cows came thronging to the pond, it had been as still as a whisper. Deep-green and smooth was the mirror of water at the shore, where the shadows of the trees cooled it; bright-red and smooth was the mirror of water in the middle, where the sinking ball of the sun set it on fire. Then a great commotion ensued in the pond when the herd of a hundred cows plunged into the water. There was a commotion in our hearts as well, when the orphan came swimming toward us between the two round suns, the calm sun in the sky above and the trembling, dancing water-sun in the pond, almost supernaturally illuminated. Foaming and spitting like a rhinoceros, blinded by the sun, she turned her black ears to our shouts while still far off, spraying colorful waterworks with her tail. She had barely reached the shadows of the trees in the water — the evening shadows were long — when she set a straight course for Velvel, her large cow eyes fixed on him. She plunged through the water with a tremulous moo of joy — it was a tone so deep and soft that it seemed to be trembling toward Velvel from the depths of the cow's heart and the heart of the pond as well; the mirror of the water folded like fine satin under this heartfelt moo. The calf did not seem to have noticed me at all. I tried quickly to change the terms of our compact: we were to keep the prescribed distance only until the orphan had ground under her feet and couldn't swim anymore, the direction she swam in didn't count — and Velvel agreed. But that didn't help at all. Stopping only occasionally to shake herself dry, the orphan went straight out of the water to my brother Velvel as though she were being pulled by a rope.

I never took revenge on the orphan for my defeat. I had sworn, it was true, and I was really afraid that my hand might wither if I raised it against her. Instead, I raised my hand against my brother. When I saw him embracing the orphan although it was dripping wet, hanging onto her head, her horns, her neck, I was simultaneously seized with a wild rage and such disgust at this tenderness that I was about to take to my heels at once. But as I began to leave I noticed my brother pulling a potato out of his pocket and sticking it into the orphan's mouth.

"You cheated, you!" I shouted and sprang at him.

"I didn't cheat," he said in his calm fashion.

"You won her with the potato!" I screamed.

"I hid the potato in my pocket," he said.

"She smelled the potato!" I shouted.

"A cow is no dog," said Velvel with precocious wisdom, like an old peasant.

"*I* didn't bring any potatoes along," I shouted, beside myself with anger.

"You didn't need any," said Velvel slowly. "I brought it along for a reward."

So he had been that sure! He had brought the reward along with him! Hatred, hatred against my brother, surged up in me and I burst into calumny.

"You've always gone to her on the sly!"

"I never went to her on the sly."

"You were never alone with her? You're a liar!"

"And you? Didn't you? It all depended. Once it was you and once it was I."

"Why does she go to you? There must be a secret reason for it. Why?" I screamed, stupid with anger. Velvel was silent. "She would have come to me if you hadn't always cheated."

"You always think that everybody has to love you more than they love me."

"Does papa love you as much as me?!"

"You're the firstborn."

"And mother?"

"Mother loves us both the same."

"No!" I screamed, although I knew very well that Velvel was my mother's favorite. "Mother loves me more than you, too. Because I'm the firstborn."

"Good. Fine. Good. Mother loves you more than me, too. Everybody loves you more than me. But the orphan, you see, the calf, you see, she loves me more," he said contrarily and laid his arm around the orphan's head. I dislodged him with a blow on the chest. It was the first time I had used the physical superiority of an older brother other than in play. In our child's play it had always been easy for me to overcome my younger brother, and I must have thought when I gave him that blow that that would be the end of it. For my brother Velvel wasn't a fighter. But how amazed I was, yes, how disconcerted, when small, easygoing Velvel not only defended himself against my blow but immediately engaged in battle, furiously fighting with all his strength.

Nor did it go well for me, either, because I was confounded by my weaker brother's attack, or because I was hindered by my desire to avoid Velvel's wet clothing, or because he was armed with righteous anger. In the exchange of blows, cuffs, pushes and bear-hugs I soon felt my brother's usually weaker childish fists hitting me harder and harder, his thin, small arms pressing me like bands of steel — my moral defeat still painfully fresh in my thoughts was about to be followed by a physical defeat as well! Then, to avoid this ignominy, I did something shameful, something so vile that it is almost incomprehensible to me now how I managed to suppress its very memory as boy, adolescent and man, until yesterday. But have I succeeded? Yesterday, in the skirmish, when my sabre flashed at the cossack's fair-haired skull — the old wound I had once given my brother, broke open . . . as though it had never healed. It was not the cossack toppling with a scream I saw: I heard my brother Velvel screaming. I saw him, not the cossack, toppling. Perhaps it was not a sabre striking the head of the cossack that I saw, but a little comb, a narrow, long pocket-comb, with which once upon a time I had disabled my younger brother — I can't say exactly.

During the childish exchange Velvel happened to strike my jacket where I kept a small comb. Was it to protect the comb? . . . No, it was apparently with the vicious intention of using the sharp-toothed comb as a weapon of war that I drew it forth quick as lightning and as quickly, clenching the comb with the sharp row of teeth in my hand, struck my brother's fair small head . . . As a matter of fact, my brother Velvel didn't really have a small head at that time; he had a long, narrow skull: in school the peasant boys called him "Long Head."

The fact that as a village boy barely twelve years old I already carried about a pocket-comb with me is something that I want to emphasize. It seems to me, now I think of it, that that pocket-comb reveals more about my character and later life than you, my son, being only twenty years old, can imagine.

iv

I do not tell you this story, my dear son, because I have undertaken at this point to confess my regret for all the shameful acts I have committed during my lifetime. Frankly, I don't know exactly how it has come about that I have told you this particular story. I do not have the peace of mind to reread what I have just written. These days my life has become so telescoped that the order in which events are recalled is all the same to me. Perhaps I just wanted to show you what a soldier's thoughts are likely to be — people imagine that he thinks only about death. Or perhaps I feel I can point out to you the source of the sorrow which pervades these pages. It does not, I repeat, come from fear of death. It comes from the memories of life. Confess? Regret? I wish to talk to you, my son. I wish only to talk to you; for I have the premonition that this is the last opportunity for me to talk my heart out to you. If you are truly my son, you will listen to me and understand. But if you are only the grandson of the Councillor of Commerce Peschek, if you are only that to me — well, then I can well say about myself: *omnis moriar*, or in plain language: I shall suffer total death. But that — now that I experience it myself — that, too, is not at all so bad. If, however, you are truly my son, you are the grandson of Judah Mohilevski, the grandson of my father, to whom I was so bad a son. Regret? Regret is nothing if it is not followed by repentance. There is no more time for repentance. Repentance is called *Teshuvah* in my father's tongue, that is to say: "turning back." Return! But return is only possible where there is a path to return on. My path, it seems to me, has come to an end. Have I ever tried to return? Although certainly no unprejudiced witness, nevertheless I venture to answer: No, I have never thought of returning. If today this forgotten thought touches me with its ghostly breath, it is attributable to external circumstances: this is war time, and war has thrust me back to the frontiers of our country. Now here I stand, a foreign soldier in the dream-landscape of my childhood. . . .

I am sitting in a village tavern. My soldiers have unsaddled. We are resting. There is a tavern exactly like this one in Dobropolia. The mistress of the tavern here might be called Czarne Gruenfeld. There is a painting of the Emperor hanging in her taproom too, an old oil impression: His Royal Highness and Apostolic Majesty, young and handsome in a white dress uniform with a red ribbon across his chest. In the room there are the same evidences of East-European poverty and East-European Jewishness. Only the anxiety in the old woman's eyes tells me that it is not old Czarne Gruenfeld. She would certainly have felt no anxiety because of me. . . Outside, soldiers are camped on a green spot of grass. One of them is playing the harmonica. Another is singing in Ukrainian:

> O Mister Emperor, O Mrs. Emperor,
> You've been discussing for three days
> What kind of a gift to give
> The brave soldiers from Zloczow.

The song has innumerable such verses. The soldier probably composed a few out of his own head. The words — well, I've translated a verse for you! But the melody is as sadly beautiful and distant as only Ukrainian songs can be. I am sitting in the tavern, writing. And I am not writing at all what I want to say to you. I am afraid I shall disappoint you in these pages. I wish I could separate myself from the outside world and be alone with you; as alone as a father can be only with his unknown son. . . But the village, the tavern, the faces, the melody, this wholly enchanted landscape — they rush into me like water into a leaky ship. Shall I be able to convey it all to you? What have I told you already? And what remains to be told? If I could now disregard a familiar melody, as, during those years of decision, I could disregard first my father's mind, then my mother's heart, then my brother's gaze — if I could do that, you should receive a clear report. But unfortunately, I cannot. Transferred to this land as though by magic, I sit quietly, trying hard to keep my self-control. But I sit here in this room with distraught eyes, and every memory dissolves into a picture — into a picture and a sound. . . Demand no clarity of thought from me, my darling.

I see — perhaps a sad, prolonged note of the harmonica carries this picture to me — I see the Long Street in Dobropolia. There is actually a street there by that name. It is a hot day. The street is very sunny and covered with a layer of dust so thick that the children wade in the soft, hot dust as in water. There are many children on the street, for it is a holiday. I am visiting Katz, the cabinet-maker's son, who is about six years older than myself and was once my teacher. We are sitting in the shade of the low, crushed-clay addition to the front wall, peasant fashion; we are too exhausted by the heat to carry on a conversation. The cabinet-maker's son is already a university student, I only a secondary-school pupil, perhaps seventeen, perhaps even younger. A prolonged melodious cry rings from time to time through the silence of the village, repeated sometimes in quick succession, at other times at long intervals: "Men-Hi-Men—Hi—Maan!" We know the cry. Koppel, the cloth-printer, comes to Dobropolia every year at this time in the course of his traveling from village to village, and for a couple of days he fills street after street with a hoarse "Men-Hi—Men—Hi-Maan!" followed unfailingly, as by a law of nature, by the barking of dogs, the yelling of children, and the cackling of frightened hens. What this word shouted through the village streets means is something I no longer know — it brings me singularly close to tears to realize that I do not know its meaning any longer . . . It belongs, at any rate, to Koppel's trade, as the lavender song belongs to the lavender women in Vienna. When this call echoes through a village street, the peasant women open their linen chests, pull out the pieces of coarse linen, out of which they make their husbands' trousers, and carry them to Koppel, who has a press in his cart and transforms coarse linen into blue-and-white-patterned trouser material on the spot, like a magician.

Koppel the cloth-printer is a bony man with two immense hands, almost as large as the stone plates of his press with which he stamps the white peasant linen blue. Various shades of blue shine all over his clothing, his hands, his boots, his beard, his cart, even on the handle of his whip. When Koppel receives a commission, he stops his cart in front of a peasant farm, and sets his press going. The peasant children stand around him, holding their breath, with their fingers in their mouths and noses, marveling at Koppel's fine craftmanship, as at pure magic. But when Koppel is finished and his horse starts moving again, when Koppel's hoarse voice is again heard in a melodious prolonged call to entice custom, the enchantment in which his craft holds their soul fades, and they are transformed into nasty, pestiferous children, howling, whistling, shouting cries of derision, singing mocking songs, throwing stones. The country rabble dances after the poor man, who walks down the sunny village street with bent back and tired steps next to his horse so slowly that it appears as though Koppel, the horse and the cart are all moving in a trance. The horse, apparently an army remount that has been mustered out of service, carries his head so high that the printer walks along under the arch of his nag's neck. One hand hangs lightly on the horse's neck and by exerting a little pressure downward, according to the exigency of the moment — that is to say, according to the direction in which stones are being thrown — he can cover his head and face by moving under the horse's neck either to the right or the left. But it was only when one came nearer that one could see to what masterful heights Koppel the printer had developed the art of self-defense. As though the stones that flew around him were no

more than a harmless swarm of gnats whom it was best to disregard, whom one chases away with a flick of an eyelid only
when they became too annoying, Koppel the printer continued
on his way calmly, his voice resounding from time to time. He
accomplished the feat of protecting both his and the horse's body
from the stones by employing the nag strategically: while he
protected his head and face behind the arch of the nag's neck,
his large, freckled, good hand moved according to the direction
of the stones, at one time protecting the left, at another time the
right eye of his horse, who was as poorly harnessed as Koppel
was clothed. Koppel the printer was certainly not a member
of the Society for the Prevention of Cruelty to Animals: he protected his nag because his own existence was bound up in the
poor hide of the nag, for better or for worse. They shared a common lot, Koppel and his remount. It was quite proper for them
to place themselves in danger for one another.

This scene was as little a novelty to my friend Katz as to
myself. But because we were sitting together, the grown lad
felt under compulsion to come to the aid of the oppressed. He
leaped into the middle of the swarm of children with a stick
in his hand, and dispersed the howling pack like a hawk attack-
ing birds. Koppel the printer halted, looked around for a
moment, ran his bony fingers through his apostolic beard, and
turned to a half-grown tormentor, who had meanwhile hidden
in a garden and, sticking out his tongue from between corn
cob stalks the height of a man, flung the customary country
insults at the printer, "Yid, Yid, Scabby Yid." Koppel spoke
to the lad with the dignity of a philosopher after this fashion:
"May it be as easy for you, sonny, to breathe air as it is easy
for me to be a Jew." Then, with a gesture of his hand, a very
expressive gesture — so expressive that it still lingers in my
memory as the wisest repudiation to all the well-meaning Aid
Committees of civilized society — he rejected my friend Katz's
help, rejoined his horse, and a few houses on the old game was
resumed.

After a while I heard my friend say: "The only question is
[138]

whether it must continue this way to all eternity." My friend poked his cudgel in the earth as he spoke, keeping his eyes fastened on it. I understood that he had not spoken to me, but had been thinking aloud. "The only question is whether one must stick to it. If it is so very hard . . ."

Ten years later I for my part disposed of this question in a radical fashion.

v

Did I do it to make things easier for myself? I think I can say with a clear conscience: No, never, never to make things easier for myself. There is in any event no all-inclusive answer to this question. A famous Russian orientalist who was a member of the staff of the Imperial Academy at St. Petersburg, was a convert from Judaism, having been a teacher in his youth, a petty teacher in a Jewish school in Vilna. He once replied to the question as to whether he had accepted baptism out of conviction, "Certainly out of conviction. I have, that is to say, arrived at the conviction that it is better to be a professor in the Imperial Academy at St. Petersburg than a Jewish teacher in a *heder* in Vilna."

I dare say that this answer contains a type of morbid humor. There have certainly, particularly in western Europe, been many instances which fit that description closely. It is quite true that in a certain segment of the Jewish upper middle-class it has been considered good social taste to embellish one's secure status by the acquisition of a "more beautiful" religion. But can we speak seriously about Councillor of Commerce Peschek? Or his wife — your grandmother — who began every other sentence with the ecstatic confession, "As a good Christian"? They adopted a "more refined religion" as they would have procured an expensive loge at a Brahms festival. Let us not speak of such cases here! Nor was I in the position of the famous orientalist who, as a scholar, could perhaps not have accomplished his life's work without coming to terms with "conviction." Perhaps I was in need of a job in the Peschek textile factory? There are some people in my circle in Vienna who see it in that light. Why should they not, when to certain Viennese circles every East-European Jew is an intruder who has pushed his way into Vienna for no more significant a purpose than to achieve a speedy fortune and a lucky match with a long-established local family. If they had been told that an East-European Jew like my father would have been loath to allow so respectable a merchant as Mr. Peschek over the threshold of his house, those practical-minded, cultured Viennese circles would have been speechless with astonishment.

There remains another motive commonly given for my apostasy which must be rejected: viz., that I had left Judaism because I had fallen in love with pretty Miss Fritzi Pescheck, who would be given me as wife only on that condition. I allowed this notion, however, to pass in silence, since my dear friend Stefan Frankl informed me that my action was unfortunately only understandable in these terms in Dobropolia, too. For though it might be all the same to me after my complete break with my family what they thought and said about me in the village, after the unhappiness and disappointment into which I had cast my family through my apostasy, it might perhaps be a slight relief to them to be able to ascribe my guilt to a passion which had overcome the influence of my parental home. But between us two, my son, between us men, I say to you: a man who can be given or not given someone he loves to wife is as good as no man at all. Pooh! I am sure you will not be such a weakling, my dear. For though you do not much resemble me — so far as I can see at this time — in a curious fashion you very much resemble your grandfather from Dobropolia. And he was a man!

Certainly your mother will scarcely have concealed the fact from you that she would have followed me to the ends of the earth, had I required it of her. And we would surely have been happy without the paternal blessing of Councillor Peschek. No! What's more, a *coge intrare* — "conversion is compulsory"

— spoken by Father Peschek at that time, would have had exactly the opposite effect. In saying this I do not wish to minimize my love for your mother, by any means. We were a very happy couple. My decision to marry her resulted in the only unmixed blessing of my life. When I separate it out of the context of my deeds and misdeeds, my marriage glows with light. Our life together was full of light and harmony throughout, even before you, my little son, lit it up with your pure eyes.

Only a great love can bring such miracles to pass. We were different, worlds different, your mother and I. She — a creature of the turn of the century, fine-nerved, unrepressed, basically ignorant, cheerful after a melancholy fashion, a trifle ironic, above all light-hearted, and yet very natural, beautiful, and full of music; while I was a youth hungry for life, hungry for education, already learned, but basically still uncultured, my instincts still unbridled.

Your mother tamed the wild thing with music, imparting a new way of life the while. O, miracles of culture, at times as great as those of nature! The daughter of Councillor Peschek was blessed with all the graces of a Viennese lady — above all, with a soft naturalness which triumphed over all the petty feminine arts of concealment. Blessed with that charm so dear to the heart, with that erotic favor which constitutes the grace of the Strauss-Lanner musical heritage, she found me an easy mark. She, whose spirit could be unlocked only by great music, led me into a world of which until then I had heard only a faint echo. Music was her domain. There I could allow her to lead me. Great music, the lofty Christian art, can seduce the spirit, as well. It seems to me that by that time I hardly needed it any longer. The seed had been sown long before, and if apparently it suddenly broke through the sod — music was really only a late rain helping the latent seed to sprout and flourish . . . Music meant far more to your mother than to most of the ladies in her social set who were under the influence of music. True, like all happily married women, she later gave up playing the piano seriously, but in the few troubled days of our marriage when misunderstanding and ill humor entered, it always struck and moved me to see how she withdrew into her music with her trouble, as though it was there that the secret springs of her life lay hidden. Be good to your mother, my son: it is true, she always has a confident and handsome appearance, our Mummy, but at bottom she is still only a helpless child.

vi

I have hesitated until now to describe the day I became that which is called by the one side a convert, by the other an apostate. I have delayed because I did not believe I had the time left to enter into a description of which I did not know where it should begin, or how long it should last, or how it should end. Now that I have been ordered back to my squadron with the patrol and have slept in a good bed for a few hours, I shall attempt to reflect in writing whether there is reason to assume that I only wished to make things easier for myself by conversion.

My difference with my father — in the course of the years we had several bitter conflicts, but I do not want to go back so far at this point since it would confuse you and myself too perhaps, and besides these conflicts were familiar enough to my friend, Stefan, who will certainly not have kept quiet about them to you — the last difference between my father and myself, which ended in a complete break and a kind of disinheritance, was over a really harmless love affair I had had with a peasant girl in our village. It was, I concede, a light-headed, trifling, youthful entanglement. I can't understand any more how I could have hurt my father so. Apparently my father could comprehend even less and he permitted himself to be so carried away as to (be it said to my shame) inflict corporal punishment on me. It was the first and the last time that it happened. He beat me with a stick, and I was already nineteen years old at the time. It was the last vacation I spent in my father's house. Still another difference with my father lay some years in the past.

I had been long separated from my family when I left Judaism. I had exchanged an occasional line only with my dear brother Velvel. I was alone in the world and could feel freed of all petty human ties — petty, that is, from the point of view of my conception of freedom at that time. It was a false conception of a false freedom, I think, now that from being a hard-hearted son I have become a soft-hearted father. I was once a religious Jew, and I have remained religious, though no longer a Jew. My education was not a religious-philosophical or theological one then and my religion has not become so now. I lived then and live now on the basis of direct inspiration — but you will probably ask me how one can move from extreme Judaism to Christianity? One reaches the point where one perceives that Christianity is nothing else than Judaism raised to a universal principle — a fact that the best Jews know as well as the best Christians — and where everything that lies between seems to be merely a contention over how best to clothe the Unspeakable. Old? New? There is nothing in the new which was not already in the old. Certainly the sun shines differently in the morning and at noon, differently at noon and at the close of day. But is it not the same sun shining at morning, noon, and the close of the day? And what presumptuous esthete dare decide when it is most lovely; at morning? at noon? or at the close of day?

You see, my son, the moment one tries to be zealous, the zeal afflicts him with pompous language as well as with a pompous spirit. I do not care for that language.

vii

My father was a Hasid of the Rabbi of Czortkow. Every year in the autumn, at the festival of the Rejoicing in the Torah, he used to travel to the Rabbi in Czortkow. My father was a silent man. It was only rarely that he spoke directly to us children, and we found it significant that he did so on certain occasions, generally on holidays. But when he came home from the rabbi he always had a great deal to tell. The camp of the Hasidim, the coterie of a miracle-working rabbi, is a true social fraternity bound by the ties of love. There, according to the old Hasidic tradition, the ancient epical Word still made the rounds.

Father returned home from such journeys wearing an expression of mild benignity on his face. He brought gifts for mother, us children, and the entire household. In addition he always brought back with him a fresh store of tales, parables and wise sayings. Until he had shared these, the mild benignity did not leave his face. This often lasted for weeks. For father went about with this store of his the way God's angel did with the five loaves of bread. He never doled any of it out on a workday, but systematically distributed his largesse on the Sabbath after prayer, in the prayer room which was in our house, in Grand-father's Room. This would take place after the blessing of consecration, when the worshipers had fortified themselves with a glass of *schnapps* and a piece of cold fish, and remained together another half-hour for an exchange of small talk, before returning home for the second Sabbath meal. Of course, we children shared the delight of the small village community that enjoyed Father's spiritual delicacies as they would divine manna. But if I remember correctly, the deeper meaning of these stories and parables did not always penetrate to us children. Occasionally, however, a traditional short saying, anecdote or proverb touched our childish hearts, as well. Even as children we were gripped by the inner voice of the tales, where the worshipful, prayerful audacity of true humility knocked on the gate of redemption. But I was no longer a child, already an upper-classman, when one Sabbath, after having returned home from a visit to the court of his rabbi, father quoted a prayer of a miracle-working rabbi hitherto unknown to us. It was a short prayer, almost merely a pious sigh, a pious ejaculation before the gates of Heaven: "Master of the Universe, redeem the Jews. And if you will not redeem the Jews, I beg you, Master of the Universe, redeem the Gentiles." — What is this? What if it was the counsel of the Lord to redeem, not the Jews, but the Gentiles; what if *they* had already been long redeemed? What if we Jews had been on the wrong path these near two thousand years? What if the Christian masters, who adorned their large cathedrals with figures, one representing the Synagogue, with a blindfold over her eyes — what if they were right to represent her as blind? What if we had patiently borne an unparalleled martyrdom — and it was not God's will? What if the thousands and thousands of deaths our people had suffered for the sanctification of the Name of God — had *not* been for the Sanctification of the Name of God — what if they had not done God's will but died against God's will? Horrible thoughts . . . .

If I had been capable of such thoughts at that time I would have been very careful not to express them in the presence of my father. But that great short prayer struck me like a blow in the chest. With trembling heart I stepped up to my father and said: "You see, Father, you see, the great rabbi who recited this prayer saw the world with different eyes from Rabbi Abba's, your great-uncle."

When the guests had gone, my father took me aside and said: "Why with different eyes? I see no contradiction. But I should not wonder if there were one. Nor should you wonder, either. For you know, our Rabbi Abba, of blessed memory, was not a Hasid."

No, Rabbi Abba was not a Hasid. On the contrary, he towered in my youth as a memorial to the war which learned Jewry had fought against popular Hasidism. He was father's great-uncle, but after I entered high school he had broken with our family. Through an accident my brother and I found ourselves in his house one winter night. Without knowing who we were he welcomed us, served us tea and questioned me at the table. I had a book in my coat pocket, and the rabbi inquired after its contents. It was a piece of fiction by an important author. I tried to explain the subject to the rabbi, but I probably explained it poorly, hindered by my awe at so great a Talmud scholar as Rabbi Abba. In spite of this, I was able to indicate

[145]

the theme; something like this: "The author raises the question whether it is permissible to sacrifice an insignificant human being for a great cause."

"Pooh!" Rabbi Abba interrupted me with an expression of remarkable hauteur. "The Gentile has written a book as thick as this about that subject! He who raises this question is himself a murderer."

The arguments from his Talmud that he afterwards advanced dealt with matters on an ethical height which I was then unfortunately not mature enough to comprehend. Nor the hauteur of his "pooh!" either, thank God ... It was also related of this great-great-uncle of ours that in the last night of his life he had played host to a stranger in whom he saw the Angel of Death come for him. He had often dreamed about this stranger, the Angel of Death. Nevertheless, after preparing his last prayers, he had had the strength to go to the table with the stranger and to drink tea with him ... this was the story. I have reason to believe it true. For my brother Velvel and I were his guests that last night. He was a great man after his fashion, was Rabbi Abba. I may have a great deal more to tell you about him. Perhaps I shall return to that night in his house in another connection. But now I must unfortunately break off. I am on duty.

viii

Perhaps you will ask how it could have come about that I, with such a great-grand-uncle as Rabbi Abba, became the son-in-law of Councillor Peschek. I have neither the time nor the strength to relate the story of my transformation at this point. It did not come easy to me and it would hardly have taken place were it not for your mother. Often I was on the point of turning back. My Dobropolia nature rebelled against the stroking hand of so-called culture. When your mother called me "Peperl" for the first time in a letter, me, Joseph, the son of Judah Mohilevski, I tore the letter into pieces. Then I packed my trunk, determined to run away, far away, back to my home village, to my father's house, there to fall at my father's feet, a prodigal son with cropped slaves-head, to scream out that I had remained his son, Joseph, his first-born, a Joseph who refused to be Peperl for anything and for anyone. But your mother tamed and stroked me with her music. And I was weak enough to unpack the trunk . . .

Now I have come to the point where I can explain to you why I did not become a Roman Catholic in Vienna, as the family Peschek expected, but rather a Greek Catholic in a small town in the East, a thing particularly shocking to Mother Peschek. They misunderstood this decision of mine, and even went so far as to spread the rumor that I had adopted this course of action simply to embarrass the family Peschek. They overestimated my ill will; their supposition was wide of the mark. Why then did I act so contrarily — as Mother Peschek thought? This time I acted for no other reason than because I wanted to make things easier for myself — with what consequences you will soon see.

Perhaps because I still retained my village hard-headedness, it was difficult for me to face the idea that I should have to learn a new Catechism like an elementary school child, to memorize new prayers — to take all the preparatory steps to conversion; the petty entry into a matter of such large moment appeared to me to be, well — a game! — a game, whose dignity I certainly comprehended with my whole soul, but a game, nevertheless, that I felt to be an experience foreign to my unaltered, this-worldly body. Perhaps, it would not be wholly wrong to assume that, without having known it consciously, I had long been inwardly prepared to adopt the Greek Catholic Church. Hence, I could avoid all these preparatory steps to conversion, since the Greek Catholic ritual was familiar to me from of old.

Although I grew up in a very orthodox home, I also grew up in a village surrounded by peasant children of Greek Catholic faith. Before I was even of school age, I knew as much about their prayers, their service and their holidays as the peasant children themselves. In addition, there were hours for religious instruction in school, Greek Catholic instruction, of course, for the school curriculum could provide for no instruction in the Jewish religion for the sake of five Jewish children — there were that few in the whole village school. I was the only Jewish child in my class and, according to the law, had the hour for religious instruction free. In practice it happened that the Jewish pupils actually did make use of this freedom — in good weather. But in winter and when the weather was bad, one remained in the classroom, with the permission of the priest, of course. Certainly, there were villages whose spiritual mentors would not tolerate the presence of Jewish children during religious instruction, so that when the weather was bad they spent that hour in a Jewish or peasant home near the school. But our admirable Canon Nikifor Horodynskyj, to whom the idea of preaching enmity toward the Jews to the peasant children during the religious hour was foreign, a kindly man who loved children, was very glad to have us in class. He was so friendly to us that in the course of time we did not dare and thought it impolite to stay away from this hour of religious instruction, even in good weather. Whenever we did so, it was stealthily and with a bad conscience, with a feeling that we were truants.

As guests we did not take an active part in the lessons. We just sat there and listened to what they were studying, the way it was being taught, and to the examinations. But when the pastor — they called him Pope there — would test the peasant children in the Bible or Bible stories, when he would receive not a single correct answer after so many hours of devoted teaching, when he would go through the class list alphabetically, calling the students by name with evangelical patience, preceding every name with his skeptical formula: "Perhaps So and So can tell me;" when at such times, already disappointed in "Mokryj, Petro," for once the Pope did not pass over the name of "Mohilevski, Osyp," with lifted eyebrows, but asked, as though the name was in place: "Perhaps Mohilevski, Osyp, can tell me?" What then? Then, the student Mohilevski, Osyp, sprang to his feet and told what he knew. Nor was his knowledge a feat. For Jewish children Bible study begins at five, and our Rabbi Motje set us much more difficult tasks. Often it happened that the Pope did not pass over the name of Mohilevski even when the question was one of the Catechism, either because he was experimenting for his own private edification, or because — and this is much more plausible — he was burdened by so many spiritual cares. It is hard to imagine the pains that a village Pope must take, the apostolic mildness he must display in one case, the taskmaster severity in another, to plant a fraction of Christianity in peasant youths called Morda and Popko and Zawyrucha and looking as though they had sprung full-blown out of the earth, breaking through its crust with their wiry hair. For the most part, they were very fine clods of earth, and close to nature. So it might have happened that the Canon did not pass over the name of Mohilevski when asking questions about the Catechism simply because he was weary. He started from his distraught state only when, amazed and hesitating, the Jewish lad who had been addressed answered, right or wrong.

To the Pope's credit be it said that on such occasions he scorned the miserable pedagogic comment — "Look here, Mohilevski really doesn't *have* to know, yet he does." He acted differently from our school director, Kopetko. The latter, though he taught subjects that were available to all pupils, only too often — perhaps using praise as a pretext — tried to implant envy and hostility against myself as a model pupil — although without visible success, for the "model student" was really nothing of the kind and his fellow students knew better.

Pope Horodynskyj's hours of religious instruction were especially beautiful during the weeks before Christmas. Then the subject of instruction was music, the prayer was song, the class a choir of mixed boys' and girls' voices, the Pope a singer of the Lord. There is no people on earth so blessed with song as the Ukrainian. There is no people like it even among the musical

Slavic peoples. I am speaking of song, not music; when it comes to song, secular as well as Church folk song, there is no people as rich. Ukrainian secular songs are wide as the steppes, with a simple, solid, heathen cossack earthiness. But at Christmas time the mild, Christlike, starry heaven of the inwardly pious Ukrainian folk song reigns over a snowy landscape sparkling with frost, truly a Christian miracle. Blessed be the millennial toil of generations of priests, of whom the Pope Horodynskyj, rich in Christmas songs, was one! Blessed be his memory — he has long been dead.

But his songs lived then, and live on, in me as well. I still remember many, if not all of them. But if I were here to copy down a stanza from one of those Christmas songs, an amalgam of word and music, compounded of the naive heart and Christian starlight — if I were here to copy four such lines, they would have a foreign, lovely but incomprehensible ring to you, my son. But to me they are four gleaming rows of stars, four ringing lines of light, which lit the sky of my life on many a winter night . . .

At this point a crack appears in my story, presenting an opportunity for someone easily to slip in with an "Aha, we see now! We see what happens when a child is placed at so tender an age in a position where he can be misled. There is little doubt that it was Pope Horodynskyj who planted the first Christian seeds in the heart of the Jewish lad." Nevertheless, this is a very erroneous supposition. Memory tends to simplify everything. Obviously, memory sees events only in profile. It distorts the image of the past by projecting one event sharply into the foreground, while thrusting another, perhaps just as important, into the background. The false vista that seems to open up at this point is certainly due to a lesser extent to the imperfection of all memory, to a greater extent to my incomplete representation of the past.

Why did things go differently with my brother Velvel? He received the same education, passed through the same experiences as I. He was subject to the same influences and dangers as I. Yet my brother Velvel was already very pious as a youth, a veritable Hasid. He married, as I have learned indirectly, a very pious wife in his youth, perhaps has children already, is the pious father of a Jewish family, and lives according to the strict orthodox tradition. Yet as a child he heard the same Christmas songs as I, absorbed them with the freshness of childhood and certainly retained them in his memory as well. I am quite sure that my brother Velvel still knows the words of that Christmas song, for example, by heart as thoroughly as myself, as well as that beautiful melody. But to him it is nothing more than a little song like many other familiar peasant songs, a childhood memory and no more.

To me, it is more. But it was only later that it became more to me, in the course of later years and by a fate that led me on quite another path than my brother's. That is the point.

Another question that rises here is whether the memory of that good shepherd, Pope Horodynskyj, was not an essential factor in my decision to convert to the Greek Catholic Church. The answer to this question, too, is associated with the distaste I have mentioned before for the preparations, the preliminary steps to conversions. Whatever the cause may be or may have been, I am positive of one thing: I was not converted by the Christmas celebrations in the house of my father-in-law Peschek. You must remember only too well the exchange of gifts that took place then, my son. Unfortunately, I cannot guess what memory you will have of it. Perhaps Christmas night at your grandparents will be a beautiful memory to you: you were always presented with grand gifts there, perhaps too grand — children are bribable, and a handsome, lighted Christmas tree always produces an effect. The effect on your grandfather Peschek, for example, was as follows: hardly had the Christmas tree lights been lit when he was seized with an agitation which stayed with him the whole of the holy night: the terror lest, God forbid, a fire might break out! — He would initiate Christmas eve with this cry, and during the course of the celebrations could never be free of anxiety, repeating his warning during and after the

meal with increasing intensity. For Peschek's Christmas tree
was really enormous, weighting the room down barbarically
with its overabundance of decorative candles, its largesse of
golden gleam and glitter; certainly it was not a pretty sight.
But to look at it all evening solely as a potential source of fire
was not quite entirely in the Christian spirit. And since, in
addition, Grandfather Peschek lisped when agitated, repeating
his constant, anxious cry: "God forbid there thould be a fire
in the houth" — Christmas eve at the Pescheks' was to me an
evening of exhilaration, though hardly religious. I hope and
fear that you, my darling, will have carried away impressions
of these evenings that are not essentially different from mine —
I hope and fear, for perhaps these impressions may be the only
ones that we shall have in common.

ix

In the Imperial and Royal Secondary School of the Dominican Fathers in the Polish Tongue in T — that was the official
name of the institution — there sat next to me on a bench
for two, from the very first day of our school career, a student
called Philip Partyka, a peasant's son, from the village of
Naboiki, near Dobropolia. We became friends immediately by
virtue of the fact that we two villagers were abashed, frightened
and overpowered by the city. The city of T — 42,000 inhabit-
ants, eight churches, two synagogues, innumerable smaller
houses of prayer, three secondary schools, a teacher's institute
and theological seminary, one infantry and one cavalry regiment, one field cannon battery, three coffee-houses, no theater,
market-day on Wednesday — is certainly no metropolis. But
for Partyka, as for myself, it will always represent a stony symbol
of the city. Like me, Partyka had never before been out of his
home village. Like me, he, too, was crushed by the city hustle
and bustle. Like me, he had never seen any other school than
the village school; and so we sat abashed in the gloomy class
of the old convent school, depressed by the unrepressed, even

[152]

insolent manner of the other city youths, the boldness of the repeaters, who had been left back in the class, who chaffed both of us unpolished villagers, and humiliated us with their superior knowledge of Latin. We both wished ourselves back in the village . . . .

During the first few weeks my neighbor Partyka, in particular, suffered from the delicate but vexatious humor of a few professors who immediately began to ride him because he was suspiciously unsure of the Latin alphabet in the written exercises, substituting the Cyrillic script to which he was accustomed, producing the while really delightful forms. The Ukrainians, who had been oppressed for centuries by the Polish landowners, had not yet at that time won the right to Ukrainian secondary schools in Austrian Galicia. They were forced to send the more talented and better equipped of their children to the Imperial and Royal Secondary Schools in the Polish Tongue when they had completed a Ukrainian public-school. Few of the children, who had been crammed with a little Polish, managed this hurdle of exchange of language without difficulty. Their principal difficulty came in the first class. My neighbor Partyka had the same trouble. The first time he was called to the blackboard he was asked to write the Latin sentence: *Terra rotunda est.* He fell into such a linguistic confusion that he suddenly resorted to the Cyrillic script and wrote: *тэрра ротунда эст.* The laughter with which forty-five youngsters in class IB greeted such Latin was — well, we were four whole years away from Homer, but our Latin professor immediately explained to Partyka the meaning of "homeric laughter."

It was easy for me to sympathize with poor Partyka. I, too, came from a Ukrainian folk-school and, though I was spared such comical performances, because I had already learned the Hebrew alphabet before the Ukrainian, and the Polish soon afterward, so that my conversion into Latin was more successful — I should have suffered with him for solidarity's sake anyhow, if he had not already endeared himself by the accident of our proximity on one bench. I began to be really fond of him

[153]

during the first written exercises. In the classroom there ruled that silence of mingled dedication and fear that thrives only in a strict humanistic school. The reflections of forty-five rosy, flushed faces shone in the clean paper of the school notebooks, distributed for the first time and still virgin pure. Soon the pens began to scratch, the noses to run — when I heard a softly suppressed groaning, a repressed sobbing. Shielding myself behind my notebook, I looked sideways and saw Partyka, sitting with bent head, his left temple on the desk, his right hand holding the pen impotently stretched out, sobbing to himself in despair. His face was wet with tears which rolled down in large drops upon the bench and — how awful! — upon the notebook as well, the new notebook. Luckily, exerting the last of his self-control, he had shielded the notebook by strategically placing a sheet of blotting paper in a position to catch and soak up the heaviest flood of his tears.

"What are you doing, Partyka?" I whispered in horror.

"Help me, brother, help me!" He gasped in a hoarse whisper in Ukrainian, a language which he ordinarily did not dare to speak in school.

"Why, what's wrong?"

"I am writing in Cyrillic again!" He gasped and turned his notebook toward me by degrees, so that I should see what he had done: I saw one and a half lines in Cyrillic which had been crossed out and stained with tears. The back cover of the notebook was already damp and rising like leavened dough.

"Mohilevski, brother, save me, let me copy," he pleaded turning a swollen face to me.

"Just be careful," I said, consenting.

With lively eyes whose blue fire had already dried his tears, he accepted my offer and, without noticeably sidling nearer to me, plucked word after word from my notebook with a tender and sure eye and the keen instinct of a village youth, as though he were capturing a very small bird. Once he pushed his blotter over to me and there scratched on it — in Cyrillic — was: "*in hortum* is wrong. It should be *in horto*." He was right.

[154]

When we received our notebooks back from our Latin professor a week later, corrected and graded, he had "good," I "very good."

"How is this, Partyka?" I said in amazement.

"I wrote *in hortum* so that he wouldn't notice."

In this way lifelong friendships begin.

We two villagers soon made out well enough. To the class and to ourselves we represented a sort of weak rear guard for the whole first semester. But how great was everyone's astonishment when it turned out at the first distribution of final grades that we two, Partyka and I, were among the first five students in the class. At first we two villagers were dumbstruck, then overwhelmed. I read my grade, he read his grade, then I his and he mine, then each his own again. The whole class gathered around us; then we were tossed: they threw us up in the air, shouting toasts. Even when the repeater Rechowicz burst into the happy tumult with the cry: "The village louts are lucky!" — it didn't bother us; we weren't village louts any more, but, equal, even distinguished, members of a variegated school society.

My friend Partyka did very well in school till our senior year. At eighteen he had the countenance, the strength, and the beauty, as well, of a Roman gladiator. Our class teacher, an excellent old classicist, Mr. de Przoworski, who was paternally devoted to Partyka, would often comment: "You, Partyka, have your diligent study of the Greeks and the Latins to thank for everything. Homer has smoothed the wiry hair, resembling the mane of a wild boar, over your Ukrainian skull. Plato has given your forehead, which once was as narrow as the tongue of a suckling, the breadth of a philosopher's. Cicero has lightened your heavy peasant tongue. Sophocles' verses have injected rhythm and harmony into your uncouth *corpus*. You, Partyka, if there were any awe in you, would devote your life to classical philology."

During the last year of school Partyka fell behind. He learned almost nothing; but he lived life to the full. He did not live it to the full like an eighteen-year-old, sipping fearfully at the cup of forbidden delights. No: he drank from the cup in great, full draughts and carried it off very well; he was well suited for passion by the heathen strength of his body. He lived so fast and full a life because he knew well enough that he would not be permitted to enjoy it in complete freedom and with a good conscience very much longer. For nothing would come of his classical or any other worldly studies. It was his father's life-dream to see his son a priest, a village Pope, with a good benefice and many red-cheeked children; that is the fondest dream of every well-to-do peasant in Eastern Europe.

Partyka tried to fend off the fulfilment of that dream as long as he could. For a time it looked as though my father might succeed in bringing old Partyka around to his way of thinking; my friend was our guest for a week every year during the summer vacation and my father had become very fond of him, probably because he was such a good son. But the old peasant obstinately clung to his dream, and his son was too obedient. When we said goodbye after our last vacation together — I was travelling to Vienna and Partyka to Lemberg to enter a seminary — he bade me goodbye with the melancholy observation: "You into life, I into the grave." It is a fact that he became a priest against his inclination.

So when, many years later, I had made up my mind to enter the Greek Catholic Church, I decided that my dear friend Partyka, and no one else, should convert me. I wrote him, he wrote back at once, and one day I set forth by train for the town of H, where my friend Partyka was a priest.

x

It was late Autumn, November. But the autumn that year was lovely and mild. The weather was fine on the day of my arrival, and it was fine on the day of my departure. There were six golden days in the week I spent in H, and they have remained so in my memory, full of clarity and mildness; but the nights were filled with terror and dreams, real Jewish nightmares.

[156]

My coming to H had not been, I perceived at once, a happy idea. If I had known the town, I would not have travelled there to atone for my sins. But I did not know it. And so, perhaps it was foreordained, I did in fact atone for my sins there . . . .

The town of H is a frontier town. The frontier divides it into two parts, one part Russian with a Russian name, the other part Austrian with a Ukrainian name. To the Russians their part of this town must seem completely Austrian, to me the Austrian part of H seemed altogether Russian. The Jews, too, appeared to me more like Russian than Polish Jews. They wore soft caps with cloth peaks, like Russians. They spoke a broader, harsher Yiddish than the Polish Jews, and their faces, too, seemed to me coarser than those of the small-town East-European Jews in my home, as well as more bigoted and even more fanatical. I was struck, at the station, by the mob of porters who grabbed hold of my luggage, how they quarreled over my person, how horribly they cursed one another before coming to a compromise over the little business the single stranger offered. The quarrel among the coach drivers at the plaza — the screaming, unrestrained in word, tone and gesture — amazed and shamed me all the more as it took place in the presence of my friend, Partyka, who had met me at the station.

"Think nothing of it," he said indulgently, "there is only one hotel anyway, and we will get there without any trouble." And, with a laugh at my vexation, he added: "There's a kind of Jew here that even you don't know."

So I already had a melancholy premonition at the station that I had not made a happy choice of the site where the sacred act was to take place.

"Unfortunately, you can't stay with me," Partyka apologized. "I don't have my own household. I live with the provost, whose coadjutor I have been for three years. The provost invites you to eat with us as long as you remain. He is a very well educated, very fine old gentleman. You are sure to like him very much."

We were by this time in the hotel, in my room. It was a Jewish hotel; I could not have expected anything else in H. My friend communicated the invitation to me in order to offer me some solace for the milieu in which I found myself. I accepted at once, for eating outside the house removed me from further contact with the innkeeper, which would have been only too painful for one in my position.

I arrived at H late in the afternoon. I had spent a cool, windy night and a sunny autumn day in a corner of my compartment. I was tired, and my friend Partyka left me to rest, promising to return to take me to dinner. The guest room on the first floor of the inn smelled of old, unused closets and drawers. It was apparently occupied only rarely; but it was clean and very roomy; and each of the three outside walls had a large window, each of which looked out on a completely different aspect of the town. From the front window you looked down on the market place, a Jewish market place in a small town. He who has never seen such a market place has never seen the grimace of true misery in his life. I had seen a few such market places in the days of my youth and later during my year of military service. Even before I looked out of the window I recognized the wretched picture that would confront my eyes from the single voice, whose droning carried the praise of a kind of pear through the window into my room: "Soft pears, Jews!" the voice droned.

This introduction was followed by the monotonous, hypnotic refrain: "A food and a drink, a food and a drink!" uninterrupted, rhythmical, like the hoarse ticking of a rusty clock — "such soft pears, a food and a drink in one" . . . The voice of the fruit-wife, already weary at nightfall, at once brought before my eyes the terribly familiar picture of the whole market in such a town. Resting on the plush sofa, I heard, saw, smelled the market place. I saw the wooden booths of the butchers, the bakers, the vegetable peddlers, the fruit-wives, the kerchief and the prayer-book peddlers. I saw the butchers with their blood-stained aprons and fox-red beards, the bakers in their flour-covered clothing, the fish-peddlers with their brown, sunburned necks, the veins of which were swollen with shouting. I saw the shoemakers looking encouragingly at peasant customers. I saw the old fruit-wives bearing the lineaments of a proud race mingled grotesquely with the ugliness of old age, made common and raw by poverty. I saw the cloth peddlers triumphantly balancing the rolls of cloth on their skilful arms. I saw the delicate prayer-book peddlers, looking with their pale faces, black beards and white hands as though they had written the prayer-books themselves. I saw the peasant men and women thronging in front of the booths with greediness and mistrust. I saw the merchants with their hats thrust back on their foreheads, half sitting back, leaning on their sticks, surveying business, like marshals on the field of battle. I saw the children with running noses, fantastically stained clothing and long earlocks, with multi-colored caramels in their mouths. I saw the calves, sheep, cattle, horses, all fearfully crowded together. I saw the wagoners and porters in dirty clothes moving through all this jumble of driving, pushing carts, thrusting, pressing and being pressed. I saw the beggars and the cripples in clothes patched in such a variety of colors as though to demonstrate what vast stores of poverty this people possessed. The heavy stink of the market place oppressed my heart. I smelled the vile air emanating from these booths, the filth of the poor small town, permeated by the breath of alcoholic peasants, mixed with the steam and stink of the animals emptying themselves in the unaccustomed clamor. . . .

Resting on the sofa, I saw, I smelled, this whole tumult over the miserable piece of bread on which they might rub a piece of garlic, and which is usually consumed on the spot on weekdays. I heard the ringing cries of the men, the sharp calls of the women, the bleating of sheep, the whinnying of horses, the cackling of geese.

Resting on the sofa, all I actually heard was the single cry: "A food and a drink, a food and a drink!" For when I rose to shut the window, I saw that the booths were cleared away and the market place was empty and even swept clean. Only two old fruit-wives remained sitting at their booths in the twilight; it was their monotonous litany about the preciousness of their pears that had unrolled the whole backdrop of the market before my eyes.

But very early the next morning I was able to convince myself that the reality of this market place accorded with my previous hallucination. I kept that window closed and curtained during the rest of my stay.

The second window set in the narrow wall offered a more friendly view. From afar you surveyed the Christian quarter of H. There were small houses, mostly of one story, high streets that were not too narrow, a church with a round dome, a school, and, in the distance, almost at the shore of the stream, a cavalry barracks, painted Hapsburg yellow, a pleasant sight in this area: you knew you were still in Austria.

The view from the third window, facing the courtyard, was very lovely. Looking over the building next to the yard of the inn, you saw the park, the town garden of H, which was astonishingly large, with old sturdy beechtrees and a long poplar alley in the center. It was the private park of Count P., who had donated a part of it for public use, really more a forest than a park, not well tended, but much too large and much too beautiful for a town like H.

The old trees had already shed all their leaves. The naked network of the branches rose gloomy-black up to the autumnal twilight sky. The forest floor, the wagon-and-foot-path, were piled in spots with leaves strewn ankle high, in spots the leaves lay piled so high that the Jewish children who played and fought here till late into the night leaped shouting into this leaf-drift, like bold swimmers into a wave. The autumn winds hurled themselves upon the heaps of leaves in sudden onslaughts, contending with the children for the playgrounds, like wild beasts bursting upon the bushes. There was a constant rustling and tumult in the wood which filled all my days and nights in H.

I shall never forget that autumn week. It was as though in the course of those six days I experienced the autumn of all autumns. As though with every leaf my heart turned sere, yellow, red, brown and finally as black as the floor of the wood, mingling in the bliss of death, simultaneously corpse and grave. It still seems to me as though never before or after in my life did I hear the fall leaves rustle so. The days rustled, the nights rustled, morning and evening rustled, and the rustling entered my dreams. . .

But I shall not anticipate the dreams. I must now interrupt. I am on duty.

xi

To the north, where the town's wood stopped at a gentle summit, there began the cloister garden enclosed by a wall. On the southerly incline of the summit stood the cloister, a blue church with sedate round domes; some fifty steps beyond it, but still within the cloister walls which were interrupted at this point by a small green gate, stood a small villa, apparently the dwelling of the provost and of my friend, who had pointed in this direction when he told me about the provost's invitation.

Pleased by the prospect of not having to pass through the town on my way to meals, I leaned forward slightly out of the window for a glance at the northern section of the town. There I saw, in the midst of a pell-mell throng of low houses, meager vegetable gardens and crooked networks of hedges, enclosed by a half-ruined wall, an imposing house of squared stone with a flat roof and a great Star of David on the front wall: the synagogue of H. So small a town and so large a synagogue? I marveled, resting again on the sofa in the clutches of weariness, as I began to sink into a pleasant, warm depth. Suddenly, like a moonbeam trembling in a deep well, a thought shuddered through me, a memory: The town of H was the seat of a miracle-working rabbi! One of a dynasty of *Zaddikim* who traced their proud lineage from a disciple of the holy Baal Shem! At once sleep was banished, all my weariness fled. I tossed for another half hour on my couch. Then I stood up, shaved, washed and dressed in haste and anxiety and, unable to tolerate the room any longer, descended downstairs to await my friend, after having locked the door and put the key in my coat pocket.

In the hall I found the innkeeper, a broad, fat Jew, in a greasy, gleaming caftan, a velvet cap on his head, in conversation with a younger man, whose hasidic dress seemed triumphantly to deny a herculean physique. The man's physiognomy was a study in lively contrasts. A face expressing humility and naiveté, earlocks flapping in pious rapture, and an ascetically neglected copper-red beard were dominated by two large powerful eyes with a hard gray-blue glint. Just as it is not difficult to recognize at the first glance a secret policeman in a crowd of hundreds of people, so one who is familiar with the milieu can easily recognize in this East-European phenomenon a *Gabbe*, the porter of a miracle-working rabbi. But the word porter exhausts neither the office nor the activities nor the character of the *Gabbe*. He is adjutant, secretary, cashier, propagandist, bodyguard, porter, messenger — in short, the *bracchium saeculare*, the earthly power, of the miracle-working rabbi. It is no simple post. But the shoulders of this man whom I encountered in the hall in conversation with my innkeeper did not look as though the post was too heavy for them to bear. The conversation broke off abruptly as I appeared, the innkeeper becoming busy with the hall lamp, which he quickly lit, although the long hall was not yet very dark. In his zeal to serve he obstructed my way, and for a brief moment I stood in the light of the hall-lamp eye to eye with the red-headed *Gabbe*, who looked over and through me with such purposeful disinterest that, with a shamed oppression at my heart, I suspected at once that I was the subject of his visit. The *Gabbe* had a thick knobby stick in his right hand, and, although the Jews in this part of the country generally carried sticks on workdays, I noted how uniquely the *Gabbe's* hand held the stick — as though the hand were held by the stick — and at once the magical image appeared before my eyes: Messenger with Stick.

"Please pardon the question, sir: Is the gentleman perhaps an

Israelite?" inquired the innkeeper, turning to me when he was through fixing the lamp, whose light he cleverly cast into my face, which he examined with a piercing look. He had spoken to me in Ukrainian, probably because he had heard me speaking to the priest in that tongue.

"No," I replied, and placed the room key, which I was about to hand over to him, back in my pocket.

"Pardon me. I didn't want to bother you. But this man" — he pointed his light to the *Gabbe* — "is looking for someone. A stranger, who is due to come to our town one of these days. He is to come from Vienna. It occured to me at once that you were not the stranger whom the man is looking for."

"No," I repeated, "I am not that stranger," and stepped slowly to the door. As I left I heard the *Gabbe* replying crossly to the reassurance of the innkeeper: "You see, you see, I told you at once —"

"Perhaps he isn't, perhaps he is. So great a cur would not fear to tell so small a lie as that."

"We shall see, Reb Goddl, we shall see," the innkeeper whispered behind my back. He stopped me at the door.

"Pardon me, sir. I forgot: please sign the register."

"Thank you," I said, and took the register. "But this can wait till tomorrow morning."

"We are at the Russian border here, sir. The regulations are very strict."

By the tapping of his stick on the stone flags, I recognized without turning around that the *Gabbe* had left the inn behind me. Walking with quick steps, I crossed the plaza, turned left and, at the town's forest, saw my friend Partyka coming towards me.

xii

I was prevented by a feeling of shame from communicating my anxiety to my friend and from seeking a kind of protection against my brother Jews from him, a priest. But I was in sore need of his counsel. Though we were on the border, almost in

Russia, yet we were still in Austria, where one cannot jest with a register. If the *Gabbe* already knew about the stranger from Vienna, the purpose of the stranger's visit to H would not be concealed from him nor, eventually, his name, either. I could picture to myself in only too lively hues what sort the Jews of this town were, particularly after the view of the synagogue had reminded me that this was the seat of a miracle-working rabbi. My horror at the fanaticism of an East European town drove away the last of my feeling of solidarity with my people, and I related the tale of the encounter in the inn to my friend.

"Red Goddl, as the *Gabbe* is called here," my friend explained to me, "is not the only Jew who knows about your arrival here and the purpose of your visit here. The whole town knows about it."

"My name, as well?" I asked, terrified.

"Your name, too."

"Then I must leave the inn," I said.

"On the contrary. It is best for you to remain," said Partyka.

"Apparently you don't know these fanatical small-town Jews. They can be driven to excesses."

"So? I do know these people. It is for that very reason that you must remain in the inn. Naturally not under your own name."

"I? Register under a false name?!" — I had lived for a decade in Vienna, long enough to be imbued with the feeling of the sanctity of a register.

"It seems to me, Josko, that you have become a one hundred-percent German. A false name! I shall fill out the register for the innkeeper myself. You will be known here as Dr. Eustach Partyka. You are my cousin and an advocate in Lemberg."

"If you fill out the register, you can write what you wish. It's your responsibility," I said.

"It's my responsibility, you German."

"A register is an official document."

"Perhaps in Vienna. Not here. The innkeeper would probably not have set one before you if he were not eager to discover whether you were Jewish."

"But he had already asked me."

"You see! I hope you said no."

"I did. I simply lied without knowing why."

"You didn't lie at all. Five days from now, on Friday, you will no longer be a Jew officially, either. What would you have put in the space for 'Religion,' if you had had to fill out the register?"

"Frankly, I never thought about that."

"You see! So you must remain in the inn. That's best. I have thought this over. Red Goddl will find out tomorrow that you are Eustach Partyka, an hour later the whole town will know that you are not the other person — and you will be let alone. That is the reason why we decided that it is best for you to stay in the inn."

"We?"

"The provost and I. I am only the coadjutor here."

"You should have written to me what the situation here was like. I should never have come here in the first place."

"I was happy, Josko, at the opportunity to see you once again. Besides, you exaggerate everything. We could easily be rid of these small-town Jews, if we informed the political authorities. But under certain circumstances that might develop a pogrom mentality: we are on the Russian border."

"That is all I would need!"

I regarded my friend with horror. Tired out from the trip, a captive to dread forebodings, I had not recognized my friend Partyka in his priestly dignity. Nine years had passed since my last vacation in Dobropolia. I had not seen my friend in all that time. For a while we had had much to write one another about, but in the course of the years our correspondence had subsided. Knowing nothing about one another, we now found ourselves in a situation to which two men who had been friends in their youth could not easily accommodate themselves. We tried to conceal our embarrassment behind the

[165]

words and jocular tone of the idiom we had employed as school-mates. In our conversation about the register we had attempted to maintain this tone, but it was quickly shattered — I looked at my friend, and a stranger stood before me.

"Have I changed very much?" he said, avoiding my eyes.

"Apparently no more than I," I said.

"At any rate you have not changed for the worse outwardly."

We walked in the pale-red reflection of an almost wintry sun-set. We stepped upon a soft layer of leaves which lay strewn over all the garden paths, as though walking on a colorful bed of a stream where, instead of water, dead leaves billowed, rising when struck by the wind. My friend led the way, deep in thought. I followed him in silence. I had expected to see my dear friend Partyka a lively young priest, a peasant's son among peasants, simple and firmly rooted, living in complete contentment; I had imagined him thus from afar. — How could I, who knew him so well, have imagined him otherwise? But I had made my reckoning without the theological seminary. His talents had apparently been early noted and he himself had soon perceived that, though he was a peasant's son, he was not of the mold of which simple country pastors are made.

An entirely different Partyka walked before me: a young clerical gentleman with a sharp profile, calm and strict eyes, a Catholic priest physically and spiritually of unusual stature. Only a line of mild resignation about the mouth reminded one of the passionate graduate who had grown as wild and stub-born at the prospect of a theological seminary as a young village recruit at the sight of stone barracks.

"Are you not going to marry?" the question occurred to me, and I expressed it, breaking the silence.

"No," he said, smiling. "I do not intend to wallow in the domestic bliss of the lower Greek-Catholic clergy. You are engaged, I believe?"

"Yes," I said.

"Is it because of the woman?"

"No, not because of the woman."

[166]

"But your bride is not Jewish, your father tells me?"

"You have seen my father?!"

"Yes. A year ago, in the summer. I was at home on leave, and I paid a visit to your father."

"How is . . . your father?"

"Quite well. Still a vigorous peasant despite his white hair, thank God."

We passed a pack of children playing; they were throwing leaves at one another and yelling. At sight of the priest they stopped quickly, removed their caps and greeted him with "Praised be Jesus Christ." The Jewish children lifted their hats, too, and stood for a while with bared, close-shaven heads and waving earlocks, looking with shyness and curiosity as the spirited little girls pressed close to the priest for the honor of kissing his hand, according to the country fashion. When the children had leaped back to their play, my friend put his arm around my shoulder and said in a soft voice:

"Listen here, Josko. I know you long enough to realize that you know full well what you are doing. As a priest it should be my duty to offer you salvation, even if you did not yourself desire it. But my father writes me —"

"Your father knows that I am here?"

"He knew that we were expecting you here."

"But how did he know that?! I wrote only to you asking you urgently — and now everybody knows!"

"Calm yourself, Josko. I shall explain everything. Let us follow this path here on the left; it will take us roundabout, but we still have a half hour. I must first tell you something about the provost, so that you will know how to behave with him. He is not at all so simple a priest as our fine Horodynskyj. Do you still remember old Horodynskyj? . . ."

"What did your father write?" I desired to know.

"He asked me — well then, he wishes you to be told that your father is already an old man and cannot survive another blow —"

"Do they know in Dobropolia, too, that I am here?! This is horrible! How do they know that?!"

"My father told them, apparently."

"And your father — how does he know it? Did you tell him, Philko? Did you?"

"No, Josko, not I."

"Who, then?"

"It was the provost who wrote to my father."

"The provost?"

"Yes, the provost. He wrote my father, and my father spanned his horse and drove hurriedly with the message to Dobropolia. Your father pretended that the news was not a great surprise. It was all the same to him, he shouted, whether you married this baptized Jewess one way or another. He dismissed my father quickly. But your brother asked my father for the exact details: how and where and when it would take place. And I think it must have been your brother who wrote to the rabbi here."

"My brother? Wrote to the rabbi? Are you sure of that?"

"Yes. I'm certain. We have a Christian counterpart of Goddl here who knows everything. He is our sexton Onufry and he brings us all the news of what's happening in the Jewish quarter."

"But you should have written to me, Partyka! If I had known that you have this sort of provost, I should not have come here!"

"You believe that the provost acted with bad intentions?"

"How else?"

"You'll soon understand. The provost is an old gentleman. A prominent theologian. Twenty years ago he was a very important man in the diocese, the right hand of the bishop, whose librarian he was. There was a great career open to him."

"Listen, Partyka, don't be angry at me. But at this moment I have not the patience to hear the biography of your provost, interesting as it may be. First tell me! Why did he inform your father? What did he think to achieve by doing that? What did he gain by that?"

[168]

"If you insist, I'll tell it to you in brief: the provost wanted to prevent your baptism."

"Prevent baptism? A provost?"

"Yes, there are such provosts as well as the other kind. At any rate, I know only one who thinks that way."

"Is that the extent of his aversion to Jews?"

"On the contrary. That is the extent of his partiality."

"Is this your influence?"

"Not in the slightest. Personally, I like Jews; but I have never thought about the so-called Jewish question. I take the point of view of the church."

"But the provost thinks otherwise?"

"Yes. He is of the opinion that Providence has saved Israel for the end of days, and we have not the right to interfere. He has also declined to administer the sacrament to you. I shall do so."

"So he is against the baptism of Jews?"

"Yes. And that is what I wanted to speak to you about. Do not enter into any disputations with the provost, although, as I have been able to see from your last letters, you are almost as well versed as a theologian. He will take the Jewish point of view and it will not be hard for him absolutely to refute both of us. So no disputations, I beg you. He will not begin them. Let it continue to appear that you wish to become a Christian out of love for a woman, and that will be sufficient."

"That's acceptable to him?"

"As a regrettable, but venial human weakness. The provost is a very human man. You will see for yourself."

We had reached the green gate set in the cloister wall. My friend unlocked and opened it, and nodded toward the small house which I had discovered from the window of my hotel room.

It was here that the provost and my friend Partyka lived. First he led me through a dark, flagstone-paved path into his own dwelling. We sat in his work room side by side for a while, two silent shadows. I was depressed by my first conversation with the friend of my youth, a conversation which had turned out badly, perhaps through my own fault, and I felt better separated from him in the twilight. I tried to bring order into my thoughts, which had been disjointed by the information my friend had imparted. I was full of displeasure, anxiety and wrath at Partyka. It was good to sit side by side, shadow by shadow, in the enveloping evening twilight which gradually thickened into darkness. I saw him clearly for the first time in the darkness. What had become of the hot-blooded, imaginative, good-humored, clever Partyka? He had turned into a cold pusher. Not a peasantlike, fatherly priest like Horodynskyj. My Partyka had become a strict, ambitious cleric, a cool, rational career-seeker. Why had I come here, to a cold friend who sat calmly by, allowing messages to be sent to Dobropolia, knowing full well the effect of such tidings? Why had he let me come here to this dark town where a small fanatical Jewish community, already prepared for the event, lay in ambush for me, informed through the unpardonable negligence of a friend, who by his own admission knew only too well the inciting effect of such an incident on so small a town.

"I suppose you want to be a bishop, Partyka?" I suddenly hurled an insult at my friend, which fell into the darkness of the room like a stone into a well.

Partyka did not answer. He sighed deeply and audibly. It was only after a long moment of silence that I heard him rise and walk around the room with heavy steps, as though he were retrieving my words, which had gone lost in the darkness. He stopped in the middle of the room, a match flared up and I saw him lighting the petroleum lamp, which shook at the apex of three thin chains, secured to the ceiling by a hook. Now I saw Partyka's nearly bald head between the chains of the hanging lamp, almost touching the ceiling, his pale, bony face and a tired look in the blinking eyes which met mine searchingly. As though the light he had made slowly and circumstantially had put out my dark question, my friend

passed lightly over it. With a look around him and with outstretched arms, he indicated the room and said in a sunken
voice:

"I have been living here for three years now."

"You have it very pleasant here," I said just as softly, and
debated whether I ought not to beg his pardon.

"When I came here three years ago your question would
have caused me embarrassment, for fear the provost might hear
it. Now I have no more secrets from him," said Partyka. He
sat down at his desk and smiled in a melancholy reverie. I
looked around me. It was a large room, very simply furnished,
with bare, white walls and two pretty windows, in which the
trees of the cloister garden, already bare, swayed like shadows.

"You have it very pleasant here, Partyka," I repeated,
shamed by my friend's forbearance.

"When I came here, the provost was not in a good position.
They were very dissatisfied with him, his removal was only a
question of form. They had been dissatisfied with him for
years. He had administered his office here with too much
mildness, with too little rigor. I was sent here not so much to
help him out as to supervise him. I was to act vigorously. The
provost had previously performed a trick which was the subject of various legends circulating in the countryside. But he
had fought that situation through, and has since settled with
me, too, — me and my ambition. Now he is a tired old gentleman; I a resigned young vicar. We get along very well."

I was very sorry to have interrupted my friend's previous
speech, in which he had begun to tell me about the priest. He
must have felt it, for he added immediately:

"I should have been glad to tell you about the situation I
mentioned before introducing you to the provost. It concerned
the baptism of a Jew, and you would have understood what the
provost is like. But now we must go to him; he is an old gentleman, accustomed to having his meals very punctually. I'll tell
you that story another time."

· · · · · · · · · · · · · ·

Alfred, the third in the series of readers, now looked at Velvel and said:

"The first part comes to an end at this point. The second is written partly in pencil. I shall ask Pessa to fetch a few more candles. There isn't enough light. The penciled lines are too faint, and the lamp is hanging too high."

Uncle Stefan and Yankel looked at Velvel, who scarcely appeared to have heard what Alfred had said. Velvel sat on the sofa next to Dr. Frankl, his left hand over his eyes, the elbow resting on his right hand. He had listened throughout the whole reading in this position. Velvel had read but a few pages himself, for when he came to the passage which described the quarrel over the calf, Velvel pushed the notebook back to Dr. Frankl with a look of pleading, then leaned back, shading his forehead and eyes with his left hand, and remained in this position throughout the rest of the reading.

Alfred rose and slowly left the room to speak to Pessa. The others sat silent for a long time. Then Velvel said, "You were quite right, Yankel. It is better for us to hear the testament here. Unfortunately, there is not much in it that would be in place in Grandfather's Room."

"Let's wait till the end, Velvel. All has not yet been said. You are usually an optimist. Let's wait."

When Alfred stepped back into the room, Velvel rose and went to meet him: "If it is all right with you, my dear, let's hear the second part of the testament tomorrow. Perhaps tomorrow evening, if you please. Of course, you can read on alone tonight. What your father writes you is intended for your eyes, and I can well imagine that you are very eager to read further. All of us here are. But it's late —"

"All right, Uncle Velvel. Let's leave the rest for tomorrow evening. Naturally, I should like to find out everything that is in it at once. But I had rather we all heard it together for the first time. We should have to interrupt anyway, for Pessa has been cooking and baking all this time —"

"O, wonderful Pessa!" said Yankel. "She always does everything at the right time. My stomach is gaping."

Pessa did not keep them waiting long. For some time she had been worried about how to interrupt the prolonged reading. Now she was happy that Alfred had been able to prepare the men for the meal that she had improvised after a consultation with Donja. She appeared, followed by Donja, and covered the table, apologizing, "It is already past midnight, God help us!"

Then, aided by Donja, whose face, like Pessa's, was aglow with the heat of the oven, and whose beauty attracted the admiring attention of Dr. Frankl, Pessa brought each of them his favorite dish, according to her own counsel. For Dr. Frankl there was the groat cream-cakes of which he had so loudly expressed his favorable opinion after his first meal in Dobropolia; there was, on a separate tray, a hen ragout in sweet and sour sauce for Velvel, a delicacy which he ordinarily enjoyed only once a week, on Friday, for lunch as an entree to the Sabbath; and there was a goulash, sharp and hot, for old Yankel and Alfred. All these special dishes were served in individual plates large enough so that each of the three meat eaters could share his favorite dish with the others.

With an appetite that they all found amazing, the men applied themselves to the delicacies, and were loud in praise of Pessa.

"The girl is a perfect beauty. Is she a peasant?" Dr. Frankl inquired, his eyes turning to Alfred.

"Yes," said Alfred, and halted. "She is — her name is Donja."

"She is the daughter of our wheelwright," Yankel helped him out.

"She is not really a peasant girl . . . Her mother is a peasant. But her father is a craftsman. A very clever craftsman. An artist in his profession —" Yankel continued.

"Uncle Velvel," Alfred interrupted, "what I want to ask you is this: that calf, that orphan — how long did it live?"

All the forks stopped moving. Even Yankel, who was Alfred's neighbor at the table, turned full-face to him, forgetting to swallow his mouthful of food. Alfred fell into a state of embarrassment, as though he had said something improper.

"I mean — you don't sell a cow of that sort. What happened to it?"

Velvel bestowed a loving look on Alfred.

"It's remarkable that you ask about it," he said, and one could see that he was not saying this to help Alfred out of his embarrassment. "Your father did not tell the whole story of the calf."

"There's still more to it?" Yankel wondered.

"Yes," said Velvel, addressing Alfred: "As you know, the calf's mother died at its birth. The orphan, as your father recalled so clearly, grew into an exceptionally large and strong cow. Unfortunately, she had a, so to speak, hereditary taint. Despite all our care and diligence, like her mother, she became very weak when in labor. To our sorrow this became apparent at her very first birth. She gave birth to a large, handsome male calf, white, with a black head and black ears, like its mother. The birth took place at night, and our stall-master, Andrej, told us the next morning about the difficult birth. 'The calf is well,' Andrej said, 'but I'm not satisfied with the mother's condition. Part of the afterbirth has remained inside her. I can't guarantee anything.' We children naturally didn't know what this meant. But my father called the veterinarian. We had no graduate veterinarians at that time, of course. The village doctor tended to both peasants and beasts. He came, examined the sick cow with much circumstance, put on an important air, and said, as though he understood the case: 'The cow will either get well or die.' Your father and I never left the sick cow's side, and called the old quack back the next day on our own initiative. The cow had fever, and Andrej told us that she was not urinating.

" 'Take her for a little walk,' said Andrej, 'sometimes that helps, sometimes it doesn't.' The doctor for his part had

[174]

nothing more to say on the subject. We took the cow out of the stall, your father and I, and led it around the stall a couple of times. It was winter. The day was cold. The snow lay high. The walk didn't help. To spare us the sight of the pining cow, my father called in a slaughterer from Kozlova and sold him the cow. We cried, your father and I, but we had to give in, since there was nothing more to be done.

"The next day a drover from Kozlova, a tall, Jewish drover, arrived. We saw in him the angel of death come for our poor orphan. Our clever orphan must have smelled it, too. She was not to be moved from her spot. Her apathy left her for a while, and she wouldn't let the drover take her out of the stall. We had to step in, crying, and help the drover. She calmly left the stall with us. Then old, sympathetic Andrej said to us:

"'Children, take your coats and go along a ways through the village. The orphan is afraid of the strange drover. Perhaps that will help. If anything should happen, just take the cow away from him and bring her back.' We dressed quickly, stole out of the house and followed the cow and drover.

"It wasn't snowing that day, but it was frosty and the road was covered with ice. We passed through the village and left it behind. When we walked next to the cow, she kept moving. When we stopped to catch our breath, she stopped, too. The drover kept urging us to go back home, for it was late in the afternoon and he was in a hurry to arrive in Kozlova with the cow before nightfall. I don't remember any more how long we accompanied the cow, but we went to the next village, till Poljanka. Just before we reached Poljanka, it happened. Our orphan crooked her backside, spread her back legs and — we were saved! Our joy was great. We seized our cow by the horns to tear her away from the drover. But the silly man, who foresaw a good piece of business for his master, the slaughterer, refused to let this stroke of good fortune escape him, and would not let go of the rope. We begged him, we cried — nothing helped. Now that he knew the cow to be healthy, he became nasty and tried to drive the cow on by striking her with his stick and shouting.

" 'You run back,' your father said to me at first, 'and fetch Andrej.' But we immediately calculated that the drover would have driven our orphan to Kozlova before I should have reached Dobropolia. So we both remained with the cow and soon arrived in Poljanka. Then we ran quickly into the nearest peasant home and told the peasant that a strange man from the city had stolen our cow. The peasant, who knew us children, naturally took our word for it! Besides, since a strange man from the city was involved, he willingly came to our help. We had no end of trouble protecting the drover from the peasants, who would otherwise have given him a sound drubbing. He made haste to escape, that drover did, and we jubilantly led our orphan home.

"Meanwhile it had grown dark and now it began to snow. We became somewhat depressed. Andrej at home also became a bit anxious. He went to my father and told him that we had followed the cow on his advice. So it happened that we encountered a sled halfway between Poljanka and Dobropolia when it was already night. We couldn't recognize the horses in the darkness. But when the sled stopped we saw that it was ours and that our father was in it. With great excitement, each trying to outshout the other, we told him what had happened, and only began to breathe freely when we noted to our astonishment that our father was not angry at all. 'Where is the drover?' he asked. 'He ran away,' we said. 'Stupid boys,' said my father, 'You're no wiser than the drover. The slaughterer would have sent the cow back tomorrow. Is this the first cow I've sold him?!' We saw at once that we had really been foolish. But still we were not so foolish as to tell our father the whole truth. The fact that we had misrepresented the drover to the peasants as a cow-thief was something we wisely kept from our father. We didn't have much sympathy with the drover, anyway. The stupid man must have known that his master would not have quarrelled with our father over a cow. That time it turned out all right. But —"

Here Velvel interrupted his tale, and the company listened with him to the rumbling of a motorcycle that could be heard through the open window. The rumbling came closer and closer, and now they could hear it in the poplar alley, leading to the farm buildings. Pessa stepped into the room again. This time she was alone. She walked to the table as though she had come to clear it. But she reconsidered and, casting an anxious look at Velvel said, "It must certainly be one of the two members of the investigating commission."

"But they left on the Sabbath," said Velvel.

"Yes," said Pessa, now looking at Yankel," but one of them came back this noon. And Bjelak's daughter —"

"Dear Pessa, we have no time for Bjelak's daughter," Velvel interrupted her. "Go to sleep, Pessa. We'll be going to sleep too, soon. I just want to finish my story."

When Pessa had stepped hesitatingly out of the room, Velvel finished his story:

"But — as I said — unfortunately, we had little joy from the orphan after that. True, she became completely well again. But at her second calving, a year later, it was even worse: this time neither calf nor mother survived . . ."

It had grown still outside.

"What's the rogue doing on our farm so late at night?" said Alfred. "Or has anyone heard him drive away?"

"No," said Velvel with a meditative look at Yankel. "What is a cyclist looking for here?"

For answer the rumble of the motorcycle was heard again. The company all grew silent. They heard it again in the poplar alley. Then it came quite near, rattling up the driveway to the house, where it became silent. They heard two men talking to one another. Then they heard Pessa's voice.

"It seems we are having late visitors," said Velvel and rose. Before he could bend over to look out the window, the door opened and in stepped Pessa, pale, and with frightened eyes; behind her came a man wearing a leather jacket and leather gaiters; behind him, in visible embarrassment, came the local policeman.

"Good evening," said the man in the leather jacket. "Pardon the disturbance, sir. We have been looking for a man on your estate. The night-watchman told us that he is here."

"So late at night?!" said Velvel. "Is the matter so pressing?"

"It has to do with a warrant, Mr. Mohilevski."

"For whom?" asked Velvel.

The man in the leather jacket put his hand in his side pocket, pulled out a sheet of paper and said, as though he were reading it:

"A warrant for the arrest of Mr. Jacob Christiampoler."

Everyone looked at Yankel, who alone had remained motionless in his seat. Without rising, he looked calmly at the man with the leather jacket and said after a while, "You are late. I expected you yesterday."

BOOK III

BOOK III

1

"YOU have a warrant for the arrest of Jacob Christiampoler, and you are doing your duty, Mr. —"

"Commissioner Guzik," the man in the leather jacket introduced himself.

"Commissioner Guzik," repeated Velvel. "You have a warrant for his arrest, that is true. You have showed it. But do you also have a warrant to break into my house at midnight?"

Velvel was far more aroused than Yankel himself, who remained seated as though this was none of his concern.

"I have no warrant to break in here," said the commissioner, "and I beg your pardon. Frankly, I should find it very unpleasant, Mr. Mohilevski, if you were to lodge a complaint against me for that reason. But I could not do otherwise. I know that Mr. Christiampoler is a beloved figure in the village, and I was afraid that the peasants would interfere with his arrest. That would have made the matter worse. Worse for Mr. Christiampoler himself, too."

"That's right," said Yankel. "So you waited until all the village was asleep. You acted very prudently, commissioner. How do you plan the rest? If I were not to go along with you now, do you think that my friend Palivoda — " Yankel pointed to the local policeman, who still stood at the door — "would handcuff me and lead me off by force?"

The policeman stopped in front of Yankel and said:

"Mr. Bailiff, I assure you I should find that very unpleasant. But you know I have nothing to say about this. I think it would be best for you to submit to the warrant."

"I shall certainly do so," said Yankel, "but not so soon. Let us come to an agreement, Mr. Commissioner. You are to appear with me before the Starosta tomorrow?"

"That is correct," said the commissioner.

"Must we appear before him at a specific hour?" inquired Yankel.

"There is nothing in the warrant on that point," said the commissioner. "Nor would it be necessary for us to leave at once — that is, if you accept my suggestion."

"If I were to order my horses," said Yankel, "— You see, I want to make things comfortable for you — if we were to travel with my horses, we should be in the city in seven hours."

"In my motorcycle," said the commissioner, "we could get there much faster."

"I am no cyclist," said Yankel. "If you want to ride in your motorcycle, you can escort my wagon. I'm traveling by wagon. Since I have not stolen a spoon, I have, I believe, some choice in the matter. — And what is your suggestion?"

"My suggestion is," said the commissioner, "that we leave tomorrow at six o'clock, provided you promise me that during the six hours that remain till then you will not breathe a word in the village about your arrest. Otherwise, I regret that I shall have to insist that we leave at once."

"Agreed!" said Yankel. "We leave tomorrow at six. And now let's all go to sleep. Pessa, give the gentlemen something to eat."

Pessa stood there in tears, but she obeyed. She invited the commissioner and policeman to come along with her, and all three left the room and entered the kitchen. Outside the room Pessa could be heard declaring: "If you imprison innocent men and let Mokrzycki run away, why don't you arrest me, too?"

They heard the commissioner laughing and assuring Pessa: "We are small people, Miss. We do our duty. We have nothing to say about these matters."

"What shall we do now?" asked Alfred, when the strangers had left.

"I have written to Dr. Katz," said Velvel to Yankel, who had stood up and taken Alfred by the arm, "and I have an answer already."

"You have written Dr. Katz? About me?" marveled Yankel.

"Yes," said Velvel. "I saw that you were acting foolishly. But you need not be worried. Dr. Katz is of the opinion that our communal secretary is not a government official. He is here on probation as a secretary and nothing more."

"You tell me that now?" Yankel shouted. "If I had known that before, I would have whipped him out of the village long ago."

"A young hotspur," said Velvel to Dr. Frankl. "What do you say to this youthful temper?"

"Where is the communal secretary now?" Dr. Frankl inquired.

"He is living with the policeman," said Yankel. "For the last three days he hasn't trusted himself out on the street. Not even in the New Village. I am responsible, that is true. If I had only known that he was not an official, my friend Palivoda would have been glad to give him a couple of boxes on the ear — off duty, naturally."

"If you are really so beloved a figure in the village as the commissioner seems to fear, nothing will happen to you, Mr. Christiampoler," said Dr. Frankl.

"Naturally nothing will happen to him," said Velvel wrathfully, his wrath venting itself on Yankel. "He will only be in prison on remand for a couple of weeks."

"What shall we do now?" repeated Alfred, still standing next to Velvel and seeming in his excitement not to have heard anything.

"I shall go along with you," said Velvel to Yankel.

"No," retorted Yankel, "you will not. You will remain here with our dear guest. You must have enough to attend to: Dr. Katz will be sufficient in the city. Now I'm going to sleep in peace. And you, Alfred, come along, there is something you can do for me."

[183]

"What will he do?" asked Velvel, aroused, and stepped between them. "Alfred must not be mixed up in this. Tell me what you want, and I'll take care of it."

"Now, no unnecessary excitement," said Yankel. "Alfred will not be mixed up in anything. All that he'll do, if he's not too sleepy, and with your permission, Velvel, is go to the farm building with me. We shall wake up Nazarewicz and ask him to drive Alfred to the countess."

"Now, at night?" asked Velvel.

"Now, at night," retorted Yankel. "That is why I want Nazarewicz to drive with him, otherwise any coachman would do. Or are you against that, Velvel?"

"Of course I'll go," said Alfred.

"He can go with our wheelwright," said Velvel. "I simply don't understand why Alfred must go at night. You won't let me ride along with you, and yet you send Alfred off to the countess at night."

"You can't help me in the city at all. But if Alfred will be so kind as to ride off at once, he will arrive at the countess' tomorrow at ten in the morning and report everything. Then the countess, who is in contact with the city by telephone, will — I assume — immediately set things in motion so that I shall not appear before the Starosta entirely unexpected. It is always better to be expected when one appears before a high official."

"As an old official I can only say that that is very wise of you, Mr. Christiampoler," said Dr. Frankl.

"Come now, Yankel," Alfred pressed him, "we have talked long enough. It's time to be doing something."

"Good night," said Yankel. "I have only one request; this time it is of all three gentlemen: if I don't remain in prison too long, I shall be grateful if you wait for me before reading any further. Good night."

"Good luck," said Dr. Frankl, shaking hands with Yankel. "I shall not leave before you come back. And as for the read-ing —"

"Naturally, we'll wait for you," Velvel quickly interjected,

[184]

shaking hands with Alfred and embracing Yankel so heartily that the old man grew momentarily pensive and his optimistic bearing was in danger of being shaken.

Velvel and Dr. Frankl now remained alone in the room. Sitting there facing one another, the dead man's testament lying open on the table, it was as if a long time had elapsed since the reading. As though by agreement, both remained silent until they heard the footsteps of the commissioner and the local policeman, who could be heard thanking Pessa, saying goodbye and then shattering the stillness of the night with their noisy vehicle. Then Dr. Frankl said, "This trick, this nasty trick that's being played on this fine old man, is that hooligan anti-Semitism?"

"What you have seen here today," said Velvel hesitatingly, "is certainly not hooligan anti-Semitism."

"Isn't this just a patriotic rationalization on your part, Mr. Mohilevski?" asked Dr. Frankl with a smile.

"Why patriotic?" Velvel Dobropolier wondered.

"Alfred tells me you are a Polish patriot."

"Perhaps Alfred is right. Our Yankel is always throwing that fact in my face. In the same sense you too, Doctor, are an Austrian patriot."

"Certainly," Dr. Frankl conceded," but I am accustomed, perhaps because of my profession, to stick to facts. You do the same, I presume."

"So far as I can judge, I do. That is exactly why I said to you that what you have been forced to witness today, to my great regret, could also have happened if a Jew had not been involved. But what has led up to it, that is another matter. There you are certainly right, Doctor. It began, as I have already explained — perhaps not very clearly — with a shabby attempt at blackmail. But the fact that so small a dog could have dared to bark at such a man as our Yankel — that could only have happened in our village to a Jew."

"Could you explain that more clearly?" asked Dr. Frankl.

"The predecessor of this clerk, a good, honorable man, kept

in our stall two cows, which were, so to speak, given board and lodging both winter and summer. It was a special privilege that Yankel, as my bailiff, granted the man, who had a meager income as the clerk of a village community. This situation continued for years, until the man died. After his death Yankel visited the widow and gave her to understand, that as far as we were concerned, of course, everything would continue as it had been. Thus the matter remained. The clerk's successor, a real ne'er-do-well who had been sent here more for political than administrative reasons, naturally had brought no cows along with him. To compensate for that fact, he approached Yankel with a remarkable demand. He wished, as Yankel expressed it perfectly, 'to milk the widow's cows.' He took the position that we had not given his predecessor a special privilege, but rather that we were duty-bound to fulfil a certain 'stall obligation' of his own invention. He continued to press this point. He came to Yankel so often with this demand that Yankel finally showed him the door. If I do not err, I called Yankel a hot-head before in your presence. He is very far from being one. He is an old fox, who could tie us all up. And he was right not to allow himself to be exploited. I learned about the whole thing only later, but I do not believe that I would have been able to change anything if I had known earlier. Since he couldn't get at Yankel, poor little Lipa had to be the victim — a misfortune, as I explained in detail in my letters."

"May I ask you something?" asked Dr. Frankl.

"Please do," said Velvel.

"If this ne'er-do-well, this successor to the clerk, had brought along two cows of his own, would Yankel have given him the same privilege he did his predecessor?"

"Of course," said Velvel, "of course. And Yankel told him that, too."

"If that is so," said Dr. Frankl, "I can't understand what you have against the behavior of the old man in this incident, or rather this accident."

"Did he say anything about it? Did he complain to you?"

"Not at all," Dr. Frankl hastened to reassure him. "That is just an assumption of my own. Please pardon me if I am mistaken."

"You have not erred, Doctor. Not in the least. Your assumption is correct. All of Yankel's superior qualities are the characteristics of a man out of another age. He still believes one need but have justice on his side to be victorious. But I am of the opinion that it is not realistic to act on that premise in our time and situation. 'If a dog bites you or barks at you,' my father used to say, 'you don't get down on all fours and bark and bite back.' I think my father was right."

"What your father said was very wise, I admit. But isn't it too lofty an attitude? You must admit that?"

"I have not seen it that way till now. I admit that you can say he was proud; but my position remains the same. Think of Koppel the printer, whom my brother remembered so clearly. Now I remember him. I can still see him before my mind's eye, with his cart and his horse. My brother made a very apt observation about Koppel. For you see, Doctor, Koppel the printer did not have it easy. But he followed my father's principle. And he was not grateful to the young university student, Katz, for his intervention. Why was it possible for him to behave in this manner? Because, despite his poverty and degradation, he did not feel humiliated. He let himself be barked at and did not bark back. On the other hand, I saw a man in Vienna in 1918 who was a doctor of philosophy, a professor, nothing less than an Honorary Councillor, yet with my own eyes I saw that man turn all colors and nearly suffer a stroke when two rascals passed by and one of them said: Look at the Jew! Which is more dignified, Koppel's pride, or the councillor's humiliation? The councillors go far with it! If Koppel the printer was proud, God bless that old pride of his!"

"Amen," said Dr. Frankl to Velvel's great amazement. "I say Amen to your blessing. But perhaps I am anticipatory

[187]

somewhat. I have a specific question to ask you: You said before that Yankel was a man out of another age. What about your father — didn't he belong to the same age?"

"No," said Velvel, "not at all. My father was a man who belonged to the tradition, our tradition, which is timeless. Like Koppel the printer. Yankel, on the other hand, never belonged to that tradition. He is still living in the age of liberalism, which is gone. Do you wonder at that?"

"No," said Dr. Frankl. "I, too, live in an age that is gone. But I know it is gone, and that is why I said 'Amen' to your dictum. However, I must admit that I would probably have behaved like Yankel, because unfortunately, like Yankel, I did not grow up in your tradition."

Both men remained in conversation for a time longer. Velvel would have liked to return to his brother's testament. He would particularly have liked to hear Dr. Frankl's opinion about a passage in the testament which had plunged him into great confusion. When Dr. Frankl had solemnly handed the manuscript to Alfred, it had seemed to Velvel as though his brother had entered the house along with Dr. Frankl. As Velvel began to read, his face expressed such devotion that Alfred had not been able to refrain from whispering to Yankel: "Uncle Velvel is wearing his Sabbath face." And when Velvel reached the passage relating the story of the calf and the quarrel that resulted between the two brothers over the love of the calf, he was not able to control his emotions, and with a pleading gesture pushed the manuscript back to Dr. Frankl. He had had during the course of the reading continually to keep himself from constantly confirming what was being read with cries of "That was it exactly! It was exactly that way!" Then he heard a sentence which fell upon his heart like a stone. It was the remark about the stranger to whom Rabbi Abba had played host on the last night of his life. Why a stranger? It had been he, his brother himself. Why had he used the word, "stranger?" Why had he not told the truth? Had he not

[188]

promised his son to tell him the truth in his testament? Had the son noticed that his father had not told the truth? Not even in the testament? Alfred must have known who the stranger had been who had visited Rabbi Abba that night. Velvel had looked at Alfred in terror. Thank God, he had not noticed! But he would read the testament again. Eventually, he would find out.

Caught in the maze of these fears it had required a strenuous exertion for Velvel to listen to the rest of the reading. It had been a relief to him to hear Alfred announce the end of the first part. The interruption was welcome. Then came the unexpected guests, and the ensuing excitement suppressed his brother's voice. But now that the rest had left, he was alone with his brother and Dr. Frankl, and he was curious to learn what Dr. Frankl knew of the stranger who had visited Rabbi Abba; he had mentioned Koppel the printer in the hope that Dr. Frankl would be reminded of the subject of the testament and return to it. But the guest's attention was apparently not to be distracted from the midnight event, and he persisted in asking for information about the social relationships in the country, a subject of vital interest to the professional politician. Meanwhile, Velvel had had time to reconsider the advisability of confiding the astonishment at that passage to this guest before they had read the testament through; the men therefore continued their political conversation, one which aroused rather than wearied them.

Suddenly they saw one another in the bright morning light. Velvel rose and extinguished the dim lamp. Through the open window Dr. Frankl saw a strip of blue water and a strip of blue sky through the gently wavering bulrushes of the small pond and heard in the room the ringing voice of silence. The golden morning call of a cock crowing into the blue was wafted through the window from a neighboring peasant courtyard, followed by the deficient, hoarse screech of a young rooster. It was as though a grating pebble had fallen into pure gold. The crowings were repeated time and again, crow after crow. Dr. Frankl turned a bright, delighted face to Velvel: "Do young cocks always crow so badly?'"

"This one is a perfect comedian. I haven't had a single good night during the last few weeks. But every morning this young singer cheers my spirits and brings me a little pleasure."

Silently smiling both men listened to the cock-crows with their cheerful counterpoint. Then Velvel led his guest into his room.

"I have promised Yankel not to leave before he returns. I intended to invite myself to remain with you over the Sabbath, anyway. Alfred has spoken very highly in his letters about the Sabbath in Grandfather's Room."

"If you remain it will be a pleasant Sabbath, one I have long hoped for. I am sure that Yankel will be back by Sabbath. Perhaps I ought to accompany him, anyway. What do you think, Doctor?"

"Let's wait two or three days. If you have no good news by then, I shall accompany you."

2

The villa of the countess reminded Alfred of the house in the *Gazon*. It was somewhat longer, and the drive leading to it ran through a larger park, but like the other, this villa, too, was in the eighteenth-century style, and this park was also laid out in the French mode. The house was well kept, painted yellow, the window frames and Venetian blinds green. The grass plots and flower beds in the park were well tended, the paths immaculate. They had arrived at ten o'clock and Alfred hesitated to have himself announced to the countess at so early an hour. But Donja's father explained that he had worked here too as a wheelwright, and resigned for no reason. He assured Alfred that the countess was an early riser and would certainly receive him at once. The wheelwright himself was in haste to disappear from the drive along with the vehicle so as not to be seen by the

countess: he feared to remind her of his irresponsible resignation and by doing so to endanger the purpose of the visit. "Great
ladies are very temperamental," he said to Alfred. "It is best
that I disappear."

Alfred followed the wheelwright's advice and entered the
house at that early hour. A man, dressed half as a servant, half
as a gardener, came to meet him in the many-windowed bright
corridor. He took Alfred's visiting card and the letter which
Yankel had given him, showing no signs of surprise at this early
visitor. After a time he came back and led Alfred through a
room to a terrace on the same level on the east side of the house
where the countess was sitting alone at her breakfast. Following
Yankel's advice, Alfred opened the conversation in French. The
white-haired, frail old gentlewoman had apparently read Yankel's few lines. Still holding the letter in her left hand, she extended her right hand to Alfred after the Viennese manner for
him to kiss and said: "You are Viennese, Mr. Mohilevski. I
do not enjoy listening to German. But if you speak it in the
Viennese manner, I should find it quite pleasant. It reminds
me of my youth. Please be seated, Mr. Mohilevski. Are you a
relation of my old friend, Yankel Christiampoler?"

"My uncle says that Yankel is our relation. But I do not know
exactly how we are related, madame."

"When did this take place?" asked the countess.

"Yesterday at about midnight."

"Was he very upset, the poor man?"

"Not in the least," said Alfred. "He was so sure that you
would help him out quickly, madame."

"Is that your own assumption, or did he tell you that?"

"He told it to me, as well," said Alfred.

"This is a remarkable world. I have known many men in my
life," said the old gentlewoman, gazing at Alfred with a melancholy look and an almost coquettish smile. "Men in my own
circles, manly men of the old race, in whose company a woman
could certainly feel secure. But I have never felt so secure with
any of them as with Yankel. This is the first time, I come to

think of it now, that I have to help *him*. But I am talking too much! You have certainly not yet breakfasted?"

"No, madame," said Alfred. "I have just arrived and I must beg your pardon for bringing you such unpleasant news so early in the morning."

The countess rang a bell which stood on the table and ordered another service. Meanwhile she ran through Yankel's note once again and asked Alfred for further details concerning the events in Dobropolia which had led to Yankel's arrest. Like everyone else in the villages around Dobropolia, she knew about the murder of the child, and it was not hard for Alfred to inform the old gentlewoman about the rest. Her very questions showed more familiarity and interest in the case than Alfred had been able to credit her with. Alfred was even more astonished at the opinions she expressed incidentally, opinions which coincided remarkably with those held by Velvel Dobropolier.

"You came by train?" she asked.

"No," said Alfred. "I would have arrived only in the afternoon if I had come by train. And Yankel was eager, madame, to inform you of the situation before he was brought to confront the Starosta in the city."

"Good," said the countess, "better early than late. Now please pardon me. I must write several letters at once. I still have a few friends in the city on whom I can depend. The letters must reach their hands as quickly as possible. It is true the facts speak in favor of Yankel. But the question is whether they will stick to facts, if they wish to give this incident a political coloration. So we shall act before that coloration is accomplished. Please pardon me. I shall return at once."

While the countess was writing the letters, Alfred examined the park, then went to the garage where he suspected the wheelwright to be. Among the different kinds of wagons in the garage there was also an automobile, which a chauffeur was polishing. Alfred ascertained from the chauffeur that the wheelwright was at breakfast in the kitchen. After returning to the terrace, Alfred waited a short while until the old countess returned with three letters. Two of them were sealed, one open. First, the countess handed the open letter to Alfred, saying:

"This letter is for the lawyer whom Yankel has chosen. He is a very capable man. I know him. Please be so kind as to give these other letters to the lawyer, as well. However, he must decide how and when they are to be delivered to the addressees. Let's act as quickly as possible. I suggest that you send your horses back home. My chauffeur will take you to the city much more quickly. Traveling by automobile, you will actually reach the city before Yankel."

Alfred took the letters, thanked the countess and was about to leave, when she called him back.

"The chauffeur will pick you up here. Wait a moment — You are probably wondering why I am not going to the city in person. I am not doing so because it is better thus. Yankel will understand. Give him my regards. And tell him not to take this matter too much to heart. Our dogs' bark is always worse than their bite. — How long have you been among us?"

"About a year, madame," said Alfred.

"Then you can't know us very well. This is all a straw-fire. Our land was enslaved for a hundred and fifty years. The men who are now at the helm of our state unfortunately are still behaving like liberated slaves. A slave understands freedom to be his freedom to have slaves of his own, and to oppress them. But that is passing. Our people's heart is fundamentally sound. They will not allow themselves to be ruled in this fashion for long. I hope to see you under happier circumstances, Mr. Mohilevski. Where will you be staying in the city?"

"Yankel told me of a Hotel Podolski. He said it is near the lawyer's office," said Alfred. He rose; the auto had just driven up.

"Yes," agreed the countess. "Send me a daily report of how matters stand. I shall send my chauffeur to your hotel daily at noon. I wish you success. Adieu."

Alfred bade the countess goodbye with profuse thanks and promised to take advantage of her friendly invitation.

"Come, come often. I should like to chat with you by the way about Vienna," Alfred heard the countess calling after him as he stood at the auto. Since he was already too far from the terrace to respond to the friendly gentlewoman without raising his voice rudely, he bowed silently and waited till she went into the house. Before stepping into the automobile, Alfred remembered the wheelwright and requested the chauffeur to fetch him. But that was not necessary, for they had to drive around the house anyway. Nazarewicz, who had already heard in the kitchen that the chauffeur was to drive the young stranger to the city, awaited Alfred at the exit gate. Although disappointed to have to travel back to Dobropolia alone, he was visibly happy that the countess was pressing Yankel's case.

He promised to give Dobropolia a complete report of what had happened and impressed Alfred with the necessity of his remaining in the city until the poor bailiff should be free.

Alfred had not traveled by automobile for a year and was amazed to see how quickly the park and the village road and the fields glided past them to the right and left. Although they were not riding on the paved road and the surface was bad, they reached the city at two o'clock. Alfred took the small traveling bag that the wheelwright had entrusted to the chauffeur, parted from the chauffeur and betook himself at once to the lawyer. As Alfred knew already, Dr. David Katz was none other than the same son of the cabinet-maker of Dobropolia who had been Joseph Mohilevski's teacher years ago. Alfred still retained the fresh memory of how Koppel the printer had refused, with an expressive gesture, the well-meaning philanthropy of the university student Katz. The lawyer, a thick-set man with an energetic face and bulging, near-sighted eyes behind thick, horn-rimmed glasses, also remembered Dobropolia, the family Mohilevski and Yankel Christiampoler well, but did not appear over-eager to discuss his former pupil, Joseph Mohilevski.

"You bear a strong resemblance to your father," he said

[194]

thoughtfully, after he had considered Alfred with a pleasure tinged with mild melancholy.

Slightly disappointed that the lawyer had exhausted his recollections of Joseph Mohilevski with this single remark, Alfred transmitted, first Yankel's letter, then the countess' letter to the lawyer, and finally the other letters. Dr. Katz read both letters addressed to him and asked Alfred for an oral report which he occasionally interrupted to take notes.

"When do you think Yankel Christiampoler will arrive here?" he asked.

"Probably in the course of the afternoon," said Alfred.

"Then you must present this letter to the Starosta at once," said Dr. Katz.

"The countess expressly stated that she wished you to forward the letters, Doctor," said Alfred.

"Why not you?" asked Dr. Katz.

"Probably because I speak Polish very poorly," said Alfred.

"How long have you been in Dobropolia?" asked Dr. Katz.

"One year," said Alfred.

"You witnessed all this?" asked Dr. Katz. "Were you on the *Groblja* that Sunday?"

"Unfortunately, I was not," said Alfred. "I came too late."

"I was born and reared in Dobropolia. I never would have believed that the Dobropolia peasants could be incited to such an act." Dr. Katz rose, took the Starosta's letter and went into the next room where his aide and secretary were. Returning, he sat down again opposite Alfred, took the countess' other letter and placed it in a drawer of his desk.

"We shall not need this second letter to the Voivoda, I hope. Perhaps it will be possible for us to defeat the action in the first stages. But it's good that the countess did not at once send the letter herself — and even better that she has not appeared in person."

"Why?" Alfred inquired. "Would it not have been better if she had made a personal visit?"

"No," said the lawyer, "it is better this way. The countess

[195]

has interceded for Jews too often during the last years. More often than the authorities care for. She naturally still has influence. But she can achieve more through her friends if people don't know that she is behind them. It were best for you, Mr. Mohilevski, to prevent the noble lady from making a personal appearance. It's to our advantage to minimize the affair. Nothing much can happen to the old man. At the worst, he will remain imprisoned on remand for a couple of weeks."

"A couple of weeks!" cried Alfred, frightened. "Why? He has done nothing!"

"We know that," the lawyer said at once.

"The whole village knows that," said Alfred, in excitement.

"We shall see, Mr. Mohilevski," said the lawyer. "I told you what can happen if worst comes to worst. It remains to be seen what can happen if the matter turns out for the best. You can rest assured that I shall do everything in my power for Yankel Christiampoler. Besides, he has opened an account for you. Do you need money?"

"Yankel won't hear of my uncle's intervening in his case," said Alfred with a smile. "You may not believe it, but old Yankel is quite proud of his case. But, as you can readily imagine, my uncle is at your disposal. If I need anything, I'll have it put to my uncle's account. Thank you, Doctor."

Before leaving the room, Alfred added; "You played an important role in my father's life, Doctor. I am happy to have made your acquaintance. When this case comes to a happy end, I hope we shall have the opportunity for a longer conversation."

"I shall be very glad to, Mr. Mohilevski. Come as often as you desire. But let me tell you this at once: don't exaggerate the role I played in your father's life. Adieu."

3

Arriving at the hotel, Alfred was pleasantly surprised to obtain a clean furnished room with solid furniture and even a private bath. The friendly clerk who showed him the room told him, "This is the best room in the hotel. We don't have many guests today. At this time tomorrow I could scarcely have been able to find you a room. Tomorrow is the weekly market day when business is livelier."

The second pleasant surprise, one which almost overwhelmed Alfred, was the discovery that the hotel had a coffeehouse. Though the hotel itself was called "The Podolski," the coffeehouse bore the international name of "Café Boulevard." Despite its French name, it was a real Viennese coffeehouse. Ladies and gentlemen sat outside at tables lacquered a bright red — more gentlemen at this time of day than ladies, and the latter not dressed in the very latest *mode*, but still dressed not at all provincially. They drank coffee with whipped cream, as in Vienna, and the coffeehouse itself, like a Viennese café, was surrounded by trees, tubs, leafy plants, and flower pots. Alfred could see all this from the window of his room and he would have gone directly to the café terrace, had he not remembered at the sight of the comfortable, roomy bed in the room that he had not slept a wink all night. He asked the clerk to wake him at five o'clock, and impressed upon him the necessity of sending all incoming mail to his room without delay. After the friendly porter had left, Alfred undressed, went to bed and fell asleep at once.

At five o'clock he awoke in fright. He saw that the clock still lacked two minutes to five. He remained in bed a little longer; then came the expected knocking at the door and Alfred sprang out of bed, completely refreshed. He would have liked to take a bath, but was too restless because of the report he expected from Yankel, which apparently had not yet arrived. He shaved quickly, dressed and went downstairs. The clerk still had no message for him. Yankel evidently had not yet arrived.

Alfred entered the café. There were no vacant tables on the terrace, but a table was free near an open window. Alfred really preferred to sit there, where he could see all the traffic outside. There were now more ladies than gentlemen on the

terrace, and among the latter fewer civilians than soldiers.
There were many men on the street, among them officers and
privates, their high caps boldly topped by silver eagles, the
cap shields pulled sharply over their eyes, as though these
soldiers wished to be alone with their all-too-combative pride.
Apparently the evening promenade on the street had begun,
for after a short time Alfred could recognize a few already
familiar faces among the passers-by. The waiters were divided
according to the Viennese hierarchy of the trade; a *piccolo*
brought Alfred an ash tray, the service-waiter the coffee, and
the chief waiter the newspapers, which, as in Viennese coffee
houses, were tied to wooden frames. At that Alfred fell into
so happy a frame of mind that he forgot about everything but
the coffeehouse, unfortunately forgetting Yankel as well. Now
he remembered how often during the Dobropolia winter, when
everything was covered with snow and ice, he had been overcome by a gnawing homesickness for Vienna. Now he knew
that he had not been homesick for Vienna, but for its coffeehouse. For as the roe loves the woods, the bird the bushes,
so the Viennese loves the coffeehouse. Alfred remembered the
last time he had sat with Uncle Stefan in a Viennese coffeehouse on the Ringstrasse. They had had a window seat and
sat in the shady cool of the place, where, as now, they could
hear the pleasant click of billiard balls cued by invisible players.
It was light enough at the window to leaf through the newspapers. Some of them were in West European languages which
Alfred understood. Although he had grown unused to reading
newspapers during his year at Dobropolia, it was still a unique
sensation to have a newspaper in his hand again, particularly
one tied to a wooden frame in the Viennese fashion.

It had been five-thirty when Alfred entered the coffeehouse.
The guests on the terrace had been protected by the artificial
half-shadow of the sunshade; the street had been flooded with
bright sunshine. But when he came to himself again, waking
from the pleasure of sitting in a coffeehouse, he saw the head
waiter turning the winch to roll the sunshade up. A cool

breeze was now passing through the still densely and colorfully populated terrace, freshening the stale air of the shaded room. Alfred looked at his watch. It was seven. He quickly paid and ran to the hotel clerk. There was mail for him now — a letter.

"Who brought this letter?" Alfred asked the clerk, as he opened it.

"A gentleman from the police," said the clerk with anxious sympathy. "The Police Commissioner Guzik."

"Wasn't there an old man with a long beard with him?" asked Alfred.

"No," said the clerk.

Alfred read the letter. Yankel wrote that he had not been given a hearing in the office of the Starosta, but had at once been surrendered to the court and now was in prison on remand. He asked that this information be communicated to his lawyer directly.

Alfred was inconsolable. If he had not remained in the coffeehouse so long, he might perhaps have been able to see Yankel for a moment and speak to him.

"Mr. Guzik is perhaps still in his office," said the clerk.

"Which office?" asked Alfred. "Where is it?"

"Commissioner Guzik is not with the criminal police," said the clerk. "He is with the political police. Ask for him at the Starosta's office."

"Where is the Starosta's office?" asked Alfred.

The clerk took Alfred to the door and showed him a building on the other side of the street. "That is the Starosta's office," he said. "If you walk through the garden here, you will see the entrance at once."

"I don't want to inquire personally. Can you send an errand boy along with me?"

"Yes," said the clerk. "Stay here. I'll send one out to you at once."

After a while a boy of about fourteen, who spoke Yiddish better than Polish, came along and led Alfred through the garden to the Starosta's office.

"Go in," said Alfred, "and ask for Commissioner Guzik."

"And if he is there?" asked the boy. "What shall I say, then?"

"Tell him that a Mr. Mohilevski from Dobropolia wishes to speak to him."

The youth ran quickly up the few steps of the outside staircase and came back at once:

"Commissioner Guzik left at six o'clock."

"Where is the court?" asked Alfred. "Can you guide me there?"

"Yes," said the youth. "It's on this street, nearby."

Alfred went along with the boy. He knew well enough that it was senseless to ask for admission to Yankel so late at night, but he was anxious at least to see the building where poor Yankel was now a prisoner. It was an old, massive structure, a typical official Austrian building. Four or five broad, stone steps, worn out in the middle by the tramping of many feet, led to an iron-knobbed, wooden door, one of whose two halves stood ajar. On the top step, in a low, armless chair sat an old man wearing the blouse of a uniform of undefinable color. The blouse was unbuttoned and Alfred saw on the collar the violet trimmings of an Austrian court attendent, worn out and weather-beaten. But it was neither the blouse nor the trimmings that threw Alfred into amazement, but the old man's face. For His Royal and Imperial Apostolic Majesty, Emperor Franz Joseph I, in the flesh, sat before the gate of this court building. The thin white beard of the old man had, like the gate of the building, two parts. The chin in the middle of the beard was clean-shaven, the mustache, bushy and far more martial than its prototype belonging to His Majesty, was neatly combed. Thousands of officials in the civil and military service, thousands of imperial councilors, thousands of bank directors, thousands of sergeant-majors, thousands of letter carriers, thousands of officials in all branches of the administration bore this mask of the Emperor through three generations of the Austro-Hungarian monarchy. There were Germans among them, Austrian-Germans and Czechs, Poles and Jews, Ukrainians and Ruman-

[200]

ians, Serbs and Slovaks, Hungarians and Croatians, Italians and Slovenes — the whole variegated mixture of the Dual Monarchy. They were so numerous that thirteen years after the death of the Emperor and eleven years after the burial of the monarchy itself, these historic masks were still being worn. Alfred had often been amazed at seeing in Vienna with his own eyes persons wearing the imperial mask who had outlived the Emperor. Now, here in front of this court building, his imagination was confounded at the vision of so authentic a reflection of Franz Joseph. Alfred's fascination at the sight of the dead Emperor's double was so great that he was frozen into a statue.

"There is no point in speaking to the old man," said the youth, who apparently misunderstood the nature of Alfred's interest.

"Who is this old man?" asked Alfred.

"He was the chief bailiff in the prison here for more than fifty years. He was pensioned long ago. But it was impossible to get him out of his official quarters in the court building. He lives there alone and every evening sits in front of the gate. The rest of the time he sits in the garden."

"Remarkable that they still allow the old man to live here," said Alfred, simply to say something. He could not pull himself away from the sight . "He must have had a successor long ago."

"Yes," said the boy, "he's been pensioned for fifteen years. Besides, he's a monarchist," he added with a smile. "He's always cursing. He says everything was better under the Emperor, but nobody does anything to him because he is so old and because he has a son who is the right hand of the Starosta. Someday he will probably be a Starosta himself."

"Is the Voivoda building also in this street?"

"No," said the boy. "But it isn't far away. Do you want to go there?"

"No," said Alfred. "But if you still have time, I should like to become acquainted with this street."

"I have time. Mr. Weiss didn't say that I must come back at once."

"Who is Mr. Weiss?" Alfred inquired.

"The clerk in the hotel," said the boy. "If we go into the garden here and keep walking in it, you'll be able to see both sides of the street at the same time. And I'll show you where all the offices are."

They entered the garden and now Alfred saw that the wide street formed a triangle in whose center the garden repeated the triangle. The street began with a church at the base of the triangle whose esplanade linked two sides of the street. It was a new church, of brick, its style the false Gothic of the nineteenth century. The first building on the left side of the street was the court building with the gloomy prison as its background. On the right side were first the prosecutor's office, then a many-storied building which Alfred recognized at once. It was the building where the chauffeur of the countess had set him down.

"The lawyer Katz lives in this house, doesn't he?" he asked the youth.

"He has his office here. But he lives in the street of the Third of May," explained the boy.

"Dr. Katz is probably not in his office now," said Alfred.

"No," said the youth. "But after dinner Dr. Katz goes to a coffeehouse almost every evening. Not to our coffeehouse. Dr. Katz always goes to the Vienna coffeehouse, where the Zionists gather."

"Is there another coffeehouse on this street?"

"Yes," said the youth. "Haven't you seen it? I'll show it to you at once."

They continued through the garden, which at this point was still as broad as a park. Here stood old acacias and chestnut trees. The green plots were scanty, and there were no flower beds. Many, too many, benches stood there, comfortable wooden benches with high backs, painted yellow. The court building was still on the left side of the street, and on the right were dwellings of varying heights: there were old one-story

[202]

buildings, but also new four story houses, and even one of six stories. At the left of the street, where the court building ended, stood two small buildings with staircases, in one of which there was a restaurant. Here the first part of the garden ended and a diagonal street broke the triangle. Crossing this diagonal street, they came to the middle section of the garden, where the herbage was younger and thinner. There were circular plots of flowerbeds, trellises of trimmed bushes, and a few benches for visitors to rest on. Here apparently the young folks of the city took their evening promenade. On the left side of the street was the coffeehouse where the Zionists gathered and a couple of houses further on, the yellow building of the Starosta's office. On the right side of the street were a bank, an apothecary, and the hotel Podolski with the Café Boulevard, which again bordered on an old building, the mayor's office. A second cross-street brought the middle part of the garden to an end at this point. It was broad, so broad that there was room for the third and last side of the triangle. Here stood the memorial to the great poet, Adam Mickewicz, after whom the small plaza was named as well as the street. It was a simple statue of sandstone, modeled after the statue of the saints that are to be found in front of churches. At this point they could no longer walk in the middle of the street, for the garden ended, and the traffic on the street was well-nigh metropolitan. They passed by the post-office building; to the left a military hospital was visible behind a white wall and in the midst of a garden which was kept as neat as a private park. From there they could survey the third side of the street's triangle which narrowed to a point. The rows of houses on the street were pressed closer and closer together, eventually merging in a small plaza, which was terminated, as at the head of the street, with a church. This church was old and beautiful. On the way back to the hotel Alfred uncovered still other noteworthy items on the street: a motion picture house, two photographer's stores, still another apothecary, and still another motion picture theater, the last of which, however, was inside the court of the Hotel Podolski.

[203]

"Now, you've seen all the offices," said the boy, who apparently assumed that Alfred had an exclusive interest in offices.

"Except for the Voivoda," said Alfred. "You kept that from me."

"We should have had to go through the street of the Third of May," said the boy. "If you want, I'll take you there tomorrow. But now the guests are already arriving for dinner, and I must help out in the kitchen."

"What is your name?" Alfred asked the boy as he gave him a coin.

"My name is Benzion Schwarz," said the boy.

"For having so beautiful a name, here is another zloty."

"For the Schwarz, or for the Benzion?" the boy inquired.

"For the Benzion," said Alfred.

"Thank you," said the boy, "thank you very much. And what is your name?"

"My name is Susja Mohilevski," said Alfred, introducing himself.

"Susja?" wondered the boy. "Your name is Susja?! I should never have thought it. But that is a beautiful name too. And tomorrow I shall show you the *Wojewodztwo*.

"Goodbye, Benzion."

"Goodbye, Mr. Mohilevski."

After dinner Alfred went to the café where the Zionists gathered. This coffeehouse was larger than the Boulevard and was as a matter of fact called Kawiarnia Wiedenska — Café Vienna. It, too, had an outside terrace, and Alfred, who arrived earlier than the steady customers, found a free table on the terrace. About ten o'clock Dr. Katz came in, but he was in company and Alfred had to wait for a time until the lawyer noticed him, answered his salutation very warmly and soon came over to Alfred's table.

"Things are not as good as I had hoped," he said.

"Have you seen Yankel?" asked Alfred.

"No," said the lawyer. "That wasn't to be expected. But I had hoped that he would have a hearing before the Starosta

[204]

and perhaps even escape imprisonment. Sometime tomorrow morning I shall see Yankel. If you come to my office at two o'clock, I shall be able to tell you more. Perhaps I can manage it so that you can see him."

"Doctor, do you think that the countess' letter reached the Starosta before Yankel arrived?" asked Alfred.

"I don't know that just yet," said the lawyer. "I hope that he hasn't received it yet."

"Why?" asked Alfred. "Why do you hope that, Doctor?" *

"Because that would be a sign that the letter has had no effect."

"Do you think it possible that the letter won't help at all?"

"Unfortunately, yes," said the lawyer. "I don't exclude that from my considerations. Tomorrow I shall also know whether the Starosta received the letter in time. Come at about two o'clock. You can always come to see me in the office in the afternoon. In the morning I am busy in the courts."

Although the lawyer left him disquieted and anxious, Alfred remained in the Kawiarnia Wiedenska till it was almost closing time.

4

The next day Alfred went to see the lawyer at the appointed hour. Dr. Katz had seen Yankel, but had nothing favorable to report. The Starosta had apparently read the countess' letter only that morning, and the only result seemed to have been that Yankel, who had spent the night in a cell, had been transferred to a room at about noon. The lawyer now seemed to take the case against Yankel more seriously than he had at the time of his first conversation with Alfred.

"The charge," said the lawyer, "is of a far more serious character than I assumed yesterday. Yankel is not charged with having spoken against the communal secretary in both villages. Such a charge, as I have already written your uncle, could easily be met with the objection that the communal secretary is not an official. However, Yankel is charged with having incited the peasants against the government."

"But that is not true," said Alfred.

"We are dealing with a charge, as I have said. No action has been brought as yet, and at this stage I can't judge the case. What we must do now is to quash the case, before an action is brought."

"How is Yankel?" asked Alfred.

"He is bearing himself very well. I have, in addition, secured permission for him to have his needs attended to privately. You see to it that he receives the proper victuals."

"May I bring him his food?" asked Alfred.

"There would be no sense in that," said the lawyer. "I could not secure access to Yankel for you; so it makes no difference who carries the food through the street. Order the food for Yankel in your hotel, and see to it that he receives it regularly."

Alfred quickly returned to the hotel and worked out an arrangement with the friendly clerk. It was agreed that little Benzion Schwarz was to bring food to Yankel three times daily. Although it was almost three o'clock, Mr. Weiss advised that a late noonday meal be furnished Yankel at once. Alfred accompanied little Benzion Schwarz to the court building. He waited for a time in front of the steps, now in the bright glow of a hot summer day. Then he retreated to the nearby park and sat down on a shady bench, where he could watch the court gate, which was now open but guarded by a court attendant. Across the way from him, on a bench in the sun, sat the old bailiff, a newspaper over his knees, a pair of spectacles on the point of his nose, nodding.

"I wasn't permitted in," reported Benzion Schwarz. "They took the food away from me in the hall, and I had to wait till the cutlery was brought back. That's why it took so long."

It was four o'clock when Alfred returned to the hotel with Benzion Schwarz. The countess' auto stood in front of the

[206]

hotel, and the chauffeur was waiting for Alfred in the clerk's cubicle in conversation with Mr. Weiss. He handed Alfred a letter. It contained only a few lines. The friendly noblewoman asked for a report. Alfred reflected whether he ought to admit Dr. Katz's disappointment, as well as his own, over the meager success of the countess' letter. He would have liked to have the lawyer's advice, but decided to inform the countess in a few lines that for the time being there was nothing of special importance to report. Having done so, he went to the Viennese café which lay on the shady side of the street. There were only a few guests there at this time of the day, and he found a table on the terrace where a few elderly gentlemen were smoking cigars, reading newspapers and chatting with neighbors at adjacent tables.

Alfred preferred this coffeehouse, not only because it was cooler there in the afternoon than in the Café Boulevard, but also because that coffeehouse reminded him of his first evening in the city, when he had missed Yankel's arrival. But he only became aware of this distaste of his when he had taken his place on the terrace and given his first order. A painful sense of despondency overcame him suddenly, and he saw in his mind's eye a clear picture of his helplessness. He saw himself sitting on this friendly street, in senseless passage from hotel to lawyer, from lawyer to court, from court to coffeehouse, day after day, week after week, month after month. He had long ago decided never to leave this city unless it was with Yankel. But was he being any help to Yankel? The waiter brought his order and Alfred looked out at the street for a while. The sight of the few passers-by slowly and reflectively going about their business calmed him slightly. How different from the large city, where often the sight of passers-by filing past had filled him with a sharp terror at their senseless restlessness. Two young ladies in white linen costumes and flat straw hats passed close to the terrace. Both were young and pretty and had laughing faces. As they came nearer, Alfred quickly rose from his seat and saw that one of the two laughing girls had also recognized him at once: it was the schoolmistress of Dobropolia, Miss Tania Rakoczy.

"You're in the city and haven't come to visit me?" she said. "You're a fine friend."

"I had forgotten that the vacation had already begun. I thought you were still in Dobropolia," said Alfred.

"This is my youngest sister, Xenia," said Tania, introducing her companion.

Her sister, scarcely more than seventeen, had Tania's figure, but was red-headed and much prettier than the schoolmistress. When Alfred shook her hand, saying, "I have heard so much about you," she blushed violently and sidled nearer to her elder sister, in teen-age fashion.

"Do you have an appointment here?" asked Tania.

"No," said Alfred. "Frankly, I am sitting here because I don't know what to do with myself."

"Come along with us," said Tania. "We have finished our business and are going home now. Come along with us; I should like to introduce you to my father." She saw the cup of coffee which Alfred had not yet touched, and added, "You can have a cup of coffee at our home, too."

Alfred paid the bill and joined the girls. They walked along the Railroad Street to the station, which Alfred had not yet seen, past the station to a plaza where a carnival had pitched its airy tents. Then they had to climb a number of steps and came to a wooden bridge high above the railroad tracks. In contrast to the station, which was old and small-townish, the railroad grounds themselves were surprisingly broad, with many criss-crossing tracks, several railroad yards and innumerable depots. This was a junction, it occurred to Alfred, who walked silently across the bridge with the girls through the smoke and steam of the locomotives rolling under the bridge, in the din and whistling of the nearby traffic.

"I shan't ask what you are doing in the city, because I know. My friend Dudka wrote me about it. I received the letter this morning and thought of you."

[208]

They now had the bridge behind them and were walking on the pavement of a small, quiet, broad street in the shade of two rows of blooming acacias, leading to a large park.

"I arrived yesterday," said Alfred, "but I am afraid I shall have to remain here a very long time."

"How is Mr. Christiampoler?" asked Tania.

"Unfortunately, I've not been able to see him," said Alfred. "You can imagine how he is."

"My father says that the affair is not to be taken very seriously," said Tania. "But you'll soon hear that from him yourself. Here is our house."

Tania opened a small gate in a fence of birch sticks and they stepped into a garden. The house was a mixture of different styles, with many turrets and romantic stairs, but the garden was lovely, with fragrant grassy plots. Alfred followed the girls around the house, walking on a paved garden path. On a plot of grass in the rear of the house a clerical gentleman sat on a garden chair in the shade, reading a small, leather-covered book with gilt edges in his hand.

"This is my father," said Tania, as the reader raised his head and took off his glasses. "And this, father — look whom I have brought — this is young Mr. Mohilevski of Dobropolia."

Alfred bowed to the cleric, who had risen to greet the guest, giving Alfred his hand. Tania's father was a tall man, who appeared even taller because of his long black *soutane* and a posture straight as a ruler.

"Welcome to my home," he greeted Alfred in Ukrainian, "my daughter has told me a great deal about you." His fine, manly voice was, in its joviality, more of a soldier's than a pastor's.

"I have long looked forward to an introduction to Your Reverence," replied Alfred, and was as happy again to speak Ukrainian, as he had been in his chats with Donja.

"Fetch a few chairs, children. We'll remain in the garden, or —?" said the father with a questioning look at Tania.

"Yes," said Tania, "we'll fetch coffee at once."

Alfred helped the girls fetch a garden table and a pair of arm chairs. They then went into the house at once.

"I am sorry," said Father Rakoczy, after they had both sat down at the table, "I regret to see you in distress, my son. But don't take it too much to heart. Who is your lawyer?"

"Dr. Katz," said Alfred.

"That is good," said Father Rakoczy. "He is a clever man. He will soon find a way of avoiding a trial. That's the point. When one has to contend with chicanery, one must employ every possible weapon. Dr. Katz will soon find a weapon. And if necessary, a small weapon!"

"Do you mean patronage, your honor?" asked Alfred.

"Patronage, fibs, bribery —"

"Bribery?" wondered Alfred, looking at Father Rakoczy in fright.

"Why not?!" said Father Rakocy, casting a look almost of anger at Alfred out of his clear, grey eyes, which were almost of the same color as his thick, close-cropped hair. "Where tyrants are masters, bribery is the last form of humanity. It was thus in old Russia. If the civil servants of the Czars had been unbribable, the tyranny would have been even more intolerable."

"I hope that in this instance we shall be able to manage without having to resort to such measures," said Alfred.

"When one is as young as you are and is as far removed from politics, it is fine to think as you do, my young friend. But don't talk your lawyer into it. He will do what he finds necessary," said Father Rakoczy.

"I am concerned about getting the old man out as quickly as possible. At his age it is really horrible to be imprisoned, even for only twenty-four hours," said Alfred.

"Perhaps it is even worse for a young man," said Father Rakoczy with a smile. "I can tell you that from experience."

"You don't mean to say, Your Reverence . . ."

"That is exactly what I mean to say," said Father Rakoczy, and his broad, fleshy face now shone with priestly mildness. "Luckily, I was no cleric at the time. Yes . . . but what I wanted to tell you was: When my daughters told me about the old man's arrest, I wondered whether I might not be able to be of assistance. I am not quite so much without influence as you might believe. If a Ukrainian had been involved, I might have been able to manage something. But as the matter stands, my intercession would certainly be harmful."

"Why?" asked Alfred. "Your Reverence, why do you think so?"

"If I were to intercede for your relative, they would say: 'The old man is a partisan of the Ukrainians.' And that would harm him even more. And if I may give you a piece of advice, my son, keep yourself well in the background. You have a Ukrainian name —"

"Is my name Ukrainian?" asked Alfred. "Frankly, Your Reverence, I did not know that at all."

"Indeed it is," said Father Rakoczy, "your name is Ukrainian. And that wouldn't matter at all, ordinarily. Many Poles have names that sound Ukrainian; many Ukrainians have names that sound Polish. But you've been in the country only a year and have already learned to speak Ukrainian. That might be given a political interpretation. So let Dr. Katz manage everything and don't interfere."

"I am very much indebted to Your Reverence. I am not at all interested in politics, and it's particularly tangled here."

"I could explain our politics to you right now. But here are my children with the coffee. I talk too much politics to my daughters. My wife always throws it up to me, and I often think myself that it doesn't do my daughters any good at all to hear so much politics. But all politicians are chatterers, and I, as you see, am no exception."

The girls covered the table, brought coffee and cookies, and the conversation took another direction in their presence.

"You are seeing only half the family," said Father Rakoczy.

"Exactly half," said Tania. "My mother and two sisters are vacationing from the city in the country, and we are here vacationing from the country in the city."

"And I am leaving for the country tomorrow," said Father Rakoczy. "But I shall not stay there long. If you wish to visit us next week again, Mr. Mohilevski, I shall be back by then."

"As much as I should enjoy seeing you again, Your Reverence, I hope not to be here next week. At that time I hope already to be on my way to Vienna."

"Will you stay there long?" asked Tania.

"A few weeks," said Alfred. "I'm also going to vacation a bit from the country in the city."

"I can understand your haste to leave Dobropolia for a while. But I fear that the case may not go so quickly as you believe."

"I should like to ask you something, Your Reverence. You must certainly know many Ukrainian clerics. Is the name Partyka a familiar one to you?" asked Alfred.

As though by prearrangement, both girls, taken aback, set down their coffee cups and looked at their father, who for his part set his cup down on the table and looked at Alfred with wide-open eyes.

"Where did you come across that name?" he asked, after a while.

"My father left me his memoirs which contain a great deal about a young clerical called Partyka, who was close to father. — But it seems to me that you are not very happy at the mention of his name. Pardon me."

"There's nothing to pardon," said Rakoczy, once again cheerful. "You have phrased it very well. We are not very happy at the mention of his name in my house. But we mention it — all too often. It is a very important name. You mean Philip Partyka, I believe?"

"Yes," said Alfred, "Philip Partyka. Now I remember his given name, too. I came across my father's memoirs a short time ago. We had just begun to read them when we were interrupted by the midnight arrest."

"Your father was friendly with Partyka, you say?" asked Father Rakoczy. "Are you sure of that?"

"It seems so," said Alfred. "My father and Partyka sat on

[212]

the same school bench in high school. Partyka often visited Dobropolia. My father tells a great deal about him."

"If that is so, my son, you need trouble yourself no further about the old man in prison. Were you thinking of that when you mentioned Partyka?"

"No," said Alfred. "Not at all. I didn't even know whether the Philip Partyka of whom my father spoke was still alive."

"And how alive he is! He is a very important man. He is a canon and one of the most influential advisors of our Metropolitan, Count Sceptycky. You must tell your lawyer everything that is said about Partyka in your father's memoirs. Dr. Katz will probably communicate with him at once."

"Where does Canon Partyka live?" asked Alfred.

"In Lwow," said Father Rakoczy. "He travels a great deal. But I know that he is in Lwow now."

"Your Reverence, do you think that the Canon would interest himself in the case?" asked Alfred.

"You may mention his name with impunity now. We have gotten over our surprise, as you see. And now I must explain to you why we were so surprised.

"The eminent dignitary Partyka and I, a small pope, are political opponents, have been for many years now. We have made it as difficult as possible for one another, to say the least. And, as far as I am concerned, I am determined to continue to fight the eminent gentleman. But that is in the area of politics. As a man and as a priest, Canon Partyka is unexceptionable and respectable. He is a cleric with the highest education, the loftiest humanity. He will receive you graciously and help you as the son of a friend."

"Thank you for your advice, Your Reverence," said Alfred. "I shall inform Dr. Katz of everything. But what I do not understand, Your Reverence, and request you to explain to me, —"

"I suspect what it is you do not understand, my son. First, I told you that I could not apply myself to your affair, because an intercession on my part could only be harmful. Yet now I

[213]

myself advise you to go to Canon Partyka in Lwow, although he is also Ukrainian. Is that what you do not understand?"

"Yes," said Alfred. "I hope I am not asking too many questions."

"Certainly not," said Father Rakoczy. "The apparent contradiction is easily explainable. I am a nationalistic Ukrainian. To me the unification of all the Ukrainians is a matter of utmost importance. Canon Partyka is first and foremost a churchman. I do not mean to say that to him the unification of all the Ukrainians is not important also. But, as a Greek-Catholic dignitary, he sees in the political unification of the Ukrainians in this country with the Greek-Orthodox Ukrainians in Soviet Russia a danger to the Greek-Catholic Church. That is why he is against the unification and against Soviet Russia."

"But you, Your Reverence, are also a Greek-Catholic priest." said Alfred. "Aren't you also against Soviet Russia?"

Father Rakoczy looked at both his daughters for a moment, as though expecting an answer from them. But the girls, who had been engrossed in the conversation, were silent and regarded their father with amused curiosity, as though to say, "Now you have it!"

"Now clear the table, children," said Father Rakoczy, casting a roguish glance at his daughters, "and fetch some photographs, that our guest may meet the rest of our family."

The girls cleared off the table and cheerfully bustled into the house.

"You have touched the heart of the problem, my son. That is good, for now you will understand me. Like my brother, who fell in the war fighting against the Poles — my daughter has told you that I, too, wanted to be a lawyer. But I decided to become a cleric in order to remain near my people. My daughters became schoolmistresses for the same reason — the youngest will be a schoolmistress too. Now I am a Ukrainian pope with a family and live with my people. Over here and over there, here and in Soviet Russia, we are the same people, Ukrainian. The fact that over there they are Greek-Orthodox and

[214]

over here we are Greek-Catholic does not make much difference to me. I am not so great a theologian as Canon Partyka. And I am not against Soviet Russia as is Canon Partyka. My Ukrainian peasants are no theologians either; you would marvel at how easily my peasants could become Greek-Ortho-dox. I tell you this as a small pope. As a politician — and here I am no smaller than the canon himself, on the contrary: there are many more behind me than there are behind him — as a politician, I say to you: There will be order here in this beloved country of ours only on the day the Red Cavalry steps in and creates order. Then the Canon, who is with the Poles and against Russia, will see which of us is the politician."

Alfred sat speechless for a moment opposite Pope Rakoczy. He was grateful to the girls who had gotten into an argument in the house, which drew their father's attention from him. They heard the younger girl speaking vigorously to her sister, who attempted laughingly to calm her.

"Excuse me," said the pope, "my children rarely quarrel this way. I don't know what's wrong." He was about to rise, but saw the girls returning to the garden, Tania coming first, still laughing, the younger girl behind her wearing a wrathful look.

"Has the Red Cavalry already marched in?" Tania inquired of Alfred.

"You see," said Father Rakoczy. "I told you I talk too much politics with my daughters."

Tania resumed her place opposite Alfred and handed him one at a time the photographs she had brought. First Alfred saw an engagement picture of Mama and Papa Rakoczy. Mama Rakoczy was slim and beautiful and looked like Tania. Papa Rakoczy was a young cossack in civilian clothes. Then fol-lowed a photograph of the whole family, the parents sitting, each flanked by two daughters. The other two girls resembled one another like two peas in a pod.

"Are they twins?" asked Alfred.

"Yes," said Tania. "Could you tell that?"

[215]

"I guessed it," said Alfred.

"I wanted to have six sons," said Papa Rakoczy, "now I have four daughters."

Finally, Tania handed Alfred a group picture framed behind glass.

"This is the photograph of the graduates of the class of my uncle whom I have told you about. Here you'll find some more familiar faces."

Xenia, who had already become uneasy as the large picture was handed to Alfred, now stood up nervously and placed herself next to her father. Alfred inspected the picture. It contained photographs of some forty youths in uniform, grouped around an inner circle consisting of photographs of instructors, under each was the name of the person in block print. With Tania's aid, Alfred found the pope's eighteen-year-old brother. He had an energetic, Slavic face with strong eyes.

"And now find your Dr. Margulies yourself," said Tania.

Alfred first looked through the faces and couldn't find the picture he was looking for. He read the list of names.

"Here!" he said. "Here is someone else whom I know."

"This one here?" asked Tania.

"Yes," said Alfred. "Morgenstern."

"Do you know him, too?" asked Tania.

"Yes," said Alfred, "He's a relative of mine. His grandmother was a Mohilevski. I often see him in Vienna."

Meanwhile Xenia had moved away from the table, and stood lurking a few steps away.

"But what happened to his picture?" said Alfred, raising the photograph out of the shadows of the trees into the light. "Someone has put his eyes out!"

"I told you so!" Xenia hissed at her sister and ran angrily out of the garden and around the house into the street.

"What's wrong with her?" asked Papa Rakoczy.

"You know well enough," said Tania. "She put out Morgenstern's eyes. She was still a child then. And now she is ashamed."

"Is that what you were quarreling about!?" said Papa Rakoczy. "I was wondering."

"The photograph hung in the children's room, and in her early teens Xenia imagined that all the lads were following her with their eyes. First she turned the picture to the wall whenever she undressed. Then one day she took the picture out of the glass and stuck the eyes out of this one head. It looks horrible. Like a dead man. At that time she was proud of it. Now she is ashamed."

"That shows that she is still a teen-ager," said Papa Rakoczy. "I always said so. Go and fetch her back!"

"She'll come back soon," said Tania, gathered the pictures together and carried them back into the house.

Alfred remained in conversation with Papa Rakoczy for a time. When Tania returned, he rose and said goodbye.

"I must get in touch with Dr. Katz in his office to tell him about Canon Partyka."

"Do that, do that," said Papa Rakoczy, "that's very important. And please visit me whenever you're in the city."

Tania accompanied Alfred.

"I'll take you to the bridge," she said, not finding Xenia on the street in front of the house.

When they reached the bridge, they saw Xenia at once; with her elbows propped on the rail of the bridge, she was looking at the trains pulling out.

"Naturally, she sees us," said Tania. "She's only pretending."

But when they came still nearer, Xenia stopped her pretense, turned around and looked at Alfred with an embarrassed smile:

"I should like to ask you a favor, Mr. Mohilevski."

"I am at your service, Miss Xenia," said Alfred.

"Don't tell your relative in Vienna that I put out his eyes," said Xenia, and now she was not smiling, but was nearer to tears.

"I should certainly never do that," Alfred assured her.

"It is terrible to imagine that someone is walking around in Vienna knowing that someone in this city has put out his eyes."

[217]

Xenia was charming in her grief. Despite her red hair, she had a dark-brown complexion with only a few freckles on the tip of her nose. Her eyes were reddish brown and her face youthfully sulky. Alfred consoled the girl as well as he could. When they parted at the other end of the bridge it was easily apparent that Xenia believed his promise not to tell in Vienna what had happened.

In the lawyer's office the room where the assistants usually sat was already empty, but Dr. Katz was still in his room. Alfred told him about his conversation with Father Rakoczy concerning Canon Partyka and was agreeably surprised to see that the lawyer, too, appeared to lay great weight on the old friendship between the Canon and Alfred's father.

"The canon," said the lawyer, "is a very influential man in our country. I don't know whether Pope Rakoczy made it quite clear to you how influential the canon is. Kostj Rakoczy is an enemy of the canon, not only a political opponent."

"He spoke only of his political opposition, but it was not hard to sense that the pope doesn't particularly love the canon. But I must say in his favor that he did not try to belittle the canon's personality. He also advised me to go to you at once."

"Was he of the opinion that you should travel to Lwow at once?" asked the lawyer.

"There was no doubt in his mind Canon Partyka would receive me. But whether I should travel or not was a decision he wished to leave to your judgment, Doctor."

"If the decision is mine, I must ask you not to travel to Lwow, Mr. Mohilevski," said the lawyer.

"You expect nothing to come of it?" asked Alfred.

"On the contrary. I expect too much to come of it. The canon is too important a personality for an affair otherwise so minor. It's not minor, for us — I wouldn't say it is. But this Canon Partyka can become a bishop tomorrow. He is, whatever Rakoczy may have told you, a notable and large-hearted man and, what is even more important for us, a friend of the

[218]

Jews. You should do well to travel to Lwow yourself sometime to see how he receives you. His friendship with your father lies far in the past. We do not know what it may mean to him. It would be worth a trip to Lwow to find out."

"Let me go tomorrow morning then," interrupted Alfred.

"I should like to have you leave today with my blessing. But I do not believe that it will be necessary to fire at the communal secretary of Dobropolia with so large a gun. I understand your impatience. I have known Yankel Christiampoler from my childhood, and what has happened in Dobropolia touches me as closely as you. Wait another day. I have found a way which can lead us to success more quickly than your trip to Lwow. To be exact, it is not I who have found the way. Come tomorrow at two o'clock."

"Good," said Alfred. "I'll wait another day. I'll be here tomorrow at two."

"Not here," said the lawyer. "Come to the Kawiarnia Wiedenska tomorrow at two o'clock. The way that I mentioned to you doesn't proceed from my office. It is a narrow, roundabout way, as you shall see. Goodbye."

Alfred went to the hotel to see after the evening meal for Yankel. But little Benzion Schwarz was already on his way to the prison. This has been a good day, thought Alfred as he walked to his room. He washed in a state of happy excitement and rested a while before the evening meal. Then it occurred to him that the countess' chauffeur had set two o'clock Thursday as the time for his visit to the hotel. Alfred sat down at the small hotel-table, which was quite uncomfortable to write on, and composed a report to the countess, since he did not know how long he would be detained in the Kawiarnia Wiedenska with his lawyer. He had not yet finished the report when he heard someone knocking on the door of his room. Little Benzion came in, flushed with joy and told Alfred.

"They let me inside today. I saw him. He was very hungry. He sends his regards to you. He said in Yiddish that you must go to the countess tomorrow. I don't know which countess. I couldn't ask, because I mayn't speak to the prisoners. An old man, but he was very hungry. What did he do?"

"Something good," said Alfred. "Something very good."

"That is not good," said Benzion sadly.

"What?" Alfred inquired.

"The fact that he did something very good," said Benzion.

"Why?"

"If he has done something good, if he has done something very good, he will stay there a very long time."

"How do you know that, little prophet?"

"The old man is not the first prisoner to whom I have brought food in prison."

Alfred arrived at the Kawiarnia Wiedenska a half hour before his appointment with the lawyer. He chose a table in a corner of the coffeehouse, because he thought he had noticed that Dr. Katz did not care to sit on the terrace. The coffeehouse was not well attended at this hour, only a few tables being occupied. At one of them, near the entrance to the billiard room, sat a man whom Alfred had often seen at that spot. He invariably sat there, insofar as he may be said to have sat. He was a peripatetic coffeehouse habitué, such as were not infrequently to be found in Vienna as well. He seemed to know all the customers, and all the customers knew him. Although there were few customers there at the time, he kept visiting every corner of the establishment holding a newspaper in his left hand, into which he cast glances as he chatted. A light stick in his right hand, he sat at his table, his legs outstretched, ready to rise to his feet at any moment. He now showed a great interest in Alfred. "There are only a few customers," thought Alfred, and having exchanged a few glances with the gentleman, withdrew behind a large newspaper in order to discourage the restless customer. The man appeared friendly and quite harmless, but Alfred was not in the mood to strike up an acquaintance. Yet hardly had Alfred finished his coffee when the gentleman rose and came over to Alfred's table, carrying his newspaper and stick with him, as though he had been invited.

"My name is Elfenbein, Abraham Elfenbein."

Alfred quickly rose, having decided to ward off the attack with a show of extreme politeness.

"Keep your seat, Mr. Mohilevski. You needn't be so polite to me. I shan't hurt you," said the gentleman. He sat down and invited Alfred to take his place at his table which — Alfred was amused to learn — had now actually become Mr. Elfenbein's table. Invited so cordially, Alfred took a seat at the gentleman's table.

"You must be wondering how I know your name."

"Frankly, I am, Mr. Elfenbein," said Alfred.

"My name is Abraham Elfenbein, but they always call me Abraham God," said Mr. Elfenbein.

"What's that? God — G-O-D?" asked Alfred, on the verge of laughter.

"Just God," said Elfenbein. "That's actually my mother's name. I used to be called by that name. Now my name is Elfenbein, after my father, but they still call me Abraham God after my mother."

"That is easy to understand," said Alfred.

"Not so easy as you might believe," said Elfenbein. "In the old days, when we were still Austrian, the government did not recognize marriages which were performed according to the Jewish ritual only. So the children resulting from such marriages legally had to bear their mother's name. Legally speaking, we were illegal. For twenty years of my life I was illegal and my name was God. Then my father decided to marry my mother legally. So now my name is legally Elfenbein, Abraham Elfenbein. But they call me God, Abraham God."

"You are right, Mr. Elfenbein, it is not so easy to understand as I thought. But now I do understand. May I order you a coffee?" asked Alfred, happy now to have made this gentleman's acquaintance. Elfenbein cast a quick glance at the wall clock and said:

"Thank you. Thank you very much. I still have a great deal of time. — So now you know: My name is Abraham God.

What you don't know is that in our city there is a saying that
runs: God knows everything, but Abraham God knows more.
Now you know how I come to know your name."

The waiter brought the coffee for Mr. Elfenbein. Without
delay he began to spoon up the coffee-with-whipped-cream
carefully and with pleasure. Now and again, he cast quick
glances into his newspaper, reading swiftly as he gulped the
white coffee down in small sips with visible and audible enjoy-
ment. Meanwhile, Alfred, completely ignored, had the opportunity to regard his remarkable table companion. His face
was constructed of three sharp lines: the line of his receding
forehead, which was crowned by curly light-blonde hair and
was bare to the middle of his rosy skull; the sharp line of a
fleshless, delicate hook nose; and the short line of a receding,
almost absent chin. His neck was long and his Adam's apple
especially prominent. He wore a white, stiff, turned-down
collar with a fantastic, flowing, black tie; a light coat of dark
blue rep material, a white vest of pique, and blue-striped linen
trousers, which un-ironed, narrowly enclosed footwear of an
abominable yellow color.

"So," said Mr. Elfenbein, after he had gulped down his
coffee and neatly picked up the last of the sugar dregs with the
point of his spoon. "So," he repeated, and threw his newspaper on a nearby table, as though the two activities of drinking
coffee and newspaper reading, were mutually dependent.
"So. Now I may advise you that I also know why you are here."

"Here, in the city?" asked Alfred, growing uneasy.

"Here in the city, and here in the coffeehouse. I am sorry.
It is a serious matter, I know. But depend on me. I shall help
you. It is now almost two o'clock. You have an appointment.
I shall not disturb you. You will see me again. You will see
me again soon."

With that he left Alfred and went to a table near the billiard
room, where he immediately concealed himself behind another
newspaper.

At a distance the omniscient Mr. Elfenbein seemed to Alfred, sitting dumbfounded and alone, quite suspect. It was not remarkable that Alfred's name should be known in a small city. The fact that the gentleman apparently knew about Yankel was also understandable. But the fact that he also knew about the appointment with the lawyer was disturbing and rendered the man suspect. Alfred at once paid his bill and decided to intercept Dr. Katz outside. But before he could do so, the lawyer entered the coffeehouse carrying a portfolio. He nodded a greeting to Alfred from a distance, but first stepped into the billiard room. At that, Abraham Elfenbein rose and, carrying his stick and his newspaper, followed the lawyer. After a while Dr. Katz returned and sat down with Alfred.

"So you have already made his acquaintance," he said.

"I am not responsible," said Alfred. "He simply came to my table and I thought him quite harmless at first."

"He spoke to you at my instructions," explained the lawyer. "I didn't want to have a rendezvous for three here."

"I was beginning to fear he was a plainclothesman," said Alfred.

"A plainclothesman! Elfenbein! How did you come to think that?"

"Because he knows everything."

"Oh, yes! He told you about his motto?" The lawyer was forced to laugh at the thought and Alfred laughed with him. "He is the most harmless man you can imagine."

"What is his business?" asked Alfred. "He says he will help me."

"He has no business," said the lawyer. "That is to say, he has all kinds of businesses. He lives on his friendships. He is friendly with everyone, and so everyone is friendly with him. As a matter of fact, he does know a great deal. He is the wandering chronicle of our city."

"But how can he help me?" asked Alfred.

"Has he already begun to give himself airs?" asked the lawyer, but didn't wait for a reply. "That is not important. Remarkable as it may appear, he has found the way about

[223]

which I spoke to you yesterday. What I mean is that I discovered the way during our conversation yesterday. Your account of the Canon Partyka reminded me of the fact that your father had a great many friends — particularly among the Christians." The lawyer looked reproachfully at Alfred, as though Alfred could do something now about the fact that his father had so many Christian friends. "But as you know," he continued, "I am a few years older than your father and don't know who were his friends and where they are now to be found. That is something I have found out this morning with the help of Mr. Elfenbein. Before two hours passed, he had found the man we need."

"Elfenbein? Was he a friend of my father's too?" marveled Alfred.

"Not that. But as I told you before, Elfenbein is friendly with everyone. Thus he has been friendly for years with a man whom you probably have already seen: it is the old man with the emperor's beard who sits in front of the court gate —"

"The old bailiff!" Alfred exclaimed. "Naturally. I see him sitting in front of the gate or in the garden whenever I pass by the court house."

"This old bailiff has a son who is the Starosta's secretary. The bailiff's name is Flisak. His son, Dr. Jan Flisak, was in your father's class at high school. He was quite poor in Latin, this Jan Flisak, and your father coached him in it. Free of charge, by the way. Our Elfenbein, who knows everything, knew this already, because he, too, often has nothing to do and sits and chats with old Flisak on a bench in the garden. Now it is up to you to get together with old Flisak, Mr. Mohilevski. But that is not so easy as you think! First, because old Flisak is already a bit senile, and it is hard to revive his memories. The second hindrance is that you can't speak Polish. Why didn't you learn Polish? You come to Poland, and the first thing you learn is Ukrainian?! What were you thinking of?"

"I don't know," said Alfred, turning red. "It just happened

that way. Whenever I spoke Polish everyone laughed. Ukrainian came much easier to me. It just happened that way."

"Well, it's all the same now," said the lawyer, in a conciliatory tone. "I can't demand that you learn Polish in a hurry now. But I do want you not to speak Ukrainian either to the old man or to young Flisak."

"I am to speak to them. But what language shall I speak to them in?"

"Speak German, French — whatever you wish. But not Ukrainian. Well. Now my task is over. You will go directly to the garden. There you will find Elfenbein in conversation with old Flisak. You will just be passing by, as though you are in a great hurry. Elfenbein will greet you very loudly by name. But you will be in a great hurry, and not stop, even when he keeps calling you. But if old Flisak should call you, go back. The rest will depend on you and old Flisak."

"Father Rakoczy urged me not to show myself at any office. I don't know whether I ought to do what you say, Doctor," said Alfred. "I beg your pardon, but it seems to me that I would not be the right partner for Elfenbein. Wouldn't it be much easier, if you were to take me to meet the son, Doctor? Why do we need old Flisak?"

"The reply to your questions," said Dr. Katz, smiling, "valid as they are, could only be clear to one who has grown up here, assuming that anyone who had lived here for any length of time would ask such questions. You can well believe that I have good grounds not to intervene personally any further. As I have represented to you, it was Elfenbein who conceived this plan. And you will see that *he* is right, not we. Mr. Mohilevski, you can spoil nothing at this point. If Elfenbein doesn't succeed in bringing you and old Flisak together, we can reconsider how to introduce you to Dr. Jan Flisak in a less roundabout fashion!"

"As you wish," said Alfred nervous, but determined. "Where is Mr. Elfenbein?"

"He has been sitting with old Flisak on the garden bench for some time."

Alfred left Dr. Katz. Holding his hat in his left hand, he walked quickly through the garden feeling as he used to in Vienna when on the way to an examination at the university unprepared. He was sure things could not turn out well, unless a miracle occurred; but he felt a compulsion to play the game with Mr. Elfenbein through as quickly as possible. The nearer he came to the garden bench, where at a distance he already saw the odd pair engrossed in conversation, the more unworthy the game seemed to him. "A provincial lawyer," he thought, wrathfully. As had been agreed, pretending haste, Alfred did not pass too near the bench. And, as had been agreed, Elfenbein greeted his appearance with a happy cry: "Whither so fast, Mr. Mohilevski?" But — ignoring the express warning — Alfred stopped at once and after a moment of hesitation, despite the despairing and frenzied mimicry of Mr. Elfenbein, walked a short distance toward the bench.

"You have spoiled everything," Elfenbein hissed at him. "You see, he hasn't heard anything."

"I am a bad actor," said Alfred angrily, turned his back on Elfenbein and hurried away as fast as he had come.

"Hey, Mr. Mohilevski! Mr. Mohilevski!" Elfenbein cried despairingly after him. He was no longer play-acting. Elfenbein's despair rang so true that Alfred could not refrain from looking around. He saw Elfenbein standing in front of old Flisak, who was attempting to rise from his seat. As he labored to aid the old man, Mr. Elfenbein called Alfred continuously by name, waving excitedly to him. As Alfred hesitatingly obeyed the incessant nods and cries, more out of sympathy with Elfenbein than anything else, he became aware to his amazement that the old bailiff was also now calling him by name, and waving to him in friendly fashion.

The rest took place exactly as the crafty Mr. Elfenbein had planned. Once the old man was on his legs, the danger that he would doze off was past, and Elfenbein, who had been so

[226]

fearful of this peril, now introduced the old bailiff to Alfred with a skill almost worthy of a man of the world. With complete modesty he assumed the function of a mere interpreter — interpreter for the bailiff more than for Alfred, whom he treated rather as a friend and patron. Alfred did not understand much of what the old man said to him as he heartily pressed Alfred's hand, which for a long while he would not let go. The first sentence, which Mr. Elfenbein translated somewhat coherently, ran: "It makes no difference, you can speak German; his Majesty, Emperor Franz Joseph, spoke German, too, and he was no German, after all." For the rest, the conversation was piecemeal and Alfred did not manage to reconstruct a consecutive whole. But it was not the fault of the interpreter Elfenbein that the conversation was confused. True, the old bailiff added a masterful "Translate this!" to every sentence. But he did not have the patience to wait for the translation; continually interrupting Mr. Elfenbein in the middle of a sentence, he left the translator in the lurch to turn directly back to Alfred, as he pushed the interpreter aside with an impatient gesture. All that Alfred made out at the time was that his father had as a matter of fact helped young Flisak with his Latin, and that old Flisak would never, never forget it. The old man reverted time and again to a certain letter for which he was particularly grateful to Alfred's father and which the old bailiff promised to show Alfred at once.

"What's this about a letter?" Alfred inquired of Elfenbein.

"Do I know?" said Elfenbein. "He keeps reverting to this letter. We'll soon see. We are now going home with him."

Flanked by Alfred and Mr. Elfenbein, silently, the old bailiff led them to the courthouse. He walked with short, shuffling steps, but decisively rejected Elfenbein's aid when the latter tried persistently to offer him his arm. Seen close up, this Slavic double of the Emperor looked far more majestic than his prototype, who in his old age looked exactly like one of the many letter carriers who resembled His Majesty. The bailiff towered a head above his walking companions. He was still well-fleshed and had a soldierly bearing. It was only his legs that refused to obey him. This was especially evident as they climbed the courthouse steps. He walked all the more vigorously through the cool corridors of the courthouse. They traversed many corridors paved with slabs of stone. The courthouse smelled, like all Austrian government offices, of the fine dust on documents and of invisible urinals. It was only when they reached the courtyard which led to the prison that the air again became clean. There were even a few old trees in the courtyard. In one of the rather charming one-story houses which connected the courthouse with the prison, lived the bailiff. They walked through a roomy, brightly-painted kitchen into a longish room with large windows, which was apparently the old man's living room. It was packed with furniture, and countless photographs of groups of men in uniform, wearing martial mustaches, hung on the walls. Nor was there lacking a youthful picture of His Majesty the Emperor, dressed in a white parade coat with a purple sash across his chest. In the middle of the room stood a table on which lay many table-cloths and a plush picture album. Hardly had they stepped into the room when the old man loudly called out toward the courtyard, without caring whether the guards in the courtyard heard him or not. Then he reverted to the letter again, and Mr. Elfenbein at last grasped the connection. And now that the old man allowed him to speak without interruption, he was able to explain it to Alfred.

"As you know, your father helped his fellow-student Flisak with his Latin gratis. That, says the old man, was very big-hearted of him. Who knows whether his son would have been able to get through the high school without his help. Only in Latin. In the other subjects he was a very good student. But in Latin he was poor. For five semesters your father slaved with Janek over his Latin in this very room. Gratis. That was big-hearted of him. But it is conceivable that someone else might have been just as big-hearted. Your father, being well-to-do, was not obliged to tutor. But one day it happened that

[228]

your father was prevented from appearing at the usual hour. So he sent a letter of apology by messenger to old Flisak, explaining his absence and assuring them that it would not happen again. This is the letter that the old man can't forget."

A young man in convict's clothes came into the room, bringing glasses and a bottle of schnapps, and the old man sat for a while tipping a small glass of high-grade brandy with his guests. He was now wearing his spectacles and examined Alfred with great pleasure:

"Now I can see you. My eyes are weak. But now I can see you. You resemble your father a great deal. Somewhat taller, it seems to me. But perhaps my memory deceives me. — Translate that!"

But hardly had Elfenbein begun to translate when the bailiff interrupted. He pushed the picture album over to Elfenbein, opened it and commanded:

"Here! Show him the pictures and explain everything to him. I'll change my clothing and then we'll go to see my son." He nodded to the convict servant and both went into the next room, where the old man could be heard cursing and groaning while the convict helped him change.

"I'll not go to the Starosta with you," said Elfenbein to Alfred. "You must pay particular heed that the old man does not sit down on the way or in some office. Otherwise he will fall asleep and forget everything."

There were only a few photographs in the album which were not of the bailiff. He had worn some uniform or other all his life. Alfred saw him first as a child in a uniform which Elfenbein explained was that of an orphanage. Next he stood in a school uniform, already as vigorous as a soldier. Then he was an infantry man with shako and parade coat. Then Alfred saw the bailiff's rise from private to sergeant. The poses in these pictures were so martial that the pictures which followed, showing him in the various uniforms of the court attendant, seemed almost civilian by contrast. At this point the imperial beard made its appearance, the two parts of the beard waxing in length and thickness with age. There were only a few youthful photographs of the deceased Mrs. Flisak. The last pages of the album were filled with photographs of his son, who — almost like his father — appeared to have been concealed behind a uniform most of his life. But, unlike his father, the son looked the civilian despite all his uniforms. Alfred, who had expected to find his father in some group picture or other in the album, was disappointed.

But his disappointment was soon followed by a compensation. For when the old man had finished changing his dress, he appeared in the doorway of his bedroom, dressed surprisingly as a civilian, and invited Alfred with a large gesture to step into the bedroom. He shook his head angrily at Elfenbein, who had risen with Alfred, and only allowed Alfred to enter alone. The room contained an iron bedstead, a clothes closet, night table and commode. The large room was otherwise bare. There were no pictures on the very high, white-washed walls, but over the headpiece of the cot Alfred saw an ebony crucifix, flanked on the right by a picture of young Flisak, on the left by one of Joseph Mohilevski, both in the uniform of lieutenants in the imperial army.

"What did he show you?" Elfenbein inquired, when Alfred returned to the living room.

"It will remain there until my death. Then my son receives the picture. Translate that to him!" the bailiff commanded Elfenbein.

"He showed me a picture of my father," said Alfred slowly to Elfenbein, who this time had not even begun to translate the bailiff's words, so struck had he been by Alfred's expression as he stepped out of the bailiff's bedroom.

"Well, now let's go," said the old man. After he had locked his home and given the key to the convict, the three of them walked through the courtyard and many corridors and out of the courthouse gate. It was only in the sunlit street that they saw how grandly the old bailiff had dressed for his visit to his son. He wore a black frock coat which extended down to his knees,

a black-striped pair of trousers which apparently were too long
for him, and high black shoes. He had put on a stiff white shirt
with a stiff turned-up collar and a black cravat. He had his
white straw hat on his head and carried a stick with a silver
crook in his right hand. When they had crossed the Street of
the Third of May, the bailiff dismissed Mr. Elfenbein with
courteous thanks.

"Be careful that he doesn't sit down and fall asleep somewhere," Mr. Elfenbein warned Alfred again in parting. He
remained standing at the corner of the street, looking after
them anxiously till they had ascended the steps of the Starosta's
office and had disappeared through the door.

Alfred breathed more freely when he noticed that the old
bailiff was received by the office attendants with great respect, even with servile politeness, and was promptly shown
into his son's office after a telephone call. The old bailiff didn't
keep Alfred waiting on the outside. When the door to Dr. Jan
Flisak's office was opened, the bailiff took Alfred's hand and
held it firm till he had laid it in his son's hand, introducing
Alfred with the words:

"See whom I've brought along. This is the son of our Joseph
Mohilevski."

That was as much as Alfred could make out. At the sight
of the Starosta's right-hand man Alfred knew at once that Yankel was safe. For the high functionary was a Slavic translation
of Ministerial Counselor Dr. Frankl. Like Dr. Frankl, he was
short of stature, narrow-shouldered, very lean, full of nervous
energy. Although Alfred knew that he must be in his middle
fifties, since he had been a fellow student of Alfred's father, he
seemed much younger. He had black hair, which was thicker
than Dr. Frankl's, and the yellow complexion of the office
worker. Yet he wore no glasses and his eyes were smaller,
livelier and harder than Dr. Frankl's. He spoke fluent German
which, he assured Alfred at once, he preferred, since he thought
it important to know the enemy's language. He greeted Alfred
with unaffected cordiality and regretted that his wife and chil-

dren were already in the country, as he would have liked to introduce his family to Alfred.

But the old man was impatient and immediately brought up the subject of Alfred's concern. He spoke long and urgently to his son, who listened attentively, occasionally directing a questioning glance at Alfred. It seemed to Alfred that the old bailiff kept repeating himself, and did not lack for vigorous invectives, for the son had to appease his father continually. At length Dr. Jan Flisak arrived at a subject on which he turned to Alfred for information.

"When was your uncle arrested?" asked Dr. Flisak, already at his desk again, his hand on the telephone.

"There must be no misunderstanding," said Alfred, frightened. "The man who was arrested is not my uncle."

"My father keeps talking about your uncle, " said Dr. Flisak, not stressing the misunderstanding.

"It's not my uncle, Doctor. It's our bailiff who has been imprisoned," said Alfred. "He is a relative," he added.

"What is your relative's name?" asked Dr. Flisak and raised the telephone mouthpiece.

"Jacob Christiampoler," said Alfred.

"Case of Christiampoler," Dr. Flisak spoke into the telephone and turned back again to Alfred. "Is this in connection with the Sunday disturbances in Dobropolia?" he asked. "Now I I remember. Were you there?"

"Unfortunately, I came too late," said Alfred.

"How old was the boy?" asked Dr. Flisak.

"Seven," said Alfred.

"Are you sure of that?" asked Dr. Flisak. "Did you know the boy?"

"It is a year now since I've come to Dobropolia, " said Alfred. "I was with the child every day. I could not have loved him more if he had been my brother."

A clerk stepped in and handed Dr. Flisak a folder.

"Excuse me a moment," said Dr. Flisak. "It won't take long," he added, leafing through the file. "I knew about the

[232]

unfortunate accident. But I knew nothing about Jacob Christiampoler. A remarkable name, Christiampoler. . . Christiampoler."

Dr. Flisak now buried himself in the file, making occasional
notes on a pad. The old bailiff waved his fist encouragingly at
Alfred. After a while Dr. Flisak shut the file, pushed it aside
with a curt, derogatory movement, rose and said to Alfred,
"Your man will be free at twelve o'clock tomorrow." Then
he turned to his father, to whom he apparently communicated
the same information in Polish. But he had greater success with
Alfred than with his father. For while Alfred rose with Dr. Flisak in happy excitement and bowed his thanks, the old bailiff
pounded on the table, hammering the folder with his fist, and
shouted lustily at his son, who again tried to appease him. It
was a while before the old man controlled himself. When his
father had calmed down a bit, Dr. Flisak said to Alfred with a
pensive smile:

"My father is an impatient man. He wants your uncle freed
today. We shall have to allow him to continue to think that
it is your uncle. But unfortunately Mr. Jacob Christiampoler's
release can't be arranged for today. I need the signature of the
Starosta. However, I could manage it alone, and my father
knows it, which is why he is so aroused. But for reasons that
are of no interest to you, I should prefer to have the Starosta's
signature. If you appear at the courthouse tomorrow at twelve,
you will find your relative there, free. Before he leaves have
him visit me here. I should like to see him. I have many questions to ask him."

Alfred thanked Dr. Flisak and left with the old bailiff, who
said goodbye to his son in fatherly fashion, but still openly dissatisfied. At the gate, Dr. Flisak said to Alfred, "I am sorry
that my wife isn't here. But if you have no appointments we
could dine together tonight. It would be more pleasant if we
could eat at my home. But there is a good restaurant in the city
that you perhaps are acquainted with. Please fetch me at eight
o'clock. I still have matters to attend to."

Alfred accepted the invitation. He was glad that he still had time to go to Dr. Katz and report the successful outcome of his visit. Elfenbein appeared near Kawiarnia Wiedenska.

"His uncle will be free tomorrow at twelve o'clock," the bailiff whispered into Elfenbein's ear. "Translate that for him!"

They accompanied the bailiff to the courthouse where, exhausted by the events of the day, he at once sat down on his customary seat in front of the gate, and having cordially said goodbye to Alfred, immediately dozed off in his Sunday clothes.

Mr. Elfenbein did not accompany Alfred to the lawyer's office. He had business to do in the coffeehouse, and he advised Alfred to appear in the coffeehouse the next day at one o'clock with his released client.

Dr. Katz was satisfied, but not surprised. As always, he was very busy, and his conversation with Alfred was short.

"I should only like to ask you one thing, " he said. "As you know, Yankel Christiampoler has known me since my childhood. But he has never asked my professional advice in any affair of his, unlike your uncle, who is an old client of mine. Can you tell me why he came to me with this case?"

"Unfortunately, I don't know that," said Alfred. "But I shall ask him, if you wish."

"Please do so and come to see me tomorrow at two o'clock."

On the way back to the hotel Alfred now discovered Adam Mickiewicz Street to be one of the loveliest streets he had ever seen. Everything was there right at hand: the buildings for the high administrative offices, the prison, the court — also the lawyer Katz and the other angels of salvation. This was only possible in a small provincial city. The fact that he had called Dr. Katz a provincial lawyer barely two hours before did not occur to Alfred now. On the other hand, he became aware that this pleasant street contained everything except a shop where one could make a purchase. In the neighborhood of his hotel, however, he discovered the photographer's studio of Herman Laub. The name seemed familiar to him. But he had glanced at so many photographs in the last two days that it was a moment before he remembered that Herman Laub was the name on the group photograph which the charming Xenia Rakoczy had been so concerned about. He stepped into the studio and asked for Mr. Herman Laub. An employee led him into a room which a small and supple man of about fifty-six at once entered, bowed and politely tried to maneuver Alfred between a camera and a background decoration. But Mr. Laub did not prove any less friendly when Alfred merely asked for information:

"How long do you keep the plates of your fine group pictures? I saw a print which I should like to have."

"Which year?" asked Mr. Laub.

"It is a photograph of the graduates of 1912," said Alfred.

"I have it," said Mr. Laub. "I always keep the plates of graduation pictures. Which high school, please? Or was it a technical school?"

"No, it is certainly not a technical school. But are there several high schools here?" said Alfred.

"We have two. There were already that many in 1912. I'll have both plates brought out and you can tell me which one you are interested in. Both are very fine."

After an interval which did not seem too long to Alfred, Mr. Laub brought him two plates of the 1912 graduation pictures. With the friendly photographer's help Alfred immediately found the plate containing the three familiar names and ordered two prints. "Send one print to Vienna. I'll write down the address there for you. And the second to Miss Xenia Rakoczy—"

"One of Kostj Rakoczy's daughters?" asked the photographer, visibly interested. "You don't have to write that address down. Every child here knows her."

Feeling that he had done a good deed, Alfred left the friendly Mr. Laub and went to his hotel. Little Benzion was unfortunately not there. He came to Alfred's room an hour afterwards.

"I am off Thursday afternoons. So I go to school then," he excused himself to Alfred. "I have come only to bring the poor old man his food."

"I'll go along with you today," said Alfred.

"What benefit does the old man have from your coming along?" said Benzion. "You had better rest."

"Good," said Alfred, "if you will promise me something."

"Certainly," said Benzion, "you can depend on me."

"If I can depend on you, I'll tell you a secret. Can you hold your tongue?"

"You can depend on me," repeated Benzion. "Ask Mr. Weiss."

"Good," said Alfred, "But what if I tell you something that Mr. Weiss isn't to know, either — can I depend on you?"

"Yes," said Benzion. "Mr. Weiss doesn't tell me everything, either."

"Fine," said Alfred. "Listen: If they let you in to the old man with the food, tell him that we go home tomorrow."

"Who?" asked Benzion. "Are you going home tomorrow?"

"You tell it to him the way I told it to you; that he and I are to go home tomorrow. Do you understand?"

"If it's not certain, you ought not to say that sort of thing. It's much worse then."

"It is certain," said Alfred.

"You have done very well. Things never went so fast before. You can depend on me."

At that he left. When he returned, he was very melancholy. This time they did not let him in to see the prisoner.

6

With the aid of the old bailiff, who accelerated the bureaucratic procedure for the dismissal of a prisoner on remand, Yankel was free at eleven o'clock the next day. When Alfred ascended the steps of the courthouse at noon he was asked by the doorkeeper to go to the bailiff's home, where he found Yankel in a vigorous conversation with old Flisak. Both men were of one mind that such a miscarriage of justice would have been impossible under the just rule of His Majesty the Emperor Franz Joseph, and they separated in friendly fashion.

Alfred, who had tried to foresee Yankel's mood after being released, had imagined two possibilities: the old man would be either very angry, or triumphant. But Yankel showed neither indignation at the injustice that had been done him nor pride at his speedy victory. On the way to Dr. Flisak's he looked as he did in Dobropolia when he had dressed for the day, after the horses had been fed, and appeared at Pessa's for breakfast without telling her in advance. Under his open smock he wore a short vest with two rows of cloth buttons, a black straw hat with pulled-down rim on his head, gray leather riding breeches, black boots with high, wide stocks which shone so bright that, as he strode slowly through the park grounds, his boots reflected variously blades of grass, stalks, flower blossoms and strips of blue heaven. He had had his boots polished by the bailiff's convict-attendant, who was as good at that as Panko. But he seemed to be happy over the opportunity to appear in the Starosta's office, and at first did not even ask Alfred how he happened to have been released so quickly.

"Did you tell the old man that I am your uncle?" Yankel inquired as he stood on the steps of the Starosta's office before going to see Dr. Flisak.

"No," said Alfred. "I'll explain it all to you later. Dr. Flisak knows who you are. I'll be waiting for you in the Wiedenska Café."

Mr. Elfenbein proved to be very proud of the successful outcome of his labors. He sat at his usual table in front of the entrance to the billiard room, a newspaper in his left hand, his stick in his right. This time Alfred took a seat at his table, and Elfenbein used the time they spent waiting for Yankel to inform Alfred exactly how he, Abraham Elfenbein, called God, had almost become a lawyer like Dr. Katz. It was, it seemed to Alfred, quite a melancholy story, but Mr. Elfenbein told it lightly and with good humor, as though it was no more than a lively provincial humoresque.

Elfenbein's father had been a small poultry-man, whose ambition was to have his son study law. As a matter of fact, young

Elfenbein did go through the fourth year of a classical high school. Poor as he was, he would have been able to pass the high school, if he had been a particularly good student; he would have been able to live on tutoring, like many poor gymnasiasts, and continue his studies. Unfortunately, however, young Elfenbein was not an exceptional scholar, though a diligent one. Then he had an idea, not bad in itself, but not quite in place in a classical high school. To earn some money, he, at thirteen, went into the schoolbook business. At the end of each semester he would buy their old books from the students and sell them again at a small profit at the beginning of the next school year after the vacation. His business prospered, but not for long; after the first semester it was discovered, and young Elfenbein was expelled from the school.

The story served Mr. Elfenbein as a vehicle for a depiction of the relationships existing in a classical high school of forty years before. He gave a dramatic portrayal of the students and professors, and was especially successful in dramatizing the strict trial of the small book-merchant which ended with his expulsion from school. The story-teller still knew by heart the speech which the director of the institution had made to young Elfenbein to guide him in his life-career, and he delivered it to Alfred with all its nuances. "If you sense in yourself an irresistible drive to business, student Abraham Gott, register at a business school. *We* are a classical institution. We educate humanists and not businessmen." On that note the director's speech, as well as Mr. Elfenbein's narration, concluded.

Although Mr. Elfenbein's account of how he had almost become a lawyer was jolly, the story made Alfred quite melancholy. Saddest of all was the fact that Mr. Elfenbein still approved of the moral the director had read into his case.

"In America," Alfred told him, "they would have photographed you, and your picture would have been published in a newspaper, as a good example for the school youth, under the caption: *Poor Student Earns Tuition Selling Books.*"

But Mr. Elfenbein rejected this interpretation.

[238]

"If I was thrown out, at least it was out of a fine classical school."

Mr. Elfenbein also displayed his pride by refusing categorically to accompany them to visit Dr. Katz, despite Yankel's vigorous urging.

"I never go to lawyers. If they need me, they know where to find me," he explained to Yankel. "Let Dr. Katz decide on my fee, and I should appreciate your leaving it with him. If you should need me again, you know where to find me."

The lawyer congratulated Yankel Christiampoler. He assured Yankel that he would certainly have won in a trial, but would have had to remain in prison on remand for a couple of weeks, perhaps months. There was no question of his accepting a fee for himself. He maintained that Yankel's speedy release was due entirely to Mr. Elfenbein, whose services he estimated to be worth five hundred zloty. But Yankel estimated them at a thousand zloty.

"I was ready to spend much more, I can tell that to you now that the danger is over," he assured Dr. Katz. "Naturally, I didn't count on your working for me free of charge."

"I am only working for you free of charge," said Dr. Katz, smiling, "because this is the first time. What I should like to know is why it is the first time. All the Dobropolia people come to me, from Velvel Mohilevski to the poorest peasant. You, Mr. Christiampoler, are the only one who has never come to me for advice in any matter. Why did you come to me this time?"

"First, because I am not arrested so often as you seem to believe. And second — second, well, why did I come to you this time?" said Yankel, and looked questioningly at Alfred.

"I don't know," said Alfred. "The doctor asked me that yesterday."

"Yes, now I know," said Yankel. "Didn't you tell Dr. Katz about your father's testament? Mr. Mohilevski's father left his son a testament, in which he mentions you, Dr. Katz. We were reading the manuscript the very night that rascal pushed his way into Velvel Dobropolier's home to arrest me. That must be the reason why I thought of you when I needed a lawyer."

"That explains why you came to me this time," said Dr. Katz, perhaps only to turn the conversation away from the dead Joseph Mohilevski. "But why did you not come to me before, Mr. Christiampoler?"

"Oh, there's a very simple reason!" said Yankel. "In the city I never go to the barber whom Wolf Mohilevski goes to; I never go to the inn Wolf Mohilevski goes to; I never go to Wolf Mohilevski's tailor. When I'm abroad I want to rest a while from the Mohilevskis and stand on my own feet. All my life I have been in the shadow of the family Mohilevski. Goodbye, Dr. Katz. Come, you Mohilevski!"

"One moment," said Dr. Katz, "I have still a favor to ask of young Mr. Mohilevski. You must promise me that at the next opportunity you will go to Lwow and get in touch with Canon Partyka. That is very important. I tell you that not as a lawyer. I tell it to you as a Zionist. I am not afraid of being in the shadow of the family Mohilevski, if something good can be accomplished by doing so."

"Good — for whom?" saked Yankel.

"For the Jews," said Dr. Katz.

"We are not Zionists," said Yankel. "Come, Alfred." He shook hands with Dr. Katz, and took Alfred's arm. But Alfred gently freed himself of Yankel's grip, walked quickly over to Dr. Katz and said to him in farewell, "But I am a Zionist, Doctor. And I shall honor your request and remain in touch with you."

"What?" said Yankel. "You? With Zionists? I shall tell your uncle!"

"I shall see to that myself. And that very soon," retorted Alfred, still in the office. On the street outside Yankel asked him:

"Why did you say that to him? Since when have you been interested in Zionism?"

"Since we buried Lipusj in Rembovlia," said Alfred.

Yankel stood looking at Alfred in amazement. Then his amazement changed into sadness. Without replying to Alfred he took his arm, and they walked silently to the hotel. They found the countess' chauffeur waiting in the clerk's booth. Yankel greeted him as an old acquaintance. The chauffeur had a letter from the countess to Alfred. Alfred opened the letter and handed it over to Yankel. The countess wrote that she had in the meantime referred to two friends, who intended to intercede on behalf of Yankel.

"Thank God, that won't be necessary," said Yankel to Alfred. "Have you telegraphed to Dobropolia? Have you ordered the horses?"

"Last night after my conversation with Dr. Flisak I telegraphed that things were all right now. I have not ordered the horses. It is now two o'clock, Friday afternoon. How could we possibly reach Dobropolia before the Sabbath begins?"

"You are right," said Yankel. "But how can we stay here over the Sabbath? We have such an important guest in Dobropolia. If we take the train to Daczkow, we'll not arrive till late at night. When does the train leave for Daczkow?"

"At three o'clock," said Mr. Weiss. "You'll be in Daczkow at five."

"See here, Osuch," Yankel said, turning to the countess' chauffeur, "does the countess need the automobile today?"

"Oh no, sir," said the chauffeur, "the countess will not need the automobile till Sunday. We travel to Dobropolia almost entirely by highway. I'll get you there in two and a half hours. The countess will be very happy to have you driven home in her automobile."

"Fine," said Yankel. "Get ready, Alfred. We'll leave at once. Or do you have something to see to, Osuch?"

"Nothing," said Osuch, "nothing at all. This is the fourth time I have been in the city this week."

"Pay your bill, Alfred. Then we three will have a bite, and then we can go," said Yankel.

Alfred said goodbye to Mr. Weiss and little Benzion Schwartz, who carried Alfred's traveling bag to the automobile, and whom he made promise that he would come to Dobropolia sometime. At half past two they drove off. As they turned into the Street of the Third of May, the car was stopped by a man with a stick. It was Mr. Elfenbein. He wished the travelers a pleasant journey and gave Yankel Christiampoler to understand that he was quite satisfied with the fee, but that an extra — a couple of sacks of potatoes, new potatoes, naturally — would be a nice surprise. It was always pleasant for a city dweller to receive something fresh, direct from the country. Yankel heartily shook his hand and promised him life-long, year-round maintenance in potatoes. "For the rest of my life, of course, not yours."

"Have you seen the city?" asked Yankel when Alfred marveled at the old Dominican church as they drove through the beautiful Dominican Plaza.

"I have seen very little of it," confessed Alfred. "Mickiewicz Street had everything I needed: the prison, the court, the Starosta's office, the lawyer, the coffeehouses, and Elfenbein. On my way to Father Rakoczy I saw the railroad station, a bridge and the city park from the distance. That's all. But I intend to come to the city more often now. It's very pretty here — "

"Pretty? Here!?" said Yankel.

They had now arrived at Lwowska Street, where they had to drive very slowly, for the city's whole population seemed to be out on the street this Friday afternoon.

"Hold up a moment here, Osuch," said Yankel to the chauffeur. "Get out. I want to show you something. We have time."

When they had both gotten out, Yankel took Alfred's arm and led him through a small street, so narrow that they could only walk single file.

"You can't go home and tell your uncle that you saw two coffeehouses, one bridge and one prison, but had no time to look at the synagogue, the famous Old Synagogue. He will ask you expressly about it. If we go down this dirty small street, we'll come straight there."

[242]

The Old Synagogue stood at the intersection of two old, bumpy streets. It was a broad, flat cube of raw stone, turned black by the weather, so that it looked as though it had been hewn out of a single stone. The dark building occupied the entire corner. But although three walls of the massive cube of the synagogue faced east, north and south unobstructed, there was no entrance on any of these sides. The entrance was on the west side of the cube. To find it one had to pass through a gate with a massive iron lattice into a small plaza, where grass grew wild between mud-piles and untended bushes. The plaza gaped like a missing tooth in the row of houses that began with the Old Synagogue and stretched on in a crooked line to the west. Hordes of children let out of school, boys with long, curly ear-locks and small satin caps, ran noisily about in the plaza. The iron-framed wooden door of the synagogue was shut, but within and as part of it there was a small door which Yankel unlatched. They stepped inside. To the right and left of the vestibule there were small rooms, full of books and long study tables. The rooms were empty.

"It's Friday afternoon and the pious Jews are now in the baths. That's why the rooms are empty," Yankel informed Alfred in a low voice. "You must have a look at the prayer room." He opened one of the large arched doors.

For a short moment Alfred believed that they had used the wrong entrance, and had come to a gallery by mistake. But soon he became aware of the fact that he was standing on the first step of a broad staircase, which descended steeply: the Old Synagogue was built deep, so deep that the prayer room was fairly twice as high as one might have suspected from the outside. They went slowly down the staircase and now stood in that great breath of silence that inhabits only high places which are built for eternity. The large prayer room was as bright as day. There were large arched windows in both walls, three on each side, completely covered by small glass panes. In the middle of the east wall Alfred saw the broad curtain of the Torah Ark with the gold-embroidered Star of David. A few wooden steps led up to the Ark, whose dark-red curtain almost filled the whole center of the east wall.

Yankel and Alfred sat down on a bench behind two prayer desks, feeling small indeed in the huge room. Then Alfred saw the platform with the lectern, and the gallery for the choir in the middle of the prayer room, on an elevation exactly the level of the entrance. The whole room consisted of benches and prayer desks, with many zigzag passages. The galleries for the women were up high, behind walls the height of a man, with a few round, glass peepholes.

"How old is the synagogue?" asked Alfred, and was frightened at his voice's loud echo.

"We must go now," said Yankel softly and rose.

Alferd rose and followed Yankel. This time he counted the steps; there were twenty-eight.

"You must see this Old Synagogue on a high holiday sometime," said Yankel, when they were outside in the small narrow street.

"Have you ever been here for a high holiday, Yankel?" Alfred inquired.

"Once," said Yankel. "When your grandfather was sick and in the hospital here. I came with your uncle to the New Year's Day and Yom Kippur service here. Thirty years have passed since then, but I shall never forget those high holy days."

They climbed into the auto and drove slowly through Lwowska Street out of the city.

"The Old Synagogue is barely more than two hundred and fifty years old," said Yankel. "It is built on the ruins of a much older synagogue, which was destroyed at the time of the insurrection of the Ukrainian Hetman, Bogdan Chmelnicky."

"So that's the reason," said Alfred. "That's why it's built so deep. That's the reason for the entrance where one would never suspect it. The Old Synagogue wants to conceal itself, so as not to attract attention. Outside it looks small, inside it's large. Now I understand the architecture. Three weeks ago I would probably not have understood so well."

"Is it already three weeks?" marveled Yankel. "Three weeks since Lipusj's burial."

"Not quite three weeks," said Alfred. "It seems to me as though it were much longer."

"Is the gravestone ready? I have completely forgotten to ask your uncle," said Yankel.

"It's not ready yet. I asked Uncle. It's to be ready this week. On my way to Vienna with Uncle Stefan, we'll stop in Rembovlia. Uncle Velvel will probably come along, and we'll arrange for the stone to be set up at once."

"I'll come along to Rembovlia, too," said Yankel.

They had now reached the height before Yanovka, and Yankel, who was traveling this road for the first time in an automobile, was amazed at the rapid progress.

"Can you drive?" he asked Alfred.

"Yes," said Alfred, "it's not very difficult."

"You must get yourself an automobile," said Yankel. "I have never been in a hurry before in my life, but it is fine to see a journey, which you thought long for sixty years, made so short."

When they had Yanovka behind them and could see nothing but fields and meadows again, Alfred said, "Yankel, do you think that my father knew the Old Synagogue?"

"What questions you ask!" exclaimed Yankel. "Behind the Old Synagogue, right behind the east wall, there's a small old house where the Rav of the city lives. Your grandfather was very friendly with the old Rav. He used to visit us in Dobropolia to rest during hot summers. When your father went to the high school, he had to promise your grandfather that he would pray in the Rav's house every day before going to school. You remember the story about Rabbi Abba, which your uncle told you in Vienna, and how your father kept his promise. Your father really did tell Rabbi Abba that he knew old Rabbi Simon."

"Yes, said Alfred, "I remember. Rabbi Abba wondered that Rabbi Simon had grown old, too. I remember."

[245]

"Weekdays and on the Sabbath your father used to go to Rabbi Simon's house of prayer. But on the high holy days he went to the Old Synagogue."

"I can't imagine how a person who prayed in that Old Synagogue could have moved so far from Judaism."

"For years we in Dobropolia tormented ourselves with that question; for decades, you might say. And we could find no answer. There is no sense in your tormenting yourself about it now. We shall hear the answer very soon."

"You still think that my father's testament will have the answer?" asked Alfred. "My father explains a great deal, but I am not sure that we'll find the reply we expect."

"I am almost sure we shall," said Yankel. "But let's not say anything to your uncle. If there should be a disappointment, which God forbid, it would be a heavy blow to him. In prison I thought about it constantly — I had plenty of time. I was anxious not to stay there so long that you would grow impatient and go back to Dobropolia. I pictured to myself the three of you reading on, and I not able to become acquainted with your father's testament."

"But, Yankel, I should have given you the testament to read any time you wished."

"These old eyes of mine can no longer read so small a script," said Yankel. "You forget that I am an old man."

"But don't forget that my Uncle Velvel made you a whole five years younger a short time ago, if I am not mistaken, Yankel," said Alfred.

Yankel smiled, and Alfred was delighted. It was the first time since the child's death that Alfred had seen the old man smile.

"Yankel, do you think that we'll read my father's testament this evening after the first Sabbath meal?"

"No," said Yankel, "your uncle won't want that. If I were sure that the testament has what we are all hoping for, I should talk your uncle into reading it today. But you probably noticed that your uncle was very depressed when your father told the story of the stranger who visited Rabbi Abba that famous night."

"I didn't notice anything," said Alfred.

"Because you read that passage yourself. That's why you didn't notice it. But I watched your uncle, and I should not like to take it on myself to spoil a Sabbath for him. But, apart from that, I am sure that your uncle will wait till the close of the Sabbath to return to the manuscript. We'll leave it up to him. At any rate, it's only a matter of twenty-four hours. We'll be able to summon patience for that long. What would you have done if I had sat in prison another week?"

They drove past a wide, long field of wheat that was already harvested. The sheaves of wheat stood in innumerable rows like the fat peasant women with their headkerchiefs over their foreheads.

"Why, look," said Yankel, as though waking from a dream, "the wheat harvest is over. Have they begun harvesting in Dobropolia, too?"

"Yes," said Alfred, looking at Yankel searchingly. "Didn't you know that, Yankel?"

"I haven't noticed a thing. I didn't notice it at all. I have not been living during the last two weeks."

"Yankel, did you know that you really have my father to thank for your speedy release?"

"Yes, that is a remarkable coincidence," said Yankel. "How did this Elfenbein happen to know that Dr. Flisak was a boyhood friend of your father?"

"That was not a coincidence at all, Yankel. You thought of Dr. Katz because he appears in my father's testament," said Alfred and told Yankel how he had inquired at Father Rakoczy about Partyka, because he appeared in his father's testament, and how Father Rakoczy had advised him to go to Partyka in Lwow, and how then Dr. Katz had discovered still another friend of his father's with the help of Abraham Elfenbein, who knew everything: "As you see, it was not a coincidence at all."

"Your father had a great many friends in his youth," said Yankel. "Many of them visited him in Dobropolia during the vacation time. I remember Partyka very well. He lived in a nearby village and often stayed with us. But I can't remember Dr. Flisak. He certainly never visited us."

"It's remarkable that my father already had more Christian than Jewish friends at that time."

"That isn't true," said Yankel. "He also had a great many Jewish friends."

"But those apparently don't like to remember father," said Alfred. "Dr. Katz, for example, was always evasive when I mentioned my father."

"Oh, Dr. Katz," said Yankel. "He was always a Zionist. But this Dr. Flisak is a very fine man."

"Yes," said Alfred. "He invited me to a Jewish restaurant for dinner last night. A very good restaurant, too. It's called Schwadron. And all evening he talked to me about my father. It moved me very much to hear him. How does it happen, Yankel? My father didn't visit this city very often after he left the high school. And yet in a certain sense he has lived on here. In photographs, in group photographs, he has remained and lived on in the friendship of his friends. In a big city, when a person goes away and doesn't return, he disappears from among the living, and is forgotten."

"I can't believe that it's very much different here. You must consider the fact that it may be easier to be true to a friendship for a person long dead than one who is alive. Friendship, too, wears out, my dear. If your father had remained here and lived on in the company of his friends and they had seen one another daily, as is the custom in a provincial city, who knows how many of his friendships would have held up? Besides, we are dealing here with a boyhood friendship, and they always last the longest, in the provinces as well as in the city."

"I am glad you have told me me this. I had already come to incorrect conclusions. I said to myself one should remain where his best friends are. When one leaves his homeland, he loses much that he had acquired in his youth, and must begin all over again."

" 'Man is not a tree,' a wise man has said. God has given man two legs, so that he can leave a homeland when it becomes hostile and wicked."

"*You* say that, Yankel, who did not leave Dobropolia for fifty years?"

"I have had no cause to leave Dobropolia. Had I had a cause, I should certainly have done so. I am no tree. Besides, do you know what Dr. Flisak said to me? I was not arrested because that man with the diploma had denounced me. 'He is a rogue,' he said; 'we know him.' And old Bjelak took my side completely in his report. But I knew that. Bjelak is a fine man."

"And yet they arrested you! Who was behind it?" asked Alfred.

"That," said Yankel, "I shall yet find out here."

"Here?" wondered Alfred.

"Right," said Yankel. "Here. We are in Dobropolia already. You have done very well, Osuch."

To their disappointment, particularly Yankel's, everyone in the house of Mohilevski was happy at their arrival, but not surprised. Pessa had as a matter of fact had a premonition — right on time, as always:

. "Bjelak's daughter came to me early this morning. She told me that her father received a telegram last evening from the Starosta's office, and that he had at once discharged the communal secretary and ordered the policeman to see to it that the man with the diploma left the village within twenty-four hours."

Pessa had informed Velvel Dobropolier of this in the morning and they knew that Yankel and Alfred would soon be coming home. Velvel's only worry was lest Yankel should undertake to drive far into the Sabbath. He was even happier now that they had arrived early.

"Pessa," said Yankel, "this is Mr. Osuch, the countess' chauffeur. Give him a good supper so he can tell the countess what a good cook you are. And don't you dare light the Sabbath candles too early today, I must write a letter to the countess at once."

"Barely out of prison, and he's giving orders," said Pessa. But her small eyes looked at old Yankel happily. Pessa was already dressed for the Sabbath, in her long, black woolen dress with three rows of cloth buttons on her sunken breast, in a whale bone corset, a white silk shimmering kerchief on her head, a heavy bunch of keys dangling from the wide, black belt at her waist.

After the chauffeur Osuch had had a good meal and been dismissed by Yankel with a letter to the countess, the company all gathered in the dining room. The table was already covered for the first Sabbath meal. The damask white of the tablecloth mirrored the house's four large silver candlesticks flanked by Pessa's two small brass candlesticks. The wicks of the white candles turned impatiently toward the sanctity of the Sabbath waiting in the twilight corners. Solemnly Pessa entered and lit the candles. She spread her hands over the six flickering flames. She gathered the light into her cupped hands and dipped her eyes into them. Three times her hands gathered the light, three times her eyes dipped into the holy balsam of the light. Then she put her hands in front of her face, and her lips, that had meanwhile begun falteringly to repeat the blessing for the Sabbath candles, broke behind the light-filled hands with the zealous ardor of the whispered prayer.

When she withdrew her hands after the last words of the blessing had been said, the pious glow of the flickering candles lay on Pessa's face, and the glow remained on her face and spread and illumined it as though Pessa in lighting the Sabbath candles had also lighted up her face in honor of the sanctity of the Sabbath.

Entranced by this magical light, Uncle Stefan, Uncle Velvel, Yankel and Alfred all looked at the flickering flames and at Pessa. Forgotten were the cares and excitements of the weekday. It was Sabbath in the house of Mohilevski.

[250]

There were many worshippers in Grandfather's Room at the morning prayer. They had all heard that Velvel Dobropolier had an important guest from Vienna. They had also heard of Yankel's arrest. Everyone pushed forward to offer the guest the greeting of peace and to congratulate Yankel. It was a fine Sabbath for Velvel Dobropolier. But Alfred was secretly uneasy when Velvel, who read from the Torah in the absence of Aptowitzer, called Dr. Frankl to the Torah as the eighth reader, the *maftir*. Alfred was not sure whether Uncle Stefan knew the proper blessing and in his excitement remembered his own first Sabbath in Grandfather's Room, when Mechzio had almost miraculously rescued Alfred as he stood before the Torah in great distress. Now Mechzio was not there, and Uncle Stefan looked so tiny in the folds of the prayer shawl Yankel had loaned him, a mere novice. He was temporarily relieved when he heard Uncle Stefan's faultless, confident, indeed even melodic chanting of the first and then the second blessing. But Alfred was still anxious. For, as the eighth reader, the *maftir*, Dr. Frankl had also to read the selection from the prophets, a feat Alfred himself had managed only after half a year in Dobropolia. But with calm ease Uncle Stefan proved worthy of this honor as well. Relieved of his anxiety, Alfred watched with delight as even Judko Segall, the small Levite, congratulated the fine gentleman most cordially on his accomplishment: "Ah, that was good!" Dr. Frankl smiled softly and threw Alfred a triumphant look.

But when Judko Segall afterward stepped up to the reader's pulpit and began to sing the lively Sabbath melodies in his famous style, Alfred became aware suddenly of how much Lipusj was missing in Grandfather's Prayer Room during the Sabbath prayer. The liveliest melodies were death lamentations when Lipusj was not there to sing them; the innermost words of the prayer were empty husks, because the lad's high voice was no longer there to bear them to heaven; the worshippers' chorus was broken, because Mechzio's voice no longer plumbed the depths, the lad's voice no longer soared to the heights. Grandfather's Room was orphaned on the Sabbath, every worshiping voice a waif, unconsciously mourning the loss.

Velvel had invited a few guests for the third meal that Sabbath afternoon: the old distiller Gruenspan, Judko Segall, Shmiel Gruenfeld, and a few others, since Dr. Frankl was very much interested in the small community of Dobropolia. At the close of the Sabbath they were again five in the dining room, counting Pessa, and Velvel recited the last blessing of the day over a cup of brandy — the blessing that separates the Sabbath from the weekday. After he had completed the prayer and had drunk a little of the brandy, Velvel poured the rest on the bare table top, set the flame of a candle in the fluid which, in extinguishing it, was set on fire. He held his hands over the small blue flames, then drew his fingers across his eyes and his face and again dipped his finger in the flickering liquid and symbolically gathered the light into his pockets with his hands.

"What does this mean?" Dr. Frankl inquired when the liquid had stopped burning and Velvel had turned a loving, but no longer Sabbath face to his guest.

"We gather a little of the holiness of the Sabbath for the weekdays to last us until next Sabbath. — A good week to all!"

"Good week, Uncle Velvel!" said Alfred. "Shall we start reading at once?"

"Yes, certainly," said Velvel. "I can well believe that you are impatient. Fetch the manuscript. We'll begin at once. Pessa will be kind enough to prepare us a very late supper tonight. We'll stay up late again tonight, Pessa."

"A good week to all of us!" said Pessa. "I shall bring the candles at once."

Then, after Alfred had fetched the manuscript and Pessa the candles, they all took their places at the table, sitting as they had sat almost a week before: Dr. Frankl and Velvel on the sofa, Yankel and Alfred opposite them on chairs. This time Dr. Frankl and Alfred were the readers, for Velvel Dobropolier

[252]

sat so withdrawn from the very beginning that they did not dare to ask him to read. Alfred began where he had stopped almost a week before.

My friend now led me to the provost. We walked only a short distance through a dark passageway, for the provost's study was nearby. There was a connecting door between the two studies, a fact I noted only later, when Partyka took me back after supper from the dining room to his study, using the connecting door this time. The provost's study resembled my friend's, except that there were many more bookshelves along the walls, and the rugs were so thick and covered at certain places with such lovely peasant patterns that on stepping into the room one immediately became gayer and, though sitting down on a stool exactly as hard as the stool in Partyka's room, one felt oneself very comfortably settled without being able to say why.

The provost, round, white and ruddy, with a fresh face and a number of fat chins, and lively, black, sparkling eyes under a mane of snow-white thick hair, looked quite vigorous when he sat. But when he rose to greet me — Partyka stepped quickly to his side to help — and with the assistance of the younger cleric came toward me, he looked in his wide soutane like an old picture whose upper parts have been well preserved by accident, all its colors freshly smiling at us, unconscious of the damage which had been wreaked upon the eroded, creased and ugly lower parts. — The cleric received me in a very friendly fashion. He received me with the friendliness that only scholarly elderly gentlemen exhibit to young people — the friendliness typical of men of distinction, who, free of the yoke of professional interest, live their own contemplative life in deliberate isolation.

"My young brother," he was referring to Partyka, "my young brother," he said, after the salutation, "has told me a great deal about you." And casting a quick look at Partyka, who displayed a sign of unrest at these words, he interpolated with the hasty birdlike look of an old man: "One tells a great deal to one's companion when one lives so close — and so I had heard a great deal about you even before you notified us of your intended visit. I am very happy to receive the son of a pious man in my house, a man whose hospitality my young brother has praised so highly."

"You must understand," Partyka quickly inserted, seeing my confusion, "that hospitality, the relationship between piety and the forms of hospitality, is His Reverence's special interest. During my frequent visits to Dobropolia, which have remained my fondest memories, I was in the happy position of noting the venerable forms of a hospitality which is older —"

"The hospitality of the pious Jews," the provost interrupted, and continued in the same decisive tone. "For the rest, in his haste my young friend has not informed you quite correctly: My special field is not hospitality. The subject about which I have thought a little and have made some notes is the distinction between piety and devotion. As far as I know there is no university where a course is given in this subject. Do you know of any?"

"I am unfortunately not informed on that subject," I said. That, I still remember clearly now, was the first complete sentence that I could compose.

"I believe that I have investigated carefully, by human standards: there are no such courses. If not the future theologians, the philosophers at any rate ought to have thought about it. One says 'a devout Christian' or 'a pious Christian' — whichever word occurs first, devout or pious, as though they both signified the one and the same thing. But devotion and piety are quite different matters."

My friend Partyka sat looking relieved and winked at me, as though to say, "Now the old man is on his hobby-horse, the worst is over."

"Often a man is devout without being pious, which is generally the case with most men. And a man can be pious without

[254]

being devout. That is a rarer case, but not too rare. Devotion is a condition of the soul or the spirit, whichever you prefer. Devotion is a matter of organic constitution. But piety, indeed, what is piety? Piety is service. The service of God in the broadest sense of the word. But one does not always attain to a knowledge of this distinction, as you may perceive, from the study of theology. In my case, at least, it was not so. I arrived at this distinction, which I have elaborated in a small work, plainly and clearly, if I may say so, through a completely profane chance event. And it has not become a matter for theology. My work will not be published in the near future. It might perhaps create some misunderstanding in high places. His Eminence has shown me too much patience, too much grace, for me to take it upon myself to cause His Eminence anguish again through something I have written. No, I would not even think of publishing this work. And that is perhaps the reason, you see, why I speak about it so frequently. But in the end it is all the same what theme an old man takes to chatter about — he will chatter in any case."

"Your Reverence," I said with real enthusiasm, "Your Reverence is not wasting his teaching: I am very much interested in this distinction."

Holding his head bent to the side, a smile on his face, which appeared so white as if it had been powdered, His Reverence was silent for a long time, appearing to reflect on his own words. Then, as though he had come to a decision, he resumed his discourse:

"My researches may not interest you very much, but the impulse that led me to my work will certainly interest you in particular. Several years ago I read in a Russian newspaper — a purely literary newspaper — an account of a talk involving Leo Tolstoi, a conversation at table as related by an author whose name I now no longer remember."

As though the name of the great author were the catchword, Partyka rose, nodded encouragingly to me behind His Reverence's back, then, while the provost continued without interruption, busied himself at a glass closet, fetched spirits and glasses, had hot, fragrant cakes on a tray handed him from the kitchen through a hole in the wall covered by a wooden slab, sat down with us again, filled the glasses, and served us, as though he were a host who did not wish to forget his guests' physical welfare during an intellectual discussion.

"An author had sent a newly published book to Yasnaya Polyana which compared the master and Dostoievsky to Nietzsche. It was a piece of hack-writing that aroused both controversy and anger among all those who shared the table talk. There was apparently someone in the learned company, one of those flattering Tolstoians who were always saying what they thought was the sage's opinion, without having grasped the true Christian sense of his teaching. Well, this individual was of the opinion that the author of that work must be a Jew. 'Hardly,' said Tolstoi, reflectively. 'No, he does not seem to be a Jew. There are no unbelieving Jews. You can't name one . . . No.' It was a learned company at table, men like Anton Chekhov and Maxim Gorki sitting with the master, and a few important Russian scholars. But no one opened his mouth. None of them could name an unbelieving Jew. If I had been there, I could have named a dozen — that was my first thought. But the more I reflected upon the master's comment, the fewer names occurred to me. Soon I was able to name none. I saw light. All at once I saw the new light, emanating from the word "faith" as Tolstoi uttered it. All at once I understood —"

The glass pane in the hole in the wall was removed with a disturbing noise, a broad face aglow with all the warmth of the kitchen hearth filled the gap and a motherly voice announced that the evening meal was ready. The old gentleman at once broke off his discourse and ordered the food to be served, his eyes hurrying to the good cooking in the dining room even before my friend Partyka quickly stepped forward to help His Reverence stand up. He did this so unobtrusively that the old gentleman hardly noticed, and I marveled at my friend's tenderness as with feminine suppleness he tended to the old man's need. It was a service which youth can display to age only by dint of a great love that does not make the burden of age too pointed through all-too-patent sedulousness, and thus by the display of youth augmenting the burden of age.

"But how have I gotten on my hobby-horse so soon?" asked the provost, smiling, as he took our arms, and once on his feet, accompanied us into the dining room with an astoundingly firm step.

"We were speaking of hospitality," Partyka reminded him.

"Yes, yes, hospitality," repeated His Reverence, "hospitality," while his eyes measured the length and breadth of the covered table from a distance as he turned his snow-white head.

"Hospitality is a part of service," he added, having taken his seat at the narrow side of the table, in a voice already refreshed as though having tasted the dishes before they had been placed on the table. "Hospitality is a part of service. In the good age it was a very important part of service. The good age was the good rural age of humanity. The rural age was the age of the founders of religion. All religions arose in the rural age. The sciences, the arts and philosophy thrive in the cities. But no religion will ever arise in the city."

"Yes," I said, struck by this insight. "Yes, that is so. There is a rural atmosphere in all the testaments of all the religious creators. There is a rural atmosphere throughout the holy testaments."

"You have expressed it well. There is a rural atmosphere in all the holy testaments. Very well put, my son. You are once more heartily welcome."

The old gentleman had been very friendly to me in his study. A friendly smile had shone on his white face, like light on porcelain, yet I had sensed that he was only paying his outward respects to me, while inwardly he was detached from my presence.

How I bloomed with pride at his praise and a tremor of joy ran over my face at the repetition of his cordial welcome. My friend Partyka, who sat facing me at the left of His Reverence, also appeared proud of me. His eyes favored me with an open, warm glance, again the honest, bright eyes of the peasant youth, eyes I had so loved in my friend, which I had painfully missed ever since my arrival in H. He was encouraging me as he had once upon a time in the classroom, when I engaged his personal enemy, our Latin professor, a conceited man, who knew everything except Latin, in a dangerous debate, to the delight of the whole class. I was almost happy for a moment. But my joy did not last long, for the soup was immediately brought forward and my triumph was, so to speak, drowned in soup.

There entered — I remember it as though I was at the provost's table yesterday — there entered a gigantic village belle with flat face, small Mongolian eyes and flashing teeth, the maid, who had waited at the service window — there was one such in this room too, the provost apparently laying great stress on many and direct connections with the kitchen. She had waited in front of the service window till we had taken our seats at the table and the master gave her a sign to bring the food in. Now she set a large, steaming soup tureen on the table. His Reverence seized the soup tureen carefully, first pushed it slowly still nearer to his place, then placed his thin, trembling hands around the round-bellied pot, which rested in a tender embrace between his hands and black-sleeved wrists, and suddenly assumed the dignity of a supremely precious object. His eyes flashed at Partyka and at myself with a bright demand — as though inquiring: Well, did I do it right? — and he raised the steaming tureen ... Then I saw my friend Partyka vigorously shake his head, reddening to the roots of his hair. He shook his head again vigorously, as though he wished to beg His Reverence, indeed to implore him, to leave off playing with the soup tureen. At that the provost set aside the tureen and, his arms and hands repeating the game with the soup bowl, he said in a soft voice to me alone, as though Partyka were not there at all:

"Since we were talking about hospitality before: My young brother has often told me of your father's great hospitality.

One tells one another a great deal, when one lives alone together the way we two live here. In the very style and manner in which your father hands his guests bowls of soup, in this very gesture there is so much seriousness and dignity — all your father's piety and the whole essence of hospitality are perfectly united in this one gesture. Thus I have often heard my young brother relate . . . . Your friend has had some fine experiences in your father's house. He has never forgotten them. As a boy he saw hospitality embodied in your father, and through him I also have learned to see it with a child's eyes. Now your friend is no longer a boy, but he has remained a good son, and he visits his father every year. And every year, whenever he goes on leave, I ask him to visit Dobropolia and pay his respects to the venerable Judah Mohilevski and observe with the eyes of an adult the style and manner in which this great host hands his guests their bowls of soup. I know very well that such a thing is not learnt from externals. I know well I am slight in hospitality compared to your father. But I have learned about him through your friend, and your friend has encouraged me time and again saying, 'Today you are holding the bowl in your hands almost like old Mohilevski.' Now, my son, you be the judge. As the son of your father, you be the judge."

His Reverence had been speaking softly to me. But at the last sentence his voice rose and, as he called upon me to be the judge, he held my eyes in his, which now pierced me like two black flashes of lightning, and, putting out his hands like a magician before performing a trick, he grasped the soup bowl and put it with a solemn motion in my hands, which, enchanted as my eyes, obeyed him involuntarily . . .

My father's hands were different from His Reverence's. My father's hands were not white. My father was a countryman. His hands were bony, brown and powerfully calm. But Partyka had apparently observed closely and reported fully . . . The black sleeves of the soutane framed the white porcelain like the sleeves of my father's black caftan. I still wonder today where I found the strength to prevent the bowl from falling out of my hands. I had traveled for a day and a night, the autumnal sadness of the landscape resembling my home had made me weak. I had not eaten on the way; seeing Partyka again had stirred me to the depths; the town, the inn, the market place, Red Goddl had terrified me . . . Now this certainly well-intended and well-considered reminder struck me like a blow on the head. With lowered head I sat before my bowl from which, meanwhile, I had unconsciously drawn a few spoonsful of noodle soup. My cheeks flushed and shuddered. The spicy aroma of the broth conjured up for a moment all the family warmth in my father's house, the family security, the sweet holiness of the holiday evenings in Dobropolia . . . My shoulders and chest were convulsed by a cramp, the spoon fell out of my hand. I burst into tears, I sobbed . . .

"Cry, my son. Don't be ashamed. It is only when we cry that we become like children. It is only when we cry like children that we know what we owe our father," I heard His Reverence consoling me and I felt his hand touching my shoulder. It was an ineffably delicate, ineffably pleasant touch. Completely stupified by his touch, I stammered a really childish apology:

"In our home in Dobropolia we only have noodle soup at the first Sabbath meal, on Friday evening."

xiv

The kindly old man had apparently proposed to influence me without direct persuasion. And he might perhaps — I now see this as a possibility — he might perhaps have succeeded. His respect, indeed, reverence, for my father, whom he knew only from my friend's accounts, powerfully impressed me. And his imitation of the gesture of the hospitable man, for which, as a child, I had loved my father, a gesture executed with almost magical identification, was like a blow on the chest of the bad son, who by that time already had so much to apologize for to his father. I do not wish to exaggerate this shock — the hot

[260]

noodle soup must have played no small part in it — but the youthful rebellion against strict patriarchal fanaticism which had driven me to the West and sustained me for a few years in a brighter and happier world, the youthful insurrection against a tyrannical father who never wished to understand his son was given a slap in the face. And for the duration of the evening there was an astounding calm; calm and amazement at my unconsidered course during the last few years of my life. What, I asked myself, bent over a bowl full of noodle soup which I swallowed with tears — what if the tyrannical villager, whom so highly placed a man as the provost respected — what if my father was not the fanatical satrap of my youth, but the dignified and pious man whose face could light up so mildly with all the glow of all the candles of all our holidays: the kindly father of childhood and boyhood, the provider and host whose house stood open on all four sides to the poor traveler, like the tent of our forefather, Abraham — my father? . . .

But that which the Christian priest almost mended was immediately afterward ruined again by the Jews of this miserable town, ruined by Goddl the *Gabbe* with a blow. To be exact, with many blows. For this creature of fanaticism actually dared to raise his stick against me . . . And he did so the morning after a night filled to overflowing for me with terror, causing me such confusion that I — I! — received a hail of blows from the messenger of a small-town miracle-working rabbi, without smashing the bones of both of them, the servant and master. It was a stick that weakened me. Not the stick with which Goddl the *Gabbe* beat me. But another stick — the stick of a miracle-working rabbi, a magical stick, the rabbi's stick and my father's stick in one . . . .

xv

Two golden autumn days followed that first evening, mild and unearthly clear days such as are to be experienced only in this country, where the sun often sheds the consolation of her

[261]

last warmth with exaggerated mildness before delivering up creation to the violence of a harsh winter. For years I had longed for the autumn days of my homeland; now I wandered about the landscape like a dreamer. During those two days I lost sight of the purpose of my journey to H. Happily I spent the days in the town forest as though I could there find again all the lost gold of the autumns I had missed. As in the imaginative life of my boyhood, lost in the landscape I imbued myself with all the dazzling colors of the fading and expiring year. All the joy of the years when one is growing, when one has the imaginative power to wither with every withering leaf, to fall with every falling leaf, to shudder at the cold with every unleaved tree — all the intense grief of the autumn tide of my childhood returned. As in the forest of Dobropolia, I bent to the fallen foliage and lifted the leaves marked the loveliest by death. There were leaves still half-green with yellow spots, yellow leaves with brown spots, brown leaves with red stains, red leaves with black stains. And the stains and the spots were the variegated leprosy which was their ruin. There were leaves which had turned all these colors and already were dung heaps, black as the earth on the floor of the forest. The floor of the forest itself sparkled with color, no longer really a floor of the forest, but a splendid deathbed decorated yellow-brown-red, bedded ankle-high with millions of leaf corpses. Yet the trees were so rich with life that, despite the millions of sacrifices they had offered to the floor of the forest, they did not stand completely naked. There were old beeches which still held fast with their last strength to their flashing copper shields of leaves. There were young beeches to whose branches green leaves still clung. But when one looked more closely, one saw that these green leaves were also marked for death. Their flesh was still green, but their veins were already gleaming with dark violet rot. A delicate birch with lemon-yellow leaves trembled at the verge of the forest, weak and pale as a candle of death under a blue sky. From the great sun which once was the spring of vitality, the forest, dedicated to death, now could receive only light — no,

[262]

only illumination and a bit of faint warmth for its decomposition. Nevertheless, so monstrous a life burned in this brown, yellow, red, purple, black dying of the forest of foliage that the solitary fir-trees and spruces stood there in their dress of pines, untouched by the breath of death, like green-varnished dummies, giving in the midst of the rustling and intoxicated death of the foliage the impression of lifelessness.

For two days I wandered under the cobalt-blue sky, two mornings and two afternoons, which, interrupted by the meals at the provost's hospitable table, seemed as long and full as two years and as short as two happy minutes. But on the evening of the second day, the sky clouded over, cold winter winds suddenly burst into the forest, the pure sky was overcast in the space of a moment by stormy fragments of clouds, behind which the golden sun blanched and sank and drowned like a moon. Driven away by the sharp November wind, I said farewell at the window of my room to the forest that had given back to me the autumnal landscape of my youth for two unforgettable days, the landscape of my homeland, with all the colors, all the fragrance, all the joy, all the rapture and all the abandon of childhood. With pain I watched for a while longer as the winds stormed the forest, disturbing the calm of the forest which had so beautifully bedded itself for death — as they stirred it up, jolted it, noisily threw down the last adornment of the trees — as they forced down the crown of the trees, and grubbed up the forest floor. Like flocks of birds, the fallen and freshly detached leaves flew in all directions; they fluttered and quivered, they rose and sank over the town for an astoundingly long time, astoundingly far, and their sick flight carried them beyond the town.

I had collected a bouquet of purple beech leaves and taken it back home; my coat, my clothing, my hands, the whole hotel room smelled of the fragrance of the forest. An odor that was a mixture of withered grass, moldering leaves and expiring roots filled the room. It smelled of the forest: of the moss of the summer and of damp mushrooms which had long departed thence. And it smelled of fresh cool snow, which the storm clouds were bringing. As though these odors had not only been imprisoned in my clothing and penetrated my mind, but had also filled my whole soul. Weary and refreshed, intoxicated and clearsighted at the same time, I walked around the table in my room, where the purple bouquet shone in a pitcher of water, as though the landscape of my homeland, the mistress of my youth, had entered my heart with the autumn fragrance of this forest.

And I heard myself sigh: How beautiful the forest of Dobropolia is on autumn days like these . . . Who said that? The self who had journeyed to the town of H, to his friend Partyka? Or that other self, who had settled himself in my heart and was already preparing to set forth on the journey to Dobropolia? . . .

Then I heard someone breathing behind the door of my room, and immediately afterwards a knocking at the door. A loud and angry knocking, obviously repeated in impatience. Then while I tried, still bemused, to guess who the impatient visitor might be, Goddl the *Gabbe* stepped in. He closed the door behind him and remained standing before it.

"What do you want?" I cried, surprised at this intrusion.

"Joseph ben Judah of Dobropolia —" Goddl began in a solemn singing intonation, as though he were not speaking to me, but rather calling me up to the Torah reading.

"That is not my name," I said.

"Joseph ben Judah Mohilevski," he began again, as though he were not calling on me, but someone concealed behind me.

"I am not the one you want," I interposed quickly.

"Joseph ben Judah!" he repeated, now in a warning voice. "Joseph ben Judah! That is what our rabbi calls you. So that is your name. And the rabbi calls you to come to him."

"I don't know him," said I and wondered whether this pretext did not already betray a weakness.

"Our rabbi knows *you*! Our rabbi commands you to come at once."

"I *will not* come!" I cried in a loud voice. Nevertheless

my voice rang weary, as though I was too weak to prevail even over the brush of hair on this messenger's face.

"He whom the rabbi calls comes. You, too, Joseph ben Judah — you, too, will come."

"It is not me the rabbi is calling. He is calling someone else."

"The rabbi knows full well that you are about to become another. The rabbi demands that you return. It is time, Joseph ben Judah. There is still time to return. Your first step is to come to the rabbi."

"But what if I will not go!" I shouted.

"If you will not go, the *Zaddik* will conjure you to him," said Goddl in his calm voice, although as he spoke he had raised his stick.

It was not the same thick knotty stick on which he had leaned in the hall of the inn on the evening of my arrival. It was an old, light stick with a soft, broad, bent crook, which, smoothed down by the palms of many who had borne it, gleamed pale and waxen like the forehead of an old Talmudist. The *Gabbe* had indeed raised the stick at me, but not with a threatening gesture. He had not grasped the stick by the crook but somewhere in the middle, and he held it high with two hands, not one. The thick fingers of his two bearlike paws embraced the slender body of the stick as though it were a holy relic. From the first moment of his entrance into the room, Goddl's solemn bearing had surprised me: a messenger with a stick — thus he appeared to me. And thus I now saw him. I had also noticed the old stick in his hand and had wondered at once what the stick reminded me of . . . During the exchange this question had vanished; but now, at the sight of the raised stick, it reappeared.

"The rabbi has not the power to conjure me," I said this sentence in my defense, to face the lifted stick, and at once repeated it again.

"True, our rabbi is still young in years," began Goddl with a smile of regret that extended over the copper-red brush of his beard with a gleam of melancholy. "But however young he may be, he is the great-great-grandson of the great *Zaddik* Rabbi Shmelke of Szarygrod, blessed be his name. As a sign of which, behold this stick; it is the stick of the holy Rabbi Shmelke, blessed be his name. You know what that means —." As he spoke, Goddl had come nearer and nearer and lifted the stick of the great *Zaddik* higher and higher.

"I know, I know," I said quickly, at which Goddl let his arms and his stick sink a little. The handle of the stick was now suspended at about the height of my chest. I perceived that Rabbi Shmelke's stick was of the same wood, and formed and curved exactly like the stick of my great-grand-uncle Rabbi Abba. My father had taken that stick from the house of mourning after the death of Rabbi Abba and preserved it in his room as a precious heritage. Rabbi Shmelke's stick looked like a twin of that of my great-uncle. But it was the same stick with which my father had beat me when he learned of my love affair with the peasant girl whom I had refused to give up. Though years had passed since that event, I had not forgotten the final reason for my flight from my father's house. I could not forgive my father his chastisement, nor my father me for having brought him to misuse Rabbi Abba's stick in such fashion . . . This was not a happy association for Rabbi Shmelke's stick.

"How old is your little rebbe?" I questioned Goddl.

"Our rabbi is still very young in years . . ." murmured Goddl, disconcerted by my tone, as well as the slighting designation "little rebbe," and fell back two or three steps.

"Well? How old?" I asked. "How old is the little rebbe?"

"Our rabbi is nineteen years old," said Goddl and I heard the anger at the insult choking his voice. "Our rabbi is only nineteen years old," he panted, "but if you say 'little rebbe' again —"

"So? He is nineteen, this miracle-worker of H? And a brat like that is going to conjure me?!"

A wave of blood rushed across Goddl's flat, bony face, turning his forehead and cheeks as copper-red as his beard. The wave

[266]

of blood visibly oozed into his beard and earlocks, for the paler his face grew, the bloodier his beard flamed. The veins in his bull neck swelled, and with a gurgling sound from his chest, he shot forward two or three steps toward me. I thought at once that Goddl the *Gabbe* would really dare to lay his hands on me. There was no doubt that he could overpower me. But despite all the changes that had passed over me — a Dobropolier seldom avoids a brawl, and along with the gold of my youth the forest of H had apparently brought back to me during those two fine days its combativeness as well.

But it did not come to that. About to grab me with one of his paws, the *Gabbe* reconsidered and let me go. For a moment, still panting and with knit eyebrows, he appeared to be consider-ing whether he ought not to leave. But at once he pulled himself together with imposing self-control; I was impressed no little by how quickly and completely a porter about to commit the most extreme act of violence was transformed back again into the dignified messenger of a miracle-working rabbi. He now set the stick — whose handle he had been pressing against his chest, as though to protect the relic from desecration by hiding it in the padding of his caftan — he now set the stick at a distance, and with outstretched arms, both hands leaning lightly on the crook, resumed the conversation. But, as though drowned in the flood of his anger, his voice completely deserted him at first. For a while his heavy lips moved tonelessly and dumb, as though conjuring the lost voice to appear again for the service of the mes-sage. Then his voice returned dark and deep, but calm and mild:

"This morning after the morning prayer, the rabbi said to me: 'A stranger has arrived in Nuchim Shapira's inn. This stranger is a Jew.'

" 'Rabbi,' I said, 'true, a few days ago a stranger did arrive in Shapira's inn, but this stranger is no Jew. No other guest has arrived in our town.'

" 'The stranger who is staying at Shapira's is a Jew,' said the rabbi. 'His name is Joseph. He is the son of Judah Mohilevski of Dobropolia.'

"'Rabbi,' I said, 'I have seen this stranger. That is not his name. He has a Christian name. I have seen this stranger. There is not a single Jewish feature in his face.'

"'A face can be deceiving, Goddl,' said the rabbi. 'The stranger is an educated man, a doctor. He comes from far off and is thinking, God forbid, of turning from the true way. You will go to this stranger at once, Goddl, and you will say to him: "The rabbi has known for a long time what you have been contemplating, Joseph ben Judah. The rabbi is fasting and praying to break your evil urge. Young in years and accomplishments is the rabbi, and his power over souls is as slight as his merit. But the rabbi wishes to know what it is that speaks evil to your mind, Joseph ben Judah, evil against us and our faith?"'

"'Rabbi,' I said, 'this stranger, this doctor, has already adopted a Christian name, he takes his meals with the pastor, may the Almighty preserve all Jewish children from doing so!' Thus I spoke. 'Rabbi, if a Jew has come that far, will he heed us?'

"Then the rabbi went into the corner of his room where the stick of his great-great-grandfather, Rabbi Shmelke, blessed be his name, stands against the eastern wall, and the rabbi took the stick and handed it to me with the words: 'Go to the confused one and say to him that I command him to come here to me. My merits are as slight as my power. But I have fasted and prayed that the merits of my father, Rabbi Salmen, and the merits of my grandfather, Rabbi Moshe, and the merits of my great-great-grandfather, Rabbi Shmelke, will stand me in good stead — the merits of the great *Zaddik*, Rabbi Shmelke, who was a grandson of a disciple of a disciple of the Baal Shem Tov, the names of the saints be a blessing for us all. Say that to him! And he will come.'

"So I have the stick, and I bring the message."

"But your rabbi did not say that he would compel me!"

"I am a bad messenger. It pleased the Master of the Universe to punish my sinful heart with wrath. I was a bad messenger. But do not blame our rabbi for his bad messenger."

[268]

With bent forehead, his eyes downcast, the giant stood before me, and the humility of his plea made the rabid porter almost handsome.

"For two days the rabbi has not partaken of food. His disciples pray day and night, and fast with fervor. There are delicate Jewish children among them, and they are wearying their souls to break the urge to evil, and to turn away the shame from our city, from your family, from all of Israel. You will not succeed, doctor! You will pay heed. The stick of Rabbi Shmelke!"

I did not think much of Rabbi Shmelke's stick, as you may well imagine, my dear son. But though I had already lived a decade among Viennese Jews, who looked down from the shaky towers of their western culture with disgust on Polish Jewry and with the wealth of their refined phantasies cover every caftan with Galician lice — nevertheless, the two days I had spent in H with the landscape of my childhood had also freshened my memory of the piety of that childhood, of the sweet meditative morning hours in the house of prayer of Rabbi Simon, the Rav of T, under whose kindly supervision I, as a secondary-school student, worshiped daily early every morning year after year in the company of the most pious children of the city . . . .

We students would arrive in the house of prayer at seven o'clock and would have only a half hour for the long morning service. We were among those not-too-beloved worshippers whom the pious with denigrating irony called *Bne Rano. Bne* means "children" in Hebrew; *rano* means "early" in Polish. In this very coupling of the Holy Tongue with a secular one there lay a lively, benevolent, but still a very clear setting of such worshipers at a distance. They were considered to be fulfilling their duty, true, but with a silly exaggeration of the importance of secular businesses, by performing their morning service at a very early hour, worshiping quickly in order to plunge immediately into their workaday affairs. They consisted mainly of poor people who came early to the house of prayer, handicraftsmen, small shopkeepers — even this seven o'clock quorum was not the earliest. Many people worshiped even earlier, and there were houses of prayer for the small people where the worshiping began at the break of day. But in the *rav's* house of prayer the élite of the pious and well-to-do assembled who could afford to make their morning prayer more important than their businesses. There were also among them some who had been blessed so meagerly with earthly goods that they had no businesses to be late for. True, this élite came to the house of prayer early, but before addressing themselves to the collective prayer each addressed himself to his own individual service, which really had a secret routine, but which daily greatly impressed us children as a voluntary regimen of psalms, and one of vast extent. In this house of prayer we, the secondary-school students, were the *Bne Rano*. But the others were glad to see us. I suspect that one or another of the élite came to the house of prayer so early on especially cold winter mornings for our sakes, in order to complete the quorum of ten, if it were necessary.

A young man who had no beard, but to make up for that had a deep manly bass, and whom we very much loved, favored us with his particular affection. It was he, Reb Hershel, who always saw to it that the quorum of ten was quickly assembled, and that we came to school on time. If the quorum was not yet assembled when winter frosts were fierce, Reb Hershel, who loved children, would run out to the street and come rushing back with some one going to market or with a water-carrier, and the service would begin. Rabbi Hershel himself was our cantor; his fine voice filled the house of prayer with soft warmth, the blue ice-ferns on the window panes began to dew with the breath of his singing. The winter morning, still blue with night and pale with snow, opened its icy blue eyes, believing it to be day, and the fervor of the young cantor miraculously removed all anxiety about the coming day from our small hearts — that great anxiety that lurks in the hearts of small Jewish children who attend schools where many of them are forced not only to answer the teachers but to disarm them as well . . . .

On the Sabbath and on holidays, when young Rabbi Hershel

sang even more beautifully than on weekdays, we remained so long that we had to run to school. But in the corridor of the house the venerable old wife of the *rav* would block our path. Already dressed in her Sabbath silks early in the morning, she would wait for us with Sabbath cakes that the cook Jitte had arranged in a basket. And as she stuffed our pockets with Sabbath cakes while we stood impatiently by, she whispered the words of farewell, of both solicitude and blessing: "Go in good health. With God's permission, may you remain good Jewish children. Go in good health . . . ."

No, it was certainly not the magical power of Rabbi Shmelke's stick. It was the voice, the voice of young Rabbi Hershel who loved children which had almost persuaded me . . . The rabbi of H, who was still so young in years — perhaps he looked like our pious Rabbi Hershel who loved children — the rabbi was praying for me. Perhaps he prayed with such fervor as Rabbi Hershel? And he was fasting for me. And his disciples were fasting, while I ate at the provost's table.

I turned my back on the red-headed *gabbe*, that he might not notice my mood, and I said, "I am here visiting a friend; if I should need advice, I shall be glad to come to the rabbi. Deliver that message to the rabbi."

Behind my back I perceived from Goddl's hard breathing what relief this evasive answer afforded. He was silent for a time, as though thinking over what else the rabbi had in mind, then he said: "I shall come again tomorrow. If you are still not ready tomorrow, I shall come again and call you for a third time. And the third time, with God's help, you will obey the rabbi."

With that he left.

xvi

It was on this evening that I had the feeling, as I sat to the right of the provost at the table, of again being free and able to hear references to apostasy and religious conversion without a sense of oppression. For, since my childish conduct on the first

[271]

night, the old gentleman had contented himself with casual references, which for the most part had very slight and remote bearing on my case. On this evening I became aware for the first time that even the slightest reference to my situation apparently troubled my friend Partyka very deeply, for he did not even try to suppress his anger. He was a master at lending his anger the appearance of sorrow, with a taut expression. But the corner of his eyes flashed now and again an icy blue. I was forced to marvel at Partyka's impudent impatience· and asked myself whether, involved in my own troubles, I may not have failed to note other changes in my friend's mood.

But this time the provost gave Partyka very little cause for vexation at table. The old gentleman had read a book that afternoon, whose author, according to the provost, a master of exegesis, had made very bold statements about the question: Why had the followers of the Greek-Catholic teachings — such as the evangelists — always completely differentiated between the Mary who poured oil on Jesus' feet and the other Mary to whom the Lord cried: *Noli me tangere* — while in the very earliest traditions of the Western Church, Mary, the sister of Martha, and Mary the sinner had merged into one person. Taking the pleasure in another's talent which only one who is himself a master can do, the old gentleman described the author, whose genius and knowledge he could not praise highly enough, although he himself developed a radically different theory for us. But my friend Partyka also amazed me by expressing brilliant opinions I would never have believed him capable of producing. For the first time I could not free myself of the suspicion that Partyka was deceiving not only me but His Reverence as well by pretending to be merely a young priest who would be content with his modest post in H under every circumstance. There was as little doubt that he had developed his knowledge and acuteness to no small extent in the provost's school, as there was of the excellence of that school. True, Partyka wore the demeanor of a student during the erudite discourse, but he was a student only in the presence of his master. And although the material was strange to me, I understood enough to comprehend that Partyka's views remained basically those of the Greek-Catholic Church.

The old gentleman spoke, after his fashion, without sharpness, as though his real thoughts were somewhere on the way in a brighter landscape, from whose light now and then a small beam was detached and reflected in the flow of his words. Partyka, on the other hand, debated like a young student, who in his fiery zeal uncritically jumps from one field to another, if necessary, to find a sound argument. I was unable the very next day to say by what leaps the conclusions of Partyka brought the conversation from the cultic distinctions to the distinctions between the Western and the Greek rituals. I can only remember now that by the time we were at the dessert the conversation has passed to the subject of proselytes, to conclude with numerous anecdotes about conversions and converts.

But at the conclusion of the evening, when the old gentleman had already given us permission to leave and was about to retire, he told the following story:

"The sage of Yasnaya Polyana had a Jewish friend who was a frequent visitor. As was his custom, among other things the author spoke to his Jewish guest about the evangelists, naturally without the intention of converting his guest. One day he received a letter from Petersburg in which his Jewish friend informed him that he had accepted Christianity. The author was very much taken aback by this news. With shaking hands he handed this letter to his secretary: 'See, I may have burdened myself with a deadly sin.' And he burst into tears."

And, with the guiltless face of a child who has recited his evening prayer correctly, His Reverence bade us goodnight and disappeared behind the door of his bedroom.

"You see," said Partyka, when we were in his room afterward, and had settled down to our evening instruction in the catechism, "you see how deceitful he can be."

"Why deceitful?"

"You don't know him. You're far from knowing him. He

built up the whole of today's table talk to deal us out this literary anecdote at the end. You still don't know him."

I could hardly tell which feature exactly in my friend's face made me uneasy as I looked at him, amazed at his hard words. I carry so many pictures of Partyka's face, all representative, that it would not be possible for me to describe how the Partyka looked who spoke thus about a remarkable man. Perhaps, I thought to myself on that evening: I know the old man very well, but you, my friend, I don't recognize you any longer, when I hear you speak thus. But all I said was, "Let well enough alone! This man is not deceitful. And the anecdote — well, it makes me think."

"The poison's already beginning to work!" cried Partyka, in anger.

"What poison?"

"He is no longer a servant of the Church. Years ago he played a similar trick."

"What trick?"

"I'll only tell it to you when you're out of danger."

"I don't feel that I'm in danger at all."

"But you are speaking differently today from yesterday, and completely differently from the first day. He promised me he would not influence you. Yet every day he injects a drop of poison."

"But, Partyka! The nonsense doesn't become more sensible the more you repeat it. He has his own views."

"He is a Tolstoian, that's becoming slowly clear to me. And a Russophile, too. If you wished to become a Greek-Orthodox, he would say nothing against it."

"But, Partyka," I remonstrated. "That Petersburg Jew turned Greek-Orthodox."

Partyka thought, smiled and sat down, apparently calmed. We sat each in a corner of the sofa, an ashtray between us, smoking, each busy with his thoughts. When our hands met once over the ashtray, Partyka rapped my hand with his finger a couple of times and said, again friendly and confiding:

[274]

"Nevertheless, Osyp! Nevertheless, I am not wrong, you were completely different at the table today than usually. Today you were sitting on his side, not on mine."

"I am not aware of that, but it may have been so. But His Reverence is not responsible for that at all."

"Nor *I*?"

"No. There's an entirely different reason."

"You must tell me about it."

"I had a visitor today."

"One of your people?" cried Partyka and sprang from his seat.

"Oh no, Partyka! Goddl the *Gabbe* visited me today."

"Oh, the redhead! Well, well. And?"

"The rabbi is calling me."

"And you will go?"

"Perhaps. I still have time to think it over."

"Well. Time to think it over?" Partyka reflected. He walked back and forth in the room, taking long steps, and repeated a couple of times: "Well, well. Time to think it over."

"Today was my first good day here, so I was a bit soft with Goddl, although at first he didn't treat me so softly."

"Yes, yes. The Jews here are impudent. And do you know who is responsible for that? His Reverence!"

The apostate's humiliation overcame me for the first time as I heard Partyka speaking about Jews as though they were enemies in my presence. He had never done that before.

"You wonder, naturally. Yet it's true. I'll tell you in due time the trick he played, even before my time. Since then the Jews have become even more impudent. But this once they aren't going to carry the day. — Excuse me, I'll be back soon."

"You're not going to do anything against the poor Jews, are you?!" I cried after him.

"Oh no!" he cried back, already outside. "I shall only give my sexton — *our* Goddl, you know — a commission. This has nothing to do with you."

I had no grounds to suspect my friend of a lie or a falsehood.

It did not appear so singular that he had a commission for the sexton, though it was late in the evening. The sexton lived in the cloister, Partyka had no long trip before him, he was not inclined by nature to be a comfort-loving pastor. Nevertheless, my friend lied this time.

But that night I thought no further about it. Left alone, I stretched out comfortably on the sofa and in the tired frame of mind which usually follows an excellent meal that has satisfied a keen hunger, I breathed in the sounds of the November night with my drowsy senses. Behind the windows was wind and silence, rustling and silence, whispering, and silence.

xvii

As though the very silence had transported him into the room, Goddl the *Gabbe* suddenly stood before me. Gigantic, Reb Shmelke's stick in his lifted right hand, his left hand sported a bunch of beautiful beech leaves which were attached to the girdle of his caftan.

"Come," he said soundlessly. I read the words on his lips.

"Where?" I asked foolishly, like a student repeating a question in an examination to gain time.

"The rabbi is calling," said Goddl.

"But you were not to call me the second time till tomorrow!"

Then Goddl stretched out the stick and touched my chest with the crook. I felt my heart and my chest expanding, and, inhaling one long draft, as though with my chest the deep draft had lifted my couch up high, I slid off the sofa and stood, wavering, in front of Goddl.

"Come," he nodded to me with a slow turn of his head.

"But I have won time to think," I cried, trying to escape.

"When the rabbi calls, there is no time to think, you fool," I heard Partyka's voice, and he himself stepped forward right behind Goddl and nodded at me, like the *Gabbe*.

"Are you coming along?" I asked, overjoyed at his appearance.

[276]

"Surely," said Partyka. "I have been called, too. Come!"

Goddl was already standing at the door. Without troubling to use his hand, he unlatched it with a press of his elbow. We followed and stepped behind him into the night.

There was a fine moonlight. The stars hung in the deep, dark sky, remarkably pure, plastic and angular, like golden Hebrew letters on black parchment. See, I can read the stars like a book! — I wanted to tell Partyka, but my enthusiasm over being able to read the stars subdued my voice. The air was as light and silent as though we were walking behind Goddl in a closed room whose ceiling was painted to resemble a starry sky. The moon, however, was not to be seen. The sharp sound our feet made in the foliage forced us to keep in step and, although Partyka and I walked very carefully, I had the feeling that we were murderously pursuing the great night silence which fled and ran before the harshness of our clattering footsteps, trying to save itself in the forest. Striding ahead of us, Goddl used the stick as a support, like an ordinary stick — Reb Shmelke's stick! . . . . I was ready to cry with shame when I saw it. Why did he do it? The misused stick nevertheless kept its unique dignity. It slipped over the strewn foliage, vertically suspended, as though pulled through rapid waters against the stream. The stream of leaves hissed at the touch of the stick's steel point. Zrrr, buzzed the leaves. Topp — the point of the stick tapped on the leafy bed of the path. Zrrr — Topp — Zrrr — Topp — : it was as though the stick was measuring and counting our steps.

We entered the forest.

It was a moonlit, clear night in the forest too. But if the silence thought it was safe from us there, it was ill advised. A great rustling greeted us at once in the forest. Perhaps it was the silence which produced the rustling in which to hide itself from us? The forest rustled quite differently from the way it had in the afternoon, when the storm had arisen and driven me out of the wood. The gusts of the wind were no weaker, perhaps even stronger than they had been in the early evening, but they were bright and mild gusts. Perhaps the moonlight made

[277]

the gusts of the wind mild, the flowing, flooding light of the still invisible moon, for even the howling of the wind sounded bright as the moon flowed so mildly over it. From the trees, which seemed completely unleaved at first glance, the foliage fell in an uninterrupted downpour. In the clear moonlight many trees showed naked skeletons from which the wind had gnawed the flesh; but many still had a good deal of foliage to lose. The deeper we pressed into the forest, the thicker fell the leaves. At first they fell in drifts like snow, but wherever the wind blew the leaves fell in complete columns of silver. They fell soft, lightly rustling, but so thick that Partyka and I had to hold our hands high before our heads to draw our breath unhindered behind the protection of our palms, as we pressed through the sharp leafy drift.

Past all the beautiful trees which I had seen during the three beautiful days, past every one of the trees which I knew, led the road to the rabbi. There stood the young birch, all its leaves shuddering before the storm, and, like the girl in Schubert's song, the delicate birch pleaded with wild death: Touch me not. The tall aspen kept its proud bearing during the storm, too. However impudently the storm might seize her fine-leaved boughs, she stood there in her dignity, a tall noble lady, giving the forest plebeians an example of how to die. But I had not seen the aspen at all during the day. And there stood lindens and all manner of maples and plane-trees, sparkling in an innumerable variety of leaves! All the trees of the Dobropolia forest and of the *Gazon* were suddenly here! Even the weeping willow which extended its boughs so wide over the small pond — it, too, was to be found here . . . O, you trees of my childhood! How large you were! If Goddl weren't walking so sharply ahead, I could greet you all here, O trees of Dobropolia! . . .

"Where is Goddl?" Partyka suddenly asked.

"He just disappeared behind the bend," said I. "Don't you hear the stick going zrrr — topp — zrrr — topp!?"

"Let's not lose our way," said Partyka.

"But you know the way," I said.

[278]

"Which way?" he asked.

"The way to the rabbi," I said.

"Goddl is taking another way," he said.

"If the stick of Rabbi Shmelke is leading him, this way leads to the rabbi, too," said I, confidence filling my heart.

"Have you seen the trees?" asked Partyka.

"Yes," said I. "They are all here, and I love them all."

"All the trees of Dobropolia are here," whispered Partyka. "There's something wrong here."

"Where these trees are, the road is good," I exulted.

"Thank God, there's Goddl!" said Partyka.

We had almost — for Partyka was pressing hard ahead — reached the bend of the path at a trot. On the right side the forest now became thinner. Goddl strode by the edge of the forest, along the clearing, the steel point of his stick shining in the moonlight over the strewn foliage like a silver glow-worm. Meanwhile the storm had subsided. In the sky, behind a thin veil, the crescent of the moon floated clear in the midst of the star letters, like an initial beginning the book of the sky.

"Look, Partyka, the crescent of the moon is like a large letter!"

"Yes," said Partyka, "like the large Hebrew *Bet*, with which the Holy Testament begins: *Bereshit*.

"You know Hebrew, Partyka?" I wondered.

"Of course," he said. "But I can't read the book of the sky. The letters are too large there."

"I can!" I cried superciliously.

As a matter of fact, all at once I could! Walking, gliding, my face turned up to the sky, I read the large golden lines of stars, ravished by the beauty of the words whose meaning opened itself up to my heart with wonderful ease.

"There, see, that is the line of the Dobropolia forest," Partyka whispered to me.

As though the words had put out the moon and the stars, suddenly it was dark. The clearing was behind us. We were again in the forest. Although the forest was very thick and very dark here, everything appeared very clear: the tree trunks, the boughs, the leaves on the twigs and the leaves on the forest floor — all appeared very clear, much clearer and nearer than it was in the full moonlight of the forest clearing itself. In the silence to be found only in very old forests, I sensed at once the soft rustling and murmuring of the brook; but I could not see the brook. I was trying to look away from Partyka's index finger, persistently pointing in one direction, when suddenly the brook came into view, dark but peculiarly clear. No wonder I had not been able to see it at once. There was no water at all in the brook, but only sere leaves! Wearing a thick coat of fallen leaves, the brook moved slowly through the forest, distinguishable from the strewn floor of the forest, which also consisted of corpses of leaves, only by its movement. Like a gigantic caterpillar heavily furred with leaves, humping and stretching, contracting and expanding, the stream crawled through the dark clarity of the forest. I should have recognized it at once, like Partyka, by this very load of leaves. This brook was in the forest of Dobropolia. When in November, swollen by the rains breaking out of the forest, it leaped down the precipice to the valley and flooded the meadows, it carried so heavy a load of leaves of the forest that the peasants jested, "The master is distributing fuel for the winter to us."

"How did you see it so quickly?" I asked Partyka, for I was annoyed that he had discovered our stream, not I.

"Oh, I don't trust this Goddl," he said darkly. "Who knows where he may be leading us, this bad man?"

"Don't worry, Partyka," I said. "He may be a bad man, but he has Rabbi Shmelke's stick! It is the stick that is leading us, not Goddl."

"We are falling behind, Josko," Partyka reminded me, worried. "Look how far away Goddl is. If he gets out of sight —"

"Let's run for a while," I suggested, for all at once I, too, felt that Goddl's lead had become disquietingly large.

We held hands and ran for a stretch. Gasping, for racing

through the deep piles of leaves was more tiring than we had expected, we came to within ten steps of Goddl, calmly striding ahead, but stopped when Goddl, walking faster, looked back to us.

"We are to keep our distance," Partyka whispered to me, and I construed Goddl's warning look in the same way. So we held up and walked for a time at the distance we had reached behind Goddl, whose back, however, despite the distance, towered in front of us broad and heavy like that of a coachman on his box. Then Partyka felt secure again at the sight of Goddl's back, and let go of my hand, which he had held in a convulsive grip while we ran. Although the forest grew continually denser and our way was full of bushes, nevertheless it was easier going. All at once I felt that Partyka was hanging on my neck with both arms as he walked, and laying his head heavy on my shoulder, his teeth chattering. My voice tightened by fear, I asked him, "What's the matter?"

His voice deserting him, his lips trembled in my ear, "Josko — Josko — the stick — the stick — is marching — it is marching by itself — Goddl has disappeared —"

"What are you talking about, Philko," I cried and looked past his head in the direction of the stick.

"Oh!" I heard Partyka groan, and saw — on the beaten path, clearly distinguished from the forest floor and its higher bed of leaves, the stick of Rabbi Shmelke walking all by itself, as it had been before at Goddl's side! . . .

Vertically suspended, it glided over the leaves as though pulled through a rapid brook against the stream, and the leaves hissed at the touch of the stick's point. Zrrr! — buzzed the leaves, topp! — the stick tapped on the leafy bed of the path, as though reminding us not to stop. Despite our paralyzing fear, we did not stop. We followed the stick, Partyka with both arms on my neck, I with my eyes on the stick walking by itself. Yet I perceived — and I perceived this with enthusiastic and solemn astonishment — that the stick was inducing in me not a state of alarm, but rather one of enchantment! Was it not Reb

Shmelke's stick, which was summoning us to a trial and constraining us? What wonder that such a stick could lead us to the court of justice by itself without the need of a poor human accompaniment?

"Don't worry, Philko," I consoled my friend, "the stick will take us the right way. It is a Jewish stick."

Partyka wanted to object, but there was no time. For, a sudden wind arose in the forest and — as though it no longer trusted the path which disappeared in the leafy drift — springing aside over the whirling heaps of leaves, the stick continued on. Turning the crook to face us as though it were nodding to us to follow, the stick hopped quickly toward the brook, whose rustling and gurgling were now louder than the storm itself. At once, all of us, first the stick, then I, then Partyka, who still clung to my neck, were seized by a strong current which glided off with us.

It was as though we were flying through the air. Yet we were standing upright on the leafy back of the brook as on a floating ice-floe. There was a rustling above us, a roar that filled our ears and eyes. The falling leaves swirled around us, the sere leaves snowed so thick that Partyka tucked his *soutane* up high, so we could breathe on the raging voyage. Large wings as of birds slapped over our heads.

"What birds are these?" I heard myself asking aloud.

"They are no birds, Josko. They are maple leaves."

"So large?"

"They are not single leaves. Maple leaves hold fast to one another when they fall, to die with their comrades," Partyka instructed. As he spoke, he pressed my hands, as though he wished to indicate that we two had been given an opportunity to imitate the maple leaves and to die as comrades. Although I did not share his fear, the pressure of his hands caused a shudder to run through me, and I began to sing psalms into the night in a weak voice. Then I perceived behind closed eyelids and through the uproar that the forest was clearing, and I peeped out from behind the protection of Partyka's flapping *soutane*.

Everything was bathed in a bottle-green light. In the green sky the moon and the stars were small and without a light of their own, as though sunken and drowned in the vast distance. Was it still night? Was it already morning? All at once the picture was jumbled: sky, moon and stars were below — forest, fields, meadows above. I shut my eyes, and all my senses were numbed. Partyka's voice revived me:

"Morning is coming, and a village is in sight."

"There's something —" I said — "but it is no village, Partyka."

"No," said Partyka, "it is a town."

"But is is not our town."

"No," said Partyka," it is another place."

"When did all this snow fall?"

It was a town. But the houses were so snowed in that they lay as small and dispersed in the blue twilight as village huts. Over the town there was night and snow and storm.

"There's a house up there with a light still shining," said Partyka, pointing with outstretched arm to a rise in the ground where a weak light blinked over the snow. Was the house so low or the snow so high? Or did the light come from a lantern standing on a snowdrift?

As we peered far off toward the light of the house in the snow-drifts, suddenly the house was next to us, indeed almost imme-diately already behind us, and Goddl the *Gabbe* strode with his stick through the snow drifts up to the small house. We sprang quickly into the snow and plunged deep into it. Lying there, we saw that our path glided on; it was the brook, strewn with foliage, the caterpillar which had borne us hither, which raged ahead. As we worked our way out of the soft depths of the snow, we noticed for the first time that the whiteness was not snow, but leaves, high heaps of drifts of foliage; leaves silvered over by the light of the moon which shone round and full here. The snowdrifts before the little house, too, consisted of fallen leaves, the whole house was covered with a drift of silver foliage. From the lighted house came a tender, slow song, so tender and so slow that at first I believed it to be the humming breath of sleepers, singing with sleepy lips. But we soon heard the words of the song, which in contrast to the sad tune, were quite jolly:

> Rejoice, O Hasidim,
> Happy times are nearing for you.
> The rebbe is coming,
> The rebbe is coming —
> The rebbe is already here!
> He has a stick,
> Ah-ah-ah-ah!
> He will wake you up,
> Ah-ah-ah-ah!

"Oh, what a sad tune," said Partyka, as though the sadness of the song made him sorrowful.

"But only the tune," I consoled him. "The words are quite jolly."

"Who is it singing so sadly here?"

"The disciples. For the rabbi has disciples."

"Why do they sing so sadly?"

"Because they are fasting."

"They are fasting?! Why? Is today a fast day?"

"They are fasting for me. They want to smash the evil inclination in me, so they are fasting and exerting their souls. Tender, good Jewish children."

"Why, you are crying, Osyp!"

"No, Philip, I am not crying. The tune is so beautiful."

"But sad. Too sad. We Ukrainians have sad songs, too, really sad. But what these Jews are singing is too sad. Why?"

"Yes, my friend: sadness can kindle as much fire, yes, as much jubilation in us Jews, as joy. That's the way it is with the Jewish heart."

"I am afraid, Josko."

"Of the rabbi?"

"Yes."

[284]

"Don't be afraid, Philko. I will not tell him that you want to waylay and mislead me."

"I? You? I wish to mislead you?! You!"

"Yes. You do."

"Why, you traitor! You want to betray your God, your people, and your family for the sake of a woman!"

"Yes, because you've misled me, you devil!"

"I'll tell the rabbi everything, you woman chaser!"

"I'll show to His Reverence as evidence of how you mislead me —"

"Oh, you traitor!" hissed Partyka, and ran up to the house.

"Oh, you seducer!" I hissed, and followed him.

We knocked on the door, Partyka and I. At the first knock the door opened of itself, immediately closed behind us, and a gust of wind drove us through the dark hall into a room whose door had also opened itself of its own accord, then at once closed behind us soundlessly.

xviii

It was a long room, very quiet and so warm! The floor, of pressed clay, was yellow like saffron; the walls green. There was little furniture in the room and many books in the wooden bookcases standing along the eastern wall which rose up to the dark, wooden-raftered ceiling from the middle of the wall. There were many more books in the room than in Grandfather's Room, to which it bore more or less of a resemblance in that both looked more like prayer-and-study rooms than living-rooms. The room was dimly lit. True, a large lamp suspended from three chains hung over the long and narrow table, but a broad lampshade gathered almost all the light and cast a very bright arc onto the middle of the table where two documents lay. It was bright in only one corner of the room, where Goddl the *Gabbe* sat in front of a fireplace which he fed with the dry leaves he took with his large hands from a pile of foliage and strewed over the glow in the fireplace, without the pile becoming smaller. It was a sad, beautiful sight when the large maple leaves fell into the flames and blazed bright, for a moment still showing their glowing veins in the perfect purity of the fire like the veined outline of a hand held against the sun. Whenever a fresh cast of foliage hissed in the chimney and beat up the flames, one saw Rabbi Shmelke's stick in the corner of the room across the way hanging from a silken bow, flanked by two other, ordinary sticks, which were not secured by silken bows. As after a long and perilous journey one is moved and thankful at the sight of the good, tired horse resting and feeding in the stall at home, so Partyka and I felt looking at Rabbi Shmelke's stick, and we were struck by the unique form and structure of this apparently ordinary stick. We had forgotten our quarrel in front of the rabbi's house.

"What are those documents on the table?" asked Partyka, his words more of a loud sob than a loud question.

"They are records," I said, already bending over the documents on the table.

"Can you read the handwriting?" asked Partyka.

"Yes," I said. "On the cover of one of the documents there is written: A false priest."

"That is I," said Partyka.

"On the second, it says: A heathen."

"That is you," said Partyka.

"Why heathen? Why am I a heathen?" I tried to ask, but my voice deserted me.

"Here is someone standing before the court with bared head," I heard a soft voice say, and reached both hands to my head.

"A Christian priest knows that one must not stand here with bared head; does not the son of Judah ben Sussja know it?" the same soft voice inquired.

"Rabbi," I said, although I saw no one in the room in addition to Goddl and Partyka, "Rabbi, forgive me. In the forest, when I saw Rabbi Shmelke's stick marching by itself, my hair stood on end with terror, and I lost my hat."

Then I felt Goddl's breath on my neck and something quite

light covered my head. It felt like two light wings around my forehead and, as though only now worthy of seeing it, I saw — the Court of Justice.

xix

"Philip, son of Ivan," said the younger judge in a mild voice, and Partyka stepped forward. This judge, a rabbi still very young, with a narrow, pale face and black, wooly beard, was the prosecuting judge.

"You are a priest?" asked the second judge, who sat next to the prosecutor. He was a rabbi of about forty years of age; he had very long, curly, brown earlocks and large, brown eyes; he was the examining judge.

"Yes," said Partyka, "I am a priest."

"You are accused," said the prosecuting judge softly.

Now I saw that the judges wore white garments — the garments of death.

"Yes," said Partyka, "I was summoned."

"How did you become a priest?" asked the examining judge.

"My father wished me to become a priest," said Partyka. "And I obeyed my father."

"Your father meant well," said the prosecuting judge. "He could not have known that you are not called. But you knew it."

"I knew it," said Partyka.

"Your father is a countryman. He dreamed of your being a priest. But you had the choice: Speak, why did you choose falsely?" asked the examining judge.

"I love my father," answered Partyka, "I was not free."

"That is true," said the prosecuting judge. "Do you understand the language of the Scriptures?"

"Yes," Partyka answered, "I have studied that which a priest must study."

"He has studied," said the prosecuting judge. "But that is only grounds for clemency."

"Do you know what the stork is called in the language of the Scriptures?" asked the examining judge.

[287]

"Yes," answered Partyka, as though he were in school. In the Holy Scriptures the stork is called *hasidah*."

"What does that word mean?" asked the examining judge.

"*Hasidah* means 'the pious one.' "

"Do you also know why the stork is called thus?"

"No," replied Partyka, "I do not know."

"The stork is called 'the pious one' in the language of the Scriptures," said the prosecuting judge, "because the stork shows love to its kind. Nevertheless, the stork is one of the unclean birds."

"Do you also know why the stork, although it shows love to its own kind, nevertheless is one of the unclean birds?" asked the examining judge.

"No," said Partyka, "I have never learned that."

"Because the stork shows love only to its own kind," said the prosecuting judge.

"I see I have a bad case," said Partyka.

"Not so bad, my son," said the examining judge. "Do you still show a true son's love to your father, for whose sake you became a priest?"

"I visit him once a year," said Partyka softly.

"Your father visited you more often," said the prosecuting judge.

"Do you also look after your father?" asked the examining judge.

"When he has a bad harvest, I send him something," said Partyka, very softly.

"Your father always sent you what you needed and fed you regardless of his harvest, so that you became the strongest of your fellows," said the prosecuting judge.

"That has nothing to do with it," a harsh voice suddenly said, speaking as though in anger — I now saw for the first time that the court did not consist of two, but of five judges. In the middle sat a little ancient. To his left sat the prosecuting and examining judges, to his right the narrating judge and a judge who smiled; the smiling judge was an old man with a beautiful beardless face,

[288]

black eyes and snow-white hair. But one could only see within the lamp's arc the judge who was speaking at the time. All the judges were of a sudden visible in the arc of light only when the little ancient spoke.

"That has no weight on our scales," repeated the little ancient, as in anger. "That is a matter of human nature: When a father gives to his son, both laugh; when a son gives to his father, both cry. Proceed!"

"My father must appear here as witness. My father will support me," said Partyka.

"He supports you, my son," said the examining judge. "But with what can you exculpate your diminished filial love?"

"I bore the yoke of a calling to which I was not called. Large and stringent duties oppressed me. That has withered my heart. I do not know how it will all end, " Partyka broke into a lament. But he did not whimper and did not plead for grace. There was a strong, manly note to his lament.

"Enough! The judgment!" called the little ancient in his angry fashion. All four judges rose and stood silent in their white garments in the arc of light of the judges' table. Then the little ancient raised his index finger and gave the smiling judge a signal.

"Philip, son of Ivan," the smiling judge announced the judgment. "You have the heart of a son and the mind of a father. That is why you have become a bad priest. For the true priest possesses the heart of a father as well as the mind of a father. So you must be sentenced. But you shall be sentenced to a punishment which will not set in all at once, but will come gradually in the footsteps of your ambition. You, a good son of a good father: You shall become Archpriest! And with that, God be with you!"

Partyka bowed low before the judges, who reciprocated, all bowing toward the arc of light and, withdrawing, disappeared all at once. With the court of justice the document also disappeared from the table, the record with the inscription: A false priest.

It had grown dark in the room, even the arc of light over the court table was pale. Only now and again a red reflection flickered convulsively on the walls when Goddl strewed fresh leaves over the glow of the fireplace, and the flames sprang high. Partyka stood before the fireplace, beating his chest with both fists and praying.

"Why, you have a mild punishment, Philip," I said to him. "You are right to thank God."

"A man cannot be found guilty," whispered Partyka, as in prayer, "but an Archpriest — how easily an Archpriest can be found guilty. Oh God!"

"*Boze*! *Boze*!" a sob burst forth from Goddl's broad chest in Ukrainian. He was sitting on a footstool, drinking tea and cutting thin slices of bread with a pocket knife. "Oh God, oh God!" he sobbed in sympathy with Partyka. All at once he set his glass of tea quickly aside and signalled me. It had grown bright again in the room. I turned quickly around — and there I stood before the court of justice.

"Yosef, son of Yehudah!" the examining judge addressed me, and by the softness of his beautiful voice I now recognized him; the examining judge was Rabbi Hershel, that man who loved children and had been our cantor in the House of Prayer of the *Rav* early every morning! But had not Rabbi Hershel died in the bloom of youth?

"Someone must have misunderstood me," I said quickly, even before the prosecuting judge could speak. "I am no heathen."

"You speak like one who has been found guilty," said the prosecuting judge. "It is not a good sign that I must speak so early in this proceeding."

"Why have you leaves in your hair, if you are not a heathen?" asked the examining judge. I felt my head and felt the leaves with my fingers.

"I lost my hat in the forest," I said. "It was only here in this room that my head was covered with a wreath."

[290]

"That is beside the point," said a voice, and it seemed to me as though the examining judge, who had kept his eyes low, were of the same opinion.

"I am no heathen," I repeated. "I know all the Psalms of David by heart," I added softly and I was ashamed, for one could see how things stood with me.

"Was he a good student?" asked the examining judge.

"His father gave him a piece of gold for every psalm he learned, and he bought a canister of tobacco for the milker Andrej with the money," said the prosecuting judge.

"That is beside the point," the little ancient interjected in his angry manner. He remained henceforth within the arc of light the whole time and I could see his face. "That is the way children are. He was a good student — that is not to be disputed."

The little ancient's face was held together only by the bones of his forehead, his cheeks and his nose. It consisted entirely of a confusion of wrinkles and puckers. But his skin was not yellow, as that of old men usually is. The skin of his face was white; almost as white as the small, thin beard which had naked spots around his chin, as though it had been plucked. His eyes, too, gleamed white under inflamed lids, smouldering with lymph.

"He was a good student in our schools and he remained a good student in the secular schools as well. He has already forgotten everything that he learned in our schools. Yet he should be examined," said the prosecuting judge.

"The fifth book of Moses, the thirty-third chapter, reads —" began the examining judge, but I interrupted him, for at the sight of the little ancient my memory became white and clear.

"The thirty-third chapter, second verse reads," I interposed, " 'The Lord came from Sinai. . . at his right hand was a fiery law unto them.' — isn't that right?"

Then all the judges looked at me almost with affection, and an inner voice cried within me: "Show them, show them your knowledge. Only knowledge can help you here!" Yet it was perhaps my own inner voice which deceived me concerning the nature of this trial.

"You have studied well," said the examining judge, and his face promised me succor. "Perhaps you also know how our commentators interpret this passage?"

"The *Pesikta of Rav Kahana* says: Rabbi Yohanan said: 'Everyone who applies himself to the study of the Torah may be regarded as though he were standing in fire,' " I knew the reply and said it with a student's zeal.

"As a child, as the son of your father, you stood in that fire," said the prosecuting judge. "And see where you stand now!" he shouted at me.

"I could not stand the fire of the Law, Rabbi. I longed for the images of the myths, for the figure of the legends," I confessed.

"A heathen!" said the prosecuting judge. "You speak like a heathen."

"Let me speak like a heathen," my pride replied, "before this court even a heathen must be exculpated. Our courts show great clemency to heathens. Is our law in force here or is it not?"

"It is in force," said the examining judge. "You may invoke it."

"According to our law, a Jew, if he wishes to win the salvation of his soul, must fulfill six hundred and thirteen commandments and injunctions. But a heathen has stood the test of our law, if he has fulfilled only three commandments."

"Which three commandments? Do you still remember?" asked the examining judge with all the great mildness of his personality.

"The heathen may partake of salvation, if he loves God, does what is right, and speaks the truth. Is that correct?"

"It is correct," said the prosecuting judge. "Do you wish the proceedings to take a turn in that direction?"

"He does not see the abyss," said the examining judge, casting a look at the little ancient. "He must not be pushed."

"He is not being pushed," said the little ancient. "He is running ahead. His nature is to run ahead."

"Our sages show clemency to the heathens. There was a great man among the heathens who was treated with conspicuous

[292]

mildness, indeed, with benevolence," I interjected, for it seemed to me as though an easy path to salvation lay before me, as though the path were begging me to take it.

"Whom do you wish to name?" asked the examining judge.

"I name Alexander the Great as an example. He was a great hero, but he was a heathen, though one of the greatest of the heathens. Nevertheless, he is highly praised in our writings, and till this very day pious Jews give his name to their sons, while there is hardly a Jew in all the world who would ever name his son after Joab, who was a great warrior-general, and Jewish, as well."

"We have not named our children after warriors for a long time, you are right in that," said the examining judge. "However, we make an exception in the case of Alexander the Great. But do you know why?"

"No," I said.

"Do you know the story of Alexander the Great?" asked the examining judge.

"Certainly," I said, "Who does not know it?"

"He knows the story!" said the prosecuting judge mockingly. "You know how the great Macedonian cursed his father, how he stabbed his friend in the heart with a lance at his banquet, how he — "

"He found the way to India," I interjected.

"A great matter! The way to India!" the prosecuting judge mocked. "Our King Solomon knew the way to India long before the Macedonian, though he refrained from sending hordes of warriors to India, but sent rather messengers of peace and merchant caravans."

"So you do not know the true story of Alexander?" said the examining judge, and looked at the little ancient, as though awaiting his decision.

"You shall hear the true story of the great Macedonian at once, soldier!" the little ancient cried to me. "Narrating judge!" he called out in a solemn voice, "tell him our story about Alexander, which is the true story."

And now something happened which so enchanted me that I forgot the place, the trial, the court, and myself. In the round semi-circle of judges the narrating judge rose. And this judge was a child! He was a boy of not more than ten years of age dressed in a white smock, white trousers, white stockings, with a white cap on his black curly hair. His face was narrow and as white as the whitest of his garments — as white as the white silken girdle which enclosed his small caftan. Two large, black eyes shining in his bloodless face looked at me with a broken, bright look, as deep as a ravine. At an almost tender nod from the prosecuting judge, the child stepped up to the little ancient, sat himself down on the footstool at the feet of the supreme judge, and began to narrate. The child's voice was strong and sweet and laid the words visibly in the air, as though the voice were writing a pure track of white letters with a nimble point on a black background. And as though he were relating and writing simultaneously, I heard and read at the same time the story the narrating judge related concerning Alexander the Great:

"It happened that the king whom all people called Alexander the Great, having conquered the land of India with his powerful army, made halt at a river called Physon. The river was broad, its current rapid. The people who lived on its banks told the king that the river Physon had its source in Paradise, and all the lands which it watered were rich in fruit and grain. The houses where those who dwelt on the banks of the river lived were covered with leaves which were longer and broader than the leaves borne by trees whose roots are in the earth. During the day, when the sun warms these leaves, their fragrance surpasses all perfumes.

"King Alexander said to those who inhabited the river banks, 'Where do you pluck the leaves which cover your houses? From what tree? From what bush?'

"They answered the king: 'The river Physon brings us these leaves on its waves from its source in the Garden of Eden.'

"When the king heard mention of Paradise for the second time, he grew thoughtful and said to his captains, 'Truly, I have

[294]

conquered the whole world, but what are all my conquests, if I have not gained the delights of Paradise?'

"And he chose from his men five hundred fearless warriors, proven in many battles, gave them each equipment, sword and shield, and with them got on a ship that was equipped with all manner of provisions for the voyage and return. And he sailed up the river Physon with his warriors, and they rowed powerfully day after day.

"On the thirty-third day their strength left them and their ears became deaf with the roaring of the waters. The warriors pulled in their oars and said, 'Our strength is gone, our ears are deaf. Master, let us turn back, or we shall die.'

"But the king said, 'Endure, O my brave men, for but one more day!'

"On the next day they saw the white and golden roofs of a city, and as they came nearer they saw that the whole city was encircled by a high wall on which there were no towers and no guards for its defense. But from the bottom to the top the wall was grown over with a green shield of moss which covered all the stones of the wall and all the crevices between the stones. For three days longer the warriors continued to row alongside the green wall against the strong current. On the fourth day they saw a narrow window in the wall and halted. And the king chose seven warriors from the band and ordered them to climb into a boat and row over to the window.

"The seven warriors climbed into the boat and rowed over to the window. They knocked on the wooden shutters and after a short time a bolt was pushed back and a shutter was opened. An old man showed himself and asked them in a mild voice: 'Who are you and whence do you come? And what do you seek in this place?'

"The warriors replied, 'We are messengers. We are messengers, but not from one of the many kings whose province is a single land. We are sent by the king of kings, the ruler over all provinces and all rulers, the unconquered Alexander, the great Macedonian. The king wishes to know the name of this land

and who inhabits it. And King Alexander wishes you to know that you must pay him tax and tribute like all the lands of the earth. Or he will beat you with the sharp edge of his sword!'

"The old man answered the warriors, 'Do not make threats here. Do not make threats and wait till I return.' And he shut the window.

"After a few hours he opened it again. In his hand was a precious stone in the shape of a human eye, from which a powerful light shone. He handed the stone to the leader of the king's seven messengers and said to him, 'We send this stone to the king as a memento of his voyage on the river Physon. He may regard this precious stone as a gift or as a tribute — as he wishes. And tell the king: This stone is sent to you, O King Alexander, out of love for humanity. Learn to know its nature, and you will turn away from all the goals to which ambition and insatiable lust drive you. And also tell the king: Turn about and hasten away, or else a storm will rise and you and your companions will perish on the river Physon.'

"The old man shut the window. The king's messengers rowed quickly back to the ship, handed the precious stone to the king and told him the message. And the king turned around and returned to his camp, which was in the city of Susa. There he called the sages of the land to him, that they might interpret the nature of the precious stone in the shape of a human eye. Yet though the sages spoke much, they could not interpret the nature of the stone and the essence of its power. The great Greek sage, Aristotle, who was the king's teacher, would perhaps have recognized the nature of the stone from the Garden of Eden, for the Greek sage had read the works of King Solomon. When King Alexander conquered the city of Jerusalem, he made his teacher Aristotle caretaker of the library of King Solomon. And Aristotle read the Scriptures and returned and read them again, and he could not bear to part from the library. So he remained in Jerusalem and did not accompany King Alexander to his camp in Susa.

"But there lived at that time in Susa a pious learned man,

[296]

called Rabbi Pappas. He was an old man and walked about in his house on crutches. When he heard of the king's desire he said to his servants: 'Carry me to the king in a sedan-chair.' And the king allowed Rabbi Pappas to enter his throne room, and he sat Rabbi Pappas at his right hand, for he was in awe of the sage. And the king asked Rabbi Pappas, too, concerning the nature and power possessed by the stone in the shape of a human eye.

"Then Rabbi Pappas said: 'Glory be to you, O King Alexander! For you have succeeded where no one else has ever succeeded: You have been at that region where the souls of the righteous tarry until the end of all time.' With that, he took the stone out of the king's hand and said: 'Let a scale be brought and all the gold of your treasury.' And so it came to pass.

"Then Rabbi Pappas laid the stone in the shape of a human eye in one scale, and all the gold that could be borne was laid in the other scale. Yet all the gold could not raise the stone as much as the shadow of a shadow. The king marveled greatly and asked: 'What does this mean?'

"But Rabbi Pappas caused an even larger scale to be brought and heaps of gold to be piled on one scale, and set the stone in the other scale. But the stone outweighed the gold. Again the king marveled, but he was silent.

"With that Rabbi Pappas took the stone, placed it again in one scale and strewed dust upon the stone — and now a single gold piece raised the stone — yes, a feather raised it!

"Then Rabbi Pappas explained to the king the nature of this precious stone, saying: 'The eye of man, O great king, is as this stone. It cannot be filled with all the gold in the world, till it is covered with dust. O King Alexander, you are this eye!'

"Then the king embraced Rabbi Pappas, sent gifts to his house and put off ambition from his own soul. And he sent away all his warriors and lived in peace till the day of his death.

[297]

"This is our story about King Alexander whom all the peoples of the earth call The Great. May the merits of Rabbi Pappas support us. Amen."

This story was familiar to me from the Talmud, but I had never grasped its meaning till that moment. As the narrating judge related the story, it seemed to me to have only one meaning. But this impression vanished at the end of the narration, and when the child's lips stopped moving, I felt myself in the grip of a great sadness in which all my thoughts disappeared. A hopeless lassitude bound my consciousness and made me so dull that for a time I forgot the scene of the event, the court, the trial and the arraignment. Only my eyes retained the strength to cling to the eyes of the narrating judge. But such a power issued forth from the broken light of the child's eyes that all that was murky became clear again, and the story's pure contours shone forth once more.

Meanwhile, the court proceeded to the explication of the story. It was clarified, explained, given a commentary and analyzed according to the rules, and in the very singsong, in which the Talmud is studied. But I was not able to distinguish the individual voices of the judges, for whenever I tried to turn my eyes from the boy's bright gaze, everything again became murky for me, and lassitude gained the ascendency over my consciousness. So I bound my eyes again to the light of the boy's eyes and followed the singsong of the interpreters and explicators, whose manifold resonances dinned in my ears like a musical anthem played on a distant organ.

"The beginning of a story is important."

"The ending of a story is important."

"At the beginning of the story it is related that the king said to his captains: 'True the whole world is subject to me, but what good are all my conquests if I have not achieved the joys of Paradise?' Is this a heathen's speech?"

"At the end of the story it is related: 'And he put off ambition from his soul and sent away all his warriors and lived in peace until the day of his death.' Is that the action of a heathen?"

"Because he knocked at the gate of Paradise, he was deemed worthy to receive a gift from the Garden of Eden."

"Because he received the stone as a gift from the Garden of Eden, he was deemed worthy to have children named after him in every age."

"Thus his name was purified."

"Because he was drawn to Paradise."

"Because he put off ambition from his soul."

"Because he sent away his warriors."

"Because he understood Rabbi Pappas' interpretation and lived in peace until the day of his death."

"But the middle of a story must not be forgotten because of its beginning."

"And what is the end of a story, if its roots are not in the beginning, its sap in the middle?"

"The middle of a story is important."

"As important as the beginning, as important as the ending."

"For a story grows like a tree: It has its roots, it has its stock, it has its leaves. If it does not have these, it is a bad story."

"And as at the sight of a tree one does not think of its roots, but marvels only at the growth of the stock and rejoices in the green foliage, thus often one does not consider the beginning of a story, being too happy with the growth of the stock and the green foliage."

"Therefore the wise commentators and interpreters first consider the roots of a story!"

"By which it is not intended to be said that the beginning of a story is more important than the middle."

"But how does the middle of our story about King Alexander run?"

" 'On the fourth day they became aware of a narrow window. And Alexander chose seven from his warrior band, and ordered them to climb into a boat and row over to the window.' That was an error for which there is no forgiveness."

"At the very entrance to the Garden of Eden, he sends out messengers."

"He did not climb into the boat and knock at the gate himself."

"And his messengers flung threats at the gate-keeper of Paradise."

"But that was a comparatively minor sin, that did not count heavily against him. True, the messengers were stupid enough to threaten. But it is not said that it was the king's command for his men to threaten the gate-keeper. This would be a sin and there would be repentance."

"That he did not knock himself —"

"That he sent messengers —"

"That at the decisive moment he allowed himself *to be represented* —"

"That — that is the only reason why the king could not pass the trial —"

"That is why he was not let in."

"He found the way to the Garden of Eden. And he voyaged through great danger —"

"And he was able to reach the entrance —"

"But since he believed that one can allow himself *to be represented* there, he was not let in."

"And he had to turn back."

"To turn back hastily."

"For he was in great danger."

Here the narrating judge nodded to me. The boy's white face was now stern, sterner even than the faces of the four adult judges. With a nod that was at the same time a warning and an encouragement, the narrating judge freed me from the bonds of his eyes, and in his last broken bright glance there was all the holiness of life and all the rejection of death. Yet the nod was the sort a school boy gives as encouragement to a comrade who is standing in front of a teacher. I now saw that the explication and analysis were nothing else than the court's proceedings against me, and with trembling lips and weak voice I interjected:

"But the stone? The stone from the Garden of Eden?"

[300]

"The stone was a moral."

"A moral for the king."

"The moral for the king is explained in the story."

"The story itself is a moral for us."

"And what does the story teach us?"

"It teaches us that there is no representation in salvation."

"All our stories teach that. Those that do not teach it are bad stories."

"That is the moral."

"And the Messiah?" I dared. "The Messiah — is he not to redeem and lead the exiles home?" '

"Of the Messiah it is said: The Messiah is sitting in front of the gates of Rome. He is bleeding from a thousand wounds, and he keeps binding his wounds and tearing them open again. For Israel continues to sin in the Exile. But the *Shekhina*, too, went into exile with sinful Israel, and the departed Glory cannot return home, until Israel has done penance. For there is no representation in repentance. Only when Israel enters the realm of repentance, purified of sin, will the exiled *Shekhinah* return home. As a sign of that repentance, the Messiah will appear and lead Israel home from the Exile. The Exile makes atonement for the sins of the sinful, it is said. But man must work at the redemption of the world. He who does not work at redemption increases the Messiah's wounds, delays redemption, and lengthens the term of the Exile."

"And must we bear the pain of the Exile till then?" I shouted. "Like Koppel the printer, mocked, insulted, stoned, to move on and smile like an exiled king mocked by the vulgar?! That smile is a worm in my heart! I wish to tear out that worm, put off the shame of the Exile from my soul. I wish to come to terms with this world — on its terms. I wish to live like the children of happier nations. I wish to be a serene part of this world! May this world be a serene part of me! I do not wish to bear the worm in my heart —"

"Enough!" the little ancient shouted at me. "He wishes the world to be a serene part of him," he repeated my words in great sorrow, deeply shaming me. "Is that your moral?" he turned questioningly to the smiling judge.

"Satan is the prince of this world. He who expects his reward in this world is lost. That is the moral we draw from this world. He is not speaking for us. He is speaking like a heathen," said the smiling judge.

"And he sat as a child over the Scriptures," said the little ancient man. "And he was a good student. In his youth he tried to deceive me. I said: 'You are really a soldier!' 'No,' said he, 'I am a student.'"

"A heathen," said the prosecuting judge, took the document and laid it before the little ancient. It was the document with the inscription: A heathen.

"He felt the fire of the Law," said the little ancient to himself, disregarding the document. "He knew the *Pesikta* and he knows the Psalms. Yet he wished to deceive me: 'A student,' said he, 'I am a student, Rabbi, a student and no soldier.'"

"Perhaps he was trapped in his own deception?" inquired the examining judge.

"Enough," said the little ancient, and he spoke as in wrath again. "The judgment!"

The judges rose. The arc of light shone so powerfully that the darkness around me was like a burning pain. I wished to open my mouth and vindicate myself at the very last moment. But my lips were frozen. I wished to grope my way nearer to the arc of light, but my feet were rooted to the spot. And then came the judgment:

"Yosef son of Yehudah, you wished to deceive me, but are yourself deceived. The judgment ought to be strict, according to the letter of the law, that the deception may be voided completely. But since you sat as a child over the Scriptures and tasted of the fire of the Law, the judgment shall not be spoken in words, but rather shown to you in images." The little ancient was speaking: "For the letters are the elements of the world; in their connections, in the words themselves, the inwardness of reality is contained. Your reality, you heathen, is such that you can bear only its external shape. Therefore the judgment will be shown to you only in images. See!"

He took the document with the inscription "A heathen" and breathed upon it. The inscription was extinguished like a light. Then he held the document before me with both his hands, which were as shriveled and small as the hands of a sick child. On the first page I saw a snowbound winter landscape, as even and white as the page, with low-growing bushes towering above the snow. Through the snow ran the yellowish track of a narrow path, and on the path a young man in a uniform was walking with a regular military stride — I myself wore a similar uniform as a student! The striding youth looked piercingly at me, nodded to me briefly with his eyes and went ahead; the snow grated sharply under his feet.

"Where are you going?" I asked him.

"I am going your way," said the student.

"This is no way for me," I said.

"What do you know about your way?" said he.

"What do you know about my way, student?"

"I am no student," said the student.

"No," I said. "You are no student. You have a violin bow in your hand. You are a musician."

"I am no musician," he said, "and as to what I have here — look: Is this a violin bow?"

"I see," I said, "that is my cello bow."

"It was a cello bow. Look carefully: What is it now?"

"You are really no student," I said. "You are wearing a soldier's coat."

"Yosef ben Yehudah," said the soldier. "I am you. And you are a soldier. So I am a soldier, too. And I am going your way."

"I wish to go with you," I said.

"You are already going with me," said the soldier.

"Where does the path lead?" I asked.

"The path is short," said the soldier. "How soon it will come to an end! . . ."

All at once the snowy landscape grew dark, and I felt myself sinking slowly in the snow, deeper and deeper. I screamed for help. I screamed with all my strength, but my voice was dumb. A dark ravine sucked me into itself, deeper and deeper.

"The prosecuting judge was the rabbi of H," suddenly I heard Partyka's voice warm in my ear.

"Are you still sinking, Philip?!" I shouted.

"Yes," said Partyka, "we are sinking in the foliage."

"Where are we, Philip?"

"We are outdoors. Don't you see the sky?"

I saw the sky, the moon, and a star near the moon, a beautiful, green, polished star, which outshone the moon. And I felt that I was not sinking any longer. We were sitting in a high pile of silver foliage in front of the courthouse. And again the tender, soft song, as soft and as tender as the humming breath of sleepers singing with sleep-heavy lips, issued from the house. There was great solace in the song.

"The prosecuting judge was the rabbi of H," I repeated.

"And the smiling judge was His Reverence," said Partyka.

"Yes!" I cried out happily. "Now I know it too, His Reverence, the good man."

"But who were the other judges?"

"The examing judge was dear Rabbi Hershel, who loved children."

"And who was the narrator of the court?"

"A child with a bright gaze."

"But why was the child granted such a distinction?"

"Perhaps because only a child is graced with the clear gaze."

"And who was the little ancient? A strict judge. Oh, how strict he was!"

"He treated you mildly."

"Not you, perhaps? You merited death, and came out with your life."

"Life is no goal, Partyka. Life is a path. And my path is short. Did you see it, the path in the snow?"

"No, I saw nothing. I only heard the judgment."

" 'Soldier,' he said. 'Soldier!' You know, Partyka, it seems to me as though I have heard the voice of the little ancient somewhere before!"

"Who can he have been?"

"Let us investigate. There is still a light in the house."

"I am afraid."

"I am not afraid. After all, I am a soldier."

Sinking in the foliage to my waist, I worked my way to the golden-yellow slab of light in the window and looked inside. The long judge's table with the semi-circle of high-backed judge's chairs had disappeared. The room was dimly lit. Only one corner, where a prayer-or-study stand stood, was bright. Before the stand, his arm propped on it, stood the little ancient. On the stand lay a large, open book. The letters in the book were so large that I could read them. I read the line: "He who kills one living being, kills a whole world. For the world does not exist for its own sake. The world exists only for the sake of living beings. And it exists as many times as there are living beings in it. Hence, he who kills a living being, though it be the slightest being, kills a whole world." At that the little ancient reached for his spectacles, put them on with his trembling, shriveled old man's hands, and shading his spectacles with one hand, as though looking at the sun, looked out of the window. Then I recognized him. "Why, that is Rabbi Abba, my great-grand-uncle," I tried to cry out. Then both halves of the window opened, a powerful gust of wind threw me to the floor, and a mountain, an avalanche of sere foliage, burst out of the window upon me and buried me in night and darkness. About to choke, I let out a scream and —

I was lying on the sofa in Partyka's room. My friend had apparently just stepped in. He was still standing in the moonlight at the open door, battling a vigorous gust of wind which almost tore the doorknob out of his hand, filled the whole room with cold air smelling of the forest and sere foliage, and pleasantly cooled my flushed face.

"Well," said Partyka, shutting the door with a bang, "now you'll not be bothered by Red Goddl any longer."

There is nothing in our dreams, my dear son, that is not in us. The image of my soul as it was at that time and everything that affected it in those days is comprised in this dream. My dream will surely seem to you confused and incomprehensible, for you do not know, as you must to understand it, about an important experience in my youth, an experience that violently and fundamentally shook me as a youth, and in the course of later years ran through my dreams as a man, the immanent motif of all my nightmares. Almost every man has one such constant dream motif that haunts his dreams in various disguises and needs be no mystery at all. In my dreams the story of Rabbi Abba's, my great-grand-uncle's, death is such a motif. I say is; for that dream was not the last into which the story of Rabbi Abba entered. Unfortunately, I have omitted to tell you that story. As a matter of fact, I began to tell it — and you will, if you leaf back, find an attempt at the tale — but it seemed to me when I began to write these pages that I had not the time to manage the tale and I broke off at the point where I mentioned Rabbi Abba. And now, my dear son, I really have no more time to make good this omission. But the damage is not so great: your uncle Stefan knows the story, I told it to him in that chatty mood which is not infrequent among good friends, probably told it to him repeatedly — he will certainly still remember it. If my friend should not remember the story, ask him to show you one of the notebooks I scribbled in Polish in my youth as a sort of diary: the complete story of the death of Rabbi Abba is to be found in one of those notebooks — you can have it translated. Those notes will describe the most fearful night of my life better than I can tell you in my present haste — I am very tired and my memory leaves me in the lurch, while I labor to stay awake.

The fact that nevertheless I remember the dream about the court is not surprising — I dreamed it three times that night, and I no longer know whether they were completely dreams, or partly day-dreams. After I had awoke as Partyka entered and had mastered my stupefaction to some extent, I rose and immediately betook myself to the inn. Partyka, who ordinarily accompanied me to the door of the inn every evening, did not this time — perhaps he was still too much under the sway of the remarkable events in the dream . . . .

You see, my dear son, I am talking pure rubbish already. How could he be under the sway of my dream? Neither that night nor later did I ever speak to Partyka about my dream. I had no more time to do so, for in the day and a half longer that I spent in the town of H no personal conversations passed between us. You will hear why at once.

That night I walked alone through the town forest to the inn. It was stormy and there was a storm of feelings and thoughts in my soul, too. In the short time it took me to walk through the forest I came to the speedy decision: Tomorrow, without first waiting for the messenger's call, I would go to the rabbi — then I would leave; but not back to Vienna — first of all, I would travel home to Dobropolia! Tomorrow I go home, I said aloud to myself; tomorrow I go home, I kept repeating as I undressed and went to bed. Tomorrow I go home, something inside me rejoiced. And with these words on my lips, like the words of the prayer before sleep, I fell into a blessed sleep, blessed with the happiness of homesickness that had burned secretly in my heart for a decade, controlled, but never stilled, never completely repressed. I slept well that night, although the dream of the forest and the trial passed through my sleep twice with pictorial clarity, twice interrupting my sleep. I slept till late into a morning which refreshed my hotel room with its blinding white reflections: the first snow had fallen that night. Already awake and still in bed, I pictured to myself the journey home and my arrival in Dobropolia, already glad with my brother's gladness, happy with my mother's happiness, strong with my father's power.

But fate broke into the middle of these reveries of mine. It assumed the dark face of Goddl, the porter, and with one blow all the threads which still tied me to my family and my people were torn. With one blow — that is putting it mildly, for I received many many more blows from the *Gabbe* of the rabbi of H. They were blows in an actual, not in any metaphorical, sense: real blows with a stick! With Rabbi Shmelke's holy stick, which had worked such potent miracles in my nightly dream passage through the forest.

xxii

I was standing half naked in front of the wash-basin, running my razor over the strop, and waiting for the warm shaving water I had ordered. I was thinking about my visit to the youthful rabbi, and I was proposing to visit his disciples who were fasting for me, as well, the pious children. I must have been humming a song as I thought — perhaps it was that song in the dream of the Hasidim who were so merry because "The rebbe is coming, the rebbe is coming" . . . Red Goddl must have heard my voice outside in the hallway, for he burst into my room with a shout of rage, "So thou singest hasidic songs?! Scoundrel! Liar! Traitor!" and furiously beat me with the stick.

The attack came so suddenly that I could not make the slightest move in my defense. It was not the fact that I stood there half naked, shoeless, while the aggressor, besides far surpassing me in strength, was booted and armed with a stick — that was not the true reason for my helplessness; you can try to defend yourself even against someone who is stronger than you. It was the circumstance that the *Gabbe* had addressed me with the familiar "thou" that rendered me completely defenseless. That "thou" revived a horrible experience from my childhood. Let me recall it briefly at this point to explain to some extent the effect of that "thou."

At home, in Dobropolia there was an old park, called the *Gazon*. In this park there was an old uninhabited mansion. But several rooms were still in good condition, in fact, very well furnished. Officers used to be quartered in these rooms when there were military maneuvers in the area. When I was twelve or thirteen years old, it happened that an officer committed suicide in one of these rooms. The old gardener came running to my father and told him about Captain von Scholz, who had been tired and off duty for a couple of days, about a shot, and about a locked door. We all ran there. The soldiers had decamped, there was no doctor. But my father, taking care of all eventualities, had picked up a peasant on the way who had some skill with wounds and was called "The Surgeon" in the village. First we knocked and listened at the locked door. It was quite still inside. Then my father had the door broken in, and while the surgeon and the gardener went ahead into the officer's bedroom, my father stayed behind with me in the parlor. In the awful silence of the house we soon heard the voice of the surgeon: "What has thou done, thou?"

Then my father took me by the hand and quickly led me away.

"Father," I asked, "perhaps he is still alive? Perhaps he can still be helped." Captain von Scholz was a jolly gentleman, and we children loved him very much.

Father shook his head and said, "If Ivan Pjetuch calls him 'thou,' Mr. von Scholz is a dead man."

The fact that Goddl the *Gabbe* called me "thou" was a sign that I was dead as far as Judaism was concerned. This recognition came to me as suddenly as the blows from the stick of Rabbi Shmelke; suddenly and nevertheless not surprisingly. Had I not once dreamed it as well? Had I not experienced it? A day of early winter snow; exhausted autumn storms refreshed by the first breath of winter; Jews, dark as swallows, who had not fled in time before the white death; and I, alone in the falling snow, in which the others walked as though safe at home — I alone with my fate . . . I did not try to defend myself, be it not said to my shame. I was overcome with the fear of the beast which is driven back to the right road by a hand beating it and, though recognizing the road, pays no attention to the stick. I knew: This was the moment of fate. Goddl the *Gabbe* was its messenger. He knew not what he did — I knew better than he. After he had spent his wrath on me, the *Gabbe* left, no less exhausted from his violence than I. I went back to bed. I lay there all day. My limbs burned, but my head was cool. There was a short circuit in my head. I had nothing further to think about. The *Gabbe* had beaten me out through the gate of Judaism with Rabbi Shmelke's stick; I myself had no further decisions to make. I could not arouse myself that day to the same anger at the dark fanaticism of small-town Judaism which had often overcome me since my earliest youth. It seemed to me as though I had died on a trip and lay on a bier in the room of a strange inn; soon the pall-bearers would come and carry me out through the door, feet first; but the pall-bearers would not be Jews . . . .

In the afternoon my friend Partyka came running to me. I had forgotten that I was invited to His Reverence's table that day, too. I had completely lost the sense of time. I told Partyka not a word about what had happened in the interval. I begged off, claiming an upset stomach, and Partyka believed me; luckily there were no marks of ill-treatment on the visible parts of my body. Partyka regretted my indisposition all the more since, he now informed me, he had already fixed the day of the conversion. "Your godfather will be inconsolable," he said thoughtfully. "He must leave on Saturday."

"I shall be quite all right tomorrow," I assured him.

We had nothing more to discuss, so Partyka soon left and returned only late in the evening.

The next day I partook of the happiness of the mystery which affords salvation.

My godfather, an elderly gentleman who lived on an estate only a quarter-mile from H carried me off in his coach. Although the snow was falling in thick clumps, there was still no sled path, so we rode to church in a carriage. Our way ran through the market and the main streets of the town. Luckily our carriage was shut tight because of the snowfall. But when I looked out of the window of the coach door, I saw that the market of H looked exactly as in my hallucination the first hour after my arrival. But I looked only once. I was much too weak to bear the sight of this town and its Jews. This physical state may also have been responsible for the fact that I can not remember much about the conversion itself. I still remember only the white, red and gold of Partyka's vestments; the childishly blissful eyes of the old gentleman, my godfather; and the blackness of my garment's sleeve, which hung on me unwrinkled and lifeless, like the black sheet over a corpse. Thus I was baptised. But perhaps my memory deserts me for profoundly sacred reasons. Baptism is a rebirth. A rebirth is a birth — who can remember his own birth? After the conversion I felt as though I were new-born. As it is written: "And I will sprinkle pure water upon you, and ye shall be clean from all your uncleanness."

xxiii

That afternoon I left. My godfather accompanied us to the railroad station, for Partyka was traveling as far as Lemberg with me. For the last time I rode through the town in the carriage. It was a Friday. The whole town was up and about. The snow-covered market place was black with caftaned figures who stared cursing after the carriage that slowly rolled over the doughy snow, trodden down by feet hurrying on business. When I cast one look out of the closed carriage, I saw them spitting, heard them cursing. They did so with great fear. They made all sorts of pretenses, but I understood perfectly that their curses and imprecations were intended for me. This time I glanced out at this fanatical uproar more than once, for it did me good to feel how indifferent I was to these vexations now.

After a short farewell visit with His Reverence, we drove quickly to the station. It, too, was swarming with black figures. There, too, they bustled about busily, the traders and the brokers, singly and in groups. There, too, they waved their slender sticks, as though scaring off snapping dogs. Only one who understood their crude curses could be aware that I was the dog at whom they brandished their sticks both stealthily and playfully at the same time.

Partyka semed to notice nothing. But perhaps he was only pretending. For he was in a great hurry to climb into the train and he advised the old gentleman, my godfather, not to wait for the train, which was lingering too long in the border station H. We sat quietly in our compartment for a good half hour, our hearing the only part of us still in the town of H, till the bell rang. As the train slowly began to roll, I rose and stepped to the window, to take a last farewell look at the beautiful town forest of H. I wish I had never done so! For the sight I saw on the station with that last farewell look left deep tracks in my heart. All the wounds I carried away from the town of H have healed, leaving no trace. But that, the last wound of all, left a scar that has never closed. And the very smile of forgiveness with which I now conjure up that sight is the scar . . . .

Rows of Jews were standing on the railroad station by the slowly rolling train. I did not know that so many of them had assembled on the platform. But they were not shouting now and were not brandishing their sticks. Their eyes were all looking for my compartment in the slowly rolling train. Someone saw me at the window and let out a loud cry; then at once, as at a command, they all raised their sticks, and the train glided past a complete forest of threatening sticks. I had in the meantime so armed myself with indifference that this pronouncement of popular wrath would not have made the slightest impression on me, had not a stick on the periphery suddenly fallen into my field of vision — a stick which I recognized at once. It was not Rabbi Shmelke's stick as, still calm, I suspected at first glance. It was an old stick with a lightly bent handle, smoothed down, bone-pale, gleaming languid like a stone in the sun. True, it was not Rabbi Shmelke's stick, but it was the stick of Rabbi Abba, my great-grand-uncle . . .

And behind the black sleeve that threatened me, extending

[312]

this stick with the smooth crook upwards, I saw the face of my brother, the face of my brother Velvel, deathly pale . . . .

As though struck upon the head by a blow from that stick, I fell backwards to the floor unconscious on the spot.

xxiv

Later Partyka told me how cunningly he had contrived to deceive the Jews. The evening I lay dreaming on the sofa in his room he had made a trip to the sexton and charged him to inform Red Goddl that I was, indeed, the one he was seeking in the name of the rabbi of H, but that I had already been baptised in Vienna and was staying here only for a few days as a guest of His Reverence. Now I understood for the first time why Red Goddl had wreaked his wrath on me, and why he had called me a liar. Had I not promised him to respond to the call of his youthful rabbi? Hearing this report and giving it credence, must not Goddl have thought my promise nothing but a shameful mockery of his master?

I do not mention this as a charge against my friend — he did his duty and believed he must set me on the right path by a white lie when I seemed to be wavering at the decisive moment — nor do I say it with the idea of excusing myself. If Partyka's white lie must excuse one of us, let it be the Red *Gabbe*. I am telling you this as an example of how fate employs petty means as well as great, and now and then bares the meaning of its dominance through those very things that we men call misunderstanding. How wisely spoke the old man in my dream: Forget what is immaterial.

xxv

Still another example, my son: All my life I have thought it was only a misunderstanding, though a fatal misunderstanding, that my great-grand-uncle Rabbi Abba took me for a soldier when I sought and found refuge in his house one bitter winter night.

I entered his house together with my brother Velvel, but since I was wearing my high-school uniform, he believed I was a soldier. And the old man — he was then ninety-two years of age — had often dreamed about the angel of death who would appear to him at the end of his days in the shape of a soldier with a knife in his hand to anounce his death; he saw in me, presumed a soldier, the bringer of his death, and — died in my arms that night . . . Two years later I was called up with the reserves. I was a soldier; I wore the Emperor's coat, but inwardly I was very far from thinking myself a soldier. What am I doing as a soldier? I said to myself. Like all students who were in good physical condition, I had been drafted for one year, had done my civic duty and served my year, but remained for the nonce what I had been before, a student. I was then promoted to be an officer and called up every other year for maneuvers; I was an officer in the reserve, but it seemed to me to resemble a game and pretense. I remained a civilian, no soldier at all. Rabbi Abba had erred in seeing his dream soldier in me, I said to myself. It had been a misunderstanding.

Now the war is here. Again I wear the Emperor's coat and it is a game no longer. Many who, like me, obeyed the call of the fatherland and with enthusiasm may still feel that their soldier's uniform is nothing but a disguise; I am not in that mood — I feel now that Rabbi Abba saw clearly. I am a soldier. Had I only always been a soldier, perhaps much that was error would not have happened! But these are only idle thoughts. If I have not lived as a soldier, I shall die as a soldier, anyway. It is only now that I can grasp the real context of my frequent dream about the court. Only now do I understand the judgment that was shown me in a picture: The soldier whose path seemed to me so brief is I. Translated into words, the judgment must mean: a soldier's death. The judgment is, viewed strictly, only an explication, an interpretation of the fifth commandment: Honor thy father and thy mother, that thy days may be lengthened. I have broken this commandment, so my days are not lengthened, but shortened. A just judgment.

A lenient judgment. The leniency consists in the fact that my days are to be shortened by my dying a soldier's death. A just judgment, a lenient judgment, perhaps a heavenly judgment, and not an earthly one at all. For with the mitigation, at the same time a severity was given to the judgment. For next to the picture of the judgment, I was shown another picture, that of the Scriptures. But what part of the Scriptures was I shown? The letters of that dictum which begins, "He who kills a living being kills a whole world." To be a soldier during war and carry that dictum in one's heart is no easy matter. But perhaps in this very severity lies the true grace of the judgment? Perhaps a soldier like me, who feels far more horror at killing than at being killed, will yet find compassion before the Supreme Judge?

xxvi

You see, my dear son, Rabbi Abba, blessed be his memory, was right: I am a soldier. I am a soldier and I do not believe that I have become one only through a transformation or an accident. There are no accidents. It is no accident that I am with a troop that is defending this particular border of the fatherland, the border between Austria and Russia, the border between the light of Europe and the darkness of the Czar's empire. This war is the last war of the peoples. As a child I heard a prophecy from my father's mouth, a prophecy by the great Rabbi of Kobryn, who said: "When the Messiah comes, he will first appear in Russia, because here the need has already become as great as the need before the end of time."

xxvii

I shall not be able to write any more, my dear son. Till now there have been only small border skirmishes, but now it seems that something larger is taking place. From close up, everything seems different than from a distance; not only a mountain and a river and a man, but the war, too, seems different from close up from what one imagines to himself. Yesterday we pulled into a village, a small village on the border, a village like Dobropolia. The first thing we saw were gallows. And on the gallows there hung a priest, a Greek-Catholic priest. They call them "popes" here. A Hungarian detachment, which had been here before us, had learned that the Ukrainian pope was a so-called "Russophile." He was said to have signaled with lights during the night to the enemy artillery. I have known many such popes, and there were many Russophiles among them — that is indisputable. But the notion of a priest giving the enemy artillery signals with a lantern seems to me as grotesque as the sight of these gallows. But this is war. My God, I hope my old provost is no longer living. He, too, was a Russophile.

xxviii

The first battle has taken place. It was a battle between Austrian and Russian cavalry. We in Austria have thought the Russian army backward. That's what our generals were sure of. Our cavalry paraded into the enemy's territory in red pants and lively tunics. The cossacks had field-green uniforms and light machine guns — and we had red pants and carbines. The inevitable happened. We are no longer in enemy territory — we, the remains of a few cavalry divisions. I am lying in a hospital in Zloczow. A good fifty per cent of my regiment were Ukrainians. Most of them peasant boys. They were stuck into Austrian uniforms and arrayed against the Russians. Across the way even more than 50 per cent of the Russians, the cossacks, were certainly Ukrainians. They were stuck into Russian uniforms and arrayed against the Austrians. The only difference between the Ukrainians on this side and those on that side is that ours are Greek-Catholic and theirs are Greek-Orthodox. They attack one another very bravely. And both on this side and on that the priests have blessed the weapons. We are now in the year 1914 since salvation —

[316]

I have wished to tell you so much, my dear son. I wished to write a great deal about my life for you. And what have I told you? Dreams. But I feel it is right thus. Without having planned it in advance, in telling you dreams I have remained within our old tradition. Dreams have played a large role in the history of our people. The fate of our people was woven out of dreams from the very beginning. In a dream the Lord appeared to our patriarch Abraham and said to him: "Go and seek a land!" In a dream our patriarch Jacob saw the ladder of heaven. Dreams decided the fate of his son Joseph. And not only our own dreams but the dreams of others, as well, have often rescued us. A dream that the King of Gerar dreamed rescued our Father Abraham when he was in danger. A dream of Laban's helped our Father Jacob when he was in danger. And the dreams of Pharaoh helped our Joseph out of prison in Egypt. As you see, my dear son, I am in good company with my dreams. To be sure, I cannot say whether my dreams have led or misled me. And the other's dream, Rabbi Abba's dream, did it direct me, or did it misdirect me?

However it may be, whatever I may have to rue, I do not rue the fact that I have told you dreams. It was good so. Death cannot be fooled. I see that, now that I am so close to it . . . I am lying in the garrison hospital in Zloczow. The Russians are advancing. Our army is in retreat. The hospital is being evacuated. The doctors say they will take me along, too. I do not believe them. The badly wounded will be left behind here. I shall fall into the hands of the Russians. It is the last chapter. And let the last sentence in this last chapter be according to our old tradition, the life-and-death cry of our people: "Hear O Israel, the Lord our God, the Lord is one."

God be with you!

Your Father.

BOOK IV

BOOK IV

1

I<small>T WAS</small> bright morning when Alfred tore his glance from the concluding word of the testament and raised his eyes. Through the open window he saw a strip of blue water and a strip of blue sky between the gently waving bulrushes in the small pond and heard the ringing of the quiet silence in the room. He felt now, as he had felt all night while reading, everything that was going on in the room. He knew without looking that Uncle Stefan had taken off his spectacles to conceal his agitation and was carefully cleaning the lenses, while his naked, nearsighted eyes wandered blind about the room. He sensed that Uncle Velvel was sitting with his head sunk low, his face in his hands, frozen at the table, as though in a separate room, lonely in his sadness. He heard Yankel's slow, whistling breath and knew that soon, at once, now, the old man would open his mouth and say something nasty about Jews. Alfred even knew exactly what he would say. Old Yankel was the only listener who during the reading of the testament had been unable to refrain from giving vent to his feelings. With heavy sighs, loud clucks, hoarse, unarticulated exclamations, Yankel had followed the description of the small-town Jews of H with particular interest. At the conclusion of the story — at the description of the emergence at the station, among the many threatening sticks raised against the apostate, of the stick of Rabbi Abba and of Velvel's deathly pale face — old Yankel had completely lost his self-control and shouted at Velvel:

"You were there?! You threatened him?! With the stick?! With Rabbi Abba's stick?!"

Without raising his head, Velvel had motioned to him with

[321]

a small spiritless gesture of his hand, and Yankel had controlled himself with a fierce grimace. Only his violent breathing told how upset the old man still was. Now, in the prolonged silence, after the last word had been read, Yankel's whistling, hoarse breath was audible like an unending hoarse scream. Nevertheless, Alfred had only one wish: that this semi-silence might be maintained forever, never to be torn and defiled by a spoken word.

After what seemed an eternity in which there was no word, in which the old man's agitation, overawed by the silence, resolved into slow breaths, Alfred dared to thank him with a glance. Though his eyes did meet Yankel's, their glances did not, for Yankel's old eyes had simultaneously disappeared inwards. Dr. Frankl's naked eyes, undressed without his spectacles, were as impenetrable as clouded glass. Velvel Dobropolier concealed his face in his arms, which lay lifeless on the tablecloth; it seemed as though his head and his arms had fallen asleep, but his breath panted in slow, gulping sobs, interrupted by alert, hearkening pauses for breath. Thus the four of them sat, separated and yet profoundly bound by the almost visible presence of a fifth, of the man Joseph Mohilevski, who had died a long time before, yet was bound with so many black strings of sadness and so many golden strings of love to life. They sat in the fresh silence of the morning, which flooded into the room through the open window. They did not look at one another and were silent, lest the voice of the dead, which had spoken to them with living words a night long, be frightened away. All at once, as though a call to awake had passed among them, all the birds outside awoke, and in a singing chatter announced cheerfully and quickly the dawn of a hot day.

Then the door opened slowly and inaudibly and Pessa entered. She was followed by Donja, walking on tiptoe even more cautiously than Pessa. Now that the birds outside were clamoring that it was day, the women dared to say good morning to the disturbed men. With the women, who brought in trays of hot bowls and steaming pots, an extremely pleasant odor of food

[322]

freshly cooked, freshly roasted and freshly baked filled the room and assailed the nostrils of the men who had not slept all night. Pessa had not gone to sleep that night. Although at first she did not know what the men were reading for so long — her prophetic soul had deserted her this once — Pessa had wakefully but calmly remained on her post in the kitchen. But she was called late in the evening at Yankel's suggestion to decipher an illegible, blurred and partly crossed out sentence in the testament — it was the passage where Joseph Mohilevski told of the preparatory instructions in the catechism which he received from Partyka — and smoothly performed this magic, to the particular astonishment and delight of Dr. Frankl. Afterwards, she fell into such a state of excitement that she aroused Donja, half nodding, half awake with her protectress, to share the sensation as well as the excitement with her. Although it was already midnight, Pessa did not dare — now that she knew what was being read — to push her way into the room with the evening meal that had been ordered and disturb the reader. For a time she chatted with Donja in their common bedroom, then they both lay down at the open window of the kitchen and listened in the night. True, they heard voices reading — once it was Alfred's voice, another time it was the strange voice of the distinguished guest — but Pessa understood not a word of what was being read. The voice came from close by in the still of the night, but the words were no clearer and no more comprehensible than Velvel Dobropolier's monotonous recital of Psalms in Grandfather's Room during the nights before the high holidays. The cool night air revived and awakened Pessa but the excitement of waiting perhaps to be called once more to decipher an illegible page did not desert her. All at once she could no longer bear the torturous idleness and, making fires in the hearth and in the baking oven, began to cook and bake and roast as for the Sabbath. Although she did not particularly hurry and, in the fervor of creativity, quite forgot the unusual cause of her night activity, with Donja's help early in the morning almost all the Sabbath-like preparations were already finished — and the men

[323]

had still not yet gone to sleep. But they were no longer reading, they were silent. Now Pessa was happy: now she could go in without first being called and add her improvised contribution to the events of the night. So it happened that Dr. Frankl was again able to taste on Sunday before sunrise the small dishes and delicacies that he had come to know and value with Velvel Dobropolier as entrees to the physical delights of Sabbath.

But it was old Yankel rather than the guest who was the first to succumb to the odor of the delicious refreshments. After Pessa and Donja had set the table, served and left on tiptoe, a clear rumbling became audible in the room, which out-clamored the jubilating birds.

"There's a hole in my stomach," said Yankel excusing the noise, and looking furtively at Velvel.

Velvel Dobropolier heard nothing. After having saved the testament from the hands of the women busy at the table and gathering it to himself with an abstracted motion, he sat at the table absorbed in his thoughts, his hands crossed over his chest, pressing his brother's testament to his heart. His eyes were opened wide, but his ears were deaf.

"Velvel," began Yankel after a while, "please forgive me, I asked a stupid question before. A really stupid question. How could you have threatened Yossele with the stick? You weren't even there. I remember how it was. You wanted to go. But they wouldn't let you."

"Had I only gone. . ." whispered Velvel with trembling lips. "Had I only gone."

Meanwhile he had risen and stood a while in front of Alfred, sunk in thought. Then he stretched forth both hands, holding the manuscript, looked questioningly at Alfred, as though begging for permission to keep it, and with a quiet step left the room.

"There's a hole in my stomach," Yankel repeated immediately, pushed nearer to the table and, representing Velvel as the host, served his guest and gave him a good example by helping himself. They ate twice, first with the sharp appetites of men

[324]

who had not slept for a night, then with the keen hunger of men who had been deeply shaken. There were only two eating, for Alfred had immediately unobtrusively followed Velvel out of the room. They ate in silence, for they had too much to say to one another. Afterwards they betook themselves to their beds to rest. But only one of the four men was able to sleep for a few hours; it was Alfred.

Dr. Frankl spent the afternoon in the company of Yankel. Together they went to the farm, and the cow stall, and Yankel explained the entire business to the guest. Then he led him over the Groblja to the *Gazon* and showed him the old house. As Alfred had done when he saw the old park and the house for the first time, Dr. Frankl marveled at the fact that so beautiful a house was being allowed to fall into ruin, and wished Yankel to tell him how long it had not been inhabited.

"Originally, the family Mohilevski rented this estate, for how many generations I do not know exactly. They always lived in the tenant's house where Velvel now is living. The estate itself belonged to a family Zabilski, who had fallen heir to it through some branch of the family. They never had their family seat here. But one of the Zabilskis, inspecting the estate once, liked the pond here so much, that he built a summer house here and laid out this park as well. I did not know that Zabilski. He lived in the distant past. But I did know the last of the Zabilskis, and I still remember him. I saw him as a child. Velvel's grandfather, Susja Mohilevski, was still alive then. The last Zabilski was a Polish nobleman of the old school. He hated Austria and always called Emperor Franz Joseph, 'the German.' He had leased out most of his many estates after the fashion of the Polish nobility. He managed one estate, which was his seat, himself. He was rich and childless, and how oddly he managed his estate, I heard from Reb Susja Mohilevski himself.

"During the sixties, perhaps it was earlier, perhaps, later, I don't know exactly any longer, a state monopoly for the production of liquor was introduced here. The landowners who ran distilleries were allowed to produce certain yearly quotas. Production of an excess over the quota, which was strictly controlled by the finance office, was punishable by a monetary fine that depended on the quantity that had been illegally produced above the quota. Now, the measuring apparatus was not very exact, and the foremen of the liquor distilleries, who were not graduate engineers, made every conceivable error during the first few years. Naturally, the office of control knew that the quotas were being exceeded because of such errors and was clever enough to overlook the fine in such cases. The procedure was simple enough: Every distillery had printed forms where one had only to report one's error, and with that the case was closed. Once an error crept into the calculations of the foreman of the Zabilski liquor distillery. The man filled out the form and placed it before Zabilski for his signature.

" 'How much is the fine?' Mr. Zabilski asked his distiller.

"The man figured out the fine and showed Mr. Zabilski the sum: 12,000 guilden.

" 'What?' said Mr. Zabilski, 'shall a Zabilski bow down before the German for 12,000 guilden!' He refused to sign and paid the fine."

"Did this Zabilski live in the house here?" asked Dr. Frankl.

"No," said Yankel. "The house was uninhabited then. But there were several well-furnished rooms where the last Zabilski stayed for two or three days whenever he inspected the estate. He used to inspect Dobropolia once every five years, like a bishop inspecting the diocese. When he was here the last time, I saw him. I was twelve years old then. I had the honor of dusting off the old gentleman's shoes when he came out of the stalls. It was this Zabilski who sold Dobropolia to Susja Mohilevski. That happened on the occasion of his last visit. He only stayed for two days then. Before riding off, he called Susja Mohilevski to him on the *Gazon* and the transaction was closed. As he bade Susja goodbye he said:

"I have learned from the family documents that the Mohilevskis were tenants here in Dobropolia before the estate belonged to the Zabilskis. This treasure was appended to some great grandmother's dowry. My grandfather, who liked to fish in the big pond, built this house. I have no heirs, and you, Susja, have an industrious son. It is my desire that this estate shall not fall into the hand of strangers.'

"And after a hearty handshake he added: 'I give Dobropolia over to you, because you come of a venerable, long-settled family, and because you are a Mohilevski. If you were called Rosenfeld or Rosenkranz or any other German name, I would not leave the estate to you, despite everything. But Mohilevski and Dobropolia — they go very well together. God bless you and your family.'

"At that he rode off and we never saw him again.

"I still see him before me: he was a small, sturdy man with a snow-white Van Dyke and a fine lion's head. He always wore white spats over his shoes and carried a stick with a golden handle. He called everyone by the familiar 'thou,' even Susja Mohilevski, who was not much younger than he. He was friendly with no one. But he respected old Mrs. Elka Mohilevski very much. 'I don't really come to inspect the estate, but to enjoy your *gefillte* fish, Mrs. Mohilevski,' he used to say whenever he arrived. As a matter of fact, he always appeared Friday afternoon and ate all three Sabbath meals with the Mohilevskis."

"But why didn't the Mohilevskis move into this house on the *Gazon* instead of letting it go to ruin?" asked Dr. Frankl.

"The house and the park were kept in good condition until 1914, the year of the war. During the war soldiers of every nationality were housed here, Austrian, Hungarian, then Russian, then Austrian again, and German. You know how soldiers live. You can imagine how it looked after four years. I was here the whole time. At first I tried to do something, and had the place cleaned and cleared up after each troop of departing soldiers. But finally I had to give up. Velvel lived in Vienna as a refugee during these four years, and when he came back in the Fall of 1918, after the break-up of the monarchy, I talked to him and begged him to have the house renovated and to move. But, as you know, Velvel lost his wife and his children in the war. He came back alone, in mourning. Nothing could be done with him. He did not wish to give up his father's house, particularly Grandfather's Room. That is understandable. It would be understandable even if our dear Velvel was not such a clerical ... But Alfred was exactly as impressed as you, Doctor, when he saw the house for the first time. And I think it probable that he will put this old house in order again."

"But is it certain that Alfred will come back if he leaves now?" asked Dr. Frankl. "Our Alfred changes his spots very quickly. You've only known him for one year. I've known him longer."

"He has changed considerably. Don't you find that to be true?" said Yankel.

"He has changed, and that not to his disadvantage. He has almost become a man during this one year," Dr. Frankl conceded.

"Yes, he has almost become a man. That is why I firmly believe that he will come back. If he does not come back to his uncle and his studies in Grandfather's Room, perhaps he will come back to me and the farm," said Yankel thoughtfully.

"And if he does not come back to me and to the farm," he added, as though considering this event for the first time, and paused for a long time before the conclusion: "he will come back to the girl, Donja — that is as good as certain."

"The beautiful girl?! Do you really believe —?"

"She is our wheelwright's daughter. But by the time Alfred is back here, she will be a real peasant wife. Pessa and I, we have provided for all eventualities."

"When one provides for all eventualities, sometimes things go all wrong," said Dr. Frankl lightly; but he regretted his words when he saw the consternation that passed over Yankel's face. "And yet it is prudent to provide for all eventualities," he quickly added.

"Yes, one must provide," Yankel agreed, relieved, "provide for all eventualities, and, for the rest, be prepared for everything to turn out differently. As in farming."

[328]

On the way home Yankel showed the guest the spot on the Groblja where the misfortune had taken place, and told him about Lipusj and about Alfred's great love for the child.

"It's good, sir, that you brought his father's testament at this very time. I should not otherwise be so sure that Alfred would still come back to us after the loss. My imprisonment came at the right time for me, too. It tore Alfred away from his melancholy, and, frankly, put me on my feet again. It's good that you came. You have helped us a great deal."

"Are you so sure, Mr. Christiampoler, that the testament influenced Alfred the same way?" asked Dr. Frankl. "When I took the document in Vienna to bring it to Alfred here, I was not only concerned to fulfill my friend's last wish — I could have waited with that till Alfred was back in Vienna. I was under a compulsion to have my friend share the unexpected dispensation of the fate that led all of us into the house of the dead man's father — this house to which the dead man was bound despite everything, as we have seen, with so painful a love, to his last hour. Let him be with us, I said to myself. And what we have learned from our dead friend's testament this night gives us reason to suppose that he would have preferred it so. But I am not clear how things stand with Alfred."

"I'm not very worried about that," Yankel hastened to reassure his guest. "But perhaps I am not worried because, frankly, I did not understand everything in the testament. I don't say that to ask you to explain it to me. I know very well that if one doesn't understand something in his old age, he doesn't understand the explanation either. But now that we are talking about the testament, I shall ask you anyhow: Doctor, you were very close to Alfred's father during the last years of his life. Did you know or even suspect that he was so unhappy?"

"It is remarkable that you ask about that of all things. There is much in the testament that would have moved me, even if he had not been close to me. What moved me most deeply was to see fifteen years after a friend's death how unhappy he was. I lay down this morning, but I could not shut an eye.

How is it possible, I asked myself, how is it possible, that one can be so close to a friend and still not know how unhappy he is at bottom. Perhaps because all his life he was too proud to share himself completely with a friend."

They had arrived in front of the house and they were silent.

3

The next day Alfred sought a conversation with Uncle Velvel and persuaded Dr. Frankl to go into Velvel's room with him. They found Velvel bent over the table, writing. On the table were spread out the notebooks containing the testament and Velvel was busy copying. He would have preferred to keep the original in Dobropolia and give Alfred back only the copy, but he did not dare to express such a wish. He honored the legitimate claim of Alfred's mother, the widow, to the possession of the original, and did not grudge her, to a certain extent, a direct view of the hand which had signed and sealed in a document the last and final triumph of the Mohilevskis over the Pescheks. That this was the second, implied meaning of the document was something Velvel believed with all the fervor of his faith; nor would all the truth in the world have been able to shake this faith.

"Why are you making this work for yourself, Uncle?" asked Alfred. "I was beginning to wonder why you had disappeared."

"I am copying the most important passages. Unfortunately, I can't copy the whole thing so fast," said Velvel, and asked Dr. Frankl and Alfred to sit down.

"Time enough for that, Uncle," said Alfred. "I want to have a copy too, and I shall make one. But, Uncle, you shall keep the original and preserve it in Grandfather's Room with your other papers."

"That is very fine of you," said Velvel with a tender glance at Alfred. "This testament belongs in Grandfather's Room. But I had assumed that you would take it to Vienna with you and show it to your mother."

[330]

"No, I won't do that," said Alfred with a questioning look at Dr. Frankl. "What do you think, Uncle Stefan?"

"I had also assumed that you would take it with you. But now I think that you are right. You mustn't hurry."

"I don't think that it will do my mother good to read this testament. My mother always used to tell me how successful and happy my father was until the war broke out. She believed it, and she made me believe it, too. Now I see how terribly she deceived herself. I think it will be better to spare her this disillusionment."

"You are right, Alfred," Dr. Frankl hastened to agree. "At any rate let us give ourselves time to think further about it. What do you think?" he turned to Velvel.

"I do not think that I may venture an opinion on this subject, Doctor," said Velvel, his look wandering between Alfred and Dr. Frankl. "We shall leave that to Alfred. Do you know the day of your father's death?"

"What do you mean, Uncle?"

"Do you know the date?"

"Mother says it was the seventh of August, 1914."

"The Information Bureau of the War Ministry in Vienna gave me the same date. But it can't be right."

"Why not?" asked Dr. Frankl. "Why do you think so?"

"I think it scarcely possible that my brother could have composed this fairly voluminous document in so short a period after the outbreak of the war."

"That never occurred to me," said Dr. Frankl.

"Nor to me," Alfred concurred.

"As my brother says: from close up everything looks different, even the war. It was always thought that my brother died on the third day of the war. But that can't be right. We shall settle the date at the Soldiers' Cemetery in Zloczow. Then I shall reckon the date according to the Jewish calendar, and we shall both say Kaddish after him every year on the anniversary of his death, Susja."

"Yes," said Alfred, "we shall."

[331]

A long silence followed this decision. Uncle and nephew looked one another long in the eye, asking, searching, expectant. All at once they both stood up as at a command, and a close embrace affirmed briefly their inner accord.

When Velvel and Alfred had resumed their seats, Velvel explained his decision, his voice now fresh and powerful like that of a man who has overcome a serious illness, passed the crisis and is suddenly convalescent.

"Once a man came to a great rabbi and complained: 'What shall I do, Rabbi? My son has stopped believing in God! What shall I do?' 'Love him even more,' said the rabbi. We have all sinned against Yossel — may he rest in peace."

"I am glad to hear you say so, Uncle. Besides, I remember that you have always suspected and even admitted that. I see now how right you were to tell me the story about Rabbi Abba in Vienna during my very first visit to you. Yankel was very much dissatisfied with you at the time. Indeed, only now do I understand fully the far-reaching importance of that night with Rabbi Abba."

"I too understand its full importance only now," said Velvel. "We all erred: my father, your father, and I. Each in his own way. My father erred on the side of strictness. Your father erred on the side of pride. He was always an impatient man and a proud one. I erred on the side of prudence. I have always been prudent — even as a boy. Your father described me very well in the testament. It was not good that I was so prudent. I have already told that to you, Alfred. It can be as bad for a young person to be prudent as for an old one to be imprudent. Isn't that so, Doctor?"

"You have put it very well, my friend. The description fits me very well, too. I have gone so far as to make a profession of prudence. Amazing, how correctly your brother saw all of us — even himself."

"I have understood almost everything in my father's testament. I know very well that I have been able to understand it only because I lived here this year with you, Uncle Velvel. Otherwise I could scarcely have suspected that my father passed through an experience that was nothing less than gruesome. In Vienna I would have read this as a novel written at the beginning of the century. Now, for the first time, fifteen years after his death, I have found my father. But though this testament is directed to me, my father tells a great deal, in his dreams, as well, that only you two can explain, Uncle Velvel and Uncle Stefan."

"For example?" asked Velvel. "What are you referring to?"

"For example, the story about Alexander the Great which takes up so much space. One really can't dream such a story. Or can one?"

Both uncles regarded one another for a while. Then Dr. Frankl said:

"I also don't entirely believe that he could have dreamed this story as he presents it. Perhaps it was in part a day dream. Your father did, as we know, prepare to go to the rabbi and expected an argument on matters of religion. Besides, this story about Alexander the Great was a favorite of your father's. During the years when he had to adapt himself to a new language, your father often translated this story and read it to me in various versions. Perhaps he dreamed it as well, though not in so detailed and clear a form as he described in the testament. I assume that he wrote it down for you expressly that you might know his favorite story and might understand what thoughts he wrestled with during the decisive days of his life."

"Yes," said Alfred. "It may have been so. Another thing I don't understand is this child, the narrating judge. All the other figures in the dream are explained. We know who the little ancient was, we know who the other judges were, but there is nothing else in the testament about the child."

Again both uncles regarded one another for a while. Then Velvel said, "Perhaps I can explain that to you. You know

Dr. Katz now. You know that he prepared your father for the entrance examination to the secondary school and also played a role in his life. It seems your father didn't care much for the cabinet-maker's son."

"That feeling seems to have been mutual, Uncle, from what I established in the city," Alfred interjected.

"But the cabinet-maker Katz had a younger son. This son was younger than your father. He was a delicate, very gifted child; the younger son of the cabinet-maker looked like your father's description of the narrating judge.

"Your father loved this child, as you did our Lipale. The child died of consumption at the age of twelve. Your father saw him in his white shroud, and it made an indelible impression on him. He was still speaking of the boy years after his death. So he sees him in the dream as he had seen him for the last time."

"What was the child's name?" Alfred inquired.

"His name was David. I still remember him very clearly."

"It is remarkable, Uncle Velvel. Since reading the dream, I keep seeing our Lipusj in two shapes: in his own shape, and in that of the narrating judge."

After a moment of oppressive silence Alfred turned to Velvel again with a sudden question:

"Uncle Velvel, do you also believe in *Gilgul*?"

"*Gilgul*? Who told you about that?"

"Avram Aptowitzer believes in *Gilgul*."

"What is this *Gilgul*?" asked Dr. Frankl, and he addressed his question to Velvel.

"*Gilgul* means about the same as the transmigration of souls," said Velvel.

"Do you believe in *Gilgul*?" Alfred repeated his question.

"I don't believe that I believe in *Gilgul*," said Velvel.

Alfred took the answer quietly, but seemed somewhat disappointed.

"How is Mrs. Aptowitzer?" he asked after a while. "Have you any news from Avram Aptowitzer?"

"Unfortunately she isn't very well, Alfred," said Velvel. "But she is a very sturdy woman. Let us hope for the best."

"I shall take a turn over to Kozlova this afternoon and say good-bye to the Aptowitzers," said Alfred.

4

Towards evening, when Alfred had come home from his sad goodbye visit to the Aptowitzers in Kozlova, Pessa brought her protegé, the horse-trader's younger son, into his room.

"Well," Pessa said to the boy, "now you can tell Alfred everything," and withdrew.

"Young master —"

"What is it, old master?" said Alfred.

The boy smiled despite his excitement. To accustom Lipusj and the other children in the village not to address him as "Young master," Alfred used to counter with "Old master." It was a familiar game, and the joke encouraged the boy, for it reminded him of the good old days when he and Lipale and the other children daily rode to school with Alfred.

"I mean to say: Mr. Mohilevski —"

"That's better already," said Alfred.

"I mean to say: Alfred —"

"Now we are on the right track," said Alfred.

"I mean to say: Alfred, please send me to the Talmud school in Kozlova," he burst out with his request all at once, quickly and tearfully.

"Why do that?" asked Alfred. "Isn't Reb Salmen a good teacher?"

"Reb Salmen is a good teacher," said the boy. "Reb Salmen is a very good teacher. But my father . . . my father has become a pork merchant . . . He has cut off his beard and now he is going to deal in pork."

"I have already heard about it," said Alfred. "That is very sad. But there are other men who have cut off their beards, Leib Kahane, for example. On the other hand, there are some who have no beard at all, like Shmiel Gruenfeld, who is smooth-shaven, and myself — I have no beard, either."

"But you are not dealing in pork," said the boy, already in tears.

"Your father isn't really dealing in pork yet," Alfred comforted him.

"But he will. He said so himself. He came back from the city with his beard cut off and he said, 'Now I shall deal in pork.'"

"He said it, I know," said Alfred. "But he's not doing it yet. Let's wait a while. If he really does it, then we can talk about it again."

"If you don't want to send me to Kozlova, young master, then at least take me to Reb Wolf," said the boy. He was disappointed, but he controlled himself and didn't cry any more. "Reb Wolf will send me to Kozlova. I want to speak to Reb Wolf."

"Good," said Alfred, "come. I will take you to Reb Wolf at once."

The small boy was dressed as for the Sabbath. He was wearing shiny polished boots and long pants, his coat was neatly buttoned and on his head he wore the black hat he wore only on holidays.

"You must tell Reb Wolf everything," the boy said to Alfred when they were already in the hall. "I can't talk so well."

"You told me everything very well," said Alfred.

"But you must help me," whispered the boy, quite upset again.

Velvel was not alone in his room. He was in conversation with Dr. Frankl and Yankel. Alfred took the boy by the hand and presented him to Velvel.

"We have a matter to discuss with you, Uncle Velvel," said Alfred.

"Reb Wolf," began the boy, "Reb Wolf, I have come to you . . . My mother sends me to you, Reb Wolf . . ."

"But you didn't tell me that," interrupted Alfred.

"I didn't tell you. I forgot. But it's true. My mother sent me."

"Fine," said Velvel. "Your mother sent you to me."

"To the young master . . . to Alfred, and to you, Reb Wolf."

"Well then, your mother sent you to Alfred and to me," said Velvel. "And what message are you to deliver to us?"

"I am to deliver the message, my mother said, I am to ask you, Reb Wolf, to send me to the Talmud school in Kozlova."

"Have you already told Alfred that?" asked Velvel.

"Yes," said Alfred, "he has already told me that."

"I only forgot to tell him that my mother sent me."

"He wants to go to school in Kozlova because his father has said that he will deal in pork."

"My father cut his beard off," said the lad, and looked at all the men, including the strange gentleman. Suddenly he burst into sobs. "My father . . . has . . . become a pork merchant."

"What a yowling," old Yankel intervened. "Shabse Punes has finally become a pork merchant."

But Velvel quickly silenced Yankel with a nod.

Dr. Frankl, though an experienced diplomat, did not now know whether he should be serious with Wolf Mohilevski or cheerful with Yankel.

"If your mother has sent you," said Velvel, "you did right to come to me. But I cannot send you to the Talmud school in Kozlova at once. First I shall speak to your mother. I shall also speak to your father. Though he is going to deal in pork, he is still your father, and I can do nothing without his consent. But you can rest easy. I shall try to persuade him, and perhaps it will be possible for you to be sent to school in Kozlova. And now go in peace. You are really a bright lad. I shall call you when I have talked everything over with your parents."

"Thank you, Reb Wolf," said the little one very seriously, and he was not crying any more now. "I knew that you would send me to school in Kozlova." With that he left, well-behaved and dignified, as though he were already a Talmud student.

[337]

At the door he turned around, bowed and wished them all, "Good night!"

"If I have understood correctly," said Dr. Frankl, "this lad wants to leave home because his father has become a pork merchant?"

"Yes," said Yankel, "you understood. This child is already as fanatical as an old clerical."

"Why fanatical?" said Velvel. "He is a well-bred, pious child. Why does he have to become a pork merchant, this Shabse!"

"Why he is becoming a pork merchant?" Yankel said heatedly. "Because horse-trading doesn't bring him a livelihood any more. Why should the rascal not be allowed to deal in pork?"

"It is not the custom in this part of the country for Jews to deal in pork," Velvel explained to Dr. Frankl. "Our bailiff is usually no friend of this horse-trader, but when there's something against the Jews, he places himself, as we have just seen, on the side of pork."

"Doctor, can you explain to me, why the Jews have been waging a thousand-year-old war against pork?" said Yankel.

"In Hungary," said Dr. Frankl, "Jewish pork merchants are no rare occurances, to the best of my knowledge."

"We haven't progressed to that point here," said Velvel, "but with the help of Shabse Punes and Yankel Christiampoler we shall attain that rung of civilization, too."

"Can you explain to me, Rabbi Velvel, why a Jew may trade in horses and not in pork? From the ritual standpoint the horse, too, is an impure animal."

Velvel cast a glance at Alfred and they understood one another without words: If he was already inveighing against the Jews, he was the old Yankel again. Both were happy and Velvel resumed his peaceful battle with Yankel. He fought him as a father his son:

"Unfortunately, I am no rabbi. A rabbi could instruct you more soundly. So far as I know, the pig in its original state is a beast of prey, which is not true of the horse. Or do you know better, Yankel?"

[338]

"Beast of prey?" said Yankel. "But the Christians don't eat beasts of prey, either. I have often dined with my friend Krasnianski — in my younger years, of course — I don't do that any more for your sake — and dined well. He never gave me a cat goulash or a wolf schnitzel. That can't be the reason. There must be another reason for the Jewish hatred of pork. You, as a clerical, should know about it."

"Perhaps I do," said Velvel pacifically, "but I won't tell you. We have a beloved guest and it is not customary to quarrel in the presence of a guest. That isn't the custom among pork-eaters, either."

"I suggest a compromise," said Dr. Frankl, obviously amused by the conversation. "The Jewish hatred of pork is, I think, not personal. I should like to believe that we Jews hate pork, not because of what it is, but what it represents: piggishness."

"If my opponent — or shall we say rather: — the opponent of the Jews — accepts this striking explanation," said Velvel, "I am ready to accept the compromise with thanks."

"I accept," said Yankel, "there's a hole in my stomach. Let's eat. Pessa has set the table long ago. Whenever there's talk of pork, I develop a wolfish hunger."

At table Yankel came back to the subject of the family Punes.

"It's remarkable that this Shabse has such a good, pious child. A wonder!"

"If you know his mother, you know it's no wonder," said Velvel. "I don't understand why she didn't come along."

"That is easy to understand," said Yankel, "because she is afraid of her tyrant."

"If one knows her brother, this child's uncle," said Alfred, "one begins to understand how such a child could have grown up in the house of the horse-trader. It's a shame, Uncle Stefan, that you haven't met Mechzio . . ." Alfred began to tell Dr. Frankl about Mechzio. He described his first Sabbath in Grandfather's Room, the great distress he was in the first time he was called up to the Torah, and how pious, ox-eyed Mechzio had rescued him from his dilemma. Velvel and Yankel listened to

[339]

the story with amazement and the more Alfred related the sadder they became, for they began to perceive how much Alfred really missed the runaway Mechzio.

"He will come back," said Yankel, trying to comfort Alfred. "He ran away once before and came back. You'll see — when you come back from your vacation you'll find Mechzio here again."

After eating Alfred took Yankel aside and asked him, "Who has the key of the old house?"

"Of which house?" Yankel wondered.

"Of the old house on the *Gazon*," said Alfred.

"What do you need the key of the old house for?" asked Yankel.

"I want to see it from the inside," said Alfred.

"You mustn't do that," Yankel warned him. "The house is dilapidated. It is dangerous to go into it."

"I won't go alone. I have a ten o'clock appointment for tomorrow morning with the carpenter and builder Srul Peczenik to meet on the *Gazon*. I shall also take our Nazarewicz along and the smith, to settle how far gone the house is. I don't believe it is dilapidated. But we shall see about it tomorrow."

"And what if it isn't dilapidated?" asked Yankel. "What will you do with the house?"

"I'll tell you that tomorrow, Yankel," said Alfred.

"Do you hear, Velvel," cried Yankel, beaming with joy, "Alfred wants to renovate the old house on the *Gazon*."

"I didn't say renovate. First I want to see it and find out whether it is really dilapidated," said Alfred.

"But you *should* renovate it!" Yankel advised him. "You should marry and furnish a fine home, as is only proper."

"Have you already found a bride for our Alfred, dear Yankel?" Velvel inquired.

"If you were not such a clerical, I would suggest one."

"Whom, for example?" asked Velvel.

"Winterstein's youngest daughter, for example. She will come into two estates."

"Well, well," said Velvel, "personally I would prefer Kasja Kobylanska to the daughter of the pork-eater Winterstein."

"May I say something?" Alfred interposed.

"Please do," said Yankel, "Please say something. After all, you are the bridegroom."

"As the bridegroom, if I may speak up, I should like to agree with Uncle Velvel. Rather Kasja Kobylanska than Winterstein's daughter."

"I knew it," said Yankel, and turned to Dr. Frankl. "In this one year he has become a clerical just like his uncle."

"Do you really intend to renovate the old house?" asked Velvel.

"I'll tell you that tomorrow, Uncle: you and Uncle Stefan and Yankel. Tomorrow at twelve, after I have thoroughly examined the house with experts."

5

The following morning, Alfred, accompanied by the wheelwright Nazarewicz and the smith, went to the *Gazon*. There the builder, Srul Peczenik, called "the Goat" in the village because he looked like a buck goat, was waiting for him. He had three instruments of his craft with him: a measuring rod, which he had stuck into the leg of his boot, a small wire spit with a handy handle, and a hatchet.

"The house has a fairly deep cellar and usually we would first go into it to inspect the foundation," said Srul Peczenik. "But since everybody is afraid to go into the house because it is said to be dilapidated, it's even more dangerous in a cellar. So first let's inspect the ground floor."

The smith opened the door on the north side and they stepped in. It was bright and cool in the corridor; there was pale grass growing between the stone flags of the pathway; and on the inside of the window frames, too, sickly moss was rampant, as well as on the outside. The parquet floors of the rooms were swollen, and as the four men slowly stepped through the rooms, chalk and mortar rained from the ceiling.

"All this sounds more dangerous than it really is," Peczenik reassured them. "This house has a skin disease, so to speak." And he went into a corner, where a tremendous tear gaped in a wall, chopped off the unsound plaster with his hatchet and tapped the sound masonry with satisfaction.

There were six rooms on the ground floor and a large, hall-like room with a large windowed door to the garden terrace, where Alfred had often taken cover with Donja on rainy days in the fall. On the first floor they walked through eight rooms, which had kept much better than those on the ground floor. In three rooms they found the remainder of the furniture: the ruined scaffolding of a four-poster — Srul Peczenik's opinion was that the bed wasn't lost either — a half-cracked mirror, a couple of easy chairs with torn slipcovers, a long, still solid table in the library room, where the wooden paneling on the walls was falling to pieces.

"This is a fine piece of work," the builder affirmed almost with regret. "But it can't be saved any longer."

Under the guidance of Srul Peczenick, who was the only one who spoke, they afterwards climbed down to the cellar floor, where they found first a large kitchen and next to it a smaller one, and many rooms for the servants. All these rooms had shady green light from the windows, which were on a level with the lawn of the *Gazon*. The cellar itself was a couple of steps deeper than the adjacent rooms. It was so dark there that they had to wait a while until their eyes became accustomed to the darkness. To their amazement, and even that of the expert Peczenik, there was no grass growing and no moss rampant in the cellar, which was airy and dry.

"Here is the secret," said Peczenik. "I never thought this house was dilapidated, but now I can see why it has kept so well. The good sub-cellar, the sound foundation — that is the secret. If you give me three or four months, Mr. Mohilevski, you'll not recognize the house again when you return."

The wheelwright Nazarewicz and the smith agreed with the builder's conclusion.

[342]

"What this house needs is a new roof," said Nazarewicz.

"The house simply has to be shoed again," decided the smith.

Outside on the *Gazon* again, they took another complete turn around the house, and Srul Peczenik, who was already in his sixties, summarized his opinion: "The enemy of this house is the grass. My father used to say: 'When you become old, a beard grows on your boots.' Grass does the same to a house. If you had not come here, Mr. Mohilevski, another twenty years, and that grass would have completely swallowed this fine house."

While Alfred was inspecting the house in the *Gazon* with his experts, Velvel was sitting at breakfast with his guest and Yankel.

"I wonder," said Velvel, "that you didn't go along, Yankel. You were always in favor of having the house renovated."

"You think that I was afraid to go along?" said Yankel. "Naturally, I was afraid. I am already too dilapidated myself to plod around old houses. But why didn't *you* go along?"

"I was never in favor of renovating the house," said Velvel.

"But if you suspected that I was afraid to go along, why did you let Alfred go?" asked Yankel.

"I never thought the house dilapidated. Besides, you can depend on Srul Peczenik."

"That's right," said Yankel. "I also depended on Srul Peczenik and still I didn't go along. Because I would rather be here to talk to you, so that Alfred will have no trouble if he wants to make the house livable again."

"So you think, Yankel, that Alfred wants to renovate the house to live there?"

"Why else?" wondered Yankel. "If you renovate a house, you want to live in it."

"What do you think, doctor?" Velvel turned to Dr. Frankl.

"I don't think that Alfred intends to renovate such a house for himself. I should be very much surprised if that were the case," said Dr. Frankl.

"You see, Yankel," said Velvel. "I am all the more positive that Alfred has other intentions with the house than you believe.

I don't know what he has thought up. But I am glad that you were afraid to go with him, otherwise a worse argument would now be taking place on the *Gazon*. We shall soon see who will be more surprised, you or I."

"I am not so easy to surprise," said Yankel. "What can he do with the house?"

"It will surprise you to learn," said Velvel, "that Alfred decided a couple of weeks ago to change his studies. He does not want to be an architect any longer. Now he wants to study agriculture."

"That's the end of Dobropolia!" Yankel cried out, laying down his fork and knife. "A learned agrarian! That's the end of Dobropolia!"

"What's the end of Dobropolia?" asked Alfred, who had just come into the room.

"I have told Yankel that you wish to study agriculture," said Velvel. "You see what he thinks of it. Just look at him!"

"But why, Yankel?" said Alfred, and sat down at the table at Yankel's side. "You yourself attended agricultural school in Slobodka Dolna."

"The school in Slobodka was a very good practical school," said Yankel sullenly. "They turned out no doctors there. But how do you know that I was in a school? I never told you."

"Uncle Velvel told me a year ago," said Alfred. "Uncle, what would you say to the idea of founding a practical school like that here, nothing as big as Slobodka —"

"Where will the school be, Alfred?" asked Velvel. "On the *Gazon*?"

"Yes," said Alfred, "the house is not dilapidated at all. Peczenik 'the goat' thinks that he can fix the house in three or four months. There is room in the stall and in the coach houses on the *Gazon* for forty students."

"Peczenik figured that out?" asked Yankel angrily.

"No," said Alfred. "I didn't go that far with him. I figured that out myself. I have in the meanwhile told Peczenik nothing about the school. First I wanted to talk to all of you."

"Well, now we know," said Yankel. "What do you say to that, Uncle Velvel?"

"First I should like to hear what you have to say to it," said Velvel. "You're the expert on agricultural schools."

"I — as for me," said Yankel fiercely, "I'm leaving. I'm leaving Dobropolia. I'm returning to the post where I began fifty years ago. What is it Nazarewicz says when he's had enough? 'I'm giving notice!' I'm going back to the countess."

"When did you conceive this plan?" Dr. Frankl inquired.

"I planned this a long time ago," said Alfred. "But I intended to wait until ending my studies before undertaking it seriously. Something like five years from now."

"He had a five-year plan," Yankel interjected.

"Yes," said Alfred, "a five-year plan. I am not suited to be a landowner, that is clear."

"Whom is that clear to?" asked Yankel. "What *are* you suited for?"

"You yourself, Yankel, gave me to understand often enough that I was no real landowner."

"And that you are not," said Yankel. "But I also had a five-year plan. What is not now can still be."

"I don't believe in landonwers, in general," said Alfred. "That is an obsolete form of agriculture. It won't last. Not only here in Dobropolia — it won't last anywhere. Your countess is right to sell her estates piecemeal or simply give them away."

"You know that, too?" marveled Yankel.

"Yes," said Alfred. "That's what I've been thinking. I've known for a long time that I am no landowner. For a time I thought that if I must be one, I would force myself, for Uncle Velvel's sake and yours, Yankel. But after what happened to our Lipusj on the *Groblja*, I realized that I had something more important to do than to establish myself as a landowner here. I'll start a school here, I said to myself, and we'll give agricultural training to young people who wish to emigrate to Palestine."

"You thought that through," Dr. Frankl interposed, "and

you decided to wait five years with this plan. May we know what has caused you to undertake it now?"

"I have you to thank for that, Uncle Stefan," said Alfred calmly. "My father and you, to be exact. You brought my father's testament, and we all read it. Before hearing this testament I said to myself, 'If I should approach Uncle Velvel and Yankel with my plan for a school, Yankel will be positively against it, and Uncle Velvel may be for it; but Yankel will win out, as always. In that case,' I said to myself, 'I should have no alternative to my great regret than to leave Dobropolia.'"

"Good" said Dr. Frankl, "we understand that. You made a plan and weighed all the possibilities. That was very sensible, I must say. But how has your father's testament changed matters?"

"My father's testament changed matters insofar as Yankel can scarcely win out this time. Now I shall remain in Dobropolia even if they are against my plan. I shall remain and do what I think right."

"You read that out of your father's testament?" Dr. Frankl marveled.

"Yes," said Alfred. "Before you brought my father's testament into the house, I was here as a guest. I was very well treated. Everybody was good to me. Perhaps too good. I lived here as in a fairy tale. Everything here was for me. I had to learn, I had a great deal to make up for — and have learned and have made up for a great deal. And I am thankful to everybody. But this catching up made me a child again. That had to be so, because I actually had much to learn which I should have learned as a child. I was here as a sort of adopted child, and I was a guest. Now I have become acquainted with my father's testament and I no longer feel myself a guest. I am no longer here in the role of a child. I now belong to this house. I belong to this house by right, like my father, who did penance and now also belongs to this house by right. I am here in this house in the name of my father who left me his testament, here, and I take up his claim."

"If I understand you correctly, you, in the name of your father, are making a claim to his inheritance?" Yankel exclaimed and rose, staring at Alfred.

"If you wish to put it that way, Yankel," said Alfred in a calm tone, rising at the same time, "if you wish to put it that way — yes."

"Alfred!" Dr. Frankl shouted at him in indignation. He was about to rise and step between Yankel and Alfred, but controlled himself, took off his spectacles with nervous fingers and with great embarrassment peered with his naked, sad eyes at Velvel, who calmly remained sitting, softly smiling in reverie.

"This is my training!" Yankel cried, beaming with joy, to everyone's surprise. "That's the way I like it!" he said to Alfred, and laid a tender hand on Alfred's shoulder. "Now I can tell you: I have always been very fond of you. I liked you straight off in Vienna when I met you. But I never took you seriously. Do you know why? Because I never take to young men who at the age of twenty aren't seriously interested in money and possessions. Such whippersnappers are always very suspect to me. In the best of cases they are fools. Now you have spoken like a man, like a real landowner. You are right. Now you can be taken seriously — you and your plan. What kind of a school are you going to start here? I'll help you. I am at your disposal. All my means are at your disposal. And if you must start an inheritance suit against your uncle, I'll help you too. You know, I am a kulak. I have fifty-five acres of land. You helped me with my trial — I'll help you with yours."

"So far as I know, you had sixty-five acres just a few days ago," said Alfred smiling, and looked at Uncle Velvel.

"Apparently he sold ten acres when he armed himself for battle against the communal secretary," said Velvel. "But we shall not need his help. If you have settled so quickly with Yankel, I shall not stand in your way. But the plan you have described is not so easily carried through as you appear to assume. We must talk about all this in more detail. I am glad that you no longer feel yourself a guest here. I have not offered you your father's inheritance, because, as you know very well, I had thought for a long time of the whole estate becoming yours. Just as you were acceptable to me before as my heir, you are now acceptable to me as a fellow-master. The school you spoke about you can establish on your property. As for me, I shall wait a while with my property, and see how you manage. If you are successful, I shall join you. In any event, you can have the house on the *Gazon* renovated, and we shall not quarrel about the rest, either."

"That is very fine of you, Uncle," said Alfred with great relief. "Thank you very much. Frankly, I expected nothing else. I was afraid only of Yankel."

"So? Afraid?" said Yankel, turning to Dr. Frankl. "I immediately offer him help against his uncle, and he was afraid of me."

"Despite that, Yankel, while I continue my studies you will be the head of our school, and I shall have to be afraid of you for another couple of years."

"I have already put myself at the head of the school," said Yankel. "Where will you study?"

"When I told Uncle Velvel that I wished to study agriculture, I was thinking of the college for agriculture in Vienna. But I have changed my plan in that respect, too. I shall remain in this country, in Lwow, or some other city. True, I shall have difficulty with the language at first, but it will soon be overcome. And now I am going to Panko, to say goodbye to him."

After Alfred had quickly left the room, the three men remained in silence for a time. Then Dr. Frankl said:

"Now we know: he is remaining. He is remaining here."

At that old Yankel rose and with outstretched arms went over to Velvel who had risen at the same time and went to Yankel with outstretched arms. For a moment they embraced as they used to only once a year when they danced together at the festival of the Rejoicing of the Torah in Grandfather's Room. But this time they did not dance. With ecstatic faces they stood opposite one another, beard facing beard.

[348]

"You — u — u see?" asked Velvel, prolonging the "you" so that it sounded like a sigh.

"You see — ee — ee!" answered Yankel, prolonging the "see" so that it rang like a song of triumph.

6

Alfred did not remain long with Panko. The invalid was doing well, and Alfred stayed only long enough to inform Panko that the park on the *Gazon* would be tended again.

"If your brother is home from his military service in the fall," Alfred promised Panko, "he will become coachman in your place and you will work on the *Gazon* and be a real gardener."

Panko was very happy to hear this, thanked Alfred and said goodbye, "A pleasant trip, Mr. Mohilevski. Come back soon. Everything will be all right here. Only little Lipusj will be missing. He would have been so happy to watch me working on the *Gazon*. Perhaps he might have become a gardener, too."

"Everything will be all right here," thought Alfred. "Only Lipusj will no longer be here. Neither Lipusj nor Mechzio." And, as on Sabbath at prayers, Alfred was again shrouded in all the black veils of mourning. He was on his way home, but he did not go there. He went first to the *Gazon* and then into the forest; he sought all the dead boy's favorite spots; in all the familiar paths in the forest and in the *Gazon* he celebrated a ceremony of farewell, and every spot, every path, was a place of bereavement.

Towards evening the sun was going down behind a motionless bank of clouds, and Alfred was sitting on the banks of the small pond on the spot where, hardly a year ago, little Lipsuj had recited the poem about the stork and had asked whether the stork was really an accursed bird. Suddenly Alfred was startled by a shout; it was Donja's voice calling him. He sprang up and saw that it was really she. But she had not called him. She had remained standing under a tree in the poplar alley until

[349]

she was positive that Alfred must see her. Now she came towards the *Groblja*, walking with quick steps. Alfred ran to the verge of the *Gazon* and waited till she came up.

"Where are you going, Donja?" he called, spying her through the green lattice of the twigs. Although they were no more than ten steps apart, Donja pretended not to hear him. She had on her Sunday dress, but there was a kerchief on her head and she walked with her face averted. She walked so quickly up the *Groblja* that Alfred had trouble keeping step with her in the bushes of the *Gazon*. By her walk he recognized that she was very angry. She was not walking with her customary calm, proud, peacock step. Striding short and hard, she walked along the *Groblja*, and even the heels of her boots seemed to be regretting that they could not beat out loud on the soft, deaf ground. Alfred worked his way out of the clinging bushes, ran up the path to the entrance gate of the *Gazon*, and, craning his neck, saw that she carried a small satchel in her hand and had the appearance of a runaway.

"Donja," he called her in an undertone, "come in here, Donja!" She made no answer, but, just as she was about to walk past the entrance gate, disregarding him, she turned and, without favoring Alfred with a glance, stepped into the park. There, as though pursued by Alfred, she ran to the terrace of the old house, where in bad weather, particularly in the fall and early spring, they had often sat alone together — and there stood still, without looking back at Alfred. Alfred took her by the shoulders and with tender force turned the obstinate girl around: she stood hard and wooden, her eyes looking angrily over him and away.

"Where are you going?" he asked.

She was silent and drew her eyebrows together, like her father, the wheelwright, in a fury.

"Where are you going, Donja?" he asked.

"To the city," she answered curtly.

"Now? Towards evening? To Kozlova?"

"A militia man is not a soldier, a goat is not cattle, Yankel is no bailiff and Kozlova is no city," she recited nastily, completely her father's daughter. "I am going to the city."

"To the city?"

"Yes. To the city. Where there are big barracks and many soldiers. I want to have a soldier sweetheart."

"What do you want to become?" he asked her. Dark wrath choked his voice. He stepped so near to her that his knee pushed the satchel. "What do you want to become?!"

She looked at him with her comprehending eyes, took a step back and sang innocently:

"I want to be a soldier's sweetheart. I shall wait in front of the barracks, and when the Uhlans come out, I shall go with everyone who winks at me like this."

Although somewhat hindered by the satchel she held in front of her with both hands, she rose on her toes, straining her breasts flirtatiously and winked one eye roguishly at Alfred . . . Never was Donja lovelier, never more ravishing than at that moment. The dazzling light of the sunset flowed around her lovely figure; her face flamed. She stood facing Alfred, her pug nose trembled, and she said insolently, "I shall never have anything to do with the infantry. That would aggravate my father."

Alfred felt a lustful desire both to smash a clenched fist into the snub nose in the insolent face and so to strike her that no damage would be done to the dear face . . . In this dilemma, he lifted his foot and pushed the satchel out of Donja's hand. The satchel fell with a din to the stone flags, the lock crashed, the cover spring opened and a yawning abyss was revealed. There was nothing in the satchel, no dress, no jacket, no middy, not the smallest ribbon — simply nothing.

Alfred looked at Donja. She held her face low, her shoulders slouched, her fingers twisted, and Donja was thoroughly ashamed of herself.

"You," he said.

"I wanted to say goodbye," she said, without looking up.

"I gave you a signal Friday, but you hid behind Pessa."

"I was so angry. It has been weeks that you haven't cared for me."

"It was because of Lipusj," he said.

"What do you care about strange children," she said. "We can have some of our own."

"What are you saying, Donja," he cried.

"You don't have to worry. I only talk that way. It's been weeks since you've stopped coming into the kitchen in the evening."

"I can speak Ukrainian already," he said.

"Oh, so you only came to learn Ukrainian?"

"You know why, Donja. Don't make it too hard for us. I shall come back after the vacation. Then things will be different."

"Yes, they will. Things will be altogether different by then. That is sure," she said and henceforth looked him directly in the eyes.

"Why are you so despondent? I'll come back very soon, Donja."

"They want to marry me off," said Donja.

"What? Who? How? To whom?"

She saw his consternation, and a tender trace of a smile hovered around her lips.

"Miss Pessa and the bailiff want to marry me off. To young Kyryllowicz. In the fall. When you come back, I shall already be Mrs. Kyryllowicz."

"Nonsense, Donja! Old Kyryllowicz will have something to say about it."

"Old Kyryllowicz has already given his consent. That's just — "

"Who could have brought him around so fast?"

"The bailiff. He promised him ten acres as my dowry, so to speak."

"Ten acres? Oh!"

"Yes. Ten acres. To lease for ten years. Without paying

rent. True, Kyryllowicz didn't say yes, but he hasn't said no, either."

"And you? What do you say?"

"My mother is very proud that Kyryllowicz hasn't said no any more — "

"What do *you* say? That's what I want to know!"

"My father is always cursing the peasants. But in the end it's what mother wants that counts."

"And you? You have nothing to say here?"

"If I get ten acres as a dowry — "

"But only to rent!"

"To rent at first. For a poor gypsy girl that is a great deal."

"Donja — Do you want to marry Kyryllowicz, or don't you?"

Donja looked at Alfred for a long time. Her eyes were hard and strange. Suddenly she shouted, "I should rather be engaged to death than to this Kyryllowicz!"

"If that's the case, don't worry, Donja. You are still young. Only nineteen. You still have time. I'll give you ten acres, if you don't take this fellow."

"Give me fifteen!" she demanded in wild resolution.

"Why fifteen?"

"Bjelak's daughters get that much. With fifteen acres I can sit around for ten years and be as choosy as Bjelak's eldest. She is twenty-six years, and still has the best suitors. With fifteen acres — "

"Good, Donja. You shall have fifteen. I promise that to you on my word of honor."

"You must write it down for me. So my father will believe me. He knows what there is between us, anyway. You don't have to worry, my father is on my side.."

"Good, I'll write it down."

"But where will you get fifteen acres, Fredziu?"

"That will be arranged. I'll speak to Yankel."

"Ah, you've got the right idea! But it's Yankel who wants to give the ten acres for rent — "

"Who told you that?"

"I heard it myself. They hatched up a plot against me."

"Who?"

"I've already told you — Miss Pessa and the bailiff. Miss Pessa has always wanted to marry me off to Kyryllowicz, even before you came to Dobropolia. She means the best for me. She has discussed it with the bailiff. They didn't mind my being there at all, because they spoke Yiddish. But I understood everything."

"You understood?"

"Yes, Fredziu, every word. Almost every word. I have tried so hard all year."

"You understand Yiddish, Donja?"

"Yes, Fredziu. You learned the language of my people for my sake. So I learned the language of your people, for your sake."

And to show him how well she had learned, she began to talk, using Pessa's intonation and vocabulary, a mixture of Yiddish and Ukrainian, swallowing her words hastily like a child in school. All at once she halted. Conscious of the speechless delight with which Alfred was enjoying her animated speech, she stopped in the middle of a phrase and was silent. Then she cast down her eyes, as she had the first day they met in the field at harvest time and began to be ashamed in his presence. Alfred saw her fingers twisting and untwisting. The beautiful girl's hands were no longer so hard and toil-worn. Donja no longer looked like the daughter of her hands, but the sister. This too was Pessa's work. He stepped close to Donja.

"Donja," he said.

"Will you come back, Fredziu?" she asked.

"Yes, Donja," he said and took her hands and kissed her. Then she began to cry.

7.

Donja and Alfred came home late that night. Both felt it to be a stroke of luck that they were to spend the last hours before his departure under one roof, in one house, though separated by some walls; both felt it and expressed it, and so they took farewell of one another with confidence. Pessa had preferred to go to sleep and not to wait for the stealthy couple. Her prophetic heart told her that "the children" were together, but she did not worry any longer, since with Yankel's help she had half won over old Kyryllowicz to her plan for a fine marriage for Donja, which, as we know, preceded Alfred's stay in Dobropolia.

In his room Alfred found his suitcase packed, his traveling suit neatly laid over an easy chair, and everything ready for the journey. He ate some of the cold food which Pessa had left on the table for him and drank a great deal of water, for he was very thirsty. Then he undressed and was about to go to bed when he decided to try on his traveling suit, which he had not had on for a year. The pants still fitted, but the jacket was completely unusable: too short in the sleeves, too tight in the chest, cramped in the shoulders. He hadn't noticed that he had grown physically as well as otherwise in Dobropolia. With this pleasant thought he went to bed, forgetting the strict rule which Pessa had taught him like a child in the course of the year: First blow out your lamp, then say your prayer. Pessa knew Alfred's habit of falling asleep with his light on, and she worried about the kerosene lamp. Half-asleep, Alfred heard Pessa whispering outside behind the window, "First blow out your lamp, then say your prayers. . ."

"Thank you, Pessa," he tried to whisper back, but his lips were paralyzed. Men grow accustomed to all sorts of new things, the words ran through his head: men grow accustomed to a new sky, a new earth, a new sun, new people, new birds. But it is hard for men to grow accustomed to a kerosene lamp.

"It is easiest for men to grow accustomed to new birds," a voice whispered through the window.

"Ah, Pessa, go to sleep, dear Pessa."

"I am not Pessa. Look this way!"

"You are, I know it already, you are the dream voice. Let me be. I am so tired."

"I bring you a fond greeting."

"You come from my father's dream."

"I come from near here. I am the stork."

"What stork?"

"Jarema's stork. A friend of your friend Klipusj!"

"His name is Lipusj. Not Klipusj, but Lipusj."

"In the language of the storks he is called Klipusj."

"Are you really a stork?"

"Look this way!"

Alfred looked. On the window ledge stood Jarema's old stork. He held his wings outspread, the drops of the night dew dripped like diamonds on his feathers in the reflection of the moon.

"Yes. It is you. What greeting do you bring?"

"Many fond greetings from Klipusj."

"That is nice. How is our dear friend?"

"Well. He is well. He is learning the Torah from Metatron, the Angel of the Presence. He has already been named the narrating judge, our Klipusj."

"That is fine. Oh, that is fine."

"He is wearing a white smock, a white cap and white shoes. And everybody loves him."

"My father did that for him. My father has a great deal to say there. Because he fell as a soldier, you know."

"It's good that I can still tell it to you today. For to morrow — "

"Tomorrow I leave."

"Yes. Tomorrow you leave. I suppose you are very happy."

"I am happy to go back to the city where I was born, and I am deathly unhappy to leave Dobropolia which I love as my second homeland."

"You have expressed that well. We migrant birds understand that. We have taught men that one should have two homelands. But few of the children of men have hearts strong enough to bear our wisdom."

"I shall learn it."

"So I shall trust you with a secret."

"Please do, dear stork."

[356]

The stork lifted a foot and rubbed its claw over its beak, like an old man rubbing two fingers over the bridge of his nose before speaking a sententious phrase.

"We storks have two homelands. We love them both. But the high tide of our stork life is neither here nor there."

"Where is it, then?"

"Listen and be still. Both here and there we live in the swamps. By the Nile and the Strypa our beaks grub in the swamps. That is our life and it is good. But the high tide of our life is the path, the flight, the passage. We swing up high. When it storms we sail. When there is a calm our wings clap high. We hear the din of our pinions, our breasts cut through the great sea of the air. In our bellies the power of one homeland, in our eyes the sun of the other homeland: — that, child of man, is our life! Then our stork hearts become as wide as the world. . . ."

"Stork, *hasidah*, pious one! The Holy Scriptures are right to name you thus."

"Do you, too, know why we are so named?"

"Because you show love —"

"That is the small truth. You do not know the great truth."

"Tell me it."

The stork spread out its pinions. Although the peasant Jarema had clipped its wings, they were broad enough to fill the frames of the window and to hide the reflection of the moon.

"What do I look like now?"

"You look like Judko Segall, the small Levite, when he covers himself with his prayer shawl on the Sabbath, you look pious and beloved."

"That is our great truth. Because we are white and black, because we bear the colors of the prayer shawl, that is why we are called in the holy tongue, 'the pious.' "

"That is a beautiful truth. You must tell it to our friend Lipusj."

"Klipusj now knows more than you and I will ever know. But do me one favor."

"What favor?"

[357]

"I have confided two large secrets to you for the sake of a favor which you must do for me."

"I'll do you any favor you want."

"You must do this favor. Klipusj has commanded it. Do you hear?"

"Yes."

"I adjure you, O short-nosed creature, do it with your hand, with your almighty hand, put the disgrace away from me."

"What disgrace?"

"See my wings! A great disgrace was done me: My wings have been cut."

"They meant well by you."

"Man often means well, and acts disgracefully. Tear out with your almighty hand my dead feathers, that new ones may grow. How can I continue to live? I cannot swing myself up to the sun."

"They will kill you!"

"Who?"

"The storks!"

"They will certainly do so. That is their right. That is my right. But only this once I wish to swing up and die as a stork in the air, not like an old drake in a small pond. Do me this favor. It is a service of love."

"If Klipusj wishes it, I will do it."

"Klipusj wishes it. He began to do it. See, a new black and white feather is growing already."

Alfred stretched forward his hand, to do Lipusj's friend the service of love. But hardly had his finger touched the out-spread stork's wing, when the bird plunged its beak through his hand like a dagger. A fire burned his hand. Flames shot out of the clapping stork beak.

Alfred awoke. The kerosene lamp was still burning on the night table. He had tried to turn out the lamp with a sleepy hand and in so doing touched the hot cylinder. Pessa was right. First blow out the lamp. But had it not been for the painful touch of the heated glass of the lamp, this dream would not have come. Since the boy's death, every night had been a confusion of dreams and images. This was the most beautiful. Lipusj is a narrating judge. He wears a white dress, a white sash, a white cap, white shoes. And he has a story to tell. As always. Dear Lipusj. He is well off. He has earned it. First blow out the lamp. Good Pessa, tomorrow she will cry. How beautiful is the prayer on going to sleep, how sweet the words, when Lipusj recited them. "Blessed art thou, O Lord our God, King of the universe, who drops the bonds of sleep on my eyes and slumber on my eyelids. May it be Thy will, O my God and God of my fathers, to lay me to sleep in peace and raise me to peace, that no dream of evil may scare me, nor any evil contemplation. Perfect be my bed before Thee. And enlighten Thou my eyes, lest I sleep on into death. Amen."